Mitzi,
We've had some fun
times - Thanks for
joining me on In
Book adventure
~ MettaJean

MW00886439

M.J. VIGNA

DEADLY
DEADLY

Copyright © 2013 M.J. Vigna
All rights reserved.

ISBN: 1482085925
ISBN-13: 9781482085921

ACKNOWLEDGEMENT

A special thanks to my son-in-law Paul Ruggieri.
Without your help and encouragement
this book would never have seen the light of day.

DEDICATION

I want to dedicate this book to my children. Mike, John, Greg, Kenyon, Linda Juan and Rosie. And my children by marriage, Mitzi, Candy, Paul, Margie, Teresa and David. Thank you for all the blessings you have brought me, including all of my beautiful grandchildren.

WARNING: The author was advised by the editor to consider removing the first few pages of this Forward. It does not pertain directly to the story and the editor was concerned that due to its graphic nature it could discourage readers from continuing with the novel. The author decided it was important to keep this information in the book so that the reader has a better understanding of the background to one of the main characters in the story. If you are faint of heart please begin reading the Forward several pages in or you can also jump directly to the novel. Once you have finished this story it will be a certainty that you will want to read the Forward to find out how the unusual pairing of Grady and Deadly occurred. Happy reading!

FOREWORD

In the mid-1800s, the territory from Canada down through North Dakota, South Dakota, Nebraska, Kansas, and Oklahoma was known as the Missouri Territory or Indian country. In time it was shortened to "the Territories".

It was 1845 when Joe Bob Grady age thirteen, came to the Territories with his family. John Deaton Grady, with his wife, Brenda Lee, their son, Joe Bob Grady who preferred just to go by his last name "Grady", and their daughter, April Ann, age ten. They had traveled from Kentucky, their ancestors were farmers. Brenda's family passed away, leaving their small farm, which was taken for debts. John had been on his own since eighteen, when his mother died. No other family.

John Deaton had sold all the livestock when the old farm had been repossessed. They brought as much as their old wagon could hold: a plow, starter seed for a garden, corn seed for their first cash crop. They had the two mules to pull the wagon and do the plowing, one milk cow, three wiener piglets, and a few chickens. April Ann had her pet cat.

The Grady family had few possessions. They had scrimped to pay the $1.25 an acre, the appraised value of claims in the territory. This was the number one provision of the Preemption Act. The number two provision was to live on the land and improve it.

This vast Indian country had been unexplored, except by hunters and trappers. It was home to several bands of Indians, and it was a stronghold of the Pawnee. Often a few would be seen a ways from their dugout. John and Grady kept rifles close. There were two forts, Kearny and Laramie, and the soldiers patrolled some of the territory as settlers moved in, and occasionally rode by to check on them.

Unfamiliar with the severe northern winters—blizzards so strong they were blinded a few feet after they stepped out of the dugout door—Grady ran a rope from the dugout to the barn and another to the outhouse while John split stumps and logs to keep fires burning in the dugout and the barn.

April Ann came down with a cold that lingered. She was wracked with coughing. In spite of Brenda's efforts at doctoring, she grew listless and stopped eating, she was fading away. They had raised a good crop of corn and harvested it before winter hit. It had become their main source of food: cornmeal mush, corn cakes, corndodgers and cornbread. Brenda and John thought the girl might have an allergy that weakened her body, and she could not shake off the cold, which slipped into pneumonia.

John killed a hen and Brenda made broth and spoon-fed April, but she couldn't swallow. She finally closed her eyes and went to sleep. They wrapped her little body in a blanket and put it in the rafters of the small barn. They would have to wait until spring when the ground thawed to bury her.

John had made Brenda a rocking chair when Grady was born. She had rocked both children in it. This rocker was the only piece of furniture they had brought with them. They had made a table from barrels and wood planks. Brenda kept up her cooking chores, but the heart had left her. She spent most of that difficult winter in the rocker with April Ann's cat in her lap. One night as Grady brought in an armload of wood, the cat ran out into the storm.

They buried April Ann that spring. That set the tone of desperation for the summer. They worked from daylight until dark. They planted twenty acres of wheat and twenty of corn. They mended and added to the barn. Aware of the severity of the winters, they stockpiled firewood. They were able to sell some of the wheat and corn, but they kept some for seed in the spring. They were able to buy a few necessities, including rifle bullets. Before the first storm hit, several deer were hung in the barn. That winter was hard, but they had a winter's experience to draw from. John spent most of his time checking on the barn animals and splitting stumps. Grady read. Brenda sat in the rocker and knitted.

In the spring they added a few acres to the wheat and grain fields. Brenda became pregnant in May. Spirits rose with that news.

They did well until a summer hail in June, which beat down twenty acres of the wheat. A blistering hot wind in August burned up the silks and stunted the corn's growth. Their cash crop was destroyed, but they salvaged enough corn for feed for the animals and ground meal for the family. They had no money for supplies or seed money in the spring. The piglets had grown into good-sized hogs, so they sold one to buy basic food supplies and seed for the spring. The baby would be a Christmas arrival. John butchered another pig. They would have bacon and ham for the holidays.

The only aggravation they had as winter closed in was a pack of gray wolves that took an interest in the chickens. A shotgun blast their way would discourage them for a while but they often snuck in at night. The chickens' uproar would send Grady running and yelling, as he fired shots in the air.

After April's death, Brenda had become quiet. She always helped do the work, but she had no joy or hope. With the baby growing in her she knitted for the baby and hummed as she worked. The entire family's spirits began to lift.

As the holidays neared, a record blizzard hit. And so did the wolf pack. John spent a good part of each night keeping a fire going in front of the barn door. At first his presence had kept the wolves at bay. As the storm raged on they grew braver and came closer, circling the barn. To save ammunition, John waited until they were close enough for a sure kill.

The night Brenda's baby decided to arrive, John was occupied with saving the last pig, the cow, chickens, and mules. A couple of the wolves came in close enough to kill both of them. The hungry pack fell on the dead wolves and John knew the two carcasses would satisfy their hunger. John built up the fire and hurried to the dugout to find that Grady had helped to deliver a small boy child. Brenda was clean and in a deep sleep. They had not been able to get the boy to cry. He had breathed a short while and then just stopped. Grady rose from the rocker and handed the wrapped baby to John. With tears in his eyes he went out in the storm to recover. John took his place in the rocker and with tears running down his face, rocked his baby boy. At daylight John took the baby to the barn and lovingly placed the bundle in the rafters, another spring burial. When Brenda woke he held her in his arms and they both cried.

Brenda didn't get out of bed. They took care of her, but she didn't get stronger. She bled from the birth of the child, passed the afterbirth, and continued to hemorrhage. They had little material to pack her with. Grady took over the meals and made chicken broth and spooned it into her mouth. She swallowed and smiled her appreciation for this young son, who had turned into a man long before it was time.

Like April Ann, she closed her eyes and went to sleep. They wrapped her in a blanket and put her in the rafters with the baby. Come spring they would bury her and the baby next to April in what was becoming a family cemetery.

With one less mouth to feed, their supplies would last, but hay and feed for the animals was low. John, sick with the loss of Brenda, in a fit of depression took his rifle to the barn and shot the cow. He dressed her out and hung her high in the barn. He figured when weather permitted, he and Grady would ride the two mules to a town and look for work. It was an effort to get through the winter. John was so depressed, Grady was afraid he would harm himself. Grady worked to keep John occupied with checkers and cards. He read aloud one book after another. John sat listless in the rocker, lost in his own mind.

They took turns getting wood and keeping the fire lit. They held onto the ropes as the storms' intensity blinded them. They had used up most of the cut logs and now each trip meant splitting more stumps. Often they heard the calls of the wolf pack. John sat, listless, and Grady would take the shotgun and shoot in the air toward the barn.

The frozen stumps were hard to split. Frozen hands and feet ached and made it hard to carry an armload of logs and cling to the frozen rope. Grady thanked the Lord for the rope guides he had installed that fall.

It was John's turn to make the final trip, before bed, for wood. Grady had read awhile but his eyes were tired. He brushed his teeth, pulled off his boots, and climbed into his bedroll. He was instantly asleep.

He awoke uncomfortable. Cold, his breath sent a fog of condensation. He sat up and saw the fire was almost out. He drew on his boots and threw a few logs on the fire. John's bed was empty. Fear struck Grady. John had not returned from the wood run.

He put on his winter wear, pulled the door shut after him, and grabbed the rope guide. This guide was the one to the barn. The woodpile was between the two. The blowing ice particles were blinding. He closed his eyes and relied on the guide. He yelled for his dad over and over, no answer. He felt with his foot until he hit a log. He was at the woodpile. He knew the area well. Kneeling down he felt with his hands. He ran into a stack of logs. Apparently split and stacked to bring to the house.

He continued to search and found the axe lying next to a stump. There was blood on the axe and the stump and soaking into the snow. Really scared now, he screamed for his dad.

The blood meant an accident, probably a slip of the axe. Where was his dad? If he was able to move why hadn't he come back to the dugout? Grady had gone back and forth on the rope guides, calling his dad. He was so scared but he knew that if he left the guides, to search, he would be the next disaster.

Exhausted he returned to the dugout, threw wood on the fire. Hung his winter wear to dry. Tears had dried on his cheeks. He sat in the rocker to warm himself and waited.

Every minute seemed to be an hour but finally daylight came. Still snowing slightly, he looked out at a white landscape. He found his father, off to the side, behind the dugout. He uncovered the snow from the body and saw the foot separated from the leg. John had probably put his left foot, on the stump, to hold it steady. With the axe over his head he had driven it with such force, missed his target and slammed into his ankle. His work boots had been no protection.

He had probably passed out for a while. When he came to he was weak from loss of blood. He had tried to drag himself to the dugout. Missed it, and finally given up. Grady figured he had given up when Brenda died. Grady added his dad's body to Brenda's and the boy child's.

It was pretty much a waiting game for Grady now. While he waited for spring, he carved wooden headboards for the graves. Feed for the animal was almost gone. He butchered the chickens so the mules could survive. With the cow he had way too much meat hanging in the barn. He had corn and rice and beans.

He was going to be sixteen this spring, and he didn't know what to do. He wasn't going to stay here; there were just too many bad memories. No relatives to go to. He was completely alone and needed to figure out what he was going to do.

He wanted to join a wagon train and go farther west. Maybe California or Texas, both new states. This unknown scared him but so did the thought of staying here with his family in the ground, along with fending off wolves and Indians by himself. He knew now that he didn't want to be a farmer. He wasn't afraid of hard work, just not behind a plow. He also knew that he could not handle the extreme winters here. The thought of enduring even one more was dreadful.

Digging those graves was the hardest thing he had ever done. He couldn't wait to get gone. He packed up what food and clothing one mule could carry. He saddled the other mule. Added his dad's rifle to the saddle scabbard; put his pistol in the saddle bag with any papers John had, including the claim for their farm.

He headed southwest towards Fort Laramie. In a couple of days he picked up the Oregon and California trail. Tracks were fresh; a wagon train had passed recently. By evening he had caught up. The wagons had circled, and people were starting campfires. Grady found the wagon master and asked to be allowed to travel with them. He offered to work for that privilege. He was given permission until the train reached Salt Lake. Some of the families would settle there and the rest of the train would take the Humboldt Trail on to San Francisco.

Joe Bob Grady was not a lazy boy. He had worked hard with his dad. John had instilled a good work ethic. Grady's nature was to learn and do. He did any chore asked of him and soon earned the respect of the wagon master and the families who needed help. He handled the cattle and horse herd, lit campfires, harnessed stock to wagons, hunted for meat, and helped drive wagons when needed.

This was the beginning of Grady's wagon train education. He had learned when they came to camp at Fort Laramie that his land claim could be sold—something he could look into. In Salt Lake he sold the mules and bought a horse and a holster for his pistol. He stayed with the wagon train. He could hardly wait to see California. He felt as if he was on a great adventure. Grady liked the excitement of new lands. He signed on with other haulers, cattle drives, north on the California Mission Trail, meat for miners in the gold fields. South on the Mission Trail, hauling supplies for settlers and towns along the coast.

By his twentieth birthday, Grady had established a work reputation and was welcome on any hauling or wagon train in the West. He had reached six two and was built muscular, still lean and agile. Towhead as a youth, his hair was now dark wheat colored, his eyes hazel. The ladies flirted with him; the men teased him for his good looks. He was good-natured with the teasing and didn't let it interfere with his work. Grady chose not to travel back east to the trailheads.

He would hire on in Salt Lake, where the California trail split, the Oregon Trail to the Gold Fields and then the Humboldt Trail to San Francisco.

His favorite trail was one that continued from San Diego and ran to the newly formed state of Texas. This trail ran close to the Butterfield stage route when possible. It crossed the Sierra Madre Mountains, cut through upper Mexico and traveled to San Antonio in southern Texas. Besides weather, rough trails, and mountains, this was Apache land. Texas had settlers and land was available. Cattle drives were organized and driven to San Diego or further north, to the gold fields, also back east to the trailheads.

Grady found a new interest. He liked the Texas cowboys. Soon he traded his work boots for the western boots, his farmer's straw hat for the big-brimmed western hat. He knew as much or more about cattle and cattle drives as these cowboys. He often had breaks in his trail jobs. He began to sign on at a Texas cattle ranch. His knowledge of wagon trains made him valuable to the rancher. In turn he learned to break horses and rope calves. His favorite jobs on the ranch were the line cabins, established far away from the working ranch. These cabins allowed a rider to work that area. Grady fell in love with South Texas. More and more often he worked his breaks from the wagon trains at one ranch or another.

For Grady, life with a wagon train or supply train was full of responsibilities day and night. Satisfying a wagon master or the haulers and their buyers meant constant contact more often than not with disgruntled people.

Life as a cowboy was equally tedious. The ranch owner and his foremen had to be satisfied. There was always a crew of rowdy ranch hands, with their different personalities, who had to be dealt with. This is why there were days when Grady looked forward to his turn at the line cabins. The cabins were stocked with staple food supplies. With a rabbit every now and then, he could manage fine.

He especially liked it when he was the sole camper. No boss. No sharing. Eat, sleep, and work his own schedule. He always gave his employer a full day, even overtime when necessary. Usually his job at the line cabin was to work the brush. When he ran across cattle, he checked for the rancher's brand, and they were entered in the tally book. If they carried another rancher's brand, they were entered, as so, in the tally book. If the cattle were not branded, Grady herded them back to the cabin and penned them in the corral.

Working the brush was exhausting. Herding the wild cattle back to the cabin was frustrating. He could not keep the cattle herded, open the gate to the corral, and herd the cows in, without the ones in the corral getting out. His first job was to build a smaller enclosure made of brush, which he could drive his captives into. After closing that gate he could open the corral gate and chase the newcomers in and shut that gate. Problem solved.

Every two weeks, a couple of ranch hands showed up with food supplies and helped to brand the cattle, in the corral. These were turned loose to make room for more. When the area at this camp contained only branded cows. Grady moved to the next line camp and started the search all over.

Wild brush cattle were dangerous. They fought wolves, mountain lions, and often each other for herd dominance. When confronted in the brush, they didn't hesitate to charge a horse and rider. The bull often had to be shot before the rider could move the cows to the corral.

A few weeks working the Texas line camps were like a vacation to Grady. The ranch hands disliked the isolation, but Grady loved it. He enjoyed making his own decisions and being his own boss.

Grady loved Southern Texas. He enjoyed riding the country for cattle, exploring the next hill or canyon. He loved the sunrises and the sunsets, the stars at night, and listening to the howls of wolves and coyotes.

On one of Grady's scouting trips he spotted buzzards circling in the air ahead of him. Curious, he continued to ride in their direction. As he got close he saw it was a dead bush cow. Several buzzards were already feasting.

He drew his pistol and shot in the air. The buzzards lifted and revealed a young calf, not more than a couple of days old. The cow looked old. The birth of the calf had gone wrong.

The calf was wobbly on its feet and there was a bloody place on its back where the buzzards had begun to eat. Grady dismounted and approached the calf. It was a bull calf, too young to be afraid of Grady.

Speaking softly and scratching the top of its head, Grady inspected the calf, while he ran one hand over the calf's body. It was licking his other hand and found a finger to suck. Grady shook the hand free and the calf continued to search Grady's arm up to his face, Grady shoved it away again. The calf was starving and the natural instinct to nurse made him frantic. The wound on his back seemed to be the only injury. Didn't matter, Grady was going to have to shoot the little fellow. The calf was newborn, too young to survive. A quick death was better than starvation and buzzards. Having holstered the pistol, he drew it and put the muzzle to the calf's head. The calf was reaching for Grady's face. Its searching tongue licked out and swiped across Grady's cheek. The two were eye to eye. Grady cussed and holstered the pistol. He cussed more with the effort to get his horse to settle down so he could get himself and the calf on without being tossed off. The calf kicked frantically until it found Grady's finger and settled down to nurse.

Back at the camp, he shut the calf in the cabin and went in search of a cow with a calf. Earlier he had seen a branded cow with a calf. He had added the count of the two in the tally book. He knew the cow wouldn't stray far from where he had last seen her.

By nightfall he had her and her calf in the small enclosure. He tied her head up tight to a corral post. He tied her calf, under her nose, so she could see and smell it. She fought when Grady tied a rope to a hind foot and stretched her leg out. To keep from falling she quieted down. Now she couldn't kick Grady as he kneaded her teats coaxing her to let the milk down. This was an old talent. As a boy on the farm, milking the cows had been Grady's main chore.

That first milking was tedious. All participants were exhausted. Tired as he was, Grady taught the bull calf to drink from a pail by letting the calf suck his finger while he lowered his hand into the milk. At first it went up its nose. Hunger raging, he soon learned to suck, without breathing in the milk.

That first night the calf slept on a blanket in the cabin, until early morn. It was still dark when the calf searching his face for a nipple awakened Grady. He tried to put the calf out of the cabin. The calf stood by the door and bawled until Grady got up. The trip out in the dark to repeat the milking was a lesson for Grady.

The late-night feedings lasted a couple of weeks. As the calf grew and his belly was kept full, he began to sleep at night. The problem Grady was now having was that he couldn't leave the calf by himself. He could not put him in with the cow and her calf. The cow wouldn't have it. The bull calf did okay when the cow's calf was turned loose with him. Two small and unprotected calves were wolf bait, so Grady had to build another brush enclosure under the hay shed, protected by the corral fence on one side and the enclosure where the cow was penned on the other side. This way they could be near the cow and the cattle in the corral. He could use this setup in the days when he was beating the brush. If he had cattle to pen, he had to move the cow to be able to use the enclosure for what it was built for. Both calves were growing. Grady thought of them as her calf—meaning the mamma cow's—and his calf—Grady's. He didn't give his calf a name, as this was just a temporary situation. By the time Grady left the line camp his calf would be weaned and could manage if left with a herd. He just called the calf "Calf." Often he was called "Little Shit." "Little Shit" was often in trouble. Being a newborn when he was found he had replaced his mother with Grady. Whenever he could escape he found Grady. Often he broke out of the brush enclosure and followed Grady to work. Grady would then have to take him back and repair the broken enclosure. Hours were wasted. One time he broke the latch on the cabin door and destroyed food supplies.

Despite the calf's interruptions, Grady still managed to get seven bush cows and two yearling bulls corralled. The two hands from the ranch arrived as scheduled and helped brand them. They were turned loose and their count was added to the tally book.

After the crew left, Grady packed up his little family and moved to the next line camp.

Calf weaned himself and became more obsessed with Grady. With his appetite growing, so did he. His ancestors, the Spanish longhorn breed, left by the Franciscan Padres, were agile, muscular, and long of leg. They were tall with strong lungs and a remarkable pair of long horns.

Calf was growing fast, and big horns were showing. Grady turned the mamma cow and her calf loose. He figured his calf would go with them. He did but then returned in time for evening feeding. He bawled at the cabin door until Grady put him back in the enclosure next to the two bush cows he had penned. In the morning he turned the calf loose again, figuring he would eat hay under the shed and give Grady time to get on with his job.

Grady was herding a couple of yearling calves, heading back to camp when he ran into Calf. He was on Grady's trail and would have caught up with him soon. Grady was peeved but also a little proud of the little fellow and felt a little pleased the calf cared enough to find him.

It was useless to leave the calf penned. Afraid he would hurt himself if he left him tied, Grady fed him in the mornings and left him to find Grady in the brush. After several mornings, the calf left when Grady did and grazed wherever Grady stopped to tally cattle. A couple of times Grady had to rescue Calf from an angry cow and one time from a very angry bull.

Grady kind of enjoyed the calf's company, he found himself talking to him. Of course, these were one-sided conversations, but Calf often gave him a nudge. At lunch break, Grady would find a shady spot to get off the horse. The horse and the calf would graze as he rested. He got in the habit of adding an extra biscuit to his lunch, for the calf.

In time the crew showed up again to help brand the penned cattle. They brought a message to Grady that one of his haulers needed a driver. The pay was always better at those jobs than ranch pay.

Grady rubbed Calf's back up and down, scratched under his chin, and said, "Good-bye, Little Shit."

He was riding back to the ranch with the crew. Calf was weaned and knew the area from following Grady. He could take care of himself. Grady was both relieved of the burden and sad at leaving him.

Grady and the ranch hands had been traveling about an hour, when Calf caught up with them. He had watched the brush cattle turned loose.

Watched Grady pack up and leave with the men. The camp was empty. He did what he always did. Followed Grady.

The two ranch hands teased Grady about his shadow. Grady knew it wouldn't help to take the calf back. The teasing was even worse when they reached the ranch. Grady ended up sleeping in the barn, in a stall with Calf.

Grady spent a lot of time trying to figure out what he was going to do with his calf. It was a sure thing that the rancher would kill him. Yearling steak and calf liver was a treat. The rancher didn't want a rogue longhorn brush bull for breeding.

Grady was to hook up with his hauler in San Antonio. It would take him a couple of days to get there. He took Calf with him. When he arrived in San Antonio he found the job was as assistant trail boss. The rancher had gathered a herd of twelve hundred cattle that he had to deliver north to the gold fields. The salary was agreeable, and Grady immediately went to meet the hands that had already signed on, Calf following.

This began Calf's trail education. He was tied to a wagon and thrown some hay. He fussed and fought with the rope, but through experience Grady had learned to knot the rope in a way Calf could not free untie it.

For the next week, Grady hired hands, stocked the grub wagon, helped brand the few yearlings that did not carry a brand. He made frequent trips to check on Calf, and mornings he took him a biscuit. Grady talked to him, fed him hay, and often untied him. He walked him around the camp for exercise and then tied him to a different wagon. Calf always fussed when he was tied. In time he accepted the routine but spent hours watching Grady's every move. The day the herd moved out, he was given his freedom.

Grady figured Calf would fall in with the herd, but he wasn't surprised when he fell in next to Grady's horse, which was tied to the wagon that Grady was driving. Once the herd was moving, Grady turned the wagon over to a camp hand and got on his horse. With Calf following he began his rounds, circling the herd, giving orders to the cowboys.

By the time he had circled the herd and returned to the wagons, the calf was dragging his feet. Grady realized the calf was not going to go with the herd. He tied him to the chuck wagon and told the cook, who was driving, that if the calf gave him any trouble to give him a biscuit.

"Little Shit" turned to "Big Shit" as he continued to grow. With time and repetition he began to learn trail manners. He often got into trouble, but he learned not to run through camp, not to scatter things, not to raid the grub wagon, not to turn over the water barrels. When he did these things, he got tied to a wagon, sometimes for days, according to the amount of damage. He wasn't denied his meals, but he was denied his freedom.

The calf was smart. With patient reprimands, he learned his lessons. He also learned to travel with the herd.

The herd was delivered to a buyer in San Francisco, who sold some to settlers in the area. Most of it would go onto the gold fields. There were several eating establishments that got gold in payment for meals.

Grady picked up a hauling job that took him back-trail to San Diego. There were times when Grady was without a packhorse. He decided if the calf was determined to follow him. The calf was going to earn his keep.

He made a pack rack to fit the rangy back and the hump above the calf's shoulders. He tied Calf to a tree and gently put the packsaddle on his back. Calf was uneasy but stood until

Grady started to fasten the girth. The calf threw a fit. He swung his body and knocked Grady down. The pack fell on top of Grady.

Three days later, after Calf had been tied to the tree night and day, Grady tried again. Calf did great. He had learned his lesson. He stood still while Grady eased the girth snug. Packsaddles have two girths. One behind the front legs and one in front of the back legs. As Grady, drew the second girth, under the stomach, Calf exploded.

This was too close to his privates. Grady got out of the way while Calf bawled, kicked, and threw a major fit. The pack slid down his side. The front girth held and the pack hung under his belly where he could kick it with fury, but couldn't get rid of it.

That night he was left with the pack hanging, without his night feed. The next morning when Grady showed up he had a gunnysack full of grain. He set it aside, stepped to Calf's side, and undid the girth. He put the pack back on the bull's back.

Calf's ears twitched and his tail swished in anger, but he stood still. Grady didn't tighten the back girth. Instead he opened the gunnysack and pored some grain into a bucket. He offered some in his hand. Good snacks always came in Grady's hand. While Calf chewed his mouthful of grain, Grady ran the back girth under the belly and fastened it very loosely. Grady ran his fingers through the grain in the bucket, letting Calf see him do it. He offered the calf another handful. While the calf chewed, Grady tied the gunnysack and put it on the packsaddle. He roped it on extra tight in case of another fit.

Grady tossed some hay on the ground, and making sure the calf saw him do it, poured the last of the grain in the bucket on top of the hay. He loosened the rope just enough for the calf to reach his feed.

Grady came back later in the morning, removed the grain sack, opened it, and gave the calf a handful. While Calf chewed, Grady undid the two girths and removed the packsaddle. He untied the calf and gave him his freedom.

This lesson was repeated for several days with Grady increasing the load on the packsaddle. The grain sack was always the last to load and first to unload, with the calf getting grain on his hay or offered in Grady's hand. In time Calf came to realize he was carrying his own special meal.

When Grady worked a wagon train, cattle drive, or supply train, he didn't need a pack animal. He and the calf grew closer as friends as he was free to follow Grady or join the herd. They settled into the morning wake-up—coffee at the campfire, and Grady never forgot the biscuit. The cook always made extra biscuits for the young bull and often snuck him one.

Calf reached his adult size. He was as tall as a quarter horse, and his legs were long. His color was a speckled red roan with white spots, like snow-flakes, over most of his hide. He had a white underbelly, black hoofs, and black horns several feet in length with tips he sharpened daily on the brush.

He often nudged Grady, on purpose or accidentally, which left bruises. The horns were deadly. He either had to dehorn the bull or cover the tips. This conversation came up frequently as Calf's horns grew. There were fewer than a thousand of these animals that still survived in the land north of the Rio Grande, and this longhorn bull was a magnificent example.

Grady wouldn't admit it, but he was proud of the bull. His respect-able growth of horn caught the attention of young and old. Whenever they came to a settlement, it was like a parade as the children followed the bull through the streets. Grady always had to put the longhorn in a corral so the kids were safe, but they could climb the fence and see him.

Grady consulted a blacksmith. The tips were enclosed in a tube with a small ball on the end. Another tube enclosed the horns halfway between the bull's head and the tips. With Grady always commenting on how deadly the bull's horns were the name "Deadly" just naturally attached to him, which was certainly much more fitting than Calf. Grady had the tubes engraved with Deadly on each horn. No longer was the bull called Big Shit. He answered to Deadly.

In 1857, Grady was twenty-four years of age, and Deadly was a three-year-old. That was the year Grady put together his first cattle drive as trail boss. Ever since Grady was twenty, he had put most of his wages in a bank in San Francisco.

He withdrew start-up cash. He purchased a wagon with sides on it to carry grain and all the other trail needs. Bedrolls, tools, winter wear, canvas tarps, medical supplies for humans and animals.

He bought harness horses to pull the wagons, extra horses for the hands to have fresh mounts. From his experience on trail drives, he designed and built a special grub wagon.

That was the year that Grady and Deadly became partners. They also put a down payment on a thousand acres in Texas.

CHAPTER ONE

This morning Grady didn't appreciate the rough shove of Deadly's nose. His head felt like it was stuffed with nuts and bolts, and every time Deadly shoved, they rattled loudly.

"OK, OK." Grady knew from long acquaintance that the bull would not cease until Grady got out of his bedroll, so he sat up slowly, his head pounding like a sledge hammer. He squeezed his eyes tight in an effort to steady the clanging inside. By sitting still the pain settled enough to allow him to open his eyes just as Deadly, in earnest, rammed his head solidly into Grady's shoulder. The jolt was devastating, the hangover exploded into throbbing agony. Grady staggered to his feet yelling, "Cut that out, damn it. Get the hell away from me!" Bleary eyed, Grady glared at the bull. Deadly Deadly looked back with limpid brown eyes and impatiently swished an oversized tail. The seven-foot expanse of polished horns that had given him his name, Deadly Deadly, wavered in Grady's blurry eyes. Grady stood still, hoping the old head would settle down. Deadly stamped a front hoof impatiently and gracefully waved the right horn in Grady's direction. Grady knew that even with the silver balls attached to the vicious horn tips, a nudge from one of them could leave a large bruise.

"OK, OK, I'm coming." Slowly he bent over and picked up his boots. He was impressed by the fact that he had removed them. The bender he had tied on in town the night before should have knocked him out. He was proud he had found his camp, much less his own bedroll, and really amazed to find he had removed his boots before climbing into it.

"Damn that spoiled bull," Grady cursed under his breath as he staggered to the grub wagon. Cook was banging pans irritably, and the noise was killing Grady's head. Opening the drop pantry he got a sugar lump from the canister that he kept for Deadly Deadly, and held out his hand, palm up, with the lump in the middle of it. Deadly removed the cube with a talented swipe of rough, red tongue.

Grady must have looked hung over, for Cook did an unusually kind thing for him. He poured, and delivered, a cup of steaming coffee into Grady's hands. The trail boss tried to smile his thanks, but the effort tilted his head and the bolts began to slide. Instead he settled slowly to his heels beside the morning fire. It took three cups of hot, black coffee, sipped slowly, to stop the nausea and slow down the pounding in his head.

Once he had acquired his morning sugar lump, Deadly took a sleepy stand behind Grady, dozing with heavy head hanging relaxed, and waited for his friend to start the day.

Habit had established a regular alarm clock, one that Grady appreciated most of the time. A toot in town like the previous evening was a rare fling for Grady. Not in the ordinary for a trail boss. The only time he ever let down to that extent was after a drive was completed, the hands paid off, and the herd turned over to the buyer. Last night had been such a night.

Grady surveyed the camp, deserted except for the cook wagon and the horses moving restlessly in the rope corral. Some scattered gear indicated a few of the men would return to camp after they sobered up. Piles of dung were all that was left of the herd. Another drive was completed.

Good old Deadly, he had done it again. They almost had enough money saved to pay off their piece of grassland in Texas. The herd they were to pick up tomorrow and deliver to south Texas would pay off the buying price and they could settle down on their own spread.

When his head cleared, Grady saddled his horse, ordered Deadly to remain in camp, and rode into Old Town; a picturesque little Spanish town nestled in San Diego Bay. The town had grown from an over-flow of people settling near the Mission San Diego de Alcala. A short distance away in rolling foothills was the beginning of New Town,; it's lumber buildings scarring the lush green countryside.

The meeting this morning would be a first for Grady. The herd they were to drive back to Texas was owned by a woman. She was the person Grady was to meet this morning to discuss the size of the herd, and the pay for the job.

Old Town appeared asleep when Grady rode onto the main street. The midmorning heat had driven most of the occupants indoors. The few horses tied at the hitching rails were standing at rest with drooping heads, waiting patiently for their owners to return.

A fishy odor blew in from the piers, and Grady's stomach churned. He would be glad to get back on the trail home, far away from the smell of rotting fish. If cattle were not bringing the incredible price of five hundred dollars a head farther north in the gold fields, he would never trail a herd to the California coast.

He pulled up in front of the hotel and added his horse to the ranks of waiting ones. Dust puffed up under his boots as he crossed the tiled walk and entered the cantina. In spite of his hangover, he was in time for the meeting.

As he entered the eating area of the cantina he was pleased to see a lady seated alone at a table by a window. In his opinion, this was a good sign. Most women were usually late, and he had been prepared to wait.

As Grady crossed to the table, the lady raised her head to look at him. Grady stared directly into steady gray eyes. She accepted his presence immediately as the person she was to meet. She smiled pleasantly while the gray eyes evaluated Grady's six-foot-tall, lanky frame, still clothed in the faded denims and dress shirt that he had put on the previous night for his toot in town.

He realized she was taking in the wrinkled condition of his shirt and he grinned self-consciously. "I slept in them last night."

She extended her hand, and from habit he accepted it. Her handshake was firm and brief. "I'm Grace Cecile McNamara. I'm usually called Ceci. Will you please sit down?"

Grady pulled out a chair opposite her and sank into it. "Nice to meet you, Miss Grace. I'm Joe Bob Grady. Most folks call me Grady."

"The pleasure is mine, Mr. Grady."

He was aware of the reaction to his having called her Miss Grace instead of the preferred Ceci. She had gotten even by adding Mister to Grady. They were off to an uncomfortable, formal beginning.

3

"How many cattle are you driving?"

"Seventy-five head."

"Seventy-five head!" His exclamation was so loud that his voice carried across the room to the waitress, who glanced up, startled from her work.

"Yes, Mr. Grady. Seventy-five head. Is that more than you can handle?"

Grady knew from the poker face and the cold look that had turned the gray eyes to steel that she was not putting him on. He ducked his head and sat silently with his eyes closed for a few seconds while the bolts that had scattered in his head settled, and he gained control of his voice. When the bolts were at ease, Grady left his head perfectly still and raised his eyes to meet hers. In a quiet, controlled voice he politely said, "Miss Grace, an average herd from Texas to trailhead runs about two thousand head, or more. I don't drive less than a thousand back trail. I charge five dollars a head going up trail and three dollars headin' back. It don't pay me to drive less than a thousand head."

"All right, it's agreed then. You will receive three thousand dollars for taking my herd to San Antonio, and I will pay you a bonus of ten dollars a head for each one you deliver safely. That's an added seven hundred and fifty dollars, Mr. Grady."

"But Miss Grace, at that price you will be losing money on your herd. You could find a couple of reliable drovers who would do the job for you at a fair price."

"I appreciate your concern, Mr. Grady, but you were highly recommended to me as honest and reliable. I did not bother to contact you and wait in this unruly, undisciplined, and quite dirty town, paying several weeks board for my herd while waiting for you to arrive, to have you tell me to hire someone else. I am quite aware of the price I am paying for your services. This herd is very important to me. I intend to provide the best help I can afford to get this herd to my ranch. You have given me your price, which I have met. If you have no other objections, I will have my things ready to travel by morning, and we can be on our way."

"On our way!" The waitress gave them another anxious look. Grady lowered his voice. "I thought you were hiring me to take your cattle down trail for you."

"That's right, Mr. Grady, but as I've explained, this herd is very important to me. I won't let it out of my sight until the herd is safely on my ranch."

4

"But Miss Grace, that's a hell of a trip! I beg your pardon, ma'am, it's a rough trip."

"I'm sure it is Mr. Grady, but don't worry, I'll try not to be a burden, and you might find me an asset. This will be your first encounter with my herd. They know me, and there may be times when you will actually be glad I'm along."

"I haven't agreed to take your herd, Miss Grace." Grady suddenly came to a halt. The thought of driving seventy-five head of cattle and one lady all the way to San Antonio had turned his hangover into a thudding headache, which usually meant he needed a drink.

She had evidently been prepared for just such an answer. She reached into her purse and then laid a stack of bills on the table. "I'm prepared to pay you half of your asking price up front. It will remain yours even if you fail to deliver my herd. I need your help, Mr. Grady, and I'm trying to be fair with you."

Grady stared at the stack of bills. He had received travel money for supplies before, but this was the first time a herd owner had paid half up front. He tried, through the throbbing pain, to be reasonable. He had driven many herds where the owners and their crews had stayed with the drive. The fact that she was a woman had to be erased. She was being more than fair. She was paying an outrageous price to have seventy-five head of cattle driven to Texas, besides he would need less help and there would be more profit. He and Deadly could retire in style.

"All right, Miss Grace, you're on. I just hope you don't have cause to regret making the trip."

"Thank you, Mr. Grady, I hope I don't either. You will find my herd in the corral next to the stables, except for Trumpeter and Reginald. They are the bulls and I had the stable master lock them in stalls. They are most important, Mr. Grady. They are the only two bulls for breeding I have. Trumpeter is not young, and Reginald is too young—he is still inquisitive and irresponsible, so I need Trumpeter to stay healthy a while longer. They will both need constant supervision. I shall be ready to leave at dawn. I hope that will give you time to organize. Please leave room on one of the wagons for my trunk."

With these parting words she smiled, rose, and left the room. Grady stared at the stack of bills on the table. She hadn't even asked for a receipt.

Some businesswoman! He picked up the money, folded it, and stored it in the tight front pocket of his Levi's. Then he waved the waitress over and ordered steak and eggs, country biscuits, and hot coffee.

He had to get moving. It would take him most of the afternoon to get together what was needed, but he ate slowly, enjoying the meal. He knew he might not find time to grab another today.

As soon as Grady finished his meal, he decided to take a look at this big herd they had to deliver. He was going to be the laughingstock of the country, driving seventy-five head of cattle. It was a good thing this was his last drive; his reputation would probably be ruined forever.

Grady's first impression when he neared the corral was how silent it was. A penned-up bunch of range cattle would be letting the world know how unkindly they took to captivity. He climbed the fence then stared in amazement at the seventy-odd animals standing docilely behind the adobe corral. They were short, squatty, round little animals, dark red in color. All of them were just alike with white faces, a white line up the neck, and white legs. Grady couldn't believe what he was seeing. They looked like biscuits stamped out of the same dough; same shape and cooked to the same color.

"It's a sight, ain't it?"

Grady had been so lost in amazement that he had not heard the old man come up behind him. Grady had no answer. He couldn't speak.

"Wait till you see what I got in the barn."

Oh my God! Trumpeter and Reginald! Grady climbed down from the wall and hurried inside. It took a minute for his eyes to adjust to the darkened barn.

The old man caught up with him. "Foller me. They're in the back."

That's where they were, all right, larger versions of the ones in the corral. Not much taller, but fat, with longer hair curled like someone had taken one of them curling irons and made little curls all over their hides. Short, stubby horns, and fat! Grady couldn't get over the ponderous weight on an animal that wasn't much taller than his belt buckle.

Trumpeter had to be the larger of the two. He looked more mature, even fatter than the other bull, which had walked over to the rail and lifted his nose to sniff Grady's hands. The bull's red tongue swept out and ran roughly over Grady's fingers.

"Herefords, they is. That's what she calls them."

6

"Herefords." Grady had heard of the breed from England, or Ireland, or somewhere abroad. One of the drovers had told a story over the campfire one night. The cowboys were haranguing him, and he was sincerely trying to convince them that he had actually seen a Hereford cow. This had to be the animal he had described.

"Gawd, what am I going to tell Deadly?"

"Who's Deadly?"

In a daze, Grady answered, "He's my partner."

Grady walked out of the barn into the late-morning heat. The sun made spots flash in his glazed eyes. Momentarily blinded, he stood looking down at the ground waiting for his eyes to adjust to the light after the dimness of the barn. His thoughts were scrambled, and he couldn't seem to pull his thinking together. Unconsciously he moved his boot around in circles in the thick dust of the street. He had dug a pretty deep hole in the ground by the time his head had cleared enough to decide what had to be done.

They would not be able to handle this drive like a regular drive. Those grain-fed, corral-fat cows were not going to travel with any speed and would probably starve to death on range forage. There went the profit. He would have to haul grain and supplement it with grazing. That meant two more wagons and a couple of tons of sacked feed, and two more hands to drive the wagons, which meant more grub. "Shit."

The first thing to do was to try and find some wagons and round up some hands. Docile cows like these wouldn't need watching so much as encouragement to move.

The hands were easy. Grady checked the back rooms of the saloons and found Gimpy Lou, so nicknamed because he had one leg shorter than the other which caused an uneven gait, and his son Denny. Lou had trailed with Grady for several years. This would be Denny's first drive, but he worked well with horses and was a good kid. He took orders well. Gimpy Lou was experienced in cow doctoring, and it looked like he was going to need all the experienced help he could get.

Grady explained the setup to Lou and Denny and told Lou to get started locating feed. He sent Denny to the camp to tell Cook to bring the grub wagon in and get supplies. Denny was to pick out a dozen of the best horses to take with them and bring the rest of the remuda to town. Maybe he could pick up a few bucks on the horses, probably not what they were worth, but the remuda at present was large enough to supply a dozen hands with three or four animals apiece, which right now made the horse herd larger than the cow herd. Grady found himself shaking his head in disbelief at the mess he was in. He would have to try to exchange some of the saddle horses for mules, or wagon horses.

While he waited for Denny to return, Grady located two wagons over in New Town and spent an hour dickering price. The owner got more than Grady wanted to pay but not as much as he wanted to get, so Grady figured it came out about even. The wagons were no bargain, but he didn't get robbed either. The man agreed to grease the wheels and check both wagons so they would be in good working order.

From time to time Grady ran into some of his men and told them to spread the word that he was not hiring on for the drive back, so they could get on with what they had to do. Then he ran into Little Bear. He liked the half-breed. He was a good cowhand, hunter, and tracker, and he didn't talk much. Grady hired him to drive the other grain wagon.

Lou found Grady at the saloon, where he had stopped to have a beer and ponder the next move. Lou had located feed, but it was bulk in the granary, so he had searched the stables, stores, and feed barns and had found some empty gunnysacks. The general store had empty flour sacks for sale. They were all pretty patterns for ladies' use, but hell, them sissy cows would probably adore them.

Cook showed up, and Grady took him over to the corral and showed him the sights. He looked the cows over, spat some tobacco juice on the ground, and said, "What's them things?"

"Cows."

"The hell you say."

"That's what I'm told."

"Dangdest sight I ever seed."

"Yeah, me too."

"We really going to drive them things to Texas?"

"That's what we've been asked to do."

"Then I guess we better get at it."

"Yeah, just remember when you pick up supplies it's going to take us four times the travel time, but we only got six of us to feed, you, me, Little Bear, Gimpy Lou, Denny, and the owner." Grady was dubious about telling

Cook that the owner was a woman. He would let Cook find that out in the morning. If he quit, then at least the grub wagon would have it's supplies loaded and ready to go.

It took Lou, Denny, Little Bear, and Grady half the night loading feed sacks, what with sewing the tops closed and then loading them on the wagons. When they were done they left the wagons in Old Town and rode back to camp, where Cook found some cold biscuits and bacon.

Deadly had waited patiently by the grub wagon until Grady rode into camp. The bull ambled over to greet Grady and waited while his friend unsaddled his horse. Grady gave the bull a hug around the neck and scratched the hump between the horns, their usual greeting. "I don't know how I'm going to explain this to you, Deadly, but we got to have a long talk."

Deadly waved his horns as if he understood what Grady was saying, and followed him to the fire. Cook had the coffeepot already boiling. Grady helped himself to some biscuits and bacon, slipped Deadly a biscuit, then squatted on his heels to eat and try to explain this drive to Deadly. "Now listen, Ole Pard, in the morning I'm going to have to throw you a real curve. We got a dumb job on our hands, and you ain't going to like it any more than I do, and worse yet, I may have to tie you to the grub wagon cause them long legs of yores will kill them fat little cows."

Deadly waved a horn and flicked his tail, and his eyelids closed. It was late and he was tired. Anyway, Deadly wasn't going to understand until he saw the situation with his own eyes.

Grady's bedroll felt great. He was tired, but it took several minutes before he could sleep, because he was going over the day's events and wondering if he had made all the preparations necessary for the drive. His last thought as he drifted off was: How had he allowed himself to get into this mess?

The crew arrived in Old Town as the sun came up. Cook pulled the grub wagon up to the corral and stopped. Tied to the rail in front of the stable were three of the most beautiful gray horses Grady had ever seen. A stallion carried a black, hand-tooled leather saddle with silver inlays on the skirts, stirrup leathers, and bridle. All heads turned and the stares lost none of their admiration as Grace Cecile McNamara came out of the barn.

She was dressed in black vaquero pants and vest, black boots, and a rose flowered-print shirt. Around her waist she wore a black leather belt set with silver conchas, each concha set with magnificent turquoise stones. Her rich black hair, loose and falling in dark waves the day before, was now neatly subdued in one long braid down her back. The braid was fastened with a thong tipped with turquoise nuggets.

The men were speechless. The woman's cheeks turned red. She was embarrassed by the obvious admiration. Grady forced himself to withdraw his eyes and introduce her to the crew, "Men, this is Miss Grace Cecile McNamara, your new boss."

Lou and Denny did very well. They quickly dismounted, all grins, shook her hand, and expressed their delight in meeting her. Little Bear gave her a brief nod, but remained by his wagon. Cook just sat on the grub wagon and glared.

Grace Cecile McNamara recovered from her embarrassment quickly and thanked Lou and Denny, nodded a response to the Indian, and insisted that they call her Ceci Then she walked over to the grub wagon and looked directly into Cook's eyes. Grady knew that look because he had fallen into it the day before.

"Sir, you are the most important person on this drive. We are all ineffective if we cannot depend on you. I beg you, please don't let the fact that I am a woman prevent you from making this trail drive. I so desperately need all the help I can get, and I promise to stay out of your way and let you do your job your way."

Such a silence as Cook studied those gray eyes, the serious face, then turned his head and spat a stream of tobacco juice to the ground on the other side of the wagon. "Then we better get a move on Miss McNamara. It's time we was traveling." He didn't offer his hand, and they all knew that this was a truce, not approval.

"Wait a minute, we've got another introduction and this one isn't going to be easy." Deadly had followed the grub wagon into town, as was his custom, and was waiting patiently for the drive to begin. Grady swung off his horse and walked around the wagon to him. As was their custom when Grady wanted the bull to follow, he grabbed one of Deadly's horns and pulled. Deadly turned and followed Grady around the wagon. Now it was Ceci's turn to stare in amazement. Grady silently prayed she would not take a step backward. He had seen Deadly react before to people who were afraid of him, and Grady sure would hate to spend days on the trail with

Deadly teasing Miss Grace. But she did good. She held her ground as Grady brought Deadly up to her. She knew how to handle cattle, all right. She didn't try to touch him. She just talked in a calm voice and told him how pleased she was to meet him.

"All right now, Miss Grace, I'm going to slip a rope over old Deadly's horns. You go in and get Trumpeter. I hope Deadly don't take him to pieces."

"He won't, Mr. Grady, Deadly looks like a gentleman to me. I'm sure he will realize that Trumpeter is old. With Reginald, however, we may have a problem." She turned and went into the stables.

Grady got the lariat from his saddle and slipped the loop over each of Deadly's horns and drew it tight. Deadly knew something was up because Grady rarely tied him anymore. Grady turned Deadly towards the stable door and braced himself. Ceci came out of the door, leading Trumpeter, and walked directly up to Deadly. Deadly stiffened his legs, lifted his head, walled his eyes, and snorted.

"Oh brother," Grady said, and braced himself for the stampede.

"Deadly, this is Trumpeter. He is a Hereford. He comes from Britain where he is from a long line of purebred Hereford cattle. He is going to my ranch in San Antonio. It's very important that he make this trip safely. If I can get just one year's crop of his calves, I will be most fortunate. He is not a young bull as you are. He needs your guidance, as he is in a strange land."

Grady could see the tenseness go out of Deadly's body as she talked. His eyes steadied and focused on the short-legged bull. Trumpeter reached forward with his nose and sniffed Deadly's nose. They stood for a moment sniffing each other's noses, and then Trumpeter lowered his head and returned to a relaxed stance. Deadly took a step forward and continued his investigation. He was not getting excited, so Grady slacked up on the rope as Deadly slowly made his way sniffing down one side of Trumpeter, across his rump, and up the other side. When Deadly was satisfied, he touched noses with Trumpeter again and stood quietly beside him, relaxing into the same sleepy stance held by Trumpeter.

Miss Grace looked at Grady and smiled. He breathed a sigh of relief and removed the rope from Deadly's horns. Deadly gave him a scathing look, for his friend had insulted him.

"All right, I'm sorry. How was I to know how you were going to act, you big lummox?"

11

"What about Reginald?" Miss Grace asked.

"Well, let's don't press our luck. If we can get Deadly used to Trumpeter first, we can always keep Reginald, or Deadly, or both, tied if we have to. Let's move Deadly and the herd out. You lead Reginald at the back of the herd." She nodded in agreement and left to get Reginald.

"Cookie, you better get moving. Bed down at Circle Creek tonight. I don't think any of these cows can make it any further. It's going to take days for us to build up some endurance in them."

Cook nodded, spat tobacco juice, and moved his wagon down the street.

"Denny, tie Miss Grace's mares to Lou's wagon. Little Bear, you lead out. Denny can take the remuda on up with Cook. We aren't going to need fresh horses except daily. In fact, the ones we're on will probably spend the day sleeping at the pace these fat cows will travel."

By the time they opened the gate and coaxed the cows into the street it was obvious they had never been trail driven before. For a minute Grady was afraid Deadly was going to panic when this crowd of look-alikes came toward him. But Trumpeter reached over, touched Deadly's nose, turned in a slow ponderous walk, and moved majestically down the street. Deadly moved quickly to pass him. Seventy-three cows obediently trailed after their lord and master. Grady knew Deadly intended to keep far in advance of this strange looking herd.

A crowd had collected by the time they were ready to drive the cattle through town. They moved out with catcalls and jokes ringing in their ears.

Miss Grace, bringing up the rear, turned their departure into a parade. Her elegant gray stallion, with head held high, pranced and sidestepped. Reginald even plodded along in style; lifting his head occasionally, he sent loud calls to his buddy, Trumpeter. Miss Grace waved at the people, made the stallion rear a time or two; the catcalls turned to cheers and applause. That was some gal. Grady had never met one like her before.

The anticipated nightmare began. Those muley-headed cows would not stay bunched. They acted as if they were on a Sunday stroll. Grady worked his horse into a lather trying to keep them together and was sorry he had sent the remuda on ahead. He was going to need a fresh horse in an hour if this kept up. Trumpeter began to tire. He wanted to stop and eat grass. Deadly was thoroughly confused. The cows would not follow him. He got mad, stretched out his legs, caught up with Lou's wagon, and settled into a steady rambling walk, occasionally stopping to graze and eye the circus going on behind him.

The herd was almost at a standstill. Grady rested his horse and waited for Miss Grace to join him. She had had to halt repeatedly to keep Reginald behind.

"Well, this isn't going to work. Any suggestions?" Grady pulled his kerchief off and mopped perspiration from his face.

"Why don't we try Reginald in the lead? I can keep him tied and lead him. It's obvious Trumpeter is too slow for the younger cows, and they don't know your bull at all."

"OK, ma'am. I'm willing to try anything before my horse collapses on me. I sure misjudged this herd. I needed to hire a keeper for each cow. We would have better luck leading them on ropes."

"Yes, it appears that way. But I have confidence in you, Mr. Grady. You will work it out."

There she went again, using diplomacy on him again. It looked like Grace Cecile McNamara could sweet-talk a man into almost anything. He watched as she moved forward. Reginald protested loudly, pulling back and bawling. She undid her braided lariat and flicked the young bull expertly on the rear. He shut up and followed her.

"Call Lou back behind the herd and tie Trumpeter behind the wagon where the cows can't see him," she called back.

Grady did so, and when they started up again there were at least fifty cows following Reginald. The other twenty-three felt the sting of Grady's rope several times before they got the idea. He figured if she could use a little discipline on her cattle, so could he.

Grady noticed Deadly grazing as the herd passed him by. He called to the bull, "You better keep up." Grady looked back for him later and saw him walking beside Trumpeter, behind the wagon. Poor old Deadly, he was as bad off as Grady. They both had lost their jobs.

By the time the herd reached Circle Creek, the cows had been disciplined enough that they were moving together as a herd, but it was an exhausted, slow-moving herd. Grady had never been so glad to see a campfire. You would have thought he had battled a winter storm all day, he was so glad to stop. The tedious pace had really gotten on his nerves.

They bunched the cattle and put Denny to riding herd on them, but he really didn't need to bother. Most of the cows dropped to the ground and rested. A few grazed quietly. There was plenty of grass so it wasn't necessary to feed the grain. They would need it for the desert areas ahead of them.

"Mr. Grady, come here please." Ceci's voice came from the rear wagon. Grady ran. He could tell from the anxious tone of her voice something was serious. Trumpeter was standing with his legs spread apart, head down, froth around his mouth, and his nose dripping perspiration. Even at a snail's pace the walk had been too much for him. Grady hadn't given him a thought. They had all been so busy trying to keep the herd moving no one had checked on Trumpeter. Only Deadly, who had traveled beside him most of the day, knew how much the old bull was suffering. Denny hauled water to him, let him drink a little, and then took it away. Ceci took a rag and sponged his face and back over and over with cool water, then let him drink again. When his breathing finally became regular she used dry grass to rub him until he was dry. Grady opened a grain sack and gave him a small portion of grain. The old bull was too tired to graze. If Trumpeter didn't die of exertion, he would surely die of starvation, if he was too tired to graze each night.

Tired as Grady was, a decision had to be made. They were not far from San Diego. Grady had deliberately made this first day's drive a short one. He must go back to town and figure out a way to transport Trumpeter, or they could forget that first year's dropping of his calves.

He told Denny to bring a fresh horse. As he ate a quick meal he explained to the tired faces around the fire. He told them to take turns watching the herd, get as much rest as possible, and not to worry. If he did not make it back the next day he would be back the following one.

It had taken them so long that day to reach the camp at Circle Creek that it surprised Grady how quickly he made it back to Old Town. By midnight he was fast asleep at the hotel. He awoke early and began his search. They were going to need another wagon, another hand to drive it, supplies to feed him, and another team to pull the wagon. Grady was beginning to believe this drive would cost him money.

He found a wagon that appeared perfect for what he had in mind. Its bed was not so large that the bull could not be braced. It had been a farm wagon used for family transportation. Grady took it to the smith's and had heavy metal supports built to keep the bull's weight off of the wheels, and reinforced the axles. He located a couple of extra wheels, the right size for the cart, and had them attached underneath the bed. He located a carpenter and had him build rail sides up high enough to keep the bull in the wagon. The carpenter also built a movable ramp that could be fastened across the rear of the end gate, and strong enough to use to load the bull. By late afternoon the wagon had turned into a moving box car.

He found another of the regular crew, by the name of Scratch O'Donnell, still hanging about, and he gladly welcomed him to drive the wagon back. A fine pair of work mules pulled the wagon, with an extra pair of work-horses tied on behind. What with the miners farther north yelling for work animals and paying four times their worth, the teams had cost an arm and a leg, and Grady was in a foul mood as they drove out of town.

The camp was asleep when they reached it, but Deadly came out of the shadows and stood watching as Grady unsaddled. He didn't come forward as usual. Grady knew the bull was still puzzled. All he could hope for was that the bull would understand as time passed. Deadly turned and went back into the shadows. Grady bedded down in the new wagon bed, and when morning came he looked for the bull. He found Deadly standing guard over Trumpeter, who lay peacefully at Deadly's feet, chewing his cud. The rascal had found a new friend.

Grady walked over and scratched Deadly's head. "You fickle son-of-a-bitch," he said fondly. He was glad Deadly was watching over old Trum-peter. The rest of them hadn't done such a good job of it.

The crew looked rested, and the herd had settled comfortably to graze, figuring their traveling days were over. Cook had breakfast ready, and while they ate Grady explained his plan.

"Every morning while we are fresh, we are going to load that bull. We are going to haul him all day without unloading him, if the trail permits. About an hour before we reach camp each day we are going to unload him and let him walk in. The herd will have tired and slowed to a steady pace that he can keep up with. When his legs have toughened and he's built up his wind enough to make that distance, we'll drop him out a little farther each time. After a few weeks travel, we'll be hitting some mountains and rough country. We'll have trouble hauling the wagons over it. It will take an extra team and a lot of tugging and jerking to get through. Trumpeter will have to walk through those areas, because he could easily get his legs broken trying to wagon him through. OK, let's give it a try."

Miss Grace ran to get a rope on Trumpeter. Little Bear and Scratch helped Grady take off the tailgate and reposition it as a ramp floor. It was pretty steep and Grady had his doubts they would get Trumpeter up it without a struggle. He hated the thought of having to dig a hole to back up to each morning, so he intended to teach Trumpeter to climb the ramp. He braced the wheels so the wagon would not roll.

Grady got a huge surprise when Miss Grace brought Trumpeter over. She walked up the ramp and the bull attempted to follow her, but the pitch was too high. She called out, "Give him a push from behind." Scratch and Grady fell to and in a wink Trumpeter was in the wagon.

"Well, I'll be damned." Grady couldn't believe it had been accomplished so easily.

"Don't be surprised, Mr. Grady, Trumpeter is a prize bull. He has ridden in wagons before, to fairs and shows. I have a collection of ribbons in my trunk that he's won. He's a real trouper, and you will realize before we reach San Antonio that the Hereford is a hardy, intelligent animal. That weight you call fat, Mr. Grady, is solid table meat. More meat, by the pound, than the scrawny range cattle you're used to." She was proud of Trumpeter this morning, and well she might be. Grady had anticipated having to bodily hoist the old bull aboard.

"All right, Miss Grace, you've made your point, this morning anyway. We'll see how many more delays your precious Herefords cost us," he replied.

"The idea is not to get the herd to San Antonio in record time, Mr. Grady, just to get them there, as many as possible, in as good condition as possible."

"That may be your objective, Miss Grace, but I have to keep in mind the weather. If we don't keep at it, you're going to get an opportunity, before this trip is over, to see how your Herefords bear up under trailblazing through snow. Now tie that bull's head up and let's get moving." Grady's patience was a little thin this morning, for he had not had much sleep.

He tied up the tailgate and put Denny to pulling grass and throwing it in the bottom of the wagon. In case the bull fell to his knees the grass would give him a cushion. Grady checked Trumpeter's rope to be sure Miss Grace had tied the bull's head up short and firm, to help brace him.

Satisfied that she had done the job right, Grady went to get his horse, which he found already saddled and waiting for him. Denny was a good kid. Cook had already left, hurrying on ahead to get camp set up before they reached the campsite. Grady had decided to keep today's drive as short as the first day. They had no way of knowing how their efforts to transport Trumpeter would work, and they would be in mountainous terrain by evening.

Denny took off with the remuda. Miss Grace had Reginald ready to go. Grady sent Lou on ahead and got the herd moving. Little Bear joined the wagons while Scratch brought up the rear. Grady told him to go as slow as needed, to keep up if possible, but to keep an eye on the bull to be sure he was riding safely at all times.

The herd started out the same way as before, but today it didn't take long for them to get the idea that they either moved or got a whack from a rope. Deadly had watched as they loaded Trumpeter and when the herd began to move he took his place beside Trumpeter's wagon.

All in all, it was a good day's travel. Not easy, but good. The docile cattle never gave up trying to halt and graze. Reginald took a spell of fighting the rope, pulling back and bellowing as if he had gone crazy. Cecile's arms grew tired. Grady took over her job and sent her back to work the drag. When she had her horse turned away Grady took his lariat and worked the bull over. Reginald quieted down and settled into a steady pace. After Cecile was rested, she returned to leading Reginald.

They were going to reach camp early. Scratch stopped the wagon and unloaded the old bull. Trumpeter backed down the ramp as if he did this sort of thing all the time and shook his head vigorously to relieve taut muscles. Cecile untied the rope from his halter and everyone returned to work. The herd had taken advantage of the stop and scattered to graze. Grady figured that this would be a daily roundup unless he could figure a way to speed up the stop, or keep the herd moving.

Grady kept an eye on Trumpeter as they traveled. He wanted Trumpeter to get used to the idea of traveling with the herd. Grady soon quit worrying, as Deadly had taken charge of the old bull, and Trumpeter seemed to be aware of his part in this program. When he did lag, Deadly would nudge him with a ball-tipped horn, and Trumpeter would respond by stepping it up a bit.

17

The old bull was breathing hard by the time the herd reached camp, but he was fine, and soon he and Deadly were grazing side by side. Trumpeter gradually worked into the herd, and Deadly, anxious to be with his new friend, tagged nervously along looking like a giant among midgets. Every now and then a cow would stop grazing long enough to touch noses with him. Grady really believed the old bull was trying to get Deadly acquainted with the herd.

When Cook rang the dinner bell, Deadly reverted to habit and came for his evening biscuit. Cook was glad to see him and slipped him another biscuit when he thought Grady wasn't watching. Deadly came over and nudged his friend in the back as usual.

Grady said, "Hello, Pal." Deadly stood quietly while Grady ate, then he turned and went back to graze with the herd.

You love him, don't you?" Miss Grace and Grady were the only ones left at the fire. Cook was cleaning up, Little Bear was with the herd, and Denny was keeping an eye on the remuda and hobbling the horses. Scratch and Lou had wandered off for a smoke where it would not bother the lady.

"Yeah, I guess. He's like family. In fact I guess you could say he is family." Grady picked up a stick and stirred the coals then fed the fire another small branch.

"No mother or father?"

"No, I have been on my own for awhile now,."

"Brothers, or sisters?"

"No, not anymore. Just Deadly."

"I'm sorry."

"Thanks, but I'm used to it. Gets kind of rough around Christmas, but I manage. I lost my family one by one when we moved out here to grab free land and start a farm. With the weather, Indians and wolves it took a toll on my family until I was the only one left."

"My mother and dad are gone also."

"I'm sorry. Recently?"

"Yes, just a few years ago. They were killed when their horse went wild on a mountain road. The buggy fell hundreds of feet down a cliff."

"Man, that's a hard way to go."

"My mother was killed instantly. My father was so broken up he couldn't be moved, and he refused to let us take him away from her. They were very much in love. He lived two days, but there was internal bleeding. I managed to get a doctor to him, but the doctor was afraid to move him." Ceci continued, "We all stayed camped at the accident until he passed. He held my mother's hand the entire time, right up to the end. There was nothing we could do except make him as comfortable as possible. Those were the worst two days of my life."

The conversation had become so personal that it was making Grady squirm.

"My brother was also in the buggy, but he was thrown out as it fell. Somehow his legs were badly mangled and now he doesn't have the use of them. He is all of my family that is left. We run our ranch together, with the help of a majordomo who has been with us since my mother was a very little girl."

To change the conversation to something less tragic Grady asked, "Will you please tell me what you are doing here with a herd of Hereford cattle?"

She smiled. "Yes. Our rancho is old. It belonged to my mother's family, a Spanish grant that has been handed down for generations. My father was like you, an American cowboy. He had a terrible time convincing my grandfather that he would be a good husband for my mother. My grandfather raised the finest Toro Bravo, the Spanish fighting bull used in the bullrings. My father was as good a cowboy as any of our vaqueros. He worked hard to learn about breeding bulls, and he did well, and when my grandfather was on his deathbed he blessed my father and gave permission for them to marry.

"The breeding did not go well. Oh, my father's bulls were grand and full of courage, but my father was a gringo, an American, and some would not buy from him. He tried, for tradition's sake, to keep the bloodline alive, but when he was killed we were in great financial trouble. My brother was young. Papa's majordomo is wise and can continue the breeding, but we have to have another source of income, or we will be forced to sell our home. I began with the wild Spanish brush cattle. I gradually built a tacky herd. I keep my good breeding stock away from the others. I raise a small number of fine bulls for the ring, because I promised my father.

"A rancher in Mexico told me about this herd. It was brought from Britain by a widow whose husband bred them. She believed they would improve our breeding stock, but she was unable to convince many people to buy them. My brother and I discussed it, and we decided that I should try to buy them."

"I went to see her, and she seemed to like me. Just as my mother had, she had spent a lifetime with a man she loved, and she shared his joy in cattle breeding. Now he was gone, she was old, and her precious cattle were being ridiculed. She was afraid the line would be destroyed. I told her about my bulls, and my scrub cattle, and offered her all the money I had for this herd.

"She was very kind. She said that the small amount of money that I had could never pay what the herd was worth, but that she would make a bargain with me. She would give me the herd if I put on paper a promise to continue the Hereford breed, and to keep the line pure. I could use the bulls to strengthen my range herd, but I must keep the cows bred pure. When I sell the calves I'm to give her one tenth of the price I get until I have paid the price she felt the herd was worth."

Ceci stretched her hands towards the fire to warm them. "I agreed, and here I am. I took part of the money we had saved and traveled to San Diego. I had a bad time with the man who was pasturing the cattle. I believe he had intentions of stealing them from her for a feed bill, or the like, but I figured the bill in cattle at the price the owner had figured their worth. The man was not happy with the six cows that I left him, but both his attorney and mine agreed I had paid more than a fair price.

"I had to feed them while I waited in San Diego for you. The money that I gave you was the last that I had with me. If we don't make it to San Antonio you won't get paid. I've told you that I cannot afford to lose many of these cows, and especially the two bulls. Now you understand why they are so important to me. If I am to keep my promise to this fine lady, I must reach San Antonio with this herd."

"Yes, Miss Grace, I understand your concern, but you know that if these cows have been pasturing with the bulls, some of them are carrying calves. You should be lucky enough for some of them to drop bulls."

"Of course, Mr. Grady, this could be true, but when I found the herd they were running with a very large herd of mixed breed cattle. It took days to round up the Herefords. I can't be sure the calves they drop this year will be pure. I need Trumpeter. Reginald is good stock, he's Trumpeter's son, but he is unproven. I can't tell you how ill I become when I imagine anything happening to Trumpeter." Her voice trembled.

"Don't worry. We'll get him there if I've got to walk him myself, and keep an eye on him."

"Thank you, Mr. Grady. I appreciate your help." Her gray eyes, softened by the evening darkness, glistened with tears in the light of the campfire.

Grady quickly changed the subject. "That's a great looking trio of horses you own."

"They are beautiful aren't they?' Pride replaced her worried expression. "They are Arabians, my father's weakness. I guess it runs in my blood, my grandfather and his fighting bulls, my father and his Arabian horses, and now me with my Herefords."

They laughed together, Grady's chuckle joining her infectious laugh. "Those horses will be of profit to me someday. I have shown them to breeders. I have a man who will buy all I can produce at a very good price, worth the delivery cost if I can deliver enough at one time. My herd of Arabians is small. I have been discreet in the breeding, for I had no market. I would not let them go as cowboy horses for practically nothing. I have records of the tremendous price my father paid to have them shipped from Arabia. If we make it safely to San Antonio, Mr. Grady, I may have need of your services again to take my Arabians safely to the East."

"I appreciate the compliment, ma'am, but we've a ways to go to determine if I earn my money. Deadly and I got a little spread of our own we're headed for. I doubt if we're going to make any more trips up this trail."

"I'm happy for you then, Mr. Grady, but before it becomes a definite retirement, let me tempt you. If my plans come to pass and I need a good trail boss, I will pay you in Hereford bulls for breeding stock for your ranch."

"Deadly isn't going to like that."

"Mr. Grady, Deadly is a fine bull. He is strong and sturdy for the range. He will have good calves. But this country is growing and there are more people every year to be fed, and believe me, Mr. Grady, there will be ranchers breeding for more meat to the bone. The Hereford is the answer, and you could be one of the first to introduce the Hereford strain in Texas. Your ranch and cattle would become famous, and in demand."

"You may be right, Miss Grace, but after two days with them squatty, fat, lazy cows, I can tell you they are not going to make it on the open range."

"I know you are wrong, Mr. Grady. These cattle were raised on land where the coldest of winters occur. I feel certain they will survive on open range in this country, but I care enough for them not to test them by letting them run wild. I am used to pampering prize blooded cattle, and I shall do whatever is necessary to both improve my beef herds and continue the purebred Hereford line, if I have to keep them in my ranch house."

Her stubborn little chin set. Grady laughed as he pictured Trumpeter walking about inside the house. He told her his thoughts and she laughed also.

"Yes, I guess you would, "Miss Grace."

"Yes, I would, Mr. Grady. Good night."

"Goodnight, ma'am."

CHAPTER TWO

Cecile struggled with her daily workload but found the time to study the man she had hired to drive her herd of Herefords across this rugged land. She was certain the herd was in the most capable hands she could have hired. Joe Bob Grady had been recommended highly by people she knew, and respected, and a very large load of responsibility had lifted from her shoulders when he agreed to take the job.

Often, as she rode behind the herd, she watched him work the cattle. She had to admit he rode as well, or better, than any vaquero she knew, which was hard for her to accept for the Spanish vaqueros she had grown up with were the finest horsemen in Texas.

She liked this tall lanky man and couldn't understand the antagonism that flared up between them almost every time they were together. He was handsome—not the swarthy dark handsomeness of the Spanish men she had grown up with, but Grady had the strong look of hardy pioneers. His face was not perfectly formed. Each feature, studied separately, had flaws, but all of them together formed rugged good looks that showed strong character, determination, and strength that instilled confidence in others.

His hair was an undetermined shade of blond and brown, as was that of many of the Anglos who were pouring into the West in droves. When he removed his hat an unruly cowlick would swing into his eyes, softening his sunburned face and giving him a boyish look.

His eyes were also an indefinable color, a hazel that shifted, sometimes green hazel, sometimes blue hazel, and when he was angry or frustrated, they turned a brown hazel. She smiled at her thoughts, for Grady was often angry and frustrated since he had agreed to drive her herd.

She watched him now as he sent his horse after an obstinate cow that was determined to quit the herd and find grass. She imagined the muscles bunching under his shirt as he balanced on the twisting, turning horse as it dodged after the cow, and an odd, exquisite feeling developed in her lower abdomen. She recognized these sexual desires and took her eyes off of Grady. She had been raised a lady, but she had no shame for the feelings. She knew that they were normal, for she was past marriage age, almost an old maid to her people. Before her parents had died a duenna, an always-present companion, had protected her. After the death of her parents she had no time for such foolishness. Running the rancho had changed her protected ways.

Now she determined to stop fantasizing about Grady before it got her in trouble. She shifted her attention to the incredible scenery about her. Once the fog of the coastline had been left behind, the trail wound upward through chaparral-covered foothills along a stream shrunken by summer drought. Alders and cottonwoods held cool shadows in their branches. Climbing higher the road wound through stands of lodge pole pines and they made camp in a subalpine meadow. Granite crags loomed over the trail with limber pines huddled at their base.

Several days later they reached the crest of a ridge. A few scant Alpine shrubs lay in the lee of protecting rocks. Far to the east she could see a gray-brown horizon, heat hazed and sprinkled with tan hillocks. In the distance she could see a large patch of white, the mineral residue of a dry lakebed glinting in the sun. Cecile was surprised to see vast semiarid terrain drop away before her. It was the western Sonoran desert. The shift from alpine landscapes to sea level desert plains was quick and startling.

It took only a day to descend the mountain that had taken many days of toil to ascend. It was like a toboggan ride down. She was both frightened and thrilled to watch the men lower the wagons with ropes, to slow their descent down the winding road. She was thankful they were traveling along the well-traveled Butterfield stage route, a man-made highway through the rugged terrain surrounding them.

The cattle needed little urging to travel downhill, leaving the men free to struggle with the wagons. The great sweeps of the switchbacks took the herd back down to sea level. The air grew noticeably warmer. Suddenly there were no more pines or firs. Chaparral took command. About halfway down the mountain the bushes, clumps of cactus, the slanting stems of last year's century plants, and slender wands of ocotillo that burst up from the broken slopes took over.

The switchbacks straightened, and foothill vegetation, sparse though it had been, yielded to even more scattered patches of creosote bush. The desert plains were covered with saltbush. Streaks of white alkali, looking deceptively like snow, left powdery white dust on everything. Even her skin was covered with a thin, white film of grit.

Camp was silent that night. All were tired, scratched by the brush, and hot and gritty with dust. Cecile tried to wipe some of the white powder away with a dampened rag, but it was futile. Another layer took its place. Her hands stung from scratches made by the brush. Before she retired she rummaged through her trunk and removed a pair of shiny black chaps decorated with silver conchos embedded with flawless turquoise. She regretted having to use them. A few days in this harsh desert would ruin them.

The chaps reminded her of Ramon, her brother, for he had made them for her, as he had all of her silver and turquoise ornaments. In a wheelchair, he had turned his disability into a beautiful art that had helped to finance this trip. She drifted into a peaceful sleep, dreaming of home and Ramon.

The next morning they crossed sand dunes where the early morning sun was so severe it sent heat waves spiraling upward. Cecile was glad when the dunes were left behind and the herd crossed onto a gravel desert floor where gaunt tree trunks followed sandy pathways. Now the heat could not be ignored. It grabbed her throat, and her head pounded.

It seemed almost too hot to bear. She kept reminding herself that soon they would reach the river, the Colorado River. She caught up with the grub wagon and lowered the dipper into the water barrel and drank thirstily of the tepid water. Rinsing the grit from her mouth she peered through the heat haze at the Dome Rock Mountains to the east in the distance. They looked like a cluster of blue fangs ready to bite the sky. Thunderheads hovered over them. How she wished she were under their dark protection from the sun.

She adjusted the brim of her black sombrero so that it shaded her sun-burned face. Her eyes relaxed their squint and she saw ahead what looked like trees in the distance. Even the herd seemed excited.

There were trees ahead, real trees with shade! But now she became aware of a new torment. Humidity, with the merciless 115-degree heat, was piling up the storm clouds. Sweat ran down her face, and dampened her clothes. She watched as rings of wetness appeared on the men's shirts. The cattle were quickening their pace. Dust filled the air and settled onto her wet skin. Mud came off onto her shirt when she wiped her sleeves across her forehead. Just when she was certain she could stand the heat and dirt no longer, they reached the river. Cattle, horses, men, and one hot, grimy young woman walked into the cool rushing waters of the Colorado River.

It was a different camp that night. Cattle grazed contentedly on lush grass along the riverbank. Everyone had spent a long time in the cool water. Cecile had taken soap and a towel and found a secluded spot away from camp for a bath. Nevertheless she was nervous about removing all of her clothes, because there were active communities on both sides of the river. She had watched as Yuma Indians pulled the ferry back and forth across the river. In the morning they would begin loading cattle on the ferry, and the Indians would pull them across. Grady had said it would take most of the day to ferry all the cattle, horses, and wagons across the river. Tomorrow night they would camp outside of the Yuma Army Post where she had been promised a long, luxurious bath—in a tub, in private.

They spent another day camped by the army post. Grady bought food supplies to replace the ones they had used. They filled the water barrels with river water while Cecile enjoyed looking around the army camp and through the supply depot. The camp seemed short on white men and long on Indians. There was talk of war between the North and the South, which explained the absence of white men. Many had gone to enlist. Those left were old and spent their days under a shade tree playing checkers.

Cecile wondered briefly how the war would affect Texas, but such heavy thoughts soon left her mind as she enjoyed the sights and activities of the garrison. The few younger soldiers treated Cecile with respect. A couple of them constantly sought her company.

There were a group of men, civilians, who kept to themselves and followed her with lustful eyes as they passed around a whisky bottle and whispered among themselves. Their eyes followed her every move, and she was uncomfortable with this attention. She felt as though they were mentally undressing her. The men were clean enough, their hair combed, but these men made her skin crawl. She was glad for the company of the young soldiers; their attention protected her from closer contact with the civilian men.

The last night camped by the fort, after the cattle bedded down, Cecile and the men were sitting around the campfire discussing the efforts needed to get on the trail in the morning when gunshots rang out. Yells from the Fort followed. Grady and Little Bear leaped to their feet, pulling their pistols, and ran for the Fort. Cook retrieved his rifle from under the seat on the cook wagon, and motioned Cecile closer to the wagon where she might find cover in case trouble came their way.

The sound of horses running away was soon followed by Grady and Little Bear returning to camp. They reported that a card game had led to the gunshots. "One of the young soldiers has been shot attempting to settle the disturbance. He is wounded seriously and might not make it. The kid got off a shot but no one knows if he hit anyone."

Cecile felt terrible. "I hope that young man makes it. A couple of those soldiers spent time showing me around the fort and they were gentlemen. However, there was a group of civilian men who made me very uncomfortable. Were they the ones doing the shooting?"

"Could be," Grady replied. "Didn't see the men. The riders who took off headed back across the river with soldiers after them. Glad we're headed out the other way."

CHAPTER THREE

Cecile was not looking forward to continuing the drive through the desert heat, but they were in luck. The next morning as the herd traveled away from the river the blazing sun disappeared and a rainsquall misted the mountain ranges ahead. Soon the gray broom of the storm swept across the desert.

The cattle plodded silently through the steady downpour, climbing into the rugged, barren hills as lightning bounced onto the escarpments of the small ridges. Cecile was amazed to see waterfalls spill off broken cliff sides where minutes before dry desert sand shimmered in the heat. The air became filled with an unmistakable odor, the sharp, resinous, almost aromatic smell of wet creosote bush and dampened desert soil.

Camp was wet that night, even the bedrolls felt damp, but the desert had cooled some from the rain, and the stifling dust was temporarily wet down. The next few days' travel was pleasant, and Cecile again marveled at the pronounced change in the scenery surrounding her. The sudden and dramatic appearance of saguaro cactus delighted her. As the saguaros became larger and more abundant, other forms of vegetation began to appear, including many small trees. There were palo verde, ironwood, desert willow, mesquite, cat claw, and others she did not recognize.

The desert began to promise woodlands in the distant mountain ranges. The small ranges they had passed through were insignificant compared to the Chiricahua ranges yet to come. This was the stronghold of the Chiricahua-Mimbres Apaches and their leader, Cochise, who was presently on friendly terms with the white men. The Butterfield route, called the "Oxbow," swept far south across southern New Mexico and Arizona, passing through the notorious Apache Pass in the Chiricahua Mountains where the road left the surrounding plains to wind through a narrow gap at the foot of Dos Cabezas, a smaller group of mountains that were almost a spur of the Chiricahuas. The road could have turned north and avoided the mountains all together, but Apache Pass contained the vital asset: water.

The Butterfield stagecoach route had secured the Apaches' friendship with presents, and it was rumored that Cochise's tribe provided the station with firewood, and camped nearby.

Cecile dreaded passing through Apache Pass and wished the ordeal behind them, and a safe arrival for them at Camp Bowie. The Apaches were such a volatile people, and Cecile feared them. She did not trust this talk of peace with Cochise.

It seemed as if they had traveled over the desert plains for weeks. The heat returned and with it the humidity as the sun dried the moisture from the sand. In reality it had only been days, but they were long, uneventful days. The distant mountains remained distant at each day's end. Cecile longed for the coolness of a higher altitude, the shade of a tree, and relief from the ever-tearing brush. Grady had moved the herd away from the trail, traveling parallel to it, but keeping the herd off the road so the stages could pass unhampered and maintain their grueling schedules. This was convenient for Butterfield, but painful for the crew dodging the dry brush.

Cecile longed for the green, lush, southern Texas country. She was tired of dust, heat, cactus, and monotony. A curiously protective attitude toward the herd of blooded cattle seemed to creep into all of them, even the crotchety old cook. Cecile McNamara's constant vigil over each member of the small herd became infectious, and all of them at one time or another found themselves moving through the herd and at times dismounting to examine, from head to foot, a cow that appeared in need of help. A scratch, a burr, received attention. Grady found himself running experienced hands over the coarse, red hair in search of ticks, the carriers of the dread tick fever.

Deadly eyed these pamperings with a snort and a twitch of his tail. Trumpeter, content to relax after each day's journey, ignored everything but the evening ration of grain that continued to supplement the meager grazing his tired legs allowed.

With Trumpeter's early retirement each evening because of his obvious need for rest, Reginald became the active herd bull. Deadly continued to stand guard over old Trumpeter and watched the younger bull's growing self-importance as he patrolled the tired herd, posturing and snorting.

The big longhorn knew that the young bull had a lot to learn. Right now he was secure with his small herd of cows and no contender. Deadly had learned from many years of trail drives to mind his own business. He wasn't sure on this drive just what his business was, but he did recognize that both Trumpeter and Reginald were special, and he would be severely scolded if he followed his instinct and knocked the cocky little bastard on his ass. So he kept his distance and ignored the young bull's offers to do battle over the pint-size cows.

Reginald failed to recognize Deadly's attitude as indifference. He strutted, teased, and taunted, pawing the earth, sending clouds of dust over his shoulders. When Deadly ignored him and continued his grazing, the young bull would bellow his challenge to earth and hell, over the desert, to echo against the caliche hills. When Deadly ignored his challenges, Reginald figured the range bull had backed down. He would make an important tour of the herd, pick out a young female, settle down by her side, and graze.

Deadly was glad tonight that the young bull had finally ceased his amateurish bawling. The night had stilled, and Deadly lifted his nose high and sniffed the air. Besides the normal camp odors—smoke from the campfire, cattle, and sweaty horses—there was a crispness that sent a chill along his back. The large rough tongue snaked out and swiped across the broad black nose in an effort to clean the dust from his nostrils. He then again breathed deeply of the night air.

Like a ritual, he made a slow swing, breathing deeply and testing the air with the long, slow, fillings of his lungs. He stood for a long while facing north, staring into the darkness. His tongue made frequent swipes to keep his nostrils moist.

Occasionally he continued his night grazing. The big rangy body required more nourishment than the squatty Herefords. Deadly often grazed the better part of the night, long after the rest of the herd had settled to sleep.

The camp grew quiet as each person retired to his, or her, bedroll. The fire had died down and the kid on night watch was dozing when Deadly threw up his head again and stared into the darkness, his instinct traveling out over the desert plains.

A gentle breeze had begun to blow in from the north, not serious, but it seemed to carry with it an unseen danger that made Deadly twitch his shaggy tail and taste the wind with his mouth open. The rough tongue extended and mopped once again across his nose. Then he returned to chewing his cud. He shifted nervously from one leg to another, twisted around to sample the air from the south, and then returned to stare, once again, into the darkness to the north. The gentle wind had increased.

Deadly lowered his nose to Trumpeter's curly shoulders and nuzzled him. The old bull was dozing. He opened his eyes, grunted recognition, and then returned to his dozing. Deadly thrust his nose into the breeze again, testing the air, and then he turned toward the camp. With quickening pace he skirted the grub wagon, and with the grace of a dancer made his way around sleeping people, saddles, and camp gear. He came to a halt beside the bedroll that contained his friend. He lightly touched his cold wet nose to his old friend's cheek. Grady was instantly awake. Long association with Deadly had taught him to be aware of Deadly's instincts. Grady crawled from the warm bedroll, pulled on his boots, and took the tip of one long horn in his hand, letting Deadly lead him back to the rise where Trumpeter dozed. Grady stood quietly as Deadly lifted his nose into the air and stood immobile for several moments, his tongue occasionally tasting the air. Grady felt the gentle north wind hit his face, and for a moment seemed to feel a hidden force coming towards them in the darkness. He searched the sky. The stars *were* crisp and bright, not a cloud to be seen, but Deadly was never wrong. A bad storm was brewing. A northern storm this time of year could be accompanied by tornado winds.

"Thanks, old pal." He patted the bull on the shoulder and turned to waken the camp.

"Everyone up! Get dressed, pack up, and meet at the grub wagon." He gave his orders, then hurried to tend to his own gear. The sleeping hands came alive and hurried to do as they were ordered.

Cecile was half asleep, not understanding the mid-night rousting. "What's wrong?" she called.

31

"Tell you at the grub wagon. We're moving out fast. Get moving or you'll be left behind." He could hear her stamp her foot, but she did not protest. She began putting her gear in order to move.

In no more than ten minutes the hands were at the wagon. Cook was still slamming pots and pans into side-boxes. He grew silent as Grady began to talk.

Cecile was still tucking her blouse into her riding pants as she arrived, breathless.

"We are in for a storm. It's coming from the north. We don't have any cover here. About twenty miles to the southeast there's an abandoned stagecoach stop with some walls left, and most of the old corrals are still standing. If we can make it we might find the old cellar still usable. Let's move it!"

The crew scattered. The kid went to catch up Cook's team. Cecile stood and searched the beautiful starlit sky. The gentle breeze wafted across her face.

"Has everyone gone mad?" she asked.

"No, ma'am," Cook answered, "and you better get a move on."

She shrugged and went to catch up her stallion. She was amazed at the hustle that was going on about her. Their urgency began to instill some anxiety in her to keep up with them, for it had become apparent that if she didn't get ready in time she'd be left behind.

Trumpeter, annoyed at the disruption of his rest, refused to mount the wagon ramp. Grady flicked his rump with his lariat hard enough for the old bull to lunge forward, and let out a startled bellow that brought his owner on the run.

She shouted at Grady, "What the hell do you think you're doing?"

He yelled back over his shoulder as he rode off toward the herd, "Get that damned mule-headed ox on that wagon, or he's going to have to run with the rest."

Cecile was fuming now, but she took the lead rope from Lou's hand and climbed up the ramp pulling hard on the rope. Trumpeter stretched out his neck and set his front feet. A day on this wagon was bad enough. He didn't intend to spend a night on it, too. Cecile coaxed and wheedled. Lou put a rope around Trumpeter's rump, and they both pulled. The old bull locked his knees, and his eyes walled as the ropes tightened around his throat and bit into his rump.

Deadly, who had been nervously pacing from the wagon to the top of the rise, walked over and nuzzled the old bull's neck. He snorted, and Trumpeter answered with a deep groan but stubbornly refused to move. Deadly stepped back and swung one massive horn, digging the silver ball deep into Trumpeter's side. The wind rushed from the bull's open mouth, and one knee buckled.

Cecile yelled at Deadly, "Get away, Deadly. I've got enough trouble without you two fighting." But Deadly lifted the heavy horn again, and snorted his intention to swing it even more solidly into Trumpeter's side. The old bull saw the gleaming horns lifted menacingly, ready to put another bruising thrust to his side. He leaped forward. Cecile scrambled for the wagon sides to keep from being trampled.

"Well, thanks, old fellow," she called after Deadly as he turned toward the herd.

For the first time since the drive had begun Deadly took the attitude of lead bull, working through the herd. His seven foot width of polished horns flashed in the moonlight as he goaded and threatened the docile cows to their feet. Reginald, startled by the unexpected intrusion on his herd, and the unusual night excitement of camp-breaking noises, prepared to do battle. Deadly ignored him and continued about his business. A rope snaked out of the night and settled about Reginald's neck, pulling tightly.

"Not tonight, old boy. We need an experienced hand out there." Reginald was tied to the back of Trumpeter's wagon. He bellowed at this insult, this usurping of his place, but he was ignored as the wagon pulled out at a rapid pace to fall behind the grub wagon. Reginald fought the rope for a while, but the wagon continued ahead, disregarding his protest. To relieve the strain on his neck, he finally settled into a running walk.

Grady shouted to Cecile when he tied Reginald to the wagon, "Help with the herd—use your rope and keep them moving. Don't let them lag." She didn't answer but mounted her horse and loosened her rope. She joined the men in trying to bunch the cows and get them moving.

At first they circled in confusion, but Deadly, aggravated now at their docile stupidity, swung his horns like lances, establishing his power over the small females. Panic struck the herd as the bull and the riders forcibly moved the cows out. Deadly took the lead and the short-legged little cows had to run to keep up with his gangling trot. Stinging rope burns and yelling drovers convinced the cows that the very devil was on their heels, and they bunched into a unit for the first time and moved with a rapidity that Grady had not thought possible.

Cecile rode close to Grady and yelled, "This pace will kill them."

"Lady, if they don't keep up this pace they are going to die anyway."

"Why? What's wrong? Will you please tell me what's happening?" she screamed.

Grady yelled back, "A northerner, ma'am. Deadly says it's on its way."

"Are you mad? Are you telling me you are driving my cows at this impossible pace because that bull says it's going to rain?"

"Yes, Ma'am, only a northerner isn't just a regular rain on the desert. Now get them cows moving."

He rode off into the night. It was getting darker. She searched the sky and found that half the stars had disappeared. Clouds were rolling in, the wind had increased, and a chill ran up her spine. She dug her heels into the big stallion and began working the herd.

Deadly wanted to run, but he knew that the little cows couldn't keep up. Grady had come forward a time or two and headed him toward the southeast. His instinct told him to run south, away from the oncoming storm, but from long association he obeyed Grady's orders and moved rapidly in a southeasterly direction.

The winds were getting stronger, and the stars had disappeared behind high clouds. The blackness made fast travel impossible. Deadly slowed to a rapid walk, using some age-old instinct to guide him across gullies and around clumps of sagebrush. Grady gave orders to let the cows trail down to single file. It was up to Deadly now as it was too dark for the riders to work the herd.

The wind was making it hard to travel. The herd was struggling to keep on its feet. Instinct helped them as each placed its nose to the rump ahead and kept moving, afraid now of losing its place in line, of being lost in the dark.

The rain began, and Grady cursed. He wasn't worried about the herd, but he was worried about the grub wagon and the bull cart. If this storm came on with the violence Deadly seemed to sense, the desert washes would soon be overflowing with rushing water. He hoped Cook and the men would keep their heads.

"Hey, Little Bear, go back and help Cook and Scratch with the wagons. Sing and Cook will hear you. If it gets any worse unload that bull, untie the horses, and leave the wagons."

"OK, boss. Good luck."

Grady could hear Little Bear's melodic western drawl singing "Get Along Little Doggies" fade away down the back trail. "Are you all right, Miss Cecile?" he called.

"If being soaked to the skin doesn't count, I'm fine," she answered.

Several hours later the wind was reaching gale force. The rain had not increased, but was pelting down like driven demons, so hard it stung when it hit bare skin. The desert soil had turned treacherous under the animal's hooves. The horses slipped and slid. Grady knew the cows could manage better with their cloven hooves, but not much, as water mixed with caliche and made slippery, oozing clay.

Then the lightning bolts began. The line of cattle stopped, and Grady nearly pitched over his horse's head as the horse bumped into the cow's rump ahead of him. He turned the horse aside and slowly worked his way to the head of the line where Deadly stood, head up, ears forward. Grady waited for a lightning bolt to illuminate the desert. They had made it!

"Good old Deadly. I don't know how you do it, ole chum. There isn't anyone I know could have found this spot in the dark."

Off to the left was a wooden corral that had been built by the stage line before they changed the route. It was meant to hold fresh horses for the coaches. It was small but well built of heavy four-by-eight posts with two-by-eight rails bolted on. Grady swung off his horse and dropped the reins, waiting for another lightning bolt so he could locate the entrance. He grabbed Deadly by a horn and led him into the corral and over to the far side. Like shadows, the exhausted cows followed. There was just barely enough room for the small herd of cows. The horses would have to be hobbled and turned loose.

"Oh God, from one extreme to the other, I am freezing!" A quivering voice came out of the dark.

"Sit still and I'll find you. Talk so I can locate you." Lightning lit up the sky, and he spotted her a few feet away, huddled over the saddle horn.

"Come on Deadly, let's get out of here."

Deadly worked his way through the herd, and Grady let him out of the opening where the gate should have been, then he caught up his horse and tied him to a rail. It took another lightning bolt to locate the gate. Its hinges had long ago been torn away. He dragged the gate to the opening and used his lariat to tie it into place.

The herd was secure for the moment. How many were in the corral only daylight would tell. In the dark many could have dropped out along the way.

Grady found Miss Grace, helped her out of the saddle, and tied her stallion to the fence near his horse.

If he remembered correctly, the depot house was in a straight line east of the corral. Holding Cecile's hand, he felt forward with his feet, taking advantage of each lightning bolt. He finally spotted the rotted remains of the old adobe building. A few walls had been built thick enough that they were still standing. One room might have been the cooking area because a fireplace was still partially standing. The room still had part of the sod roof over it. He cleared Cecile a place to sit, and said, "Stay here. I must see if I can find that cellar."

"All right." She was trying to sound brave, but Grady knew that she was cold and wet, and scared.

He crisscrossed the ground around the decayed adobe building until his feet hit a raised area. Soon he located the cellar entrance, the door long torn off and gone. He took his weatherproof match holder from his pocket and lit a match and went down the cellar steps slowly. These old cellars made great snake dens. With no door on the cellar, the rain was creating an underground pool, but there wasn't much he could do about that right now. He returned to Miss McNamara.

Breaking up some rotted windowsills and a ceiling beam; he got a fire going in one corner, out of the rain.

"You get out of those clothes and dry them. Keep this fire going if you have to burn the house up piece by piece."

"You aren't going to leave me?"

"Yes, ma'am. I got a couple of bulls out there, not to mention my men who are still out there also."

"I'm going with you."

"No you aren't. It's dark out there and I could lose you. Besides, those cows need someone to keep an eye on them, and we need that fire burning to find our way back. That's your job."

"OK, Mr. Grady. Good luck."

He got his horse and went back down the trail. Deadly followed close behind him, eyes and ears attuned to the dark, windy night. Grady raised his voice in the "Cowboy's Lament," yodeling and whistling taking turns with silence until he heard an answering yodel. It was Denny with the remuda. The kid had tied the horses together in a string with Cecile McNamara's mares at the head of the line.

"Keep going straight in that direction. A fire's lit, look for it."

"You bet, boss, I'm ready for a fire."

Thirty minutes later Grady came on Lou driving the cart with Trumpeter and Reginald. The cart was slipping and sliding over the desert ruts.

Lou called out, "For two cents I'd leave this fucking cart here."

"We need that ramp for the cellar door, and we better get it there soon. Where are the others?"

"Cook's way behind. I tried to get him to unhitch the horses and come on, but he wouldn't leave that damned grub wagon, something about a captain going down with his ship. Crazy fool. Little Bear and Scratch stayed to cover the grain wagons. They should be along with the two teams."

"OK, let's get these bulls on into camp."

"That's not going to be so easy, Boss. Trumpeter's about played out."

"I guess we've only got one choice then, let's get him back in the wagon."

"Hell, Boss, he can't stand up in it, and the horses can't pull in this mud."

"I know, but if we drop him down and tie his legs, he can't fall because he's already down. I will put a rope on the wagon and help pull. We've got to make better time, or we're done for."

Trumpeter was so tired he readily climbed into the wagon. It took all their strength to drop him to the floor and tie his feet together. He bawled with indignation, but the job was finally done. Then the worst of the trip began.

"Deadly, get on out." The old trail order, the words used to send Deadly out to the head of the herd. Deadly responded by taking the lead, the wagon horses following him. With Deadly picking the trail the wagon made better time.

The washes were now rushing with water. Once as water flowed over the wagon bed old Trumpeter bawled with fear. Reginald added to the tug of war by locking his legs and being dragged unwillingly into the flooded wash.

The night was nearly over as the light of the fire came into view. Denny had the remuda hobbled, and had put Miss McNamara's mares and stallion in the corral. He had collected lumber and was keeping the fire burning.

Cecile had dried out and drifted into an exhausted sleep. She woke as the men came into camp. She ran to the wagon to check on Trumpeter, and gasped when she saw him in a huddle on the wagon floor. Grady, near exhaustion, climbed into the wagon and untied the rope from Trumpeter's legs. The old bull just lay there, and Grady cussed under his breath.

"You damn bull, don't you be hurt on us now. Get on your feet."

He yelled, "Trumpeter, get up!" The bull lurched to raise his hindquarters. His blood circulation had been slowed down and he could hardly make his legs work. A second try got his back legs under him with his front knees still on the floor.

"Come on Trumpeter, you can do it," the girl pleaded.

The bull gave a staggering lurch and was up, weaving unsteadily but up on his feet. At first it looked as though he was going to crash back down, he was so wobbly, but after a few minutes he managed to get his legs steady. Grady and Lou set the ramp and brought him down. Reginald was put in with the cows, Trumpeter was taken by the fire where Miss Grace rubbed him dry.

The wind had reached gale force. Grady and the two hands used the wooden ramp to fashion a cellar door, securing it with rope hinges and tie downs.

Grady watched the sky and kept an eye on Deadly. The big bull had moved to a mound past the corral, where he stood, head to the wind, on watch. The rain began to fall harder. Drops as big as eggs thundered to the ground. The wind whistled and whined over the desert. You could see the dark clouds swirling in the sky.

"Everybody to the cellar. We've done all we can up here!"

"Mr. Grady, I can't leave Trumpeter alone in this storm."

Grady didn't answer her. He just swung her into his arms and carried her down the cellar stairs. As with most underground cellars a bench had been dug into the sides of the dirt walls. Only the floor was flooded. Denny had dug ditches to detour the water away from the cellar door opening.

Grady kept watch at the makeshift entrance. Once he left the dugout and was gone a short time, then returned. "It's on its way."

"What's on its way?" Cecile was near hysteria.

"The tornado, Miss Grace," Scratch said.

"Tornado! My God! My cattle! My horses!"

She tried to climb the stairs, but Grady wrapped his arms tightly about her. "Ma'am, that's one thing you can't win against. You just got to pray and hope somebody hears you."

The wind became a terrible roar, so deafening the girl put her hands over her ears, but they could not shut out the screaming, howling tornado. The makeshift cellar door rattled and banged until it finally lifted and seemed to float slowly across the yard. A suction pulled at the people huddled in the cellar. They clung to each other, and to whatever timbers they could find to hold on to..

They found out later that they were not anywhere near the eye of the tornado, only on the outskirts. But while it passed overhead, the people in the cellar were all sure they were going to die.

The gale winds subsided, but the rain kept falling. They left the cellar to find the adobe walls still standing, but the corral gate was open and the herd gone, as well as Trumpeter, the Arabians, and Deadly Deadly. Some of the hobbled remuda was still in sight.

Cecile was in tears. She wandered about in the rain trying to find a clue as to the direction the herd had gone. She alternated between looking for her horses, her bulls, and her cows.

Grady started up the fire while Denny went out to catch the hobbled horses. Lou fixed the corral gate, and when Denny returned with half a dozen horses they were penned immediately. He saddled two, and Grady joined him. In an hour they had rounded up all the hobbled horses and secured them in the corral.

"Did you see the herd?" Cecile asked

"No, ma'am, but don't worry, Deadly will keep his eyes on them."

"Mr. Grady, why do you insist on treating that animal like a human?"

"Why, ma'am, he's a lot more human than most of the humans I've met."

"But he's not superhuman."

"No, ma'am, but you got to admit he knows when a northerner is coming."

She looked at her feet. "Yes, I guess you're right."

"Yes, ma'am, and first things first. We got to find the men, and the other wagons. We could be gone some time. You want to come, or stay here and keep an eye out for your herd?"

"I better stay here. The Arabians will return for their oats. I should be here to catch them."

He knew she was hoping, more than certain, that the stallion and mares would return. He had his doubts. That trio was probably in the next county by now.

"OK. See if you can find some wood. Stay out of the rain as much as possible. The last thing we all need is a pneumonia."

There wasn't any trail to follow. The rain had not only washed prints away, it had filled to overflowing every dip and dry wash on the desert, and the steady downpour gave all indications that they would be waterlogged for some time. It might even be days before the weather cleared and the flooded ground dried out.

Grady and the hands took turns yelling. It finally paid off with the distant clanging of the grub wagon dinner gong. They heard Cook cussing a blue fog long before they sighted the wagon sitting high on a mound, with water running madly around all sides of it. Cook had wisely located a high piece of ground on which to halt the wagon. The flooding water could not reach the wagon bed to destroy the food supplies. But, in the dark, he could not see that the high ground was an island in the center of a desert gulch. To cross the rushing wash now would accomplish the very thing he had tried to avoid.

He ceased cussing as the men sat across the wash and surveyed the situation.

"Where are the other wagons?" Grady yelled at Cook.

"How the hell should I know?"

"Give a guess at the direction."

"I'd say over yonder," Cook pointed to the north, and waved off westerly a little.

"Close up that wagon. Pack up enough to get us by for a couple of days. Unhitch and load the horses. Go in that direction. You'll find Miss Grace. We'll have to wait for a letup in this rain, and for these washes to run off, before we can move that wagon. How come you missed that tornado?"

A blast of cusswords filled the wet desert. Relieved by his own answer, Cook yelled, "Who the hell missed it? The damned thing passed right over last night's camp and was headed right over the top of me. Man, I was making my peace when it just kind of veered off to the right. I still don't know why this wagon isn't upside down and scattered all over this damned desert, my man up there heard me talking to Him."

"It's good to see you, Cookie."

"Thankee, boss, you don't know how glad I am to see you ugly bastards."

"We're going on and try to find the grain wagons."

"Check. See you in camp."

The three men headed in the direction Cook had pointed them.

"Spread out, but keep in sight, and keep your eyes peeled."

The rain, steady and insistent, continued to add to the flooded countryside. A yell from the right caused Grady to swing in that direction. He yelled until he received an answer. Slipping and sliding, the horses fought the ankle-deep mud until they came to where Scratch sat exhausted, surveying one wagon turned upside down, and the surrounding area where the sacks of grain lay, some broken open with grain floating away in the rivers of washes. Little Bear was struggling to save as many sacks as he could retrieve from the other wagon that was tilted dangerously ready to slide into a rushing stream. The men quickly threw their lariats over the wagon wheels and pulled it to higher ground. They then sat silently surveying the contents of the other wagon, knowing that even if they salvaged the undamaged bags they would be wet through. The grain would swell, mold, and mildew and be destroyed before it could dry out.

Grady straightened up and took a deep breath; trail experience came to his aid. "What's done is done, get on with it."

"OK, fellows, let's get the wagon over and pick up what is salvageable."

The men tried to right the wagon, but it was too heavy, and their feet slipping in the mud didn't help. Grady hooked his lariat to the sideboards and mounted his horse. With a lot of slipping and sliding, cussing and yelling, horse and rider, with the help of the men, turned the wagon over.

One side of the wagon had washed away, but the important axles and wheels were intact. Best of all there were eight bags of oats under the wagon, protected from the rain, still dry. The men hurriedly loaded the bags into the other wagon.

"OK, fellows, let's pick up all the bags that are not torn. Maybe we can salvage them somehow."

They found the harness half buried in the mud where it had been stripped from the teams and dropped in the hurry to beat the storm. The bridles and reins were not there. They had been left on the horses.

The riders removed their saddles and threw them in the wagon. They hooked the harness up to their animals, Grady collected the short bridle reins and wearily turned his horses in the direction of the camp. The men climbed into the wagon bed, pulled canvas over their heads, and wet to the skin and shivering, dropped instantly to sleep, the cowboy's trained ability to grab rest when and where offered—on horseback or soaking wet in a jarring wagon. They would have to make another trip to bring in the damaged wagon.

The trail back was difficult. Grady picked high ground whenever possible. The horses struggled in the mud, and slopped through the puddles. Grady avoided the rushing washes when possible, but to reach the camp it was necessary to waken the men and put them to work adding ropes and stationing them on the opposite bank to aid in pulling the wagon across several running streams. He was fortunate in locating crossings shallow enough to allow the wagon to cross without wetting the wagon floor.

It was dark when they spotted the distant campfire. An exhausted bunch of cowboys gratefully accepted hot coffee and camp beans, while Denny unhitched the horses, hobbled them, and turned them loose to forage for grass.

Cecile Grace McNamara, a very worried lady, tried to hide her anxiety as she looked around the makeshift camp. The men were weary and too tired to dry out their clothes, but did so anyway to avoid possible colds, or pneumonia, the trail driver's dreaded disease. She took shirts and pants, and worked by the fire, turning and drying the clothing while the men rummaged in saddlebags for spares. The bedrolls and clothing were a mile away on the grub wagon.

With bare legs and feet sticking out below rain ponchos the men waited patiently, dozing by the fire while one side toasted until the heat awakened them and they turned the other side to roast.

Cook had found the wagon ramp and propped it strategically against the adobe wall giving added shelter. The rain had lessened some, but still fell steadily.

It rained all that night and the next day. Trying to take care of everything that needed tending to in the constant rain was taking not just a physical toll but also a mental one. Nerves were strained and snapping, but it was a tough crew and with tight lips they carried on doing what was required. Little Bear and Scratch went back to bring in the other wagon. Grady, Denny, and Lou went in search of the herd. Grady was certain Deadly would keep them moving in the right direction, but they were not a normal trail herd and they were not used to following Deadly.

By the evening of the third day the rain had stopped. The clouds remained, but hope that the downpour was over kept Cecile watching the cloudy sky. The night remained dry, and the wind helped to dry the ground. The water gradually stopped running in the washes. The fourth morning came with breaks in the clouds.

Horses were saddled, Cook and Lou mounted a team bareback and led two wheel horses back over the sodden trail to bring in the grub wagon. They didn't know how long it would take for the washes to dry out. It could be days before they could move the heavy grub wagon; however Grady decided to try to move the camp out in hope that Deadly was in control of the herd, and waiting for Grady to catch up.

The grain wagons were hitched, but Trumpeter's cart was left behind with a team in the corral. Lou would pick it up when Cook and the grub wagon returned. Little Bear drove the nearly empty grain wagon, and Scratch followed with the full wagon.

Cecile saddled a horse and joined Grady, her eyes searching for the Herefords. Denny followed the grain wagons with the remuda. The ground was still in deplorable condition. Travel was slow, at times impossible without the help of horses tied on to pull the wagons.

They were frustrated at the slow progress, and they constantly searched for the herd. Cecile expressed everyone's concern late in the day, "Where the hell is that damned herd?" No one answered, either from embarrassment at the unladylike outburst, or because they had all been asking themselves the same question. By now everyone knew how much that herd meant to her future. The loss would be devastating and no one wanted to give up hope that they would find them intact and well. The faith that Grady had in Deadly was the only thing keeping everyone on the positive, but as the days passed it began to look more and more grim.

CHAPTER FOUR

When the winds reached gale force instinct nagged at Deadly to move with it, to travel. But, loyalty held him stamping nervously beside the cover of the cellar where Grady had disappeared into the ground.

The wind became stronger, bushes were flying past, and Trumpeter was uneasy. He left the adobe windbreak and joined Deadly at the cellar entrance.

The wind was picking up debris and throwing it across the desert. The cellar door banged and strained against its fastenings. The corral gate suddenly flew across the yard. The Arabians, already spooked by the wind and flying brush, leaped out of the entrance and ran. They galloped across the yard, onto the desert, and out of sight. Deadly watched them disappear. He knew this was wrong, but at the moment there was another worry.

The cows left the corral and followed the Arabians. When Deadly saw Reginald trot past him he decided it was time to move.

He set out to catch the runaways, forgetting that Trumpeter was following. Fortunately the cows tired quickly and slowed to a walk, so Trumpeter was able to keep up. Deadly's instinct nagged at him. The herd was going in the wrong direction.

The gale force of the wind hit the herd knocking some to the ground, and pushing others along with it. The wind passed as fast as it hit, but it left the herd scattered in every direction.

44

Deadly doggedly tried to gather them back. Trumpeter followed him for a while but grew tired. He halted and began to bawl. The louder he bawled the more answers he received from the cows. The scattered herd had not forgotten the old bull. They answered, and from all directions came in answer to his call.

Deadly watched this gathering. To keep this herd together he had to keep Trumpeter with him. He waited patiently while the old bull rested. After Trumpeter had rested, he joined Deadly. Sixty-nine cows followed. Reginald was nowhere in sight.

The rain continued to fall, and settled into a steady pattern. The cows put their tails to the wind, and slowly followed Deadly as he carefully chose a path over the rain-soaked desert. He avoided the rushing washes and traveled always in a direction that Deadly knew would, in time, lead back to the original southern cattle trail.

Much later the mud-drenched cows began to complain, and travel slowed as they halted and bellowed discontentedly.

The big longhorn searched for high ground and led the straggling herd to it. He watched Trumpeter drop wearily to the soggy ground. The soaked cows huddled around the old bull. Some dropped to the mud, but most just turned their rumps to the pelting rain and stood dejectedly.

The herd, scared and miserable, huddled close to each other, and Deadly was relieved that, for once, the little cows were docile. A range herd would have split and disappeared in every direction when they left the corral. The longhorn remained on his feet, but he closed his eyes and dozed as the rain continued to drench his already soaked red-and-white-speckled hide.

For two more days the small herd plodded over the muddy ground, the rain falling at a steady rate. They no longer resisted Deadly's lead. He kept them on high ground when he could, crossing the rushing washes only when he could find a safe crossing. A few times he had to lead the bedraggled Herefords out of the way to get them across washes that had turned into frothing rapids. By instinct he always turned back to keep his little band of cows headed towards the cattle trail. When he could find grass to graze on he let the cows feed. They ate the soggy grass hungrily. Deadly did not hurry them. He watched the back trail for movement that could be his friend Grady. When the herd rested at night he stood staring into the darkness and listened for familiar sounds.

45

By the dawn of the fourth day, the rain had eased. The clouds still hovered over the land. Deadly nudged Trumpeter. It was time to move on down the trail. Deadly had slept little during the night. He was lonely. He wanted to walk away from the little herd and go back down the trail looking for Grady, but the strong feeling of duty Grady had instilled in him made him rouse the cows and lead them on.

Now that the rain had ceased, water in the washes was starting to subside, but the slippery clay bottoms remained dangerous. The fear that his cows would get stuck made him continue to weave his way across the desert, keeping to high ground and staying on the right course as much as possible.

They had plodded along about an hour when Deadly halted and stared down the trail. His ears turned forward as he strained to catch again the sound he had heard. The cows grew impatient and began to wander off to graze. He bawled at them to let them know they were moving ahead then resolutely turned and continued to move toward the sound. As he walked he held his head high and searched the horizon, his ears straining to overcome the noise of the sucking mud as the herd moved along behind him.

Suddenly he heard it clearly and recognized the throaty, defiant challenge of a wild range bull. Bawling, bellowing, muttering, shattering the air with his threats, his oaths of revenge sending a challenge over the hills in a basso scream.

Then Deadly heard an answering response to the bull's challenge. He could just barely hear the challenger's reply, but he knew in an instant that the response was Reginald's. He had heard this amateurish hollering many times the past days on the trail.

The range bull, furious now, let out a series of far-carrying bawls of rage. He was ready for battle. Deadly took off using a ground-covering gait, part trot and part pace. He ignored Trumpeter's bellow of protest as he left the herd behind and hurried toward the battleground.

CHAPTER FIVE

Reginald had followed the cows out of the corral while the winds were whipping the countryside into a frenzy. It was dark as the cattle ran from the campfire onto the desert. The blowing sand made visibility almost non-existent while pelting like miniature bullets into the hides and eyes of the cows. In panic they ran together until the uneven ground began to separate them into small groups. The herd branched off into desert washes that were already beginning to run with rainwater.

Reginald stayed with the small group of cows that were in front of him, no longer sure how many he followed. Fearful that they would disappear into the black night, he kept his chin over the rump of one of the cows and ran blindly, letting her lead him through the darkness.

The winds were howling, and he could feel the lash of sagebrush carried on whipping winds. The cow went down and Reginald fell over her in the darkness. In a tangle of legs they fought to regain their footing. The cow freed herself, leaped to her feet, and plunged on down the trail, running recklessly to catch up with the bunch. Reginald lurched to his feet just in time for the tornadic winds to carry a large sagebrush against his side so hard it knocked him to his knees. In the darkness the whipping branches of the brush infused Reginald with fear. He lurched wildly to his feet and ran blindly into the night. He could no longer hear the small bunch of cows over the howling wind. He was alone in the blowing fury, alone for the first time in his life, alone in the dark. He bawled in terror and tried to outrun the screaming wind.

He thrashed through brush, stumbled over rocks, and slid down gullies. With each bump and smack in the dark, he began to slow his headlong, hysterical race to a pace that allowed him to continue through the dark with some warning of obstacles in his path. He kept the wind behind him, trying to escape from the howling noise and flying debris. All through the night he traveled, until the winds quieted and the rain settled into a steady downpour.

He was exhausted. Great streams of air heaved from his nostrils as his sides swelled with the effort to regain his breath. The sound of his heart pounding interfered with his efforts to listen for a familiar bellow from his herd. But the pounding heart and the pelting rain were all he heard. The scared young bull stood straddle-legged, staggeringly tired, and waited for daylight.

Dawn came, but with the dawn the steady rainfall and dark clouds remained. The desert now ran with deep, rushing water in its low washes, and it was hard to see through the rainfall into the distance. Not knowing which direction to go, he continued to turn tail to the rain and gingerly picked his way across the rain-drenched ground, trying to stay out of the deeper washes. Confused and lost, he moved slowly, sometimes halting and gazing into the desolate country around him. Luckily for Reginald, he continued to travel in the easiest direction, away from the storm, to the south, sometimes drifting to the southeast. Unbeknownst to him he traveled a parallel course with the herd. Unhampered by the responsibility of the small herd of cows slowing him down, he was traveling ahead of them and off to the left of the trail.

On the evening of the fourth day the rain was slowing to a drizzle. Reginald heard the sound he had been listening for—the low bawl of cattle. Quickening his pace, he topped a small rise and across the valley he saw cows. It was getting dark and he began to trot, sliding occasionally in the slippery, wet clay.

As he neared the small bunch of cows he realized they were strangers, and coming to meet him was a large bull. The stranger was a glossy, dunnish brown, merging into black on the lower legs, with white speckles and splotches on his rump and a washed-out copper line down his back. His thick horns were set forward for tossing a lobo wolf into the air or ripping a belly open.

A hundred yards off, the bull stopped and began pawing the mud. He gored the wet dirt and thrust his horns into the tough stems of sagebrush. Jerking and twisting his head from side to side he broke the brush to stubble.

Reginald saw that the horns were sharpened for bloody work. They had been rubbed against trees and brush and whetted in the ground, glistening with rainwater. Reginald turned and retreated to the rise. From there he watched the bull practice his thrusts as he continued to send forth a challenge of rage that seemed to be tearing the very lungs out of him. The young bull kept his distance, and as the night drew on the enraged bull quieted to throaty, mumbling talk to himself as he paced back and forth in his war march between the cows and the young bull.

Half of the activity of a range bull was in battle or preparing for it. The Hereford was bred for begetting calves, but courage was not bred out of him. An ancient instinct nagged at Reginald. He had been practicing his challenge for weeks and he had challenged the big longhorn, Deadly, several times, only to have the big bull back down.

As the night passed, the young bull answered the challenge with boastful arrogance in response to the range bull's invitation. As the fifth day began to dawn the dun bull was in a fury, and Reginald had spent the night working himself into an eager contender for the small herd of range cows. When it became light enough to see the battleground, Reginald walked proudly and confidently down to meet his challenger.

As he came nearer he watched the dun bull practice his thrusts. Reginald tossed his horns in answer. Each seemed to wait for the other to begin the attack. Inexperienced Reginald turned slowly as the range bull began to circle, fronting his antagonist and maneuvering for an opening. They halted a few yards apart. The other cattle gathered to add sympathetic bawling to the atmosphere.

The circling bulls churned the muddy footing. Then a lunge and the impact of skull against skull shattered the early morning quiet. Reginald did well in this first contact. He was much shorter than the range bull, but he had set his legs solidly in the muck. Both bulls stood planted in the mud, neither giving way to the other. The dun bull's shoulder muscles bunched, the massive neck sinews rose almost to the height of humps on a buffalo, his back—a downward sweep of line beautiful in its grace—curved tensely. Then the range bull sidestepped to unbalance his opponent, and Reginald dropped to one knee. The dun bull backed to rush again. Reginald regained his feet and braced himself for the head on lunge. The bull backed and rushed again and again.

The battle strain began to tire the younger bull. Eyes bloodshot, mouth slobbering, with tongue lolled out and legs tired, the Hereford began to give ground. The range bull continued to back off, paw the churned mud. Then they would clash again. Reginald was backed toward a soggy mud bank. With his heart pounding and his lungs bursting he struggled to hold his ground. Another step backward and he would founder in the mud hole.

The range bull stepped back slowly swinging his horns back and forth, then launched his final drive. When he was about to collide with the young bull, he stopped still to hook one of his horns, the master horn, goring it deep into Reginald's eye. Ripping upward, he brought the young bull's eyeball out on the tip.

Reginald screamed in pain as he fell backward into blackness. He failed to see Deadly as the Longhorn thundered across the battleground. Silently, with no warning, Deadly hit the range bull squarely in the side, running one long, slender silver tipped horn through the thickest part of the wild bull's neck. The horn was so deeply embedded and the hide so unyielding that Deadly's ornate silver ball refused to withdraw.

Several hours later Grady and Cecile came upon this grisly scene. The young bull was mired in the mud, his hindquarters were settled deeply while his mutilated head lay stretched forward in an effort to keep his nose above water.

The empty eye socket ran red, staining the muddy pool. The battleground was red with the range bull's blood, as Deadly dragged his dying carcass around in circles trying to free himself. Unable to do so he had dropped tiredly to his front knees and was resting, preparing for another attempt at freedom.

Gone were the range cattle replaced by sixty-nine Herford cows and Trumpeter who worriedly circled around Deadly and the range bull, challenging the dead bull in an effort to protect his friend.

CHAPTER SIX

Grady and Cecile McNamara were anxious to find the herd and in their search soon left the remuda and the grain wagons far behind. The rains had done a good job of washing away any tracks. Grady's instinct was to head for the cattle trail. He knew that if Deadly could manage it, the bull would follow the familiar trail home. The two spread out and moved as quickly as the muddy ground would allow.

Cecile had been right about the mares. They had returned for their daily ration of oats and the stallion had followed at a distance. Denny had caught him and doubled his vigilance over the Arabians.

Cecile rode a remuda gelding today. Her fancy finery had been replaced with working skirt and boots. It was she who spotted the cow with the broken leg. From afar she couldn't see that the leg was broken and she yelled and waved her hat in glee until Grady spotted her. By the time he joined her she was sitting silently on her horse, tears running down her cheeks. The cow, glad to see someone, was coming toward them on three legs. The front left leg dangled uselessly as she slowly approached.

"I don't suppose we can save her?"

"No, ma'am. Even if we splinted the leg and packed her in the wagon we've got the mountains to go over, and we've all got to walk there."

"OK, but don't let her go to waste. Clean her and we will take the two rumps for the grub wagon." She pulled her horse around and rode off looking for the rest of the herd.

Grady waited until she was far enough away that the pistol shot was muffled. He did as she requested and removed the two rumps, tied them together and threw them over the back of his saddle. The horse protested at the smell of blood, but soon settled down. Grady mounted and rode after Cecile.

He drifted to the left of her so they could cover more ground. He was the one who found the drowned cow. He shook his head and rode on past the mud-covered animal. He didn't see any reason to show Cecile the cow. They would be lucky to find any of the cows alive. Why show her each disaster?

They had ridden much farther than the grub wagon could get in the mud. They decided to ride until dark, and then camp out. The rain had passed. He built a fire and they roasted a couple of steaks over it. Grady could hardly swallow the meat, remembering the promises they had all made to preserve the herd; it was a very expensive meal. He had to admire this woman. She ate in silence, but he knew the meat stuck in her throat.

Grady built up the fire because they had no blankets or bedrolls. He had to feed the fire several times during the night. He covered Cecile with both saddle blankets and she slept soundly until dawn. It was the fourth day after the rain.

They rode all morning, keeping each other in sight. Grady found the first sign, a cloven hoof track. He called to Cecile and they moved their horses out as fast as the slippery trail would permit the horses to travel without losing their footing. They heard the cattle long before they rode over the rise and saw the drama before them.

Cecile caught her breath then kicked her horse and rode ahead of Grady to the mud hole. Grady left his saddle while his horse was sliding to a halt. He ran to Deadly's side and saw immediately the predicament. He pulled out his pocketknife, opened it, and cut a large hole through the neck of the dead bull. He saw that Deadly's horn had entered the jugular vein and driven upward toward the backbone. The range bull had bled to death.

"Grady, help me."

Grady turned and saw the girl bending over the bloody head of Reginald. Deadly was getting to his feet. Grady ran to his horse for his rope. He bent down to Reginald and put it over his head. He cringed when he saw the empty eye socket. He wrapped the rope around the saddle horn and climbed into the saddle. Backing the horse slowly he pulled Reginald out of the mud hole while the exhausted bull thrashed.

Grady slacked up on the rope and waited for the bull to get to his feet. Reginald made a tired effort, then sank back to the ground. Grady slid down from his horse, went to the bull, and ran his hands expertly over the young animal's body, examining all of the major bones.

"Don't feel nothing broke. He's probably just tired. Look's like they had a hell of a fight." He surveyed the battleground. He walked over to Deadly and wrapped his arms around the big bull's neck. He rubbed the hair between the giant horns and said, "Good old Deadly. I knew you were on the job. Good boy."

Deadly nosed his shirt pocket and Joe Bob pulled a hard, dry biscuit and held it where the rough, red tongue could pull it into his jaws. With a pat on Deadly's nose Grady turned to the Cecile.

She was bending over the bull. She had wet her scarf and was trying to remove some of the blood from Reginald's eye area. Grady wet his neck scarf and together they cleaned the blood away from the socket.

"Hell of a mess."

"Yes, it's pretty bad, but if that is all that is wrong with him, Mr. Grady, he will still father calves."

Grady noticed that she had returned to the more formal use of his name, and acknowledged it by answering, "Your right, Miss Grace. While he is down I'll close that eye socket." Grady took a small oilcloth wrapped package from his saddlebag. Inside were dry matches, tobacco, a razor, a small packet of needles and a spool of strong black thread, the usual survival kit on the trail.

"You sit by his neck and if he tries to get up put a knee on it."

She did as she was told and Grady threaded the needle and quickly stitched together the eyelids over the empty socket. The bull didn't move. He probably had so much pain from the empty eye socket that he didn't feel the needle.

"Well, if that doesn't fester up, he'll be all right. Let's see if I can get him to his feet. Sure was a hell of a fight here, if your bull done most of it you can be proud of him. He sure showed some courage."

"Of course, Mr. Grady. I told you the Hereford has courage. Back your horse and pull and I will push."

It took a few tries, but Reginald was soon standing, legs shaking from fatigue and dazedly shaking his head as he tried to clear the blinded eye.

"Oh, Reginald," she sobbed as she gently rubbed his head. Then she brushed away a tear and for the first time turned to inspect the herd. Grady had already done a quick count of seventy. That accounted for all but three. One had broken a leg, one had drowned, and one was unaccounted for. Maybe she would turn up.

Cecile walked over to Deadly, wrapped her arms about his neck, as she had seen Grady do. She scratched the topknot and placed a kiss on the rangy jawbone. "Thank you, Deadly. Thank you so much. If I hadn't seen it for myself I would never believe that an animal, much less a bull, could be so special. I owe you everything you big, wonderful, amazing boy."

Deadly switched his tail gently, swung the big horns, and walked off to find his friend Trumpeter. The two bulls moved into the herd and began to graze.

Grady removed the cow meat from his horse and tied it high in a bush. He then put his rope over the range bull's horns, and dragged the animal into the mud hole that he had pulled Reginald out of. He pulled the bull until it sank in the mud. While they were camped out in the area this remedy would ensure that they would not be besieged with the desert scavengers and when the rains dried the bull would be buried by hardened clay.

By evening Denny arrived with the Arabians and the remuda. He hobbled the Arabians and the loose remuda horses and let them graze with the cows. He also stretched a rope between two bushes and to the rope, he tied the horses to be ridden tomorrow.

Grady got a fire going, and that night they all ate steak. They were grateful to have found so many of the herd had survived the storm and thankful for the food in their hungry stomachs.

The next morning Denny produced a coffeepot from his saddlebag, and a small portion of coffee. The three enjoyed the hot, bitter brew while they made plans for the day. It was decided that Cecile would remain with the herd. Her horse was tied and ready for her to saddle if she needed to keep the herd bunched and settled. The two men would go back over the trail to find the rest of the crew. Hopefully they would be back by nightfall.

As Grady saddled his horse, Deadly left Trumpeter's side. "No, you stay here old partner, and help Miss Grace keep an eye on the herd." He gave him a hug and a scratch, and then he repeated "shoo" several times, waving the bull back to the herd. Deadly turned reluctantly and strolled back to continue grazing by Trumpeter's side.

The ground was drying, and the horses were able to travel at a rapid walk. Occasionally they had to detour around flooded low areas, but by noon Denny and Grady were a welcome sight for Gimpy Lou and Scratch. The wagons were making better time today, but the day before had been a bitch.

They all got off their horses and down from the wagons. Squatting in a circle, sharing paper and tobacco, the crew rolled cigarettes. Drawing slowly, they swapped information. It was decided to get the two grain wagons to the camp and leave a man with Miss McNamara to help dry out some of the grain. The rest would backtrack to help Cook and Little Bear with the grub wagon and the cart.

The trip back to camp with the loaded wagons was much slower than the morning's ride. The time would double or triple, and it would be long after dark when they arrived. The men, aware that the woman was alone on the open desert, worked feverishly to get the wagons back to camp, but the trails easily covered on horseback became sucking, grasping, sliding traps for the wheels on the heavily loaded wagons. The men used their ropes and horses to aid the struggling teams pulling the wagons. They used brush to create traction through unavoidable mud sumps. The men cussed, and the louder, more abusive the language, the easier seemed the work. The horses strained and sweat lathered their necks. Froth dripped from their mouths as they chewed on the bits and strained against the harness and the pull of the lariats.

CHAPTER SEVEN

Cecile watched Grady and Denny ride away. Her feelings were mixed—foreboding at being left alone and luxuriating in the thought that she would have some time to herself. She poured another cup of the bitter camp coffee and sat, elbows on knees, to watch the cows as they went about the task of filling their bellies. At the moment they were safe. She regretted the loss of three cows but realized how lucky she was to have lost so few in such a disastrous storm.

She knew that her trail boss had done everything he could to save the herd. She was grateful, both to him and to the longhorn bull, whose uncanny prediction of the tornado had allowed them time to get out of the path of the merciless spiral.

The sun was shining and everything was fresh and clear. She had the day to herself to do with as she pleased, outside of keeping an eye on the herd as it grazed. She smiled. She wasn't sure she even needed to worry about that job, as Deadly seemed to have the direction for the herd to graze under control.

She put down her tin cup and leaned back to rest her head and shoulders on her saddle. She closed her eyes and felt the heat of the sun warming her skin, while beautiful yellow and orange sunspots drifted across her closed eyelids. She felt good today, inside anyway. The outside felt pretty grimy. She sat upright. That's what she wanted, a bath! She had been days in the same clothes. That she couldn't help, but she could get a sponge bath and rinse out her underwear.

She reached into her saddlebag and brought out her travel kit. She smiled at the difference between the contents of her survival kit and the one Grady had produced the day before. She did have a change of underwear, but she had worn it several days ago and now both pair needed freshening. She dug into the saddlebag again and was pleased to find she also had a clean camisole in the bag. Good, this would allow her to wash her shirt. She draped the shirt over the saddle and spread out her items from the travel kit.

She had a heavy Spanish comb, a bar of scented French soap, a small jar of face cream, and a travel-size pot of delicate pink rouge. A handcrafted silver vial decorated with turquoise brought her brother to mind, and she smiled with love. The vial contained a heavy perfume that her father had imported from Arabia for her mother, when he imported the Arabian horses. Her brother, Ramon, had made the vial and given it to her for her birthday last year.

She unscrewed the lid. Closing her eyes, she drew in a deep breath of the familiar fragrance. Her mother's image floated through her mind. Her feeling of happiness was replaced for a moment with sadness as she silently told her mother's image how much she missed her and loved her. The moment of sorrow passed quickly.

She returned the lid to the vial and continued the perusal of her kit. She had needles and a fair selection of thread, neatly packed for travel. She had a small vial of antiseptic and a roll of clean, sterilized rag wound tightly and wrapped neatly in oilcloth to preserve its purity, to be used for minor accidents. Also enclosed in a folded piece of oilcloth, tied with blue ribbon, were several pieces of monogrammed writing paper and a small pencil. She smiled at the absurdity of these articles out here in the middle of this vast, empty country, but she remembered how useful they had been to while away the hours when she had waited in San Diego for Mr. Grady, trail boss, to arrive. She wondered if the letter she had sent Ramon would reach him before she and the herd did. Surely so.

She set aside the packet of writing materials and put her fingers inside her kit again. She knew it would be empty, but natural human curiosity and wishful thinking made the action unconscious. She was surprised when her fingers touched two small, hard objects. She brought them from the kit with her fingertips and laughed with delight when she saw two brightly wrapped hard candies. How she had missed them before she couldn't imagine, for Grace Cecile McNamara had a sweet tooth that never would have allowed her to save the two candies had she had known that they were there.

She started to unwrap one of the candies and pop it into her mouth, but a thought stopped her. The two candies would give her something to look forward to as the day wore on. She knew that she would become hungry later and she wanted to wait as late as possible to build a fire. She would have to go all day on what was left of the cold, bitter coffee, and a hard biscuit saved from the night before. She returned the two delights to her kit anticipating the pleasure she would get when she had one for lunch and one late in the afternoon. Now she had something to look forward to, to help her keep her mind off the return of the men.

She picked up the soiled pair of underwear and the bar of soap and went in search of a puddle of water deep enough for the mud to have settled to the bottom. She found several. She bypassed one that looked absolutely marvelous; she would use that water to bathe herself.

After she had soaped and rinsed the undergarments she returned to camp and spread the bloomers on a bush to dry. She couldn't prevent a blush from seeing her unmentionables waving in the mild breeze, and she couldn't help but glance around to be sure she was alone. She laughed, "Well, what shall I do while they dry?" Her voice sounded loud out here in the open with no other sounds to interfere. Even Deadly halted his grazing and lifted his head to stare for a moment in her direction. Deciding that she had not addressed him, he returned to his grazing. She replaced the items in her travel kit and then placed the kit back into the saddlebag. She noticed the shiny, black leather was water spotted and mud spattered.

The ornate silver inlays glistened in the sun and the turquoise looked richer and bluer out here in this land of sagebrush and mud.

The scarf she had used to wash away the blood on Reginald had been rinsed clean in cold water the night before and tied to sagebrush to dry. Using it dry, she wiped over the saddle, rubbing hard on the more soiled areas, renewing the polish by heating the layers of accumulated oils that had been rubbed into the leather over the years. It was a makeshift job, and the saddle would need proper attention when the wagon arrived, but an hour later the saddle had resumed its lustrous appearance. She shook her saddle blanket vigorously; loose horsehair, dried dirt and horse sweat dusted the air. She stretched the blanket over a bush to air.

She checked on the herd and was surprised to see how far away they had grazed while she labored over the saddle. All looked well so she went to the bush displaying her undies and found them to be nearly dry. By the time she bathed, starting from her hair down, they would be ready to wear.

Now she had to make a decision. The only vessel she had that could be used to pour water over her hair and herself was the coffeepot and that still contained a couple of cups of coffee. The small metal cup hooked to the handle of the pot would take all day to rinse with. She poured herself another cup of the cold, bitter brew and poured the rest onto the ashes. From the saddle she removed the camisole and soap, grabbed up the coffeepot, and headed for the water hole that she had picked out earlier. The cattle were drifting enough that she knew she would soon have to saddle up and join them, but now she intended to thoroughly enjoy her bath.

First she removed her shirt and quickly soaped and rinsed it then hung it on the nearest bush to dry. Loosening her thick black hair from the turquoise thongs she ran her fingers through it carefully got it un-braided. Taking a deep breath she quickly dumped the coffeepot full of chilly water over her head.

She gasped as the water hit her body. She had debated about heating the water over the embers of the campfire, but had been reluctant to prolong the time before she went to check the herd. She soaped her hair and then walked around surveying the land in all directions while she scrubbed her scalp, enjoying the feel of sun and soft breezes on her bare breasts as they rose and fell with the vigor of the scrubbing.

To keep the water as clean as possible, she made many trips to the puddle to fill the pot and then walked away a few feet to pour it over her head, rinsing the soap away. It was awkward and she soon realized that her riding skirt and boots were about to be drenched. Throwing all modesty away she stayed bent over and removed first her boots and stockings, then her riding skirt and underwear. She backed up to the bush and tossed the garments on it to keep them off of the still-muddy ground.

Completely nude, white flesh glistening in the sun, she returned to the tedious job of rinsing her hair, one pot at a time. She stood upright and let the soapy water fall down her body. She used her hands and lathered herself from head to toe, over and over until the long hair rinsed clear of soap. Then she stepped into the water hole refilling the pot numerous times to rinse her body squeaky clean. Without a towel she would have to air dry so she rinsed the pair of undies she had removed, and took them back to camp to hang on the same bush as the previous pair. She got her comb from the saddle kit and spent another half hour removing the tangles from her hair. She braided it while it was still damp, and refastened the thongs.

Now dry, she put away the comb, pulled on the clean underwear and got the camisole and riding skirt. She carried the wet socks to join the undies on the bush by the camp, and returned the soap to her kit. She filled the pot with a final load of water, picked up her boots, and returned to sit on her saddle blanket where she rinsed her feet with the water, then sat relaxed while they dried in the sun.

She felt wonderful. She could never remember a bath feeling so glorious. She closed her eyes, and soaked up the sun. It was getting hot at midday. She opened her eyes and searched through very bright sun for the herd.

"Good Lord, they are nearly out of sight." She pulled on boots over bare feet, bridled and saddled her horse, removed the lariat pegging rope, wound it up, and tied it to the front saddle tie. The coffeepot was secured to a back tie. The beef rump was heavy, but she got it down and tied it across the back of the saddle. The wet laundry she wound up in the shirt, and climbed into the saddle.

The cattle were farther away than she realized, but she soon caught up to them. Ahead, in the direction they were grazing she spotted some good-sized bushes and rode on ahead of the herd to spread her laundry on them and put the meat in the shade.

Then she dropped her reins to the ground and let the horse loose to graze. Having been tied all night, he fell to a steady cropping of grass.

The rhythm of the cropping soon had Cecile looking for a spot to lean back. She found a rock at the base of a small mesquite tree, sat on it so she could be off the damp ground, and leaned back on the slender tree. She had counted the cattle as she passed through the herd. Satisfied that all was well, she closed her eyes, listened to the steady cropping of grass, and drifted off to sleep.

Startled, she opened her eyes. A rifle muzzle was touching the tip of her nose. She jumped, forgetting where she was, and the trunk of the mesquite tree scraped hard into her back. The pain brought her instantly awake. She looked up into the eyes of a stranger, a big, handsome man. Handsome, that is, in the manner of a western man. He didn't have the exquisite handsomeness of the Spanish men. He had a nice grin and beautiful teeth. They appeared to flash as he smiled at her. That was all she could say nice about him. His clothes were filthy. He had probably been caught in the storm. The fingernails on the hand that held the rifle were black with filth. She didn't remember Grady having dirty fingernails, even when he was doing the dirtiest work. She looked from the man's hands back to his eyes, only to find them running insultingly over her bare shoulders. The camisole was scant, designed to wear under her clothes, and it barely covered her full breasts. The thin straps over her shoulders allowed her slim neck and smooth shoulders to be viewed openly by those hungry eyes.

"Hey, Vince, come 'ere. See what I got!" His eyes never left her breasts as he called the other man.

The man came from behind her, leading her gelding. "No, man, you look at what I found. Man, look at this saddle. What do you suppose a saddle like that is worth?" The runty little man had taken a quick look at Cecile and turned back to gloat over the silver mounted saddle. The rifle didn't move, and neither did the man watching her.

"Where's yore menfolk, Lady?"

"They'll be here shortly."

"Yore lying to Ben, darlin'."

"No, I'm not. They had to get the grub wagon out of a ditch, but that was hours ago. They will be back any minute."

"Ben, don't press your luck. That breed of woman ain't out here alone."

"Shut up!" The smile turned to a snarl, and Cecile saw for an instant an uncontrolled insanity flash in his eyes. He quickly resumed the smile and turned his head slowly to study the silver mounted saddle. He took in the greedy way Vince was running his hands over each turquoise mounted silver inlay. He didn't like Vince doing that, but he would handle that later. Right now he had something more important on his mind, and he turned his attention back to the girl.

Cecile hadn't moved a muscle. She was afraid of this man. This was a dangerous man, possibly mentally deranged. A man like that was unpredictable. Anything could set him off, trigger his anger. So she sat perfectly still, appearing calm, while praying silently, "Grady, where are you? Please come."

The rifle remained unwaveringly on the tip of her nose. He reached forward with his other hand and flicked a ribbon from the front lacing, out of the cleft of her breasts, the finger moved lightly over the curve of the breast following the lines of the camisole, until it reached the braid of hair hanging forward over her shoulder. He felt its softness between his fingers. His eyes left hers to study the thong decorated with turquoise nuggets. His attention came back to her eyes, the grin fixed on his face. He lifted the braid over her head and pulled it tight.

"Move slow, ma'am. Get up." The rifle followed her face as she reached behind to use the tree trunk to push herself up. Slowly, hand over hand she rose, bringing her feet under her. When she was upright she still had to look up to watch the man's eyes. He was a big man.

He backed up, pulling her forward by the braid. The rifle muzzle had raised some; she was staring right into the end of it. She followed obediently into the opening past the horse and the other man. When her leader stopped, so did she. For the first time, the rifle moved away from her face.

He held onto the braid and began to circle around her. His eyes studied everything, her ears, her neck, her camisole, her riding skirt, and her boots. He dropped the braid and ran his hand searching over her hips and down her leg. He slid the hand between her legs, waited for her to protest. When she stood still he moved the hand down her leg to the top of her boot. He ran his fingers around the inside of both boots, then up the inner side of her leg, only this time in under the skirt. Near her crotch he tightened his fingers on her flesh and waited for her reaction. She stood firm, although it took all of her concentration to keep from flinching. She reasoned it best to be passive, and inactive, hoping not to excite him by fighting. He completed his inspection, running his hand slowly around the other side, then ran his hand over her camisole, lifting each breast in turn. The rifle was again pointed at her nose.

"Tie that horse up and see what else you can find," he ordered the other man. She could hear the man moving to do as he was told.

"Where's yore men, darlin'?"

"I told you, they should have been here already."

"I ain't dumb, ma'am. I know a woman with yore class ain't going to be out here alone. What I don't know is, where they are, and how many of them there are."

"I just told you, they should be here any time, and there are nine of them."

"Little darlin', yore lying to Ben."

"Why are you holding that rifle in my face?"

"Well, little darlin', I didn't want you to get scared of Ben and scream, or do something Ben would have to hurt you for. Menfolk are funny about their women, and I don't want any trouble with nine menfolk, now do I, darlin'?"

His hand drifted to her shoulder strap and traced its path over her shoulder. The fingers once again gathered her hair and she could feel them move in and out of the twisted braid.

She was in grave danger. All her life she had taken for granted the art of breeding cattle and horses. She was experienced in animal passion, and she could smell the male sex glands of this man. He would have her if he had to kill her. All that kept him from attacking her was the puzzle over why she was alone. She knew that he fully intended to rape her, but he didn't want to get caught with his pants down.

A yell came from the other man "Hey, Ben, there's a hunk of beef over here. Man, what luck. I'm starved."

"OK, Vince, cool it. I gotta think."

Vince came around the brush and walked with a limp toward them. His grotesque, squatty figure gave the appearance of an ape. His eyes were close together, and he kept them lowered to the ground.

"Let's get out of here, Ben. We can take the meat and the saddle, and run for it. Don't mess with the woman. They mightn't come after us for the saddle, but if you hurt the woman you know what's going to happen, Ben. Please don't mess with the woman. Let's get out of here." His whining voice even irritated Cecile. She didn't blame Ben when he backhanded the man across the mouth.

"You know better than that, Vince. I ain't going to hurt the woman, and I ain't going nowhere until I'm ready to go."

The rifle hadn't moved. Cecile was getting tired of having to watch the barrel to keep it from ramming her nose.

"I have to go," she said, watching the rifle.

"Go where, darlin'?"

She kept her eyes off of his grinning face, kept them glued to the rifle bore. "I have to relieve myself," she whispered.

He laughed out loud, and then scowled, and moved the rifle over and shoved it into her cheek. "Sure, darlin', Ben's going to take care of you while yore menfolk are away. See that bush over there?" He pointed to a sagebrush large enough to hide most of her. "Ben's going to keep his eye on you, darlin'. Ben don't want nothing to happen to you. Ben don't want you wandering around by yourself. Hurry and come back, or Ben's going to come after you, OK?"

"OK," she answered, but she remained still until he pulled the rifle away from her face. Then she ran for the bush, his laughter ringing out behind her. She didn't know if she could trust him, but she really needed to relieve herself. She was so scared that if she didn't she would soon embarrass herself. She quickly performed the ritual, keeping both eyes directed through the branches of the bush. Then she returned to the clearing.

As she walked slowly back to the man she scanned the trail for the herd and raised her eyes and took a fix on the sun. She must have slept for several hours. It was midafternoon or later. The cattle had had several hours to graze out of sight. The pair of men must have arrived from another direction. Her horse, dragging his reins, and being a well-trained cow horse, had stayed in the area where he had been released. She wished that he had followed the herd.

"Feel better?" The grin was lewd. She nodded and lowered her eyes to stare at the ground. He watched her for a while. Nervously she occasionally searched the trail for a glimmer of the herd. Her fear was that they would be discovered. The idea of her Herefords in the hands of these barbarians made her sick. Luckily she didn't search the back trail for Grady. The man was watching her every movement. He knew the girl would be praying for help to arrive. He saw her searching the distant horizon to the south. He thought her men would come from that direction.

He pondered. Should he take her with him, use her here, or wait to see how many protectors she had. Perhaps there was more wealth like the saddle. Vince had gone over to run his hands over the silver again. Damn moron. Ben was tired thinking for the runt. Angrily he yelled at the little man, "Find some firewood. Let's get some meat in our bellies."

Vince moved away from the saddle and began gathering shrubs and some brush logs. He made several trips to the clearing with firewood. When he had a substantial stack he turned to Ben to await further orders.

The big man shook his head, smiled patiently, and said slowly and distinctly, "Go get the horses. Tie them over there where the other horse is. Get some matches out of the saddlebag. Light the fire. Find some water. Get the coffeepot off the girl's horse and fill it with water. See if she's got some coffee in her saddlebag to go with it. Cut some beef and put it on some sticks and hang it over the fire. Would you like for me to repeat that?"

"No, Ben, I got it. I go get the horses, build a fire, fix some coffee, and cook some meat. Right?"

"Right."

Vince chuckled, pleased that he had repeated the orders correctly and then he ran off to carry out the first order to get the horses. Cecile was relieved. They had not seen the herd. They had not crossed their path at all. The cows would be safe. Now all she had to do was to take the best care of herself that she could until help came. Please, sweet Jesus, send help soon.

"Come here, little darlin'."

She jumped. She had been staring at the ground, noticing that it was still soft mud. She wondered how she could make such unimportant observations when she should be trying to figure a way out of this mess. Her eyes met his, that sparking grin again. She would see it in her sleep, but she obeyed and walked over to stand in front of him.

He took the braid in his hand and turned and walked back to the mesquite tree where he had found her sleeping. He pulled her along with him by the braid.

"Sit." He indicated the flat rock she had used before.

She sat, the hair pulled tight at the roots of the braid. It hurt, but she didn't cry out. He laughed and let the braid fall as he sank to the damp ground beside her. She turned slightly toward him so she could keep her eyes on him. He took her hand and spread it. With the forefinger of his right hand he lightly traced the lines in her hand, then straightened out her fingers inspecting each one as if it held some secret. She was revolted as the dirty fingernails traced their path, but she controlled the feeling and waited for the next move.

It came suddenly. He grabbed her braid in one hand and pulled her head to place his lips on hers. She was caught by surprise. Her lips parted and her teeth clashed painfully into his gleaming white teeth. The encounter was painful, and she cried out. He bit her lips in punishment and then released her. Cursing, he rose to his feet. He walked over to the bush she had used earlier; she figured he needed to relieve himself.

Cecile leaped to her feet, ran to her horse, ripped loose the reins and headed the horse down the back trail. Then she hit him as hard as she could to send him flying out of the camp. Why hadn't she leaped into the saddle? Instinct maybe. She knew Ben would run her down. Maybe the horse, alone, would return to his last bed ground. Just maybe, he would find some of the crew.

Ben was on her. She had never seen such rage. He struck her across the face and she fell sprawling onto the mud. Vince's arrival saved her from another blow. When he saw the ornate silver mounted saddle disappearing he climbed into the saddle of one of the horses. He yelled and sank his heels into the horse's side, sending him leaping after the gelding. Ben's horse, spooked by the noise and excited by the horses running wildly, sidestepped Ben as he reached for the reins and raced after the disappearing horses, leaving behind the man and girl on foot. Now Ben had no choice, the girl had made the decision for him. He would wait for the men to return for her.

He allowed her to return to the rock under the tree. He was angry, and he didn't like it. The anger spoiled the sensual feeling he had enjoyed earlier as he mentally undressed the girl. From his shirt pocket he removed his tobacco and papers, rolled a cigarette, put it in his lips, and lit it. Using the match, he bent and lit the firewood that Vince had piled up. He smoked and searched the land to the southeast. Someone would come from that direction. The girl had said soon. It could be anytime. Or possibly Vince would catch up with the fleeing horse and return in time.

He cut a slab of meat and propped it over the fire on a strong stick. He did not fix one for the girl. To hell with her, let her starve. Serve her right for letting the horse loose. He turned the meat a few times and added fuel to the fire. The earlier grin of amusement was gone. He didn't like being without a horse. His rifle was on the saddle; he had only the pistol on his belt. He was at a disadvantage because he didn't know how many riders to expect.

66

He gnawed at the meat, wiped his chin on his sleeve and his hands on his pants, frustration built up in him and rage formed. It was too dark to see the enemy coming. The sun was down. Soon the stars would be out. Ben was trapped, and he needed to know how many men would come. Rising, he went to the girl sitting on the rock. He jerked her to her feet and slammed a backhand blow across her face. She screamed and fell back against the hard trunk of the mesquite. It broke her fall and held her up. She threw her arm across her face expecting another blow to follow. Instead, he grabbed the front of the camisole and tore its fastening free, exposing her breasts; her nipples were firm in her reaction to her fear. In a rage he grabbed both breasts in his hands and squeezed his fingers into her flesh as hard as he could. She screamed in pain. It hurt so badly she couldn't move.

"How many?"

She couldn't talk, she couldn't scream, she couldn't move. The pain was unbearable. She could feel herself sinking into blackness. Her knees buckled adding more pressure on her breasts. She heard the screams, but she didn't know anymore if they were hers.

CHAPTER EIGHT

Deadly had grazed with the herd all day, staying out in front, keeping Trumpeter near him. The cows were not aware that they were being maneuvered to continue in a southerly direction. They drifted after the two bulls, eating, searching out the next mouthful. Reginald, in pain, stayed with the cows. He tried to eat; he was weak and needed food, but when he lowered his head the empty eye socket throbbed so he tried to keep his head as still as possible to ease the pain.

Deadly had observed the woman as she joined the herd; the sun was now high in the sky. He knew she had made camp under a small tree, and satisfied that he was in charge, he continued to graze with the herd. When the sun began to go down he became nervous. He had already spent several nights alone with this herd, and he missed his regular camp habits. Grady was back on the trail somewhere. It was possible the camp had been set up where the girl had stopped under the mesquite tree. The lower the sun went, the more agitated he became.

Nervously he circled the herd, waving the ball tipped horns at the cows. He moved them together into a holding pattern to bed down. Trumpeter had already sunk to the ground; Reginald, no longer cocky, was weak from hunger, his muscles sore and pain annoying his head. He found the old bull and settled down near him, keeping Trumpeter to the side where his good eye could see the veteran bull. His presence offered the young bull some comfort.

Deadly checked the herd again, then stretching his legs into a running walk he back trailed until he saw the camp fire. It was dark now, and the fire meant friends and a biscuit. He dropped to a slow trot. Then he heard the screams. He knew they were the woman's, but his concern was for Grady. Something was wrong. When he heard the screams again, he leaped into a gallop, racing toward the fire.

He didn't know what to expect as he neared the campfire, but repeated punishment for running through camp brought him up short just outside the firelight. He saw the girl. A stranger was slapping her face. Deadly had fought many a range battle; however, he had never before attacked a man, but an instinct of danger would not allow him to hesitate. He plunged across the opening.

Ben heard the noise behind him and turned, drawing his pistol, expecting to confront a man. His amazement at seeing the huge longhorn bull, red of eye, lunging at him out of the darkness saved Deadly's life. Ben froze and the pistol was never fired as a smashing blow in the stomach with the heavy polished horn, knocked the breath from him. He felt himself being lifted into the air. Deadly put all of his weight into that toss. The man was thrown back over Deadly's shoulder to land in a heap on the ground, the breath knocked out of him.

He tried to rise, but the bull was on him, pinning him to the ground with one mighty horn, goring and raking that "master horn" in and out of Ben's chest. When the man became still Deadly ceased the attack. He backed off keeping an eye on his enemy. Then he pawed the still damp earth, advanced, tilted a long horn to slide under the body and rolled it across the ground. He continued this ritual until he was convinced the man would not get up.

The girl was recovering, although the pain she suffered was terrible. Gingerly she massaged her breasts and sobbed. She looked around to find her tormentor, and saw Deadly standing in the fire light toying with a bundle on the ground. She rose to her feet and walked closer to the object. When she recognized the bloody body, now limp as a rag, she threw up.

"Stop it, Deadly. That's enough." The bull backed away from the bloody heap of rags as the woman came to him, wrapped her arms about his neck, and began to cry. He wasn't sure if he should stand still or move away from her. He was trying to make up his mind when Grady and Little Bear came galloping into camp. Well, it was about time. Where was the grub wagon? It was biscuit time.

CHAPTER NINE

The grain wagons soon became the object of the four men's wrath. After many struggles to move the wagons through hub deep mud, the men began to develop a system. One man rode ahead and picked a trail, cut brush and threw it over the next mud sump. One man drove the team, and the other two alternated pulling with their lariats from horseback. Wedging poles under the axles lifted the stuck wheels by hand. They traveled the fresh trail first with the lighter wagon, the one that had lost half of its grain in the storm. They would move it a quarter of a mile, then find a dry spot to pull aside and the brush cutter would rotate to driving the second wagon. The driver went to the back of a horse and the previous rider now became the brush cutter.

They would leave the lead wagon and team of horses to rest and catch their breath. One man rode back to the second wagon. The brush cutter concentrated on the ruts that had been the worst, the first time over. The heavier wagon was just as troublesome and time consuming but the men had some idea of the difficulty of the trail and could take more precautions when necessary. At times all four men cut brush or filled a really obstinate wash.

They were still a long way from the previous night's camp as the sun began to lower. The men were tired, and so were the horses, so tired that Grady called a rest stop. The men dropped about the wagon. Denny had been driving this time, and he just sank back against the grain sacks and closed his eyes, too tired even to roll a smoke. He was young enough not to be so addicted as to crave a smoke over rest. Little Bear and Scratch squatted by a wagon wheel and leaned back to relax their tired backs. Grady sat on his horse and rolled a smoke, lit it, and took a few drags before he gave his orders.

"We can't make it tonight. It's too much of a struggle even in daylight. We go it as far as we can before the sun goes down. Then we will head for camp and get a good night's sleep. We can get the wagons in early in the morning." The tired men agreed. Little Bear rolled two smokes and handed one to Lou. The crippled man had worked as hard as the other three and they all knew he was feeling pain in the gimpy leg. He didn't express his thanks for the smoke, or the light Little Bear provided, but his sigh of relief as his body relaxed was thanks enough for Little Bear.

While the men smoked and rested, Grady turned his horse and scouted down the trail. It was not bad for a way, and then he came to a wash that had a four-foot drop on both sides, and a trickle of water still running downhill through it.

The banks were treacherous and the bed could be bottomless with slacking clay.

Returning to the men he took a good look at the mud-covered cowboys. All he could see clearly were Denny's eyes; the rest of his face was covered with mud. Lou had kept his face clean, but with that gimpy leg he had spent a lot of time on the ground. His blue overalls were filthy. Little Bear had removed his boots and worked barefoot, his pants rolled to his knees. With Indian dexterity he had managed to stay on his feet. He was mud spattered, but of the four men, he had stayed the cleanest.

"Let's try to drive both wagons this next stretch. I think we can do it. Over the rise a bit there's a small river still running. We'll pack it in there. Lou, you drive the other wagon, Little Bear and I will do the muscle work."

Lou grabbed the wagon wheel and pulled himself up. As he took the seat, his sigh of relief was audible; finally he had the luxury to be able to relieve the pain from his legs and back. One of the reasons Grady liked this group was because they gutted up and did what needed doing. Grady had known Lou was far beyond needing a break but not once had he complained.

Little Bear snuffed his cigarette butt in the mud, rose, and led his horse ahead of Denny's wagon. The ground was pretty solid—damp, but not slippery. A few places needed brush added. The Indian did this job and then returned to hook his rope to the wagons and help Grady pull them over the rough spots.

It was almost dark when Denny spotted the horses running across the desert some distance away. In the evening's growing darkness they were hard to see. At first Denny thought they were wild horses, but the manner in which they were traveling made him look harder. They were not traveling together in a bunch as wild horses do.

One animal was in the lead, head high; running like the devil was after him. He had to look twice at the second horse, but he was sure there was a rider on it. Far behind the other two, a third horse ran easily, keeping the second in sight, but not trying to catch up.

"Whoa." Denny pulled up the lead wagon. Grady and Little Bear were helping Lou. "Hey, boss, look yonder," he stood up on the wagon bed and pointed to the horses.

Grady turned to see what the boy was pointing at. It took a minute to find the traveling horses. If the ground had been dry, a dust cloud would have located them. He didn't know for sure what he was seeing but he didn't want to take any chances. A rider on this desert had to be looked into. It could be somebody in trouble.

"Come on, Bear, let's catch a horse," he yelled, and kicked his horse into a run. The Indian did not hesitate. He followed, riding low over his saddle, Indian fashion. His animal was tired, but the Indian had rubbed him down several times during the day, and watered him frequently at puddles. Where the white man had rested himself, the Indian had rested his horse, and now his animal had more to give than Grady's horse.

They set a course to meet the lead horse at a certain point. As they got nearer Grady could see the black saddle that belonged to Cecile. A gunshot rang out. There was a rider on the second horse, and he was shooting at the Indian. Grady drew his pistol. The handle was slippery with mud and he nearly dropped it. His horse, running low to the ground, was following Little Bear. Grady used both hands to wipe the gun on his shirt, and then he fired at the rider. He didn't aim, at this pace he knew it would be a lucky shot if he hit the rider. What he wanted to do was to keep the rider from shooting the Indian.

He turned his horse to head off the rider, firing as he rode. As they drew nearer the rider turned his horse and rode away from Grady. Grady followed long enough to be sure the rider would keep going and not stop and ambush him.

Then he went to catch the second horse. The animal was tired, and came to a halt by himself, and waited for Grady to catch up the reins. Grady didn't recognize the horse, or the saddle. Little Bear rode up, leading the horse carrying Cecile's saddle. Grady was frightened.

"Come on, there's trouble." He wheeled his horse and they returned to the wagons. Grady swung down from his horse, and onto Cecile's gelding. Even with the run the animal couldn't be as tired as the one he had been riding.

"Little Bear, you ride that animal and come with me. Denny, you and Lou take our horses and follow as fast as you can. Leave the teams. Miss Grace is in trouble."

It was dark now and suicidal to race the animals but Grady pushed the horse as fast as he could. They slipped and the animal's back feet went out from under him. Grady stepped out of the stirrups as they went down, and landed safely. The horse scrambled up. Grady led him for a few steps to see if he was sound. The horse seemed fine, apart from heaving sides and nostrils gasping for air.

Grady mounted and rode on. He could hear the Indian in front of him now. Recognizing the possible danger at camp, Little Bear had not stopped to attend to Grady. He had wisely continued on.

The noise of the horse Little Bear rode— winded and wheezing from the earlier run—gave Grady a direction to follow. He soon caught up with Little Bear, and they traveled rapidly in silence.

The Indian spotted the campfire first. He motioned off to the left slightly, and Grady saw it. It grew brighter as they approached the camp. The Indian stopped his horse, and Grady impatiently pulled up also. He didn't want to waste any time, but he knew Little Bear was right. They would be no help to Cecile if they ran into a trap.

Slowly he followed Little Bear as he wove his horse in and out around the camp. Keeping far back in the shadows they searched for signs of strangers. They didn't find any horses, or riders, and now they could see Deadly by Cecile in the clearing. Grady forgot caution and galloped his horse into the clearing. Swinging from the saddle he ran to Cecile. He tried to take her in his arms, and she began to scream and tightened her hold on Deadly's neck. The bull bolted sideways, dragging her with him.

"Hold it, Deadly. Whoa, boy."

The bull recognized his friend and settled down. The girl screamed, her arms tightened around his neck, and Grady had to pry Cecile's arms loose.

"Easy, ma'am, it's Grady. It's all right now Ma'am; it's Grady."

His name finally penetrated the screams and her eyes began to lose the look of shock as she slowly recognized him. She grabbed his neck, substituting Grady for Deadly. He pulled the small, trembling body against his own and wrapped his arms around her. She no longer screamed, but her arms threatened to never release him. Sobs wracked her body. He petted her as though she were a puppy, smoothed her hair, crooned to her, and the sobs began to recede, but the hold on his neck remained.

As Cecile quieted, Grady surveyed the clearing. Little Bear was squatted beside a pile of rags. His horse, wall eyed, strained back against the reins to move as far away from the bloody carcass as he could. Little Bear rose, took his horse, gathered up Cecile's gelding, and then moved over to Grady.

"Damn dead, that man. Old Deadly seen to that. I'm going to tie up the horses and scout the camp to be sure we don't be ambushed."

"Good."

A shudder shook the body in his arms as Cecile gasped for air, trying to control her sobs. Her face and mouth were buried against his neck, and Grady felt the wetness of her tears. How hurt was she? He wanted to find out, but he knew that she was too hysterical to release him yet.

The sound of horses arriving came to him. He spun the girl about to face that direction, and pulled his gun. The horses stopped outside the light of the camp fire and Denny called out "It's us, boss."

"Ride on in," Grady answered, and holstered his gun.

"Don't let them see me like this, please get me away from here. Please don't let them see me."

Grady was angry, remembering the proud, haughty woman he had left that morning. That someone had turned that strong woman into the broken spirit he held in his arms made him want to lash out. He gave the men a signal to stay back and swung her legs up into one arm and carried her, still clinging tightly to his neck, into the flickering shadows on the edge of the firelight.

He held her until she began to relax. Soon she took one hand and wiped the tears from her face. She kept her body pressed against his chest. "Please close your eyes," she whispered. He did as she asked. She released her hold on his neck, and he could feel her trying to gather her camisole across her chest.

"You can put me down now."

"With my eyes closed?"

She laughed shakily. "You may open your eyes, but please don't look at me. Please," she pleaded.

Grady opened his eyes, found a dry place on the ground and set her down. He could not help seeing her torn garment. Her arms hid her breasts where the garment didn't cover them. She was muddy, and her face was swollen on the right jaw with blood on her lips.

"Please look away. I don't want you to see me this way."

"Ma'am, I need to look at you. I got to find out how bad you're hurt."

She blushed. "I'm not abused, Mr. Grady. I still have my virginity, but I feel dirty. That filthy man had his hands all over me. I was so clean. I had bathed and washed my clothes, and that trash rolled me in the mud." She was free of the fear. Now she could get mad. "Just look at what he's done to my camisole. No, don't look. Please will you get my shirt and things from that bush over there?"

He got the shirt for her, and turned his head while she replaced the torn camisole with the shirt, pulled off her boots and put on her socks, and replaced the boots. She wrapped the camisole and spare undies together and got to her feet. He heard her draw a deep breath, composing herself.

"Thank you, Mr. Grady. I'm all right now."

Grady turned to face her, seeing her clearly in the firelight, hair tangled, bruised and swollen jaw, and it looked like tooth marks on her mouth where some dried blood remained. He could only imagine what she must have been through.

"Hell of a trail boss I am. I should have my head knocked off for leaving you alone."

"No! You will not blame yourself. How could you know these men were anywhere near here. And besides, most men are not animals. It could have been others, nice men."

"Don't matter. After this you are not to be left alone. Either you will go with the crew, or Denny will stay with you."

She laid her hand on his arm, squeezed lightly, and said softly, "Mr. Grady, do you know where Denny would be right now if he had been here with me today?"

Denny lying dead on the ground flashed across his mind. "Yore probably right, but I promise that you will never have another day like this. Are you sure you're all right?"

She looked him squarely in his eyes. "Yes, beside some minor cuts, a few bruises, and hurt pride, I am unharmed, I promise you. Deadly arrived just in time. I owe my life to that bull. If that filthy man had ruined me, I would not want to live. As it is, I shall always remember those filthy fingernails on my skin." She shuddered and Grady knew her nerves were near shock.

"Come sit by the fire."

She lifted her head proudly, and walked, her arms holding the undergarments to her body. He seated her on a saddle blanket and propped her saddle behind her. She put her garments in her saddlebag, and tiredly sat staring into the flames.

Little Bear and Lou had dragged the man's body away from the clearing. They were gone a long time, burying the man, she supposed. Denny gathered fuel for the fire, and Grady cut up what was left of the beef rump and put it across the fire to roast. Denny hobbled all of the horses but one, and turned them loose to graze.

Grady took Deadly to a water hole and rinsed the blood from the bull's horns and body. He spent some time patting and rubbing the bull, talking to him. "You're too much, old bull. Two fights in two days. What are we going to do with you?" He was scolding, but his voice was filled with love and pride. He hugged the bull's big neck, and scratched the topknot. Deadly stomped a foot; he really was getting impatient. He appreciated the time Grady spent with him, and the pats of approval. But where was his biscuit?

Grady went back to the fire and turned the meat. Deadly followed him to the campfire, but Grady kept moving around, so Deadly went over to stand behind Cecile. Maybe she had a biscuit.

He waited patiently. The girl was unaware that the bull was behind her. She was lost in thought. He reached forward with his nose and gave her a nudge.

Cecile jumped, and with a start turned to see the bull. "Oh, Deadly, you scared me."

"Go on, big guy, get away from the lady. You'll have to wait until Cook gets here for your biscuit." Grady waved at the bull.

Cecile remembered the candy in her travel kit. "Wait, wait, please don't send him away." She dug frantically through the saddlebag, found the travel kit, and searched through its contents for the two candies. She found them. Removing the paper from one she put it in the palm of her hand and offered it to Deadly. He was wary. It didn't look like a biscuit, more like a sugar cube. That was all right. A sugar cube was a treat. He sniffed to make sure. It smelled different, but it smelled sweet. The rough tongue made a quick swipe, and the candy was gone.

He held it in his mouth for a moment to decide whether he wanted it, or would drop it to the ground. He decided it was good and began to work it around with his tongue. The more he moved it about, the better it tasted. He closed his eyes, felt the heat from the fire on his head and horns, and shifted the hard candy about his mouth until it melted away. He stood several minutes longer, chewing his cud, enjoying the lingering sweetness, and then he gave the girl another nudge. Maybe she had more.

She laughed, "Yes, you wonderful old bull, I have another, but that is all. When we get to my rancho I will buy you a sack full." She unwrapped the second piece and fed it to him. She remembered when she had found the candies only this morning. It seemed a long time ago. Like a little girl, she had looked forward to eating them herself. Now she watched an animal eat the small treats, and all she could think was how much she wished she had another for him.

Cecile pondered at what an unusual animal Deadly was. He was special, that's for sure. He had saved her herd, and now he had saved her. She knew, from all her years breeding and being around animals, that they each possessed a unique personality, just like people, but never had she seen it exhibited so strongly as it was in Deadly. She smiled to herself as she thought about this bull viciously killing the range bull and a man, yet knowing she was safer having Deadly near her than not.

The men ate a chunk of beef. The girl refused. She didn't think she could swallow anything yet. She did drink a cup of the hot coffee. It was as bitter as the morning pot, but the warmth in her belly relaxed her, and she soon lay back on her saddle and was fast asleep.

Denny waited until he knew she was asleep, and then he said to Grady, "Boss, I'm going back to my horses. They're tired. They worked hard today."

They need some time out of the harness if they're going to be any good tomorrow."

"No, you're a good hand, Denny. But there is another man out there—maybe more than one—and I don't want you out there alone. Besides, Scratch is with them."

The Indian squatted silently on the other side of the fire. He saw the expression on Denny's face. Slow-witted Scratch would not care for the horses. He spoke, "I go with the boy."

Grady looked from one to the other. He knew the kid was right, but his confidence in his judgment was shaken, if he sent Denny and Little Bear back to the wagons, that left only Lou and him here with Cecile. No one really knew who, or what was out there. Just because Cecile saw only two men didn't mean that there might not be more. There could be an entire robber band out there in the darkness.

Lou knew what Grady was struggling with. He didn't want to see anything happen to his boy either, but he knew the Indian was good. He rose and unstrapped his gun belt. He handed it to the boy. Denny wasn't in the habit of carrying a gun. Young and happy to work with horses, he had never taken to guns, but he took his father's gun belt and strapped it to his waist without comment. The Indian disappeared into the darkness to catch up a horse.

After Denny and Little Bear rode out, Lou went over to the saddles, took a rifle from the scabbard and said, "I'll take the first watch. You get some shut eye, boss." He walked with his limping gait into the darkness. Grady knew he would circle the camp slowly, changing his position to cover all sides until it was time to change guards. He put his saddle blanket over Cecile, threw some more wood on the fire, and lay down close enough to toast his back.

Deadly dozed by the fire until Grady bedded down, then he walked quietly away from the camp, it was time to check on his herd. He passed Gimpy Lou sitting on a rock, watching the camp. The old man acknowledged the bull, "You got work to do, too? See you in the morning, Deadly."

The bull answered with a low bawl, swung his horns to limber up his neck, and lifted his cloven hooves into a steady trot. No telling what he would find when he returned. This was the most unpredictable bunch of cows he had ever had to ride herd on.

CHAPTER TEN

Lou slowly moved around outside the camp for several hours. Occasionally he picked up a few chunks of wood and fed the campfire. Finally he woke Grady, handed him the rifle, and took his place by the fire. He was asleep before Grady left the clearing. Grady spent the rest of the night much as Lou had, changing his location often, sitting quietly listening to the night sounds, alert, not wanting trouble to surprise the poorly protected camp.

As daylight approached he went in search of the hobbled horses. They had not wandered far. He swung bareback onto his horse and drove the other two back to camp.

Lou was gathering brush for the fire. The rain puddles were drying up, and it was hard to find enough water for the coffeepot. Denny's coffee grounds were with him, so they had to make coffee with the used grounds from the night before. Lou searched his saddlebags and found a small packet of sugar. He sweetened the colored water. It would have to do.

As Grady saddled his horse he said, "Lou, get the horses saddled, and see that this camp is cleared. We wont be back here again. I'm going to ride down the trail and check the herd. You get Miss Grace up and take her with you. Keep your rifle handy. I'll catch up with you before you reach the wagons."

"Right, boss. See you later."

"I wont be long," Grady called over his shoulder as he cantered the horse out of the clearing. He picked up Deadly's tracks and kept the horse at a steady lope along the trail. The herd had traveled a long way, or maybe it just seemed long in his anxiety to assure himself of their safety and get back to the wagons. This storm had been a disaster; a shiver ran down him as he thought about what could have been if he had not heeded Deadly's warning. He loved that darn bull, and he was certainly pulling more than his fair load. Deadly had proven to be more valuable on this drive than all the humans combined.

He didn't like leaving the herd unattended. He could count on his fingers a dozen things that could go wrong, a couple of which could be theft by bandits or Indians, hungry men, hungry wolves, hungry lions, not to mention the obvious wild range bulls always ready to add a few more cows to their herd.

With the wagons scattered and everything such a mess he needed every hand available to get it sorted and bring an end to this chaos. Knowing Deadly was guarding the herd was the only solace he had about leaving them on their own.

He was relieved when he finally saw the herd ahead of him. When he reached the scattered drag he began to count. By the time he reached the leaders he had accounted for all that had survived the storm.

The three bulls were grazing together. Grady was surprised to find Reginald dogging Trumpeter's footsteps, keeping his bad eye to the bull and his good one on his open side. He was using Trumpeter as a shield for his blind side.

Deadly bawled a greeting. He was glad to see Grady. Grady rode over to the bull, leaned over and vigorously ran his hand up and down the bull's back. He crooned, "Good old Deadly. Good boy."

He surveyed the herd carefully. They all appeared in good condition. Hold it! His eyes went back over the cows he had just checked. He rode over to one of the cows and dismounted. The calm cow went on with her grazing. She lifted her head and smelled at his leg as he ran his hand over her sides and belly, appreciating Cecile for spending so much time gentling them so that this girl would allow him to handle her without being tied.

He picked a spot in her side and gave it a firm shove, then flattened his hand quickly, low on the side of her stomach. A solid thump bumped the side. Well, well, he was right. Before this trail drive was over they would need a nursery. He wondered how many more were in this condition. It was late in the summer to drop calves, but there were exceptions on all cattle drives. Why should this one be different?

"Deadly, bed them down. Bed them down, Deadly," he commanded.

The rangy bull swung his head toward Grady and saw the familiar hand signal that meant circling the herd and bedding down for camp. Confused, Deadly shook his head, ears wagging, horns waving, and waited for Grady's second command. He saw that his friend was serious, that he wanted the herd stopped.

Deadly set about getting the job done. He was annoyed. He had just gotten the herd straightened out and grazing on the trail, but he obeyed, as he had learned from long acquaintance not to question Grady's orders.

Grady waited until he was sure Deadly understood the command. The cows settled down to graze, foraging for feed without moving down the trail. They began to drift one way and another, but always staying within the confines that Deadly enforced.

"Make camp, Deadly," Grady called as he turned his horse to return back down the trail. He didn't give the herd another thought. He knew Deadly would hold the cattle where they were until he returned.

He kicked the horse and let him out to stretch his legs, covering the distance back to the camp and through it without stopping. The horse ran easily. The ground had now dried out enough to allow the animal freedom from boggy mud. Soon the riders appeared ahead. Lou, watching the back trail, saw the trail boss and halted the horses to wait for Grady to catch up.

Lou was worried about Miss Grace. She hadn't complained or said a word, but her teeth were clenched. She had tied her reins in a knot and dropped them over the saddle horn, letting her horse find its own way as it followed Lou's horse over the desert. Her arms were crossed over her chest and her hands grasped each arm tightly. A few times when he looked back he saw that not only were her teeth clenched but her eyes were shut tight as she bent over the saddle horn and fought the pain.

He was relieved when he spotted the trail boss catching up. He would be glad to turn the responsibility of the woman over to Grady.

Cecile was glad to see the trail boss as well. She was in such pain that nausea and dizziness were developing. She had been riding in fear of falling from the saddle. Even with such discomfort, she was eager to hear if the herd was safe.

81

Grady reported, "The cattle are fine, and they are all there. We should catch them tonight."

"Trumpeter?"

"He's fine, and so is Reginald. Deadly's in control, and he has done a good job."

"Thank God," she gasped, and swaying, lost consciousness and started to slide from the saddle. Grady jumped off his horse and gathered her into his arms. It wasn't long in the safety of his arms before she opened her eyes. He was shocked at the paleness of her skin, the pain lines in her face.

"Do I look that bad?" she mumbled as she regained consciousness and saw his worried stare. She could hardly open her mouth. Her jaw had swollen to twice its normal size, and was turning blue.

"Are you sure that jaw isn't broken?" he asked when he got over the shock of seeing her. Even her eye on the right side was turning blue.

"I don't think it is. It hurts something awful, but it doesn't feel broken."

He could barely understand her. It was difficult for her to speak, and saliva ran from one corner of her mouth. The place where her lip had been bitten looked like it might be festering.

"Lord, you're enough to scare a drunk," he said, trying to cheer her up.

She hunched over, her eyes squeezed tightly shut. "Don't make me laugh, it hurts too much."

"Well, how about some good news?"

She looked expectantly at him.

"The herd's doing fine. Kind of makes me feel useless. Deadly's got them going in the right direction, and all are accounted for. Reginald's eye socket is healing but it wouldn't hurt to use a little antiseptic on those stitches when we get back." He was talking to cheer her, trying to divert her mind from the pain she was trying to hide. It was hard to read the expression on her face, but her eyes thanked him. "Oh yes, Lady, do you know anything about being a midwife?"

She gave him a puzzled look.

"Well, if old Dr. Grady's right, we've got an addition coming soon to one of them little cows. I didn't have time to examine them all, but we just might arrive in San Antonio with more head than we started out with."

She smiled, but pain in her jaw made her bring her hand up to cover it. Her arm froze in midair. Her eyes squeezed tight while tears ran from under clenched lids and down her cheeks. Slowly and painfully she lowered her arm to rest across her chest.

"Ma'am, you need to tell me what hurts. I can see there's more damage than you can handle, and I intend it to be cared for. You could have something broken. Now it's either tell me, or Lou. Lou's got some animal doctoring in him. If you won't let me examine you, then it's going to be Lou."

"No, no. There's nothing either of you can do, but if you will send Lou down the trail I'll try to explain."

"Lou, you go on. Miss Cecile can't travel fast. We'll rest a bit every now and then. Tell Denny to ride back trail and see if he can spot Cook."

Lou waved and kicked his horse into a canter, disappearing down the trail. Grady lowered Cecile to the ground and squatted beside her.

He looked her in the eyes. She frowned and hesitated. She didn't know quite what to tell him, or how to tell him. She shrugged her shoulders and painfully sat up. Slowly she raised her hand to the buttons of her shirt and unbuttoned three of them. She pulled the shirt aside enough to allow him to see the bruise around her breast, without exposing the nipple. She watched his face as he studied the bruises, deep and dark in color, so defined that you could almost count the man's fingerprints. He knew without having to look that the other breast looked exactly like the one he was viewing.

Anger boiled up inside him. He stood up and walked away from the girl. He kicked a bush, put his hands on his hips and stared at the horizon. Who in hell could he hit? In frustration he drove his right fist into the palm of his left hand. He was shaking with anger. To calm down he took his makings from his pocket and rolled a cigarette. He smoked half of it before he turned and walked back to Cecile.

He had an intense desire to take her in his arms and protect her. This thought caused him to pause for a moment and wonder about these feelings. The only thing that prevented him from acting on his emotions was that he knew she was in too much pain to be handled, much less moved. All he could do was look into her eyes. Frustration and anger controlled him. He was more helpless than she was.

"Please don't do this. Don't blame yourself. You warned me, remember. You told me a trail drive wouldn't be easy. It was my fault. I fell asleep. I had taken a bath and was feeling so good. The sunshine made me sleepy. I didn't see them coming. It was my fault. I was careless."

He squatted and lifted his hand to her shirtfront, moved the shirt aside far enough to study the bruises again, and then he buttoned her shirt.

"I don't want to hurt you. Tell me the truth. Your shoulders and arms, is anything broken, or any muscles torn?"

"No, I promise. He just tried to make me tell him where the crew was. He hit me in the face a few times, but he didn't beat me. He grabbed me with both hands and it hurt terribly. He crushed me so hard I couldn't talk. The more he tried to force me to talk, the harder he dug into me, the more impossible it was for me to answer."

"I fainted, and when I came to he was already dead. Deadly was standing over him. Grady, I swear, I promise you, I'm sore all the way under my arms, and I can hardly lift them. My head aches and there is some ringing in my ears and my jaw is killing me, but that's all. I'll heal. Even my embarrassment will heal, but I learned a lesson. No one, no one, will ever catch me sleeping again. Now please, it hurts to talk."

"All right, but you are going to have to take it easy for a while. I'll see to your needs. The bruises will heal but if he tore some ligaments, or destroyed some tissue in the teats—sorry, ma'am, breasts." He blushed and looked down. "I'm around cows too much," he looked up at her and grinned. "You could get some bad complications, and that knowledge comes from handling cows, not girls."

Her eyes twinkled. She knew they had an understanding. He would help her for a few days until she recovered enough to care for herself, and his intentions were those of a cattleman nursing his cows back to health. She wondered if he could really keep that attitude.

"Are you sure about the calf?"

"She's about due, too."

"Oh Grady, I hope it's a bull, just the first one, and that it's Trumpeter's calf and not a bastard."

He laughed. He couldn't stop laughing. "Bastard? How can a calf be a bastard?"

"Oh, you know what I mean—purebred. Fathered by Trumpeter, not some tacky, half-breed ox."

Grady was overcome with laughter.

"Stop it, it hurts me to laugh. Stop this minute."

He pulled himself together. "Let's make it interesting, we'll have a bet riding on the little bastard. First we'll bet on the sex—bull or cow, boy or girl. What's your choice?"

"A boy, of course. A bull."

"OK. I'll bet it's a gal. What shall we bet to make it interesting?"

"If you win, I'll do your laundry the rest of the trip," she hoped she was not going to lose.

"OK, and if it's a bull, I'll polish your boots and saddle the rest of the trip."

"Done. That's fair enough," she agreed.

"Now if the calf is purebred, bull or cow, you won't owe me no bonus for getting him to San Antonio."

"That's fair. And if it is a bastard, bull or cow, I'll give it to you for your ranch. It will be half Hereford, and if it is a cow, she would be a beginning."

"That's a pretty serious bet. I don't want you to give up your calf."

"No, we have a bet. It's a fair one, and it will help to make the drive more interesting. I'm not going to talk any more now, my head hurts and my jaw aches." Grady helped her to mount her horse. He swung into his saddle and they continued the trip to the wagons.

It seemed as if the horses were dragging they were walking so slowly. Any faster pace would jar Cecile, so Grady kept them moving steadily in a plodding walk. It was still early morning, but he had been up since the middle of the night and made the early trip to the herd. They hadn't been more than an hour on the trail. It had to be around eight o'clock, or eight thirty, yet he felt like it should be noon.

They rode quietly for another hour. Grady's horse had taken the lead. He turned often to check on Cecile; she was fighting pain. When he spotted the wagons he was so relieved that he turned to tell her and realized that she was about to use up the last of her strength trying to stay on the horse. Her knuckles were white as she clung to the horn, her eyes were closed, she swayed in the saddle. He swung back beside her, and standing on his saddle, put one foot over behind her saddle and slid on behind her. He wrapped his arms about her and took up the reins. He leaned her back against his chest and loosened her hands from the horn. She squeezed his hand weakly, in thanks, and relaxed her full weight against him.

As he rode on toward the wagons he saw that the grub wagon and the cart were there. Smoke was curling up from a campfire, and he was sure he could smell coffee. Cook and Scratch had done the job alone. He had been sure all of them would have needed another day or two to get the grub wagon into camp. He was relieved to find it already done.

He rode into the camp, swung down from the horse, and let the girl slide off into his arms. She was limp, and at first he was afraid she had fainted again, but her even breathing told him she had gone to sleep.

The men gathered as he rode in. A bed of blankets was made near the fire—Lou's doing. He had known the girl was too injured to function. Grady carried her over to the bed and gently laid her down, covered her with a blanket, and moved out of her hearing. He gave Cook a pat on the back, and shook hands with the rest of the men. He was glad they were all together again. Cook handed him a cup of coffee.

"Man, is that great. I could eat a horse. Have you had a chance to cook breakfast?"

"Hell yes, hours ago. You done let it get cold. I'll fix you a plate."

Grady was soon squatted with a pan of pinto beans and Dutch oven bread. It tasted wonderful. He used the bread to sop up the bean juice and shovel the beans into his mouth. When he finished eating, he rolled a smoke. The men watched him eat, talking among themselves until he had finished. Now he turned his attention to the job at hand.

"OK, where are we?"

"Well, boss, the teams are hitched to the wagon and ready to move. The ground's pretty good today if we can get over this little stream. We've spent some time cutting brush and building a crossover. It's my opinion we ought to move the grub wagon over it first. Could be too rutted to get it over after all the others tear up the mud."

Grady asked Cook, "How long will it take you to get ready to move out?"

"Half an hour."

"OK, get moving. Our cows are halfway to San Antonio. Denny, I want you to find a couple of bedrolls and clean out the cart. Put the bedrolls and some blankets in the cart. Put enough to cushion the ride. We'll put Miss Grace in the cart."

"Yes Sir." The kid hurried to do what he was told.

86

"That's a good kid, Lou," Grady said as he watched Denny work.
"Thankee, boss. Takes after his ma."
"Hell, Lou, that boy's all you."
Lou ducked his head, his silence indicating his pleasure at Grady's compliment. Grady got up and beckoned Lou to follow him out of earshot of the other riders.
"Lou, I need your advice—doctoring, I mean. If you had a cow that had stepped on her teat and bruised hell out of it, what would you do?"
Lou looked at Grady, then looked over to where the woman lay by the fire. "Is that what he done to her?"
"Hell, Lou, he nearly took 'em off her. She's starting to turn blue all the way up under her armpits."
Lou snorted, threw his cigarette on the ground, and with his gimpy leg ground it into the damp dirt. "Ain't much you can do. If it was a cow, I got some liniment that heats up the skin and muscles, and draws the blood to circulating in the bruised area, which helps to break down the discoloration and eases the hurt. But hell, Grady, it might burn her skin off. She ain't tough as a cow."
"Well, we gotta do something, and she don't want the men to know, so keep it quiet. Let's go get the stuff. I'll try it on myself and see how strong it is."
The men returned to the campfire and Lou went over to the grub wagon to rummage through the box that hung on the side, filled with medicine for both men and animals on a trail drive. After a few moments he returned to Grady, who had squatted by the fire, and poured another cup of coffee. He was watching the sleeping woman. Cook came over to get the coffeepot.
"I want a good, hot, strong cup of coffee fixed for Miss Grace. Put some of that sleeping powder in it and a couple of spoons of honey."
"OK, boss. How much knockout powder do you want me to use?"
"Hell, Cookie, what do I know? I suppose it better be less than the dose you give a man, but it's got to be strong enough to keep her out until we get these wagons to camp tonight." Cook took the coffeepot and went to the medicine box that Lou had just come from.
Lou squatted down by Grady and took his knife from a sheath in the inside top of his boot. He opened the blade and used it to pry the top off the salve can. Grady reached a finger in, thought a minute, then rubbed the

ointment into the soft flesh of his neck where his shirt collar protected his skin from the sun.

"Hell! Damn! Shit!" he exploded as the ointment burned into his skin. The odor was bad enough, and fumes rose and stung his eyes. The skin grew hot as fire and turned flame red. "Damn stuff's going to burn a hole in me." He got to his feet and hurried to the water bucket hanging on the grub wagon. He undid his kerchief from his neck, soaked it with water, and scrubbed the inflamed area.

"Get me a cup half full of lard." His order was directed at the cook who was watching the trail boss with interest. Cook grabbed a tin cup and dipped into the lard bucket, then handed it to Grady, who returned to the fire and squatted by Lou, who had watched the trail boss with a touch of laughter in his eyes.

"Put enough of that cow liniment in this lard to thin the fire out of it, about half and half ought to do it. Man, if I give that stuff to her like that I wouldn't blame her if she shot me."

Lou took his knife and dug into the can, pulled out the black, gooey ointment and dropped it into the cup. When he had what he figured to be enough, he replaced the lid on the can, and with the knife stirred the mixture until it turned gray in color, and the fumes had decreased to a tolerable stench.

Cook came over and handed Grady a cup of steaming coffee, then he kicked dirt on the fire. Grady knew he was ready to move out with the grub wagon. Extinguishing the fire was always the last chore of a good cook.

"Roll it on out, Cookie. Follow the tracks and keep going until you reach the herd. Get camp set up and fix a good meal tonight. We'll need it."

Cook nodded his head and spat tobacco juice onto the mound of damp dirt that covered the embers. He climbed to the seat of the grub wagon, yelled at the team, and cracked his whip. The wagon moved out.

Grady shouted to the men, "Help Cook over that ravine, then get all these wagons moving. Denny, you help the men. I'll take care of Miss McNamara. I won't be able to keep up with the other wagons, so when you get to camp, get a lean-to set up and a place for me to bed her down. And tell Little Bear that we need meat."

"Yes, sir." The young wrangler leaped to his saddle and hurried to help the men move the grub wagon across the ravine.

When Grady turned back to look at Cecile, he saw her eyes were open and watching him.

"Sorry I woke you, ma'am, but this coffee needs drinking before it chills." He knelt down and helped her sit up.

"Oh, wow!" she groaned, stiff from the hard ground and from muscles and skin growing taut from swelling. He held the cup while she drank. It had cooled just enough to allow her to swallow it down thirstily.

"Now I'm going to go tie my horse behind the cart, and I want you to take this salve and rub it any place you feel the need for it, except your face. It will burn your eyes out of your head if you get it in them. Here's my kerchief—I wet it—wash your hands when you get through so you don't rub your eyes accidentally while the salve is on them."

She reached out to take the cup and stopped in midair, a grimace on her face. He set the cup on her lap where she could reach it without lifting her arms.

"I'm going to give you some privacy but if you have trouble call, OK?"

She nodded and smiled her appreciation. Grady turned and went to where his horse stood waiting patiently and tied the horse to the back of the wagon. With his back to Cecile, he leaned against the wagon and lit a cigarette.

Cecile's fingers were stiff. Nothing wanted to work—her fingers, her arms, her mind—but she managed to unbutton her shirt and study her injured breasts. They were swollen with blue bruises getting larger all the time. She dipped her fingers in the salve and slowly lifted her hand to her nose. "Whew!," she said out loud. Grady chuckled.

"Be sure and get up under your arms," he called.

"It's awful," she answered. Her eyes began to tear from the fumes as she slowly rubbed the ointment over her chest, around her ribs, under her arms, and up to her neck. As she rubbed, forcing the salve into her skin, a burning began. It grew in intensity until she yelled out, "It's cooking me, I'll be blistered!"

"I hope not, ma'am, but I can't guarantee that you won't be. I'm not real sure of the right mixture of the ingredients."

"Damn you, Grady. What did you use to make this hell fire?"

"Cow ointment."

"Well, if I live through this I'll be cured, but don't count on me making it. I think you're going to have to treat me for burned off skin next"

"I'm sorry, Miss Cecile, but it's the best I could think of to ease the soreness."

"Well, it does that, all right. All I can feel is fire. You can come back now."

He walked back to her, and he really felt bad. Tears were running down her cheeks, and she smelled of ointment. He remembered the burning skin of his neck and knew she was not faking. She was on fire.

"Good girl. Come on, get ready now, I'm going to lift you and put you in the cart. Hold your breath, here we go."

He lifted her and carried her to the wagon, where he carefully settled her onto the layers of bedrolls that Denny had arranged. He covered her and returned to the dying campfire. He carried the bedroll she had been lying on and spread that over her. Then he climbed to the cart seat and took up the reins. "We're moving out. Hold on."

Cecile shifted her body until she found a comfortable indentation in the bedrolls. She wrapped her arms about her breasts, bracing herself against the swaying of the cart. The burning sensation had reached its peak intensity and settled into a soothing warmth. The fumes became more powerful as her body warmed. She closed her eyes to prevent the fumes from burning them. Her lids were very heavy. The last thing she remembered as she drifted off to sleep was the swaying of the cart and the sound of Grady's voice as he coaxed the team over the washed-out desert.

Cecile kept trying to open her eyes. There was a brightness that entered her lids and she tried to open them to see what was disturbing her, but they were too heavy. As she struggled to get them open she became aware of voices talking from far away. She concentrated, and the voices came closer.

"Look, her eyes are moving. She is trying to wake up."

"Man, it's about time. I was really starting to worry. I should have mixed that knockout powder myself."

"Yeah, Cookie damn near killed her."

"I don't think it was only the powder. Her mind needed the rest, needed to forget for a while. The drops just added to the blackout."

"Yeah, guess yore right. Well, I got to get back to cleaning that harness. What a mess."

"OK, Lou, thanks for the support. I really was afraid she wasn't coming out of it."

Now she could tell the light was the sun. A ray had found its way through the branches over her head. Orange flashes filtered into her eyes as she forced them open. Someone lifted her head, and she felt warm broth flow into her mouth. She swallowed, and another mouthful took its place. Automatically she kept swallowing until the cup was empty. Her eyes were staying open now and she could tell that the branches were uniformly spaced. She was in a man-made shelter of sorts. She lifted her lids and saw the worried face of Grady.

"Are you trying to get rid of me?" Her speech was slow, and her tongue was thick and hard to move. "First you scald me to death, and then you give me sleeping sickness."

The cowboy grinned. "You don't know how glad I am to hear your ornery voice."

"Where are we?"

"With your herd."

"Did I sleep through the whole ride today?" Cecile asked in a puzzled tone.

"You bet! Not only did you sleep through the trip, but through the night and most of the day. Cook's getting supper on. If you want to doze a while longer I'll wake you at suppertime and get you out of this bedroll. We got to get those muscles moving, and I think it's about time for another dose of cow ointment."

Cecile groaned, closed her eyes, and drifted back to sleep, only now her breathing was regular and Grady, relieved, left her side for the first time since they had brought her in and put her to bed under the shelter.

CHAPTER ELEVEN

Deadly heard the wagons long before he could see them. Excitement kept him pacing back and forth from the herd to a rise, where he could watch the men and horses arrive. When they were near, he trotted out to meet them. The cook wagon came first with Cookie, who was as glad to see the big bull, as the bull was to see the cook wagon. Cookie leaned over and gave Deadly a cold biscuit from the pantry. Deadly grabbed it eagerly, and trotted on, chomping on the biscuit as he greeted each wagon. The men waved and called out to him as he passed. He was looking for Grady, and all the men knew it.

As each wagon passed, and no Grady, the big bull stood and bawled loudly, like a lost child. As Cook set up camp Deadly wore a path walking back and forth from the grub wagon out along the trail, and back again, to bawl over and over. Cook tried to pacify him with biscuits that he took eagerly, but the bribes didn't quiet the need he had to see Grady come down the trail. When he finally spotted the cart he went to meet it, his long, rangy legs covering the ground in record time.

When Deadly reached the cart, Grady called out, "Hey, Deadly, old buddy, how you been? Did you take care of those little cows?"

Deadly bawled and shook his massive horns. He then trotted around the cart and took his place in front of the horses, leading out, headed for camp. He was contented now—full of biscuits and reunited with his friend.

When they reached camp, Denny directed his boss to the shelter he had built. Grady drove the cart to it and Denny helped him unload the sleeping girl. She groaned a few times, but remained in deep slumber, her breathing slow, so slow at times that it seemed to halt. Grady didn't like the irregularity of it.

Denny took the cart out of the camp area, unharnessed, rubbed down the team and the cowpony, and turned them loose to graze.

Deadly waited patiently while Grady got Cecile settled. Grady saw the bull waiting, walked over and wrapped his arms around the bull's neck. For several moments he rested his head on the bull's sinewy muscles and drew in some heavy drags of fresh air tinged with bull sweat and camp smoke. He hadn't realized how tired he was. It had been a hell of a week.

The bull shifted his hind feet restlessly at the unusual behavior of his friend. Grady scratched the skin over the hard bone between the massive horns, ran his fingernails down, and scratched the broad space between the eyes.

"Well, let's look you over, old man, and see if you are all right." He slapped the bull affectionately on the neck and then ran his hand over the stag-like muscles of the bull's chest, up to the high shoulder top, along the ridgepole-thin backbone, across the flat ribs, and down each long leg. The bull, gentle as a lapdog, lifted each rock-hard, bright, polished hoof, and let Grady run his fingers into each split, checking for lodged stones or thorns that could work into the hoof and cripple the animal. A fast run over both narrow hips and Grady returned to the bull's head, and affectionately jiggled the dewlaps swinging from the powerful neck.

"Outside of some mud, old buddy, I guess you're in better shape than I am right now." While he talked he used his fingers and combed some of the caked mud from the thick skin covered with coarse hair. The red-and-white-peppered hide was hidden in vast areas by dried clay.

A final pat on the bull's shoulder, and Grady walked over to the grub wagon, pulled up a dipper of fresh water from the water barrel, and drank thirstily. Deadly followed and took a lazy stance by the tailgate of the grub wagon and settled into a resting position. The sweeping tail that almost reached the ground switched lazily from one gaunt flank to the other. He chewed his cud and closed his eyes, ready to wait until Grady left the wagon. The weight of the heavy horns relaxed his neck muscles until his muzzle touched the ground.

Cook was working over a stack of pans, washing the mud from them. These were the larger pans that hung from the outside walls of the cook wagon, which had collected a fair share of the wet clay. He chewed his tobacco in time to the sloshing rhythm as the pans were cleaned in a large tub filled with hot, soapy water.

He spat tobacco juice into the campfire, and said, "Beans hot, biscuit in the bin. Little Bear ain't back yet."

Grady dropped the dipper into the bucket, fished a tin plate out of the pan cupboard, found a fork and helped himself to half a dozen biscuits. He took his utensils to the pot set aside by the fire, close enough to keep warm, but not to burn, removed the lid, and dumped a couple of ladles of red beans into the pan. He squatted with his back to the fire and ate his dinner, half asleep, marveling at how hungry he was. He wondered for a moment why Deadly had not come over to mooch a biscuit, but he was too tired to coax him.

When Grady finished his meal, he sat for a while sipping hot coffee, then grabbed his bedroll and told Lou to watch the girl while he got some sleep. It was still mid-afternoon, but he needed the rest.

Deadly watched Grady crawl into his bedroll and knew the man would be deep in sleep for a few hours so he turned and moved slowly out to join the herd. Rambling in and out of the grazing cows he sniffed and touched noses, reassuring them that all was well.

He completed his tour by the side of Trumpeter, who lifted his head from tearing up the grass, and touched Deadly's nose. His tail switched as he returned to grazing. Reginald, grazing a short distance away, saw Deadly with his good eye, bawled a low greeting, and returned to filling his belly. Deadly dropped his head and soon the rhythmic chomp and chewing blended in with the cattle around him. He ceased to concentrate on anything except filling his growling stomach.

Grady slept for three hours, then woke and relieved Lou from watching Cecile. Her breathing was still slow and uneven. Grady felt her forehead to see if she was feverish. She was not. Still he didn't like the lax, slack look of her face. She was really under.

Grady spent the night watching over her, making trips to the campfire to fill his coffee cup, and to toss another cow chip, or a chunk of sagebrush on the fire. The nights were chilly since the rain. The weather could turn really ugly before he could get the herd over the mountains. It wasn't the time of year to linger. He didn't like it, but the woman needed a day or so before they set out again. He would see how she felt tomorrow.

Deadly returned to the camp and joined Grady as he watched over her. The bull chewed his cud, digesting the grass he had consumed. He listened to Grady as the man talked to him, not understanding the talk, but used to Grady's ramblings as he worked out the problems of a trail boss. He did recognize his name, and when Grady said it he would reach forward and nudge his friend's back.

These two strange companions had shared many a night watch in this manner. They were company for each other. When Grady tired of talking and dozed, Deadly returned to the herd and lay down not far from Trumpeter.

CHAPTER TWELVE

Little Bear felt good as he had some brief time to himself. Being a half-breed, he was torn between two worlds, the serious, silent, and emotionless Indian character, and the white man's constant need for company and entertainment. Today, after the joint effort of the men pulling together to reach a goal, he looked forward to a few hours alone. The white man in him wanted to yell "whoopee" when Denny gave him the boss's orders to find meat, but the stoic Indian just nodded his head and saddled up a fresh horse. He packed some cold biscuits and jerky in his saddlebag, slid his rifle into its scabbard, and rode silently from camp.

He headed back along the trail, riding easily in the relaxed manner of the Indian.

The group of wild range cattle that had attacked Reginald should still be in the area. A range bull had the habit of marking his territory, and even though a new leader would have taken over the herd, it was unlikely that they would have left the area they were familiar with. He knew that the wild cattle did not run in great herds but kept in small bunches, stayed under cover during the day, and ventured out on the desert only at night, grazing against the wind. They were seldom seen in the day time unless riders searched the thickets and scared them out. They were as watchful as wild turkeys, alert in the nostrils as deer, quick, uneasy, restless, constantly on the lookout for danger, snuffing the air and moving with elastic steps.

Little Bear watched the ground filled with fresh tracks since the rain had washed clean the trails. Crisscrossing each other he saw tracks of deer, bobcats, rabbits, ground squirrels, coyotes, and the splayed tracks of the wild cattle. He studied closely the deer trails, checking them for freshness. Some venison would taste pretty good. He intended to bring down whichever he found first.

It was nearly twilight when he came across a fresh cow trail. A small herd of cattle, possibly headed for a water hole. There were four or five cows, a couple of spring calves, and the tracks of a heavier animal, probably the new herd bull.

Little Bear pulled up his horse and stared into the direction the tracks had taken. The sun had gone down and there was just enough light left for him to study the terrain. Not much different from what he had been traveling through, sagebrush, and thorn thickets, enough cover to hide a small herd. Nothing was moving as far as he could see.

Then he caught a flash of movement several hundred feet down the trail. His quick eyes focused on a large buck, missing one horn. The deer was gone before the Indian could determine how many points were on the antler that remained. It was late in the summer for a buck to be shedding his antlers. He had probably lost it in a fight. Now Little Bear had two quarries ahead of him.

He kicked the horse and guided him along the trail, keeping the animal walking on soft ground. Little Bear's eyes, like a cat's, adjusted to the coming darkness. He stopped the horse often to listen. Once, off to his right, the thrashing brush, and the thump, thump, thump of a leaping deer striking the ground with all four feet, told Little Bear that the deer had either heard, or seen him, and that would be the last of that fellow. If he wasn't more careful he would be seeing a bunch of cows leave, too.

Little Bear climbed off the horse and squatted on his heels. It was that in-between time of night just as true darkness descends, before the moon rises high enough to offer some visibility. He would have liked to roll a cigarette, and relax while he waited, but the smoke would carry to every animal downwind. If the herd didn't get the odor some fleeing animal would alert them.

So, in patient Indian fashion, he sat still, one hand around one of the horse's front ankles, giving a slight squeeze when the horse became restless.

The other hand held the reins. He listened to the sounds around him and down the trail he heard the bawl of a calf. They weren't far away. Closer than he thought.

As the moon arose Little Bear began to define the contour of the ground around him. The brush and thickets began to take shape.

To his left was a strong little mesquite tree. He rose and led his horse to it and tied the reins to a thorny branch. He removed his kerchief and tied it about the horse's nose. This horse had been trained to remain quiet, not to call out when the kerchief was used. Little Bear knew that his horse was of no use to him now. It would be wiser to leave him behind. He had seen a wild range bull gore a horse through the lower neck. The horn had gone clear through the thickest part of the horse's thick hide. It was so deeply embedded, the hide was so unyielding, that for a considerable time the horse and bull had been fastened together, until the horse bled to death and fell to the ground.

Another time a rider, unaware that wild cattle were in the thickets where he was working rounding up strays, was surprised by the wild, rau-cous, hair-raising sounds made by an old range bull as it charged from the thicket, hit the rider's horse, drove one master horn, honed to a piercing point, into the horse's stomach and ripped upward, spilling guts all over the ground. He had so much time and training invested in this horse that he did not dare take unnecessary risks.

Little Bear took a carved cow horn out of his saddlebag, his rifle out of the scabbard, checked its load, and put some extra shells in a pocket. He took a pair of moccasins out of the saddlebag and exchanged them for his boots. With a parting pat on the horse's neck he slipped silently down the trail.

A man on foot was in more jeopardy from wild cattle than a man on horseback, but Little Bear didn't plan for the cattle to see him as he moved slowly and silently, searching the moonlit ground ahead of him, listening for the utterances of a cow to her calf. A cow has one sound for her newborn calf, another for it when it is older—one to tell it to come to her side, and another to tell it to stay hidden in the tall grass. A calf answers her, calls her when he wanders too far away from her side, and makes angry squeals when milk from the teats is slow to flow.

Little Bear could hear the herd for some time before he got near enough to see them grazing in a clearing with plentiful dried grass. They were far enough away that he couldn't determine how many, or of what the herd consisted: old cows, young cows, old bulls, young bulls, calves. For eating meat Little Bear preferred a young cow or bull, old enough for a good beef flavor, young enough to be tender.

Little Bear slowed to the slope-shouldered, squatting run of the Indian, his silent moccasins landing always on soft ground. He moved forward from one brush cover to another until he was close to the edge of the small clearing. He fell to his stomach, and inch by inch, made his way to the last bit of cover on the edge of the clearing. From under a large clump of sagebrush he studied the small herd. There were two older cows, with large calves, two yearling heifers, one young bull not yet ready to challenge the leader, and a brindle bull six or seven years older and at the apex of his prowess. His powerful neck showed a great bulge just behind the head, and his dewlaps accented his primeval origin.

The brindle had taken a position on a rise. From this vantage point he could watch the clearing, trading off with one of the cows when he grazed.

Little Bear knew that he could chance a shot, but at this distance, and in the uncertain moonlight, he could wound the bull. He knew that a wounded range bull has been known to hunt for his enemy by scent, trailing him like a dog. Besides he preferred the more tender meat of a young heifer, or the young bull.

He put the carved horn to his lips. No cattle voicings, not even those attending a bullfight, had the power, the might, and the terror of the massed blood call. The call is a succession of short bellowing cries, like excited exclamations, followed by a very loud cry, alternately sinking into a hoarse murmur, and rising to a kind of scream that grates on the senses. This performance of cattle excited by the smell of blood is most distressing to hear. Cattle will come en masse in answer to the blood call.

Little Bear had learned to imitate the blood call, and had carved, with much skill, an instrument from the horn of a bull which, blown properly, gave an exact imitation.

The blood call rang over the clearing. The brindle bull swung rapidly around, testing the sound on the night air. He swung again as Little Bear sent out another call. This time the bull had the direction of the call. He leaped from the rise and trotted toward the edge of the clearing. The small herd bunched rapidly and came to stand behind him. The primitive excitement produced by the blood call set off a bellowing that rent the night silence.

Little Bear sent out the call again, then dropped the horn and picked up his rifle. He sighted quickly on the white marking between the eyes of the young bull, who had advanced to the side of the brindle. He pulled the trigger and the bull dropped. The frightened cows jumped away from the fallen bull. Now there was a strong smell of blood.

The brindle leader, agitated to the point of charging, held his position, searching for a target. The flash of the rifle had attracted his attention to the sagebrush where the half-breed was hidden. The smell of the young bull's blood infuriated him into charging the bush.

Little Bear had, from experience, rapidly reloaded the rifle. He didn't want to drop the old bull; they didn't need that much meat on hand, especially tough bull meat. He aimed high to hit the hard bone between the horns. His aim was good and the bull fell to his knees, stunned.

The Indian sank back into the brush, and keeping low to the ground he ran swiftly back down the trail until he reached his horse. He changed back into his boots and put the moccasins back in the saddlebag. He removed the kerchief from the horse's muzzle, untied the reins, and climbed into the saddle. Now he put the horn to his mouth again and blew. Loud blasts rent the air. He made the horn sound like an Indian drum beating a war dance. Any animals within hearing would soon be miles away, including the small herd of cattle.

When Little Bear reached the clearing the herd had disappeared. Little Bear was satisfied with the young bull. The meat wasn't laced with the fat that a range bred steer, raised as a meat animal had, but it looked good. Indian style, he let the bull lie on the ground while he dressed it out. Thus, the meat would be sweeter, and more nutritious than if the animal had been hung and the blood drained out of it, white-man fashion. Under the thick hide he did find a few layers of fat tallow, which he carefully removed.

In camp he had tied to the back of his saddle several of the patterned flour sacks that had carried grain for the herd. The heart and liver, along with the tallow, he took special care to pack. The haunches and shoulder hams were wrapped separately in a sack, tied, and thrown over the saddle. He kept the ribs and the loins. If he had been taking the beef to a stationary camp, there would have been very little of the bull left.

The hide would have been cured, the horns carved into ornaments, the brains and tripe, delicacies to the Indian, were wasted on the white man. The young bull's horns would have been carved into toy horns for the children.

The load ready, Little Bear changed back into his moccasins for his trip back to camp on foot, leading the horse. He settled into the Indian's ground-covering half walk, half trot. The horse settled into a dogtrot. They would be back in camp in time for breakfast.

The half-breed took turns running and walking to rest himself and the burdened horse. It was late in the night, past midnight, when he saw far off to his right ahead of him, a light, and a campfire. He didn't feel that the direction was right, but his Indian teaching made him head toward the light. If it was not Grady's camp, then it was equally important to find out whose camp it was. After what had happened to Miss Grace, any campfire was suspect.

He slowed to a ground-covering walk, keeping the light in sight, measuring his distance by the fire as it appeared larger and began to take shape. When he was as close as he felt was safe, he tied his horse and wrapped his kerchief over its nostrils. He pulled his rifle from its scabbard and continued silently toward the campfire. He moved from brush cover to brush cover, studying the next advance, making sure the way was clear. He got close enough to confirm his suspicions. It was not Grady's camp. There were several bodies on the ground around the fire. He counted five bedrolls. There was one man half sitting, half lounging against a saddle. As he dozed, he kept a rifle lying across his lap.

Little Bear kept his distance from the camp and began to circle it. He wanted to check their horses. He bent over and walked slowly avoiding any obstacle that would make a sound and betray his presence to the man on guard. Ahead he heard the restless stamping of tied horses. Dropping low he worked closer until he could count the animals. Six only, no pack horses, no teams, no wagon, or even a chuck wagon in sight. The six men were traveling light.

He retraced his path to the spot where he had first studied the men around the fire. As he raised his head to study the camp again, he froze. He was staring directly into the eyes of the biggest dog he had ever seen. The animal's head and shoulders had risen over the legs of the man by the fire that was supposed to be on guard. The dog had been sleeping and was probably awakened by noises made by the Indian, sounds that only the sensitive ears of an animal could pick up. He couldn't see the Indian, but he knew something was moving about in the brush, possibly a rabbit. He was trying to get a scent, but the smoke from the campfire interfered.

Little Bear remained frozen. It seemed ages, but probably was only minutes before the dog, satisfied that whatever had been out there had passed on, lay his massive head back down. Little Bear continued to freeze until he was sure the dog had gone back to sleep, then he moved slowly, making sure each hand or foot landed silently as he made his way away from the camp.

When he was out of earshot he rose and quickly returned to his horse. Remaining in his moccasins, he removed the kerchief, untied the animal and led it back in the direction of Grady's camp. Now he traveled at a rapid walk, not the resting walk he had used before. When he got farther from the camp he changed to a faster pace—a hard, ground-covering trot, no longer the rapid walk.

He was in his camp before daylight. Denny had been on guard.

As Little Bear neared the camp he whistled a familiar signal, and the kid met him and helped remove the cut-up carcass from the tired horse. They unloaded the meat onto the drop tailgate of the chuck wagon for Cook to cut into usable portions, dry some for jerky, and salt some down for future use. The noise woke Cook.

He greeted the Indian with a disgruntled, "Morning." The Indian answered with his usual limited greeting that sounded like a growl. The cook went about slicing meat for breakfast, putting on a pot of beans, and setting bread to rise.

Denny unsaddled the Indian's horse and rubbed him dry, watered him, hobbled him, and let him out to graze.

Little Bear went in search of Grady. He found him dozing against the lean-to of Cecile McNamara. He touched the cowman's foot with his moccasined one. The trail boss's eyes were instantly open, and aware that it was Little Bear standing over him. The Indian beckoned, and turning, walked over to the campfire. Grady rose and followed him.

Little Bear sat on a log that had been pulled up for a seat, removed his moccasins, and stretched tired feet toward the heat.

Grady sat down beside him. They rolled cigarettes and smoked silently. Grady let the Indian rest, catch his breath, and relax until he was ready to speak.

"Six men, six horses, big dog, no supplies, short rations. Couple miles northwest."

"Are they trailing us?"

"Too dark to read," he flicked the cigarette into the fire. "We better keep our eyes open."

Denny came up and put Little Bear's saddle near him. He had wiped it clean of blood. Beside it, he set the Indian's boots and placed the saddle blanket over the log. The Indian nodded at the kid, and Denny grinned. A "thank you" and "you're welcome," had just passed between the two trail hands. Little Bear lay down with his back to the campfire, threw the blanket over his bare feet, and was instantly asleep.

Grady finished his cigarette and lit another. He sat by the fire a long time. Denny found his bedroll for a couple of hours of sleep. Now that the boss was up he didn't have to watch camp any longer, and Cook wouldn't have breakfast ready until nearly daybreak.

CHAPTER THIRTEEN

As the sun came up, Cook set up a clamor with the dinner gong that hung permanently from the grub wagon. Soon everyone except Little Bear gathered at the grub wagon, including Cecile McNamara. Grady had watched the camp while it slept. After an hour's sound sleep, the half-breed, wearing his moccasins, had taken his rifle and disappeared down the back trail on foot.

Breakfast that morning was a feast. The first real meal they had had in days. Cecile was starved. She had missed several days of food and Cook had outdone himself. Strips of thin, fried steak, home fried potatoes, hot biscuits, melted tallow with blackstrap sorghum mixed in it to pour over the biscuits, hot coffee laced with apricot brandy, a treat that Cook always kept for special occasions.

Today was a special occasion because they were all together again. The herd was safe, and soon they would be back to the job of moving the animals toward San Antonio.

They ate in silence—the biggest compliment a cook can receive, hungry folks enjoying their meal. It gave Cook a deep sense of satisfaction that he could bring a little comfort to the crew given what they had all endured the past several days.

Deadly came up and everyone greeted him. Grady gave him a biscuit and Cook slipped him another. Cecile soaked a piece in the sorghum tallow and gave it to him. Deadly was really growing fond of this new person. It seemed her treats were always on the special side, and he like that. He stopped behind Grady and listened to the humans as they rolled cigarettes and talked.

"Miss Cecile, how are you feeling this morning?" Grady asked.

"Much better, thank you. I was sure I would never wake up again. I was so sleepy. And that horrible ointment, I still smell from it, but I can move my arms some. I feel weak, but I'm sure it's just hunger. I'll be better after this grand breakfast." Cook brought her another cup of coffee in appreciation of her compliment.

Lou spoke up, "We sure are glad to see you up and hungry Miss Grace." Denny and Scratch grinned and nodded in agreement.

"From now on I insist you all refrain from any formality when addressing me. I beg you all to just call me Ceci or Miss Ceci, whichever you prefer but we have all been through too much not to be comfortable with each other now. I also want to thank you, all of you, for your help. I'm sorry I was so stupid. I wanted so hard to pull my own weight on this trip, not be a bother, but it seems I failed."

"No, ma'am, you weren't no trouble Miss Gra-uh I mean Miss Ceci," Denny stammered. Lou and Scratch nodded again.

"That's nice of all of you, but I know I have been. I just want you all to know that it won't happen again if I can help it. I don't intend to get caught napping again." The tone of Grace Cecile McNamara's voice had changed, hardened, and the men knew that she would live with her memories for a long time.

Grady had sat quietly listening to the after breakfast conversation. Cook had begun to scrape the plates.

"Cook, come join us. We need to talk."

"OK, Boss." The cook grabbed a tin cup, poured himself some coffee, and joined the group. Everyone's attention was fixed on Grady.

"We have trouble. Bear came in at daybreak with meat. He ran into another camp, could be Miss Grace's bunch-I mean Ceci's bunch."

"But there were only two men."

"We don't know where those two men came from, ma'am, and we can't account for the whereabouts of the second man."

"Are they after us?" Denny asked.

"Don't know, Bear couldn't tell. We don't know who they are or which way they are headed but from now on we keep our eyes open. We wear our pistols at all times and carry our rifles. We'll keep someone watching our back trail, and keep the night guards posted. I intended another day or two in camp to allow us all to get our gear in shape and the animals rested, but my gut tells me that we better move. I'm sorry Ceci. Do you think you could ride with Cook?"

"Yes, of course, you're right. We must move on and thanks for letting me be just Ceci, it feels much better."

Just then Little Bear came striding into camp. Everyone watched his face, hoping to read some message. He looked at Grady and Grady nodded, giving his permission for the Indian to speak.

"Ground's still wet, no dust, no movement in sight."

"No dust, huh? That means we don't know if we are being followed, or not, but the fact that they are not in sight means we could get a head start on 'em. Could be they've got their own business, not have us on their minds at all, but we know there's one man out there that wanted Ceci's saddle pretty bad. If those are his friends, it's my bet they will catch up with us sometime tomorrow. So let's pack up and move out."

"Oh, shit," Cook exclaimed. "I put apples on to soak. I was going to make Miss Ceci an apple fritter tonight."

"Sorry, Cook, but I know your powers. I've seen you come up with fritters in the middle of the night."

"All right, boss. Midnight fritters coming up," Cook grumbled under his breath, tossed the rest of his coffee on the fire, and kicked dirt over it to put the flames out.

"Denny, you get the horses hitched, the bedding out of the shelter and stored in the cook wagon, saddle the horses, and get the remuda moving."

"Yes, sir." The young boy took off in a run to catch up the hobbled horses.

"Lou, you and Scratch make sure the wagons are ready, and catch up Trumpeter and load him. Little Bear, scout the trail ahead just to be sure someone isn't waiting for us."

The men turned to do Grady's bidding, and Grady turned to Cecile, "OK, Ceci let's see what you need."

"Do you suppose there's still some warm water? I'd sure like to freshen up a bit. And Grady, if there is any of that ointment left I'll use it. It did help."

"Sure, I'll go catch Cook first before he tosses out the water." He was aware that finally he was calling the girl Ceci as she requested., and she was calling him Grady. They were working as a team, and had finally become friends instead of employer and employee.

He returned with a washbasin, a clean rag, and a bar of brown soap. He had dug through her trunk and found what appeared to be a clean work shirt. He had been surprised to run across a black leather holster made of tooled leather inlaid with the same silver and turquoise ornaments on her saddle. Digging deeper he found a black Colt with a silver and turquoise inlaid handle. In the top tray of the trunk he found several boxes of shells.

Miss Grace Cecile McNamara never ceased to surprise him. He gathered them up and took the pistol back to where she was scrubbing everything she could, without undressing.

"Here's a clean shirt, and put that pistol on. Do you know how to use it?"

"Yes, some. I used to practice with Ramon when we were children. He used to get mad at me because I could beat him to the draw."

"It isn't the draw I'm interested in. Can you hit what you aim at?"

"I could then."

"Well you better get some practice in when you can, and I don't want to see you without this on, hear me?"

"Yes, sir."

He smiled and took her chin in his hand. He studied her face. The swelling had gone down, the wound on her lip had scabbed over, but her jaw and eye were still discolored.

"How's the chest?"

"Much better. It still hurts when I breathe deeply, and I still can't lift my arms. I think moving around will help a lot.

"OK. here's the ointment and a clean shirt. Get ready, I'll go find your jacket and put it under the wagon seat in case you need it.

When she was finished, Grady took the ointment back to the cook.

"She's coming," he said, "keep an eye on her. I'm not sure that knock-out powder has worn off. I'd hate to have her fall asleep and drop off the wagon."

"Well, I ain't no nursemaid, but I think I can take care of Miss Ceci for a couple of days."

Grady smiled. Cook had been won over.

Cecile walked stiffly to the wagon, and Grady helped her up. Cook climbed up and picked up the reins, flicked his whip and moved the team out.

The herd was already moving. Trumpeter had protested the return to the cart. Reginald stayed with the older bull. All his cockiness was gone as he followed docilely behind the cart, where Trumpeter bawled in protest, but no one paid the old fraud any attention. The cows had gotten used to following Deadly through the storm, and had learned to respect the shining, silver-mounted horns that dealt out discipline unmercifully when any of the little cows disobeyed. They didn't like the pace that was set, but they responded as ordered by Grady in back and Deadly in the lead. The two wagons and the cart followed as fast as they could negotiate the deeply rutted trail.

Not far along Little Bear waited for the remuda, and directed Denny down the trail. He returned to point out the trail for the grub wagon, then rode past the herd and pulled his horse alongside Grady.

"All quiet ahead. Trail's not bad. Pretty clear. I'll take a quick look down the back trail then come back and help you push the cows."

"OK, Bear. Watch yourself."

"You betcha."

The day was uneventful. The cows grew tired and gradually began to lag. The wagons and cart soon caught up. Grady and Little Bear took turns scouting the trail ahead, and checking the back trail. In midafternoon Trumpeter was let free and he looked like a young bull as he ran to the head of the herd to travel beside Deadly. Reginald followed close behind him.

The pace had slowed so much by now that Deadly was disgusted. He walked half dozing, still aware of following the remuda tracks and the grub wagon along the trail, but sleepwalking, ignoring all else around him. Trumpeter had no trouble keeping up. The days of travel after the storm had toughened him.

Cook had built the fire in a gully, hoping its glow would not be seen. Yesterday's beans were warming and he had a roast cooking on a spit over the flames. Cecile was resting by the fire, drinking a cup of warm broth.

Denny caught up four fresh horses. Saddles were transferred and Grady, Little Bear, Lou, and Scratch mounted and set out in different directions, to scout for riders. Denny unhitched teams, checked the wagons, and gathered firewood. Soon the men began to filter back. Their horses were tied up and fed grain, but were left saddled.

The hot meal was the best. No one was terribly overworked, but the tension of watching the plain all day had left the crew on edge. Cook's apple fritter helped to loosen up the group. When the meal was over, bedrolls were shaken out and quickly occupied. Lou and Scratch took the first watch, Grady and Little Bear took over at midnight. Cook rose at his usual hour, four-thirty, and strapped his pistol over his apron. Grady and Little Bear crawled in for a couple of hours, while Cook gathered wood, patrolling in different directions, made the fire, put water on to heat, always keeping an eye searching the landscape.

There was oatmeal with maple syrup and hot coffee for breakfast. Soon the herd was on its way. Yesterday's pattern was followed with one difference; Cecile had rummaged in the bottom of her trunk and brought out a braided rawhide whip. Its handle bore the same ornate, hand tooled leather as her holster. Its butt end was solid silver inlaid with the largest, deepest blue turquoise stone Grady had ever seen.

She rode most of the day on the wagon seat, but when the herd slowed later in the day, she climbed down and walked. Occasionally she flicked the whip and snapped its fringed ends. She winced back each time she tried, and waited until the pain subsided before she tried it again. Grady watched her for a while. He could tell by the way she handled the whip that she had used it plenty before. She was equally good with each hand, even though she was not working for accuracy, but only to exercise both arms. That night, in camp, she asked to use the ointment again.

The night went pretty much like the night before. When Grady and Little Bear were on watch a band of coyotes started up a chorus from one canyon to another. The sound was lonely and beautiful.

The two riders came together after circling the camp, and stopped to listen as the coyotes answered each other. Then, to the west, a howl filled the air, deep and raucous, drawn out like the howl of the timber wolf, not accented with short, staccato barks as the coyote. Now all that could be heard was the eerie howl of the intruder. The coyotes had ceased their songfest.

"Not a wolf, Bear. Must be your big dog."

"Hell of a big dog, boss. I don't want to meet that one in the dark. He's so black you'd never see him."

"That mouth on him is enough to send shivers up my spine. If he's as big as that voice we better keep a tight circle on the herd. It looks as if our visitors are traveling to the side. I'll keep watch, you take a look."

Little Bear faded into the darkness, while Grady, shivers running up and down his spine, continued to circle the herd and the camp.

When Cook got up Grady did not climb into his bedroll, but continued to scout the camp, riding in wider circles as the sun began to light up the sky. When the breakfast gong rang, he returned to camp, hurried the meal, and got the herd moving.

CHAPTER FOURTEEN

Cecile knew something was wrong. Grady had barely taken time to say good morning. He had been everywhere, urging Lou to get the horses harnessed, and helping Scratch load Trumpeter. He had sent Deadly and the herd down trail with Denny and the remuda. Little Bear didn't come in for breakfast. Nervously she scanned the land in all directions from the wagon seat.

Her breast muscles and arms were stiff from yesterday's practice with the whip. She began to work them by clenching and unclenching her fists, bending and straightening her arms. Slowly one arm reached over her head. The other arm raised. All morning she took turns resting and exercising. When afternoon came she left the wagon and walked, once again flicking out the heavy, braided rawhide whip. Today she took aim and branches snapped and flew into the air, rocks skipped across the ground. She was actually enjoying challenging herself, unaware all the while of the crew's growing admiration of her talents.

She shifted the whip from one hand to the other until she was dripping with perspiration and her muscles were loose and moving easily. She practiced drawing her pistol. Slow, slow. She hated it and tried again and again until Grady rode by.

He called, "That's enough. You want to be laid up again?"

He was right. She had exhausted herself. She flagged Cook down and climbed into the wagon.

CHAPTER FIFTEEN

The terrain was changing. An occasional oak tree and a few fir trees began to dot the horizon. If the band of men was following, it was reasonable to assume they would wait until the small herd and handful of riders reached the mountain range. There would be more cover for an ambush, and it would be harder to control the herd.

Grady didn't like it. He had hoped those men would go on about their business, but according to the reports that Little Bear gave him, the men were definitely trailing them, biding their time. With little or no food provisions, the gang would soon have to make their move. Grady decided to strike first, rather than wait and be surprised. It had been on his mind all day, but he hadn't picked his drovers for their fighting ability. He tried to determine just what their chances would be in a fair fight. Cook was pretty good with a sawed off shotgun, but that weapon was only good at close range. The kid, Denny, had never carried a pistol. Likely squirrels were the meanest things he had ever taken a shot at. Gimpy Lou was a good hand. He could shoot straight, but he wasn't fast. Scratch wasn't too bright. He would probably get himself killed first because he forgot to duck. Bear was the only fighter he could count on not getting himself killed. He didn't even consider the girl. It was his job to keep her safe. So that left it up to Bear, Lou, and Grady. Three against six, that should be enough if they could surprise them.

They made camp that night in the open, a flatland valley that looked like the last good grass before the trail began to climb. The herd settled to graze. Cook rang the dinner gong, and everyone gathered to eat except Little Bear who caught up a fresh horse and rode lookout by riding in a wide circle, keeping the campfire in sight.

Grady gave his orders to the rest of the crew. "Denny you are to lay out the bedrolls, make them look good. Then get your horse and rifle and ride lookout away from the fire. Scratch, you take a stake-out over in those rocks where you can keep an eye on the camp. Cook, you keep that shotgun in your hands at all times, and your eyes and ears open. Ceci, you stay away from the fire. Put your bedroll under the chuck wagon tonight, and keep your pistol under your pillow. Lou, Little Bear, and I are going to check on our neighbors tonight to see if we can find out what's up."

"I don't like you men taking that kind of risk," Cecile said.

"It's less of a risk than sitting here like ducks in a pond waiting for them to look us up." Grady replied.

"I guess you're right, but you will be careful?"

"Yes, ma'am, we'll be careful. We've all been hoping that bunch of men would go away, but I don't think we can ignore them any longer and be safe."

"Just be careful," she repeated.

The men scattered to follow the trail boss's orders. The three men climbed on their horses and rode off into the darkness. Denny, with Cecile's help, turned the bedrolls into lifelike bodies around the camp. Cook hung the shotgun over his shoulder. It had a specially made sling that allowed the gun to hang under one arm with its muzzle level, facing forward. The sling allowed the cook to use both hands to continue his chores. With little effort his right hand could rise to the trigger and pull both barrels, scattering a devastating spray of shot, guaranteed to distract if not blow to pieces anything in its wide range.

Denny rode off, and Scratch disappeared. Cecile did as she had been told and made her bed under the wagon. Tucked in the bedroll was her pistol. Wrapped around her waist was the flexible braided bullwhip. For a while she helped Cook by finishing up the chores while he set bread for breakfast. She fiddled around the wagon drying dishes, moving pots and pans. Cook knew that she was nervous and trying to pass the time, so he didn't grouch at her. He went about his business, but his eyes were straining to see past the firelight into the darkness.

Cecile soon tired and crawled into her bedroll. Cook poured a cup of coffee and sat by the fire, adding believability to the stuffed bedrolls.

Scratch had settled, out of the fire's glow, in the rock pile. He wrapped a blanket around himself and settled into a comfortable position where he had good coverage of the campfire. He had his rifle propped beside him ready to grab if necessary. He watched the girl and the cook for a while, then he lay back and studied the stars in the sky with his ears tuned to the sounds about him. He heard the kid's horse pass a couple of times as Denny circled the campfire. Scratch's eyes closed, he was tired. He would rest his eyes awhile and just listen.

The herd was beginning to settle for the night. Some were bedded down, others still searched for clumps of grass but the vigorous grazing had slowed to leisurely feeding.

CHAPTER SIXTEEN

The little Hereford cow was restless. She was having some stomach pains. She ceased her grazing and slowly ambled through the herd. The Longhorn bull had left to make his nightly trip to the grub wagon. Trumpeter was down, chewing his cud. Reginald grazed near him, his hunger not yet abated. She circled back through the herd, walking slowly, dropping her head to snatch an occasional clump of grass. A cramp developed, and the small form inside of her moved. This was her first birthing and she didn't know what was happening, but instinct told her to find her secret place. She wasn't sure where it was so she circled back through the herd.

The campfire caught her eye and she stood watching it flicker for a while. The movement inside her caused her to lose interest in the fire. She walked over to Reginald, who lifted his head from grazing and greeted her with a nudge. He smelled along her side and across her rump, the mating fragrance wasn't present so he returned to his feeding. The little cow watched as he grazed, then she turned and worked her way back through the herd until she reached the outskirts.

She sniffed the air along the back trail, then slipped quietly into the sagebrush. An ancient instinct made her move stealthily. She didn't want anyone to find her secret place. She walked along the back trail, roaming from one side to the other. She wasn't sure what she was looking for, so on she went.

Then she saw it. The landscape, bright in the moonlight, showed a solid clump of mesquite. She went directly to it, circled the bunch of little trees until she found an opening, then worked her way through the thorny branches until she reached the spot. This was it, her secret place. The place where her calf would drop, hidden from sight, safe from harm. A place where she could hide.

The pain was strong now. She was frightened and she began to slobber. Instinct warned her that this was bad. Fear had an odor. She struggled to overcome the fear and concentrate on the pain. It was overpowering. She dropped to her knees and crashed over onto her side. Her eyes walled until the whites showed as she fought the pain. She refused to bawl, something might hear her and find the secret place. She kicked her legs, strained her head and neck, and pushed in silence until the infant inside her passed through the narrow passage and fell to the ground.

She lay limp and breathed deeply, relieved of the rending pain. Then curious, she raised her head and stretching, reached back to smell the wriggling mass at her haunches. She was frightened at the wet blood odor, but sniffed again, and instinct made her reach out her tongue and grab at the mucous bag that encircled the infant.

It was necessary that she remove that thin covering from the little calf encased in it. She worked at the job, as much as she could, from her side. Her rough tongue reaching out removing the membrane sometimes landed on the wet hair of the calf. The baby was healthy and active. The more he was released the more he thrashed about. Instinct told her to sever the umbilical cord.

The little cow lay back on the ground and rested. Then she raised her haunches and got her hind legs under her. A tired lunge, and she was on her feet. She turned to the calf and continued to clean it until the rough tongue had dried its hair into small curls. The gentle massaging circulated the blood, arousing the calf, strengthening it until it was ready to try its legs. The instinct that drove the cow to find a birthing place, now drove the calf to find its mother's teats and nurse.

It took awhile for the new calf and the new mother to work out the nursing ritual, but in time, with the calf's persistence, it found the teat. The young mother stood still even though the tug and the discomfort on her teats was a new experience. She swung her head and watched the baby as it attacked the teat in an effort to start the milk flowing. Her eyes wide and uncertain, she studied this new responsibility.

When the calf tired of tugging on the teat it walked about on weak, uncertain legs, staying close to the warm tongue that cleaned and smoothed it until it stumbled and fell to the ground. Tired, the calf drifted off to sleep as the warm tongue continued to polish the baby until its coat was dry and clean.

A fierce feeling of protectiveness arose in the cow toward this little black and white splash of color. The cow was unaware that the infant she had just given birth to was not pure Hereford, but a cross of Hereford and Holstein, black in color where it should have been red. It had the Hereford's white face, the only identifying mark of its Hereford heredity. The young mother was unaware of the inferiority of her calf. To her, he was beautiful.

As the infant slept the restless cow left the Mesquite clump. She needed water but she didn't want to leave the newborn calf alone. Tired, she stood guard at the brush entrance. She was drifting into tired sleep when a howl jerked her instantly awake. The hair along her spine stood on end. She had never heard the cry of a wolf, but the sound she heard terrified her. She knew there was an enemy coming toward her.

The eerie howl rendered the air again and again. She swung to face the direction from which it came. She could hear the animal running. It would soon be on her. She bawled for help, a wild, raucous plea to the herd.

No longer compelled to keep her hiding place a secret, she repeated the call several times before the massive animal appeared before her. A throwback to the huge Mastiffs that hunted the moors of Scotland, the dog stood as tall as the Hereford cow. He was thin from hunger and his mouth drooled saliva. He smelled the blood that lingered from the birthing. His eyes shone like hot coals in the moonlight.

The little cow braced herself to meet this demon. Terrified, she kept her back to the opening of the brush and her head to the monster that leaped at her nose, nipping and slashing. She lowered her head and hooked with her short, stumpy horns. She was shaking with fear and weakness. This monster was not going to pass her. She would protect the small baby with her life.

The dog, half crazed from hunger, leaped and slashed, spit out mouthfuls of thick, curly hair, tasted blood and attacked again. He tried to work the short little cow around so that he could tear at her hamstrings, but she was so terrified that she backed further into the thorny branches and braced herself for the next frontal attack.

Furiously the dog sprang at her nose and clamped his huge jaws tight. The cow screamed in pain and shook her head to remove the cause of the pain from her nose. The massive dog braced his legs. The flesh of the cow's nose tore and the blood ran. She used her front feet now, pawing in desperation. She struck out blindly, landing a lucky blow on the dog's chest. The wind momentarily knocked out of him he loosened his hold on the cow and dropped back to catch his breath.

The cow, weak from birthing and fear, pain blinding her senses, sank to her front knees. Terrified at the thought of getting down she lunged up again to face the dog as he rushed in. This time she was slow, and he side-stepped as she lowered her head and hooked. The massive jaws clamped on her neck and she could feel them grind as they searched for the jugular vein. She couldn't breathe. Sorrow filled her as blackness overcame her and she sank to the ground.

The dog, encouraged now as the cow dropped to her knees and blood poured into his mouth, failed to hear the snort of an enraged bull. Deadly charged into the battleground and lifted the huge dog on his master horn, tearing the dog's jaws loose from the cow's throat. Deadly threw the dog over his back, rearing and bellowing with rage. The bull wheeled and dropped one thousand pounds of weight onto the dog's chest. Raking his horns into the ground, wheeling and swinging with vicious force, he tried to pin the animal to the ground.

The situation was reversed now. The dog struggled to regain his feet, whining and yelping as one horn, and then the other, battered into his body. He scrambled, half crawling, to get out of the bull's reach. Deadly, enraged by the cow's calls for help, charged onward, not giving the dog a chance to regain its footing. The dog rolled and struggled to escape.

The herd arrived. Trumpeter and Reginald had also answered the little cow's cry for help. The herd had come as one, not as swiftly as Deadly, but now they ringed the battleground.

The dog panicked. His advantage over one weak, small cow had turned into an army of enemies confronting him. If he didn't get away from the fury of the longhorn bull, which was determined to grind him into the soil, he would be dead. He didn't have a choice.

Managing to get on his feet, he charged the ring, and luckily chose a group of cows, enraged but unsure of the enemy. They lunged at the dog; he dodged, ducked between their legs, and vanished into the dark.

CHAPTER SEVENTEEN

Little Bear led Grady and Lou out of camp. They traveled quietly. Only the sounds of the horse's hooves, and the squeak of saddle leather could be heard. Often, the Indian halted, and the three men sat still and listened to the night. At one stop the Indian pointed, and Grady could make out the light from a campfire some distance away.

Little Bear removed his boots and replaced them with his moccasins. Still sitting astride his horse, he stuffed the boots into his saddlebag, and then he slid from the saddle. He handed the reins to Grady, rubbed both hands over his horse's muzzle in a gentle command for silence, and disappeared into the shadows.

Grady and Lou sat motionless with ears straining, listening for the Indian's return. They would run a hand along the neck of the horses when impatiently they would begin to shift about.

The Indian's horse remained still, like a statue gazing into the darkness, in the direction his rider had gone. Soon he lifted his head with ears erect.

He wanted to greet the returning half-breed, but training stronger than the desire kept him quiet. He shook his head up and down in silence.

Grady, watching the horse, knew Little Bear would be coming out of the shadows soon so he was not startled when the Indian appeared to rise from the ground in front of them.

"Camp deserted. One man, sick maybe. On ground by fire. One horse. Tracks lead toward our bed ground."

"Shit," Grady exploded. He dropped the reins to the Indian's horse and jerked his own horse around, plunging his heels into the animal's sides. Startled, the horse leapt forward nearly colliding with Lou's animal, dodged around him, and vaulted away down the back trail. The horse was stumbling in the half moonlight and trying to dodge brush. A low whistle brought Grady to his senses. The Indian had used a recognized signal to halt his boss. Grady pulled the animal up and waited for the Indian, now mounted, to come alongside him.

"Yore going to kill that animal and have to walk back for a rescue."

"Right. Go on, Bear, lead out, but move as fast as you can."

The Indian acknowledged the order and kicked his horse into an easy, ground-covering trot that permitted the animal and the Indian to work together dodging brush, and avoiding unsure footing. The other two men followed.

They traveled at this pace for about fifteen minutes, and then Little Bear pulled his horse up. Grady and Lou halted beside him. The Indian raised his hand signaling silence. They listened, and across the sagebrush came the eerie, raucous howl of the hound that they had heard before. It came from the direction they were headed, near their camp.

Little Bear dug his knees into his horse, only now he lengthened the trot into a fast traveling pace, risking a fall in the shadowy darkness. The animal sensing the urgency, responded admirably, relying on the Indian to guide his direction. The horse kept his eyes on the ground in front of him and didn't question his rider's demand. Soon they could see the campfire and Little Bear slowed the horse. The three riders spread out and walked their animals.

Gunfire split the night air. The roar of Cook's shotgun followed as both barrels were fired. Grady kicked his horse into a full gallop.

CHAPTER EIGHTEEN

Scratch drifted off to sleep. The howl of the dog penetrated his sleep and disturbed dreams of mountain lions and wolves drifted about his subconscious. It was the bawl of cattle that brought him abruptly awake. Having worked cattle all of his life, it was second nature to respond to disturbed cows. A rider could lose his life in a stampede by ignoring warning signs.

Instantly awake, he observed the cattle moving rapidly back trail. He scanned the camp. Cook was standing by the grub wagon watching them go. Cecile was asleep under the wagon. What had disturbed the cattle? Then he heard the yelping cries of the distressed dog as it fought to escape the longhorn's attack.

Scratch had started to unwrap himself from the blanket and grab his rifle, when a voice from behind him growled, "Don't reach for the rifle mister, or I'm going to put a hole through yore head."

Scratch froze. Hell, he had sure blown this one. Serve him right if the guy did blow him away. As he waited for further orders he scanned the camp.

Coming out of the darkness behind Cook was a man with his gun drawn. Scratch's instinct was to yell a warning, but just then his companion shoved the gun barrel into his back. He gulped, swallowed the warning, and watched in silence as the man stealthily crept up on Cook. The man was about to raise his pistol and smash the butt into Cook's skull when the hissing, snapping sound of Cecile's bull whip flew from under the wagon and stung the raised hand in midair. The pistol sailed across the camp, the man screamed. Cook turned and pulled the first trigger, releasing a blast of shotgun pellets that hit squarely in the man's gut, sending him crashing backward, his insides splattering into the campfire.

A second blast hit a shadow and sprayed pellets into the darkness beyond, hitting the intruders' horses. The animals screamed with pain, tearing loose from the bushes they had been tied to. They fled into the night. The sounds of the horses retreating told the cook that the men who were attacking were now afoot, and would be even more desperate to gain control of the camp.

Cook ducked under the grub wagon, regretting that he must put Miss Ceci in danger, but not knowing from which direction trouble would come, it was useless to try to hide behind the wagon. Only from under it could he watch all sides as he reloaded.

The gun in Scratch's back dug into the flesh. "Tell the old guy to throw out his gun and come out with his hands up, or I'll blow you to pieces."

"Hey, Cook," Scratch called with a shaking voice. "Yeah, Scratch?"

"There's a fella up here with a gun on me. Says for you to give up."

"How the hell did you get in that fix?"

"Took a little nap."

"Shit."

"Knock it off, old man." The gunman was impatient. "You do as you are told, I don't mind killing this bastard one bit."

"OK, son. Just hold your horses. These old bones ain't as spry as they used to was. I'll throw out my shotgun, but you got to give me time to get my old rheumatiz back out from under here."

"Toss out that shotgun, and if you don't move fast enough to suit me I'll fix that rheumatiz back for good."

"OK, OK. Here's the shotgun." The sawed off shotgun flew from under the wagon bed and clattered on the ground. Cook whispered to the girl, "He don't know you're here. Cover up and stay still." Then he crawled on hands and knees out from under the wagon.

"Move it." The man drove the gun harder into Scratch's back. Scratch struggled to free himself from the blanket, and get to his feet. The two of them advanced into the camp.

Cecile smothered a gasp. It was Vince, the little weasel she had encountered a few days back. She drew the bedroll over her head, and slowly slid her hand under her jacket that she had rolled to make a pillow. She felt the cold steel of her pistol. Keeping her finger off the trigger, she slowly drew back the hammer. The jacket muffled the sound until the hammer was in the cocked position. Then she waited. With one eye peeking from under her bedroll she watched as the two men approached the wagon.

"Get over there by the fire, both of you, and sit on that log." Vince waved the gun at Cook and Scratch. The two men moved quietly to obey him, anxious to draw the man away from the grub wagon to protect the girl who hid there.

"Come on in, Luke."

"Coming," a gruff voice answered from the dark. Quickly two men came into the glow of the campfire.

"You were right, Vince, them bastards headed right for our camp. We ought to get what we come for and get a good head start, 'fore they get back.

"Yore stupid, Luke. That rotten dawg a yores done give us away. I told you to tie him in camp."

"Hell, Vince, if I'd a tied him in camp I might not a got back to him if we had to ride."

"Well we got to ride now, and what the hell are we going to ride on? You stupid son of a bitch."

"Christ, Vince, don't get so damn mad. I seen some horses, hobbled. I'll go see if I can fetch them."

"Well, you better hurry. That shotgun blast is going to have them cowboys back here before you can locate yore ass. Get the hell moving. Yancy, you go along that trail them riders took, and set up an ambush to slow them down. Ace, you grab and get some grub together while you keep an eye on them two. If the cowboys come back, you take the old man and stand behind him with yore gun at his head, and I'll take the other one."

"Sure, Vince, what should I put the food in?"

"Find something, idiot. Look around. I got things to look for myself," he said as he climbed in the tailgate of the grub wagon.

Cecile could hear things being shoved about above her as Vince searched the wagon. A thud as something heavy hit the dirt told her he had found her saddle. He continued to rummage through her trunk. She knew he was searching for anything that would bring him a few dollars. It was unlikely that he would find the secret drawer in the trunk where she kept her jewelry, but she knew that her concha belt, chaps, hatband, and other turquoise and silver decorated gear would not escape his eyes. How stupid and vain of her to have brought such items with her on this trip. The trouble she had caused for them all.

"Here's some sacks." Vince stuck his head out the back of the wagon and tossed some of the flowered feed sacks to Ace, who was going through the pantry. Vince rummaged around in the trunk some more, and then jumped to the ground, picked up the saddle and carried it over to where the two men sat by the fire.

"Where's the girl?"

"Yore friend killed her," Cook answered.

"The hell you say?"

"That's right. He done a right bad job of it."

Vince snickered, "Ben always did have a way with women. I guess he done paid for it, though, seeing as how he didn't catch up with us."

Cook didn't bother to answer. He was content that he had diverted the little weasel from looking further for the girl.

Horses were approaching at a canter from the direction Luke had taken. He soon appeared riding one horse, and leading another.

"These are all I could find. One of us has got to double up."

"You can double with Ace. Throw that saddle on my horse and tie the grub behind and let's get the hell out of here."

"What about the boss?"

"What about him?"

"Aren't we going to go back to camp and get him?"

"Yeah, sure, Luke. Why don't you do that, you stupid bastard."

"You better quit calling me stupid, Vince."

"Yeah, stupid. What you going to do to me?"

"Oh hell, Vince, you know I ain't good with a gun, but I could break your skinny neck."

"How you going to get close enough to do it?"

Luke scratched his head and thought awhile, and then he mumbled, "I'm going to go get the boss by myself."

"Boss, hell. Luke, the man's got a bullet in him. We got a posse after us, and he can't ride. I'm moving on as fast as I can. You do what you want to do."

"I'm going to get the boss." Stubbornly, Luke set his jaw.

"Shit." Vince grabbed the lead to one of the horses and led it over to the saddle. He picked up the saddle and slung it over the horse's back, then reached under its belly and drew the cinch. He returned to the pile of items he had on the tailgate of the cook wagon, picked up the black, ornate bridle, returned to the horse and quickly bridled it.

"Give me that grub, Ace."

"Don't you do it, Ace," Luke growled.

"Shut up," Vince said.

"He's got the best horse and saddle, and he's going to leave the boss. He'll leave all of us without food the first chance he gets."

"I told you to shut up," Vince screamed.

Luke, obviously afraid of Vince, backed his horse off, but did not shut up. "Don't you give him no food, Ace."

Ace circled the fire, tied the sacks together, and threw them across the back of Luke's horse, then he turned and headed out of camp. "Come on Luke, let's go get the boss."

Luke turned to follow. Vince reached for his guns, but his intention to shoot both men in the back failed when Grace Cecile McNamara took aim and pulled the trigger of her pistol. The bullet hit Vince in the middle of his back, cutting his spine in half. His legs buckled and he fell in a broken pile, to the ground.

The rapid fire of pistols came out of the darkness informing the group in camp that the trail boss and his men had returned and run into Yancy's ambush. Luke and Ace disappeared into the dark as Cook ran for his shotgun. Cecile rolled out from under the wagon firing wildly after the fleeing riders.

Grady, followed by Lou, rode into camp. Scratch yelled, "Two of them went that way, one's on foot. I think they got a guy to pick up at their camp."

"Hell, Scratch, they would be stupid to go after that man now that they got riders on their tail," Cook argued.

"Well, that Vince guy said Luke was stupid, and I believe him. I think he'll go get the man."

"Damn, I betcha a hat they won't," Cook growled.

"Yore on. I get to pick out the one I want," Scratch laughed.

"The hell you do," Cook protested.

"That's the bet." Scratch grinned.

"Shake." Cook said to Grady, "You heard him, boss."

"OK, Cookie." Grady gave orders as he rode out. "Let's go take a look, Lou, and see if Scratch wins a hat. Scratch, get these bodies out of this camp."

The two men lifted their horses into a lope and returned on the back trail to the gang's camp. They passed Little Bear riding and leading Yancy on foot, his hands tied behind him and a rope around his neck. Grady lifted his hand in greeting, "We'll be back after we pick up whoever is at that camp.

CHAPTER NINETEEN

Denny was scared. He had never been so scared before. He had felt almost a man since his dad had said he could trail with him this year. The trip to San Diego had been hard work, but there had been plenty of riders to share duties. No one had ever had to ride night watch alone, and no real trouble had developed, outside of a few camp fights. This night riding alone with guys out there in the dark sneaking up on a fella made Denny just a little more than scared. The hair on his neck was standing on end, and he didn't have enough eyes to watch in front, back, and at the sides at the same time.

He had made about six circles around the herd when the howl of the hound split the night. His heels dug into the horse's side with a thud. The howl, and the heels, sent the horse into a tailspin, bucking and crashing into brush. Denny held on, his fear forgotten. His only desire was to stay on his horse and gain control.

Once he had his horse under control he surveyed the area, observed the cattle's distress, tried to calm them down, but feared that his shaking voice, as he tried to sing, would only add to their anxiety. The cattle ignored him. They had heard the young cow's plea for help, and all were moving as one. All Denny could do was follow them.

He joined the ring of cattle as they circled the battleground where Deadly had the dog pinned to the ground. In the semi dark he could not see what was happening. The growls and occasional yelps of pain told him an animal was attacking, or being attacked by, the bull, but Deadly did not utter a sound. His battle with the gigantic hound was direct; he was determined to destroy his enemy.

Denny was in the path of the dog as it escaped the horns of the bull, dodged through the legs of the cows, and brushed Denny's legs as he fled from the fury of the bull. Denny could hear Deadly, and in the moon's faint rays see him, as he continued to rake his horns into the sand, pawing and throwing sand high over his shoulders. Now he sent the thundering bellow of the herd bull challenging the attacker of his young cow to return and fight.

Denny held his horse still, waiting for the bull to calm. He knew Deadly was enraged enough to attack shadows right now. He waited until the furious bellows turned to frustrated snorts, then softly he began to sing a song that he knew Deadly was familiar with.

Deadly became quiet, and Denny kicked his horse forward, passing through the ring of cows. When he came to Deadly he continued to sing as he dismounted and tied his horse to a bush. He took some matches from his pocket, and with his thumbnail struck a light, and for a brief moment the battle ground was lit up. He saw the cow, down on her knees, Deadly standing guard over her as she struggled to gain her feet. Blood was running from her nose and dripping profusely from the tear in her neck. The match burned his finger. He jumped, stopped singing, and began to cuss. He knew better than to try to approach the cow now. Deadly was still aroused.

Striking another match, Denny's eyes quickly searched for dry brush. Spotting some, he reached it before the match went out. Breaking dry branches from the sagebrush he started a fire, adding more fuel until he had a fire large enough to light the area.

The light calmed Deadly. Now he could see around him and he recognized Denny as a friend. He allowed Denny to approach the cow, which had now gained her feet. She stood dazed. Denny feared her jugular vein had been torn open. On closer inspection it looked to him as though the dog's huge jaws had reached over the jugular vein and clamped together, shutting off the flow of air, puncturing the muscles, and creating a vicious wound. The timely arrival of Deadly had prevented the dog from completing the rending tear that would rip the vein, allowing the young cow's lifeblood to flow rapidly from her body.

Denny took off his kerchief and stuffed it into the open wound, hoping that it would slow the bleeding. The cow staggered away from the boy and plunged into the thicket. Denny heard her move through the brush. He followed, trying to head her off, and came to a halt as he heard her low call to her calf. The baby answered, and Denny slowed his approach cautiously. The little cow was tamer than a range cow, but could still be dangerous if she felt the need to protect her calf.

Half crawling, Denny felt across the ground until his hands found the small, warm body. He talked softly to the cow as he gently lifted the calf, and backed slowly from the secret place out into the light of the fire. The calf bawled for his mother. She answered and followed the boy and the baby out of the thicket.

Denny slowly walked, carrying the calf, toward the camp.

He left his horse tied. The hurt cow was losing a lot of blood. He had to get her back to camp before she grew too weak to walk. He reasoned that if he kept the calf in touch with her she would follow, and she did.

Deadly bawled an order to the herd, turned and followed the boy and the cow back to camp. The herd moved in behind. Trumpeter and Reginald fell in and a strange procession moved through the darkness. Denny heard gunshots and was now really scared. He strained his eyes searching for the campfire. What would he find? Was he walking into a trap? He had to chance it. The cow was bleeding to death.

CHAPTER TWENTY

Grady and Lou caught up with Ace and Luke at the outlaw's camp. They found the leader of the bunch weak from loss of blood from a bullet wound in his thigh. The man was delirious with fever.

Ace wanted to fight and run, but Luke, concerned for the wounded man, ignored his sidekick, threw his gun aside, and gave no resistance when Grady demanded that they surrender. A well aimed shot at Ace, and the man threw down his gun and raised his hands. Lou tied the hands of both men behind them and made them sit near the fire. He gathered some wood and built up the dying embers into a bright flame so that he could see the injured man's wound.

"We need some whiskey, the cart, and some bandages, boss."

"O.K,. Lou. You keep an eye on them and I'll beat it back to camp." Grady climbed aboard his horse and traveled quickly on the path that was becoming familiar.

When he reached camp he found Denny, Cook, and Cecile working over the cow. Scratch was burying the two bodies. They had tied the little cow by her feet and dropped her to her side on the ground. Cook had poured gunpowder into the wound and lit it, searing the flesh to seal the wound and stop the bleeding. The cow had protested loudly as the gunpowder flash bit deep. Deadly paced nervously on the edge of the herd. He was not worried about the little cow, he knew her fate was in the hands of the humans, but the small herd, already excited by the attack of the dog,

131

watched as the little cow was doctored, and were walleyed and ready to bolt.

Grady's experienced eye took in the drama around the camp. "Denny, get out there and settle that herd before it scatters."

"I don't have a horse. I had to leave mine tied back trail."

"Take mine. Quiet the herd then round up a team for me."

He swung down off the horse and crossed over to the cow to inspect the work Cook and Cecile had done. "Lost a lot of blood. Looks like you've got it stopped. You better keep her in camp."

"I don't think we'll have any trouble doing that. Come take a look." Cecile was smiling like she had a big secret as she led him over to the cart that had carried Trumpeter. There the small baby had settled into a pile of prairie grass, it's white face shinning brightly in contrast to its black-and-white body.

"Son of a gun. Looks like we're going to need that nursery sooner than I figured."

"It's not Trumpeter's."

"Yeah, I noticed."

"I'm sorry. I hoped you would win this one."

"Well, I won half of it. It's a bull calf."

"He'll make your herd produce heavier meat."

"Yes. I'm anxious to see how the crossing of Hereford blood affects the upgrading of my scrub cattle. We don't know much about his other half, except you said the Herefords were pastured with some Holsteins. That explains the black color." Grady spent a moment admiring the calf, then returned to more serious jobs.

"We've got to get him out of the cart for now. I need it. Let's tie him over at the cook wagon wheel. We can't tie the cow until her neck heals, so we'll have to keep the calf tied for a while." Grady lifted the calf and carried him to the grub wagon. Cecile rummaged in the tack box and found a piece of soft cotton rope.

When the calf was secured, disturbed by the move and the rope confining it, cried for its mama. She answered from the ground.

"Let her up, Cook. Let's see if she's got the strength to stay on her feet."

Cook untied the cow and watched while she struggled to get her legs under herself. It took several efforts, but the baby's cry encouraged her, and she lunged unsteadily to her feet. Walking weakly over to the calf she began the ritual cleaning. Cecile lengthened the calf's tie rope so the calf could reach its mother's teats; the sound of sucking filled the air. Cecile, Grady, and Cook looked at each other with smiles on their faces.

"I think she'll be all right if that wound doesn't get infected. Ceci pour a little whiskey over it daily. Wash it out if necessary. There's some salve in the medicine chest that you can put around the wound to keep the flies away. Don't get it in the wound, it could soften and open up the bleeding. OK, mother and son doing fine. Let's get to work."

Grady told them what had happened at the outlaw's camp. "Ceci, get some medical supplies together, and some blankets. Cook, get me some whiskey, and get some broth going and food ready. These men haven't eaten for a while."

The cattle quieted as Denny sang to them, circling them into a close herd. As the little cow and her calf settled down, so did the herd, and Denny rode off to find the horses. Shortly he was back with a team for Grady. He harnessed the team while Cecile made a bed in the back of the cart. Denny unsaddled Grady's tired horse, hobbled it, and released it to graze.

"You want me to drive the team, boss?"

"No. I'll drive it back. You better go get your horse and keep and eye on the herd."

"Yes, sir." Denny crossed the camp and disappeared into the night as Grady drove the team in the opposite direction toward the outlaw's camp.

He found the camp as he had left it. The two men by the fire were dozing. Lou was keeping the fire burning and had accumulated some surplus firewood. A pot of water was boiling, and he had found enough coffee to make a pot.

With the whiskey to pour on the wound, and a knife heated to red-hot sterility, it wasn't long until Lou had the bullet out of the outlaw's thigh. Grady held the man down while Lou seared the wound and poured whiskey over it. He then wrapped the leg in clean bandages.

They loaded the wounded man into the cart and added the tied men to the load. Lou drove and Grady led the way. In the early hours, just before daylight, the cart returned to camp. Grady was exhausted. He knew that all the crew had put in an equally tiring night, but for the first time in days, he felt a heavy weight lift. Looking over his shoulder and waiting for an attack was over. For the moment, he was in control. Once again his herd and his crew were safe.

The men were fed. The wounded man was spoon-fed broth laced with the same knockout powder used on Cecile. Yancy had been added to the other outlaws, fed and bedded down, all three tied securely for the night. Scratch had finished burying the dead men. Little Bear took the watch while everyone in camp turned in for a couple of hours of sleep before the sun came up.

Denny had not returned from picking up his horse. Grady had the kid on his mind as he drifted off to sleep. If Denny had not returned by the time Cook started the morning meal he would go searching for him.

CHAPTER TWENTY-ONE

Denny was tired. He had debated whether to ride Grady's tired mount out and get a fresh horse and then ride out to get his horse, or walk back for his horse. He knew the job of catching up a fresh horse could take as much energy as the walk, so he decided to walk, but he took his time. It was still dark. There had been a little moonlight tonight, but it was now gone and it was difficult to follow the faintly defined cattle trail in the dark. He could feel the trampled ground under his feet and having traveled this trail back and forth several times today, he kept headed in the right direction.

It wasn't a long way to the thicket the little cow had chosen. His mind daydreaming about the day's events made the trip seem even shorter, and he soon spotted the glowing embers of the fire he had built. His horse should be tied to a nearby bush, but Denny didn't see him. He found some brush and threw it on the embers. Soon the dry branches were aflame, lighting the area. No horse.

"Shit." His voice echoed about the clearing. He searched and found where the horse had shifted his feet restlessly. The ground was churned with hoof prints. He repeated, "Shit," and then gathered more wood, threw it on the fire and squatted down to rest and roll a smoke. Tired, the hypnotic flames lulled him into staring vacantly into the fire. Denny was so deep in the hypnotic dancing of the flames that it was a while before he was aware that something was moving about in the brush a short distance away. He sharpened his senses and concentrated on the movement. He could hear brush crackle, then silence as the movement halted, then brush noises as something moved about again.

Good, it had to be his horse. The reins were probably dragging and hanging up on the bushes as the horse tried to move a-bout. Denny tiredly got to his feet and started working his way toward the sounds, talking low and calling the horse. He didn't want to scare him and have him run off into the night. That's all he needed, to chase a horse the rest of the night.

He stopped often and listened for sounds. The noises continued to move away from him. Damn that horse. Why couldn't he just stand still? Why did he have to pick tonight to cut up? He stopped again to listen. No sound. He strained to hear, and still no sound. Good, maybe the reins were snagged and the horse was halted. He went forward, eyes straining into the dim shadows.

A vicious, snarling growl scared the hell out of him. It came from the brush ahead where the wounded dog had crawled. Now cornered, he faced the enemy that was following him. Pain caused the dog to halt his escape. He had broken ribs, torn skin and one hind leg disjointed.

It had been all the dog could do to escape the battleground. He had struggled, dragging himself under the brush to get far away from the area. The broken ribs were ready to puncture his lungs, and the pain was more than the dog could bear. Weak from hunger, loosing blood, one leg useless, he had crawled on his side, pulling himself along. Froth had gathered about his jowls, and dirt was embedded in the blood on his body. He faced the man, prepared to battle until he could move no more.

Denny's eyes adjusted to the darkness of the brush where the dog had crawled. The sight of the gigantic animal, frothing at the mouth, was terrifying to the boy. Not knowing how badly injured the dog was he backed off slowly, afraid the dog would charge. He reached for his pistol and remembered he had given it back to his dad tonight when the men had gone to scout the outlaw's camp.

The dog continued to growl, but he didn't follow the boy. He was ready to defend himself, but he didn't have the strength or desire to fight.

Slowly Denny backed off far enough to realize the dog was not going to attack. The growling subsided as Denny backed further away. When the dog ceased growling Denny halted, more curious than afraid, since an attack had not been launched. What now?

The boy squatted to his heels. He could not see the dog in the darkness, but he remembered that first horrifying moment when he heard the growl and saw the huge frothing mouth full of teeth, and the eyes red in the moonlight. Devil Dog! That's what had flashed into Denny's mind. The Indians had a legend about a devil dog. Denny had thought for a moment that he had run into the legend. He was shaking from fright, so he lit another cigarette. The dog growled again, but did not move, and Denny realized the animal was hurt, maybe dying.

He used his smoke to think. The boss said for him to guard the herd. Without his horse it would be another long walk back. He would have to guard the herd on foot. Should he get back to the herd, or was the herd in more danger from the injured dog? He put that thought aside. It was too dark to do anything. He couldn't kill the dog with his bare hands, and he didn't know how handicapped the animal was. He might end up getting himself killed.

A pitiful whine came from the bushes. Denny sat still and waited. The dog whined again, he was in pain. Denny stood up. The dog growled a warning. Denny squatted back down. The two were silent for a long while. The dog tried to move, and yelped as the dislocated hip sent tearing pain through his body.

Denny waited until he felt the pain had settled, and then he talked to the dog. He didn't try to get up again, he just sat and talked quietly to the animal. For lack of a name he called the dog "Devil." "Good boy, good Devil. Take it easy, Devil. It's all right old fellow."

The dog whined and licked the froth from his jowls, keeping his eyes on the man. He tried to care for the broken places in his skin. The huge tongue cleaned blood from the open cuts. The effort moved the broken ribs and the pain caused the dog to catch his breath. Saliva dripped from his mouth. He whined in pain. Denny watched the dog. He felt sorry for the animal.

Grady found the two of them, the dog and Denny, sitting watching each other. The dog had laid his giant head on his massive paws. The boy had not tried to approach the dog again. Every movement the dog made was painful. At times his eyes closed as the young man talked.

Denny heard Grady's horse, long before he came into sight. He stood and waved the trail boss to him. The dog, aware that someone was coming, growled as the boy stood up. When the rider approached the dog tried to drag himself further into the brush. Wounds stiff from inactivity added to the wrenched muscles filled the dog with agony and he fell to his side, howling in pain.

Denny walked closer. The dog whined, pleading, expressing his fear of the man. Denny saw defeat in the dog's eyes as they pleaded for mercy.

Grady dismounted and came to stand by Denny and look down at the wounded animal, cowed now with pain and fear, unable to escape, unable to defend himself from the men.

"I'm sorry, boss. Can't find my horse. The dawg's bad off. Didn't have nothin' to put him out of his misery. Couldn't tell in the dark how bad off he was. All I could do was wait until light. Then I seen him so thin, look at them ribs. You can count them. You can even see the ones that are broken. He was just hungry. Maybe he ain't really mean. Bad mean, that is."

Grady knew the boy. He was the best hand he had ever had with horses. The kid just naturally loved animals.

"We might take on a pack of trouble if we took him with us, kid." Grady had too many problems, this was too much.

"Yeah, I know." Denny was afraid he was going to say no. Spoke up. "I have been giving it a lot of thought. I know we would all be better off if we just put a bullet in him and left him out here. But look at them eyes. They scared hell out of me last night in the dark, but I've had a chance to talk to him eye to eye in the dawning, and I don't believe he's got a natural mean bone in his body. He's big enough to scare hell out of a body, and he's desperate enough to kill for food, but I don't think he's purely mean."

Grady took off his hat, scratched his head, brushed back his hair and reset the hat. "I'm going to scout for your horse. You decide what you want to do. I'll take a chance on him, but he's got to be kept tied. If you can figure out how we can get him back without getting our hands tore off."

"Thanks, boss. I'll try to get a rope on him."

"Be careful." Grady mounted, threw Denny his rope, and rode off. Denny picked up the rope and took a step toward the dog. The animal flinched and whined. "It's all right fellow," soothingly Denny talked, using the same quiet voice he had used during the night. Continuing to talk, he approached slowly and stretched out his hand. The dog lifted his head in an effort to sit up, whined with pain, and dropped his head back down, his eyes never leaving the man approaching him. He shivered as Denny's hand rested gently on his shoulder and smoothed the ruffled shag of hair.

Moving slowly Denny continued to pat the dog, careful not to touch wounds, and injured areas. He was rewarded with a slight wag of the heavy tail. Slowly he removed his neckerchief and moved his hand up the dog's neck, scratched his ears. The crown of his head, and under his chin. A warm, wet tongue licked his fingers.

"Well, you're a pussy cat, ain't you," Denny crooned. If I'd known that, Devil, we could have had this over with hours ago." Gently he fashioned a muzzle around the dog's jaws and tied the knot over his ears.

"That's just in case the pussy cat has teeth," he continued to talk. The dog whined, and tried to raise a foot to push off the restriction about his jaws. Rib pain caused him to cry out and lie quietly, resigned to his fate. Denny realized the dog was powerless to fight, and knew he would not need to bind the animal. Devil's injuries were a more severe restraint than any rope could be.

"OK, boy, you lie quiet. I'll be back. Stay, "Denny commanded the dog, and repeated, "I'll be back." He didn't know how much training the dog had, but "stay" was a basic command usually taught a ranch dog, and it was all Denny knew to make the dog understand that he was to lie quietly. With those broken ribs any thrashing about could puncture a lung.

Denny backed away and turned to greet Grady as he came through the brush leading Denny's horse.

"Broke rein. Guess he got spooked. The dog could have scared him," Grady said as he handed one good rein to Denny.

"Yeah, that would be my guess. He's enough to scare the daylights out of a fella in the dark. I know!"

"He's some hellhound, all right," Grady sized up the dog as he lay stretched along the ground.

"I'll have to go get the cart." Denny handed Grady his lariat and untied his own lariat from his saddle. He tied one end of the lariat to the bit of the bridle to fashion a temporary rein.

Both riders turned their horses for camp. Grady knew the kid had decided to keep the dog. The decision was up to the boy. No more was said. He knew Denny was aware of the responsibility that he had assumed. They rode back to the camp in silence.

CHAPTER TWENTY-TWO

Grady put the dog out of his mind. He had more pressing problems, with four extra mouths to feed, it created a dangerous threat to the trail drive. Tied-up men to watch. Men desperate enough to take any chance, watching constantly for a way to escape. This drive, so far, had been jinxed. He should have known better in San Diego. He should have stood firm with his decision not to ramrod this drive. He shook his head to clear it. No use looking back. There wasn't time for that.

The camp was having breakfast. Denny joined the group around the fire, and they caught him up on the night's events.

Grady dismounted and went to check on his prisoners. He found the men separated and tied, one to each wheel of the grain wagon. He bent over each man and checked his bindings.

"When we gonna get fed?" Luke whined.

"Soon," Grady replied.

"How soon? I'm hongry. Last night was the first decent grub we ate for two weeks."

"You been on the run for two weeks?" Grady asked.

"Who told you we was running from anything?" Luke whined.

"Yore boss talked in his fever."

"Cragen, never. Cragen's tough. He's took bullets afore. He don't never talk." Sincere, in his own way Luke was loyal.

"He did this time." The bluff was on. It was all Grady had, he had to use it. "One of you killed that soldier."

"I don't believe you," Luke pouted, his faith slipping.

"Shut up, Luke," Ace growled from the other side of the wagon. A set, stubborn expression came over Luke's face as he glowered at Grady.

Grady knew he would have to separate the men if he wanted to get anything out of Luke, so he joined the crew at the breakfast fire.

Cook handed him a tin bowl and he loaded hot oatmeal into it, and then poured a generous helping of molasses over the oatmeal. He was about to take a spoonful when Cecile. handed him a metal pitcher. He took it and peered inside, took a sniff, and then poured a generous helping of fresh cream over the cereal, and a dash into his cup of black coffee that Cook had set beside him.

"I'd forgotten about that little cow. How's she doing?"

"Just fine. It's all so new to her she didn't protest much when Cook borrowed some milk for breakfast."

"Man, does that taste good!"

"You bet it does, boss. I had three bowlfuls. Can I take the cart now and go get Devil?" Denny asked excitedly.

"Yeah, kid, run along. Hurry though. We're going to get at least a half day's drive in."

"OK, boss. Thanks." Denny was up and running to gather a team.

"Devil?" Cecile's eyebrows rose.

"Big dog. Scared the kid's horse off last night, and I think he had the kid pretty scared until daylight. I guess they had several hours to get acquainted. The kid wants to bring him in."

"But Grady, he attacked the cow!" Cecile protested instantly.

"I know. I know. It wasn't an easy decision, but I know the kid. He will assume full responsibility for keeping the animal away from the herd."

"What good will that do if he does get loose and attack?"

"I give any of you permission to shoot to kill if the dog even looks like he wants cow meat. OK?"

Cecile drew in a deep sigh of resignation. The crew watched her struggle.

"OK, boss. We'll help keep an eye on the hound for the kid," Lou said. Bear and Scratch nodded in agreement.

"He better stay away from my cook wagon," Cook growled, his way of agreeing with the crew to accept the dog.

Grady helped himself to another bowl of oatmeal heavily doused with molasses and cream. "Delicious," he murmured as the warm gruel slid down his throat. "Looks like you'll have to make another potful for our guests. This one's nearly cleaned out."

"What are we going to do with those men?" Cecile's mind left the problem of the dog and now watched Joe Bob anxiously while he finished his breakfast, set the tin bowl aside, and rolled a smoke.

He was quiet for some time, smoking, sipping his coffee, and thinking. The crew was quiet, waiting for the trail boss to break the silence. When the cigarette had nearly disappeared he threw it to the ground and slammed a boot over it, twisting, grinding it into the dirt.

"It's a bitch, isn't it?" The men nodded in agreement.

"What do you mean?" Cecile looked from one worried face to another.

"We should kill them all," the Indian said so quietly she barely heard him.

"We can't do that!" Her eyes grew large in disbelief.

"You want this herd to reach your ranch?" Little Bear looked her directly in the eyes, his face void of expression.

"Of course I do, but we can't just murder those men."

"OK, Bear, that's enough. I know you're right, but us white men are supposed to follow the Ten Commandments, which means we don't intentionally kill those nice fellows over there."

Bear grinned. It was the first time Cecile had seen the dour half-breed with any expression on his face. Why the old fraud, he had just as much feeling and compassion as the rest of the men. Funny she hadn't seen it before.

"I hope I'm alive if you have to admit I was right," Bear said.

"Man, so do I!" Grady nervously pulled out his tobacco and paper and began to roll another cigarette.

"So what's the decision, boss?" Lou asked as he also rolled another cigarette.

"We'll have to make room on the grain wagon, and tie them on. One of us will have to watch them every moment. Means night watches continue, and don't for a moment think that fellow with the injured leg ain't dangerous. I get the impression from his men over there that he's some kind a man."

"That dirty animal. How could anyone capture the loyalty of filth like those three and be a threat?" Fire and flame were ready to spew from Cecile's mouth and eyes. The men remembered the ordeal she had gone through at the hands of one of the criminals, and they didn't blame her for feeling so much hate.

"I don't know, Miss Ceci. Maybe man was the wrong word to use. Maybe I should have said animal. Just the same, don't ever let your guard down. He's dangerous."

Just then Denny drove the cart into camp and the crew rose to take a look at the dog. Even Cook joined them as they walked to the cart and looked inside.

"Hot damn!" Scratch spat tobacco juice on the ground. His mouth hung open as he stared in surprise at the dog that lay sprawled on the cart floor, head and tail touching the seat and the tailgate. His back was against the sideboards, one leg stretched across to brace him against the other side board, the other three legs were drawn up in pain. The dog lifted his head and growled as the strangers looked over the sideboards.

"Quiet boy. Take it easy. Down." The boy laid his hand on the massive head and the dog relaxed as he heard the familiar voice. A rough, red tongue flapped loosely in an effort to caress the hand as it smoothed his head and moved around to scratch under his chin.

"Devil dog," Little Bear growled as he took in the size of the animal.

"That's what I call him—Devil. He already knows that's his name." Denny grinned from ear to ear, watching the faces as they looked in awe at the giant dog, until he spotted the worried face of Cecile McNamara.

"Miss Ceci, please don't worry. I promise I'll keep him tied. I'll watch him."

"I know you will, Denny. Please forgive me for not having more faith in you. It's just that he is so big and so thin. He must be starved."

"Yes, ma'am, I'm sure that's why he attacked the cow. I don't think he's really mean, ma'am."

"I hope not. Cookie, do we have anything to feed an animal that size?" Cecile asked.

"I'll make a double pot of oatmeal for him and them no good dogs over yonder, only for him I'll add the last of the cream, last night's left over broth, some beans and a biscuit or two."

"I shore would hate to be on yore bad side," Lou laughed as the cook headed back to fix his prisoners their breakfast."

"To make sure this animal doesn't attack another cow, we are going to have to be responsible for keeping belly his full." The crew all knew, including Cecile, that Grady had just given a command. No rabbit, ground squirrel, or any other game that crossed their trail would be ignored.

"Ceci., you're to stay away from the prisoners. Lou will care for them. You stay with the herd today. Scratch, you drive the cart with the dog in it. Trumpeter will have to walk today. The half day that's left won't hurt him. Denny, you and Lou get this dog doctored; those ribs need wrapping, and then feed him. Lou, you get the prisoners fed. Bear, you go get the horses and then help Denny hitch up. I'm going to ride out and try to figure out how far off the Butterfield route we have wandered."

Everyone scattered to do as they were bidden. Cecile watched as Lou expertly doctored the dog. Everyone left in camp had to help hold him down while Lou set the hip joint. After the dog had been cared for Denny carefully removed the kerchief muzzle and fed the dog a large dishpan full of Cook's gourmet dog breakfast. The animal was so hungry the food disappeared like magic. The heavy tail thumped and begging eyes studied each face, hoping another pan full of food would be offered.

"Sorry, old fella, not too much all at once," Denny crooned and patted the big head. The thumping tail answered and then the dog relaxed and his eyes closed. He had found friends. They had cleaned his wounds and fed him. His night of fear was over. He was safe and now could sleep.

The herd met Grady when he returned. Cecile, Little Bear, and Denny were moving it slowly, letting the cattle graze. It had taken Lou, Scratch, and Cook longer to break camp than usual. The added chores of feeding, loading, and tying up the extra passengers on the grain wagon, making a spot to load the calf on the grub wagon, and tying the cow to the tailgate, had slowed them down. Grady could see them down the valley, under way, and knew they would catch up later in the day.

CHAPTER TWENTY-THREE

The trail was gradually uphill now, the foliage changing as they rode. Deadly, completely bored by the slow pace of the fat cows, let Trumpeter and Reginald take over the lead. He drifted away from the herd and grazed until they were far ahead, then his rangy legs stretched out and he soon walked again in the lead. He repeated this action several times until it grew late in the day and it would soon be time to stop. He walked with his head up studying the rocky slopes ahead, trying to figure out the spot that Grady would choose to camp.

Grady smiled as he watched his friend. The big bull had become so predictable over the years of trail driving that Grady knew his every action. He also put a lot of faith in Deadly's ability to choose a bed ground. They played a game, but Grady knew that Deadly was the one who made the final choice. When Deadly spotted the place to stop, he always slowed down and began to munch grass here and there, and pull a bite or two off of the bushes. The herd always followed suit. Grady would signal and yell, "OK, Deadly, bed 'em down." Deadly would halt just where he had intended to stop all the time.

The crew was irritable that night. The day had been tedious. Grady had made a dozen trips to check the ropes on the prisoners. Scratch had pulled the cart behind the grain wagon and watched the men all day. Lou had halted the wagon a dozen times and checked their ropes. Denny had slowed a dozen times to croon to the dog as he rode along side the cart. Cook brought the prisoners a drink of water later in the afternoon.

Cecil and Little Bear were the only ones that did not check the prisoners. Cecil worked steadily with her whip, and Little Bear's eyes studied the mountains ahead.

When they stopped for the night, all were quiet, speaking only when necessary. All but the prisoners, who began to complain the moment they reached camp. They had spent a cramped, uncomfortable day tied in the wagon. Sleep was not even an escape for them as someone always awakened them to check the ropes. And they were hungry.

The crew went about their jobs. The prisoners were tied to separate wagons. The injured man was conscious, and wary eyes followed each one of the trail hands as they worked. Grady had had Cragen's arms tied for the day. Now that the man was fully conscious and seemed in his right mind, he tied his feet and released his hands so he could stretch, sat him up and down a few times to circulate the blood, and then tied his hands together again.

Cragen was silent, but he studied Grady's face as he worked over him. Grady's eyes locked with Cragen's. Both men were steady as they studied each other.

Grady had to break his gaze to complete his job. Neither man spoke. They both knew that right now Grady was in charge, but he had better be careful, because if Cragen got any chance at all the odds would change.

Then Grady checked Ace; just to be sure Lou had tied the man securely. "Gawd dammit, I wish you bastards would quit tuggin' at them ropes. You've got my wrists tore all to hell," Ace's temper was genuine. Grady checked the wrists and saw the red irritated skin. He didn't answer, but he decided not to tug at the ropes again tonight.

He went over to Luke, who sat relaxed against the wagon wheel. "Yore wrists sore, Luke?"

"Hell, yes."

"Well, let me take a look and I won't pull at them again tonight." Luke leaned forward and Grady tested the ropes. They were secure. "All right Luke, grub will be here soon. Your boss is awake. If you behave yourself, I'll let you talk to him in the morning."

Luke's face lit up. "Yeah, man, that will be good. Cragen's going to live? Man, that's good."

"You really like him, don't you, Luke?"

"Best man I ever rode with. Good to Luke. Never teased me. I'm a little slow, you know. But Cragen don't mind. He always stood up for me. Wouldn't let nobody roust me."

"He sounds like a good man. How did he pick up that bullet?"

The grin left Luke's face. "Ain't going to say nothing until I talk to Cragen. He'll know what I'm supposed to say. Ain't going to answer you."

"OK, Luke, grub will be along soon." Grady walked to the campfire and sat down by Cecile.

"Cragen's conscious," Grady said.

"I know. I felt eyes on me, and when I turned to look he smiled." The memory made her shudder.

"Maybe he thought you were an angel."

"Mr. Grady, is that a compliment?"

"I guess so, lady. If I woke up and saw you, I'd sure think I was in heaven."

"Maybe I better keep my eyes on you, Mr. Trail Boss. You sound like you could become a little dangerous yourself."

Grady laughed. "Maybe you're right. I do see you in a different light these days, and I don't mind telling you I'm scared shitless, pardon the expression. Having these men along is like trying to transport a cargo of nitroglycerin, ready to blow any minute. I don't like it, and I don't trust that Cragen. I got a feeling about that man. He's one to reckon with."

A shiver went up Cecile's spine. "I know what you mean. Those eyes of his."

"You keep away from him," Grady warned.

"Don't worry. I will," she replied.

The men came in and got their bowls. They filled them from the pot of beef and potato stew that hung over the fire. There were hot biscuits in the Dutch oven to sop up the stew gravy and hot coffee laced with rich cream to wash it down. The meal was eaten in silence. As each man finished eating, he rolled and lit a cigarette.

"Thanks, Bear." Denny was the first to speak. Little Bear had shot a couple of rabbits and handed them to the kid when he gave him his horse to unsaddle. Denny had cleaned them and now he propped them over the fire with a couple of sticks, to roast. The big dog was not to be fed raw meat.

One of Denny's intentions was to teach him to come to him for his meals, instead of looking for raw meat.

Lou took a bowl and left to feed Cragen. Cook handed Scratch a bowl and nodded toward Luke. Scratch took the bowl of stew and mechanically shoveled the food into Luke's mouth. Cook came by just as the man finished. He had his shotgun over his shoulder, the muzzle pointed at Luke's head. "Untie him."

Scratch untied the man and Cook handed him a cup of hot coffee laced with the same heavy cream the crew had had. Luke drank slowly, he sipped and slurped, the two men patiently waiting for him to finish. When he drained the cup he handed it to Cook.

"I gotta go."

"Untie his feet." Cook gave Scratch the orders and Scratch carried them out. Then Cook handed Scratch the cup and put both hands on the shotgun, steadying it at Luke's forehead.

"Turn slow, and walk to that bush. I'll be right behind you. If you even look like yore going to give me trouble, my face will be the last thing you ever see."

"Yes, sir. No, sir. I won't. Man, be careful with that shotgun," Luke whined like a baby. Walking carefully, he made it to the bush, unfastened his pants and relieved himself. He turned slowly and went back to the wheel.

"Good boy. Tie him up again.

Scratch retied the man's hands and feet. Cook checked them and hurried back to the grub wagon. Scratch followed doggedly. He knew there were two men to feed yet. Lou had cared for Cragen. When the prisoners were secured for the night Cook and Scratch went back to the fire.

Denny stopped turning the rabbits. They were ready to cool so he set them aside. All eyes were on Grady, as the men waited patiently for the boss to assign night watch.

A crackling sound in the brush made them all jump, wheel around, and reach for a gun, except Cecile and Denny. Cook's shotgun aimed into the darkness and Grady drew his pistol and stepped away from the fire. Out of the darkness and into the firelight ambled the big longhorn. It was biscuit time, and Deadly went directly to the bread pantry on the grub wagon.

"Shit," Cook exploded with relief, and went to get the bull his treat.

Grady looked at the gun in his hand and grinned at the crew. A round of laughter filled the camp relieving some of the day's tension.

"This is the shits," Lou said as he picked up the still smoldering cigarette he had dropped to the ground to free his hand as he drew his gun.

"Yeah, the shits," Scratch repeated.

"Who wants first watch?" Grady asked.

"I'll take it, boss. I got beans to soak tonight," Cook answered.

"OK, Cook, you hang in a couple of hours, then get me up. Lou can take over at midnight tonight, and you can get the early a.m. shift. Tomorrow night, Scratch and Bear can handle it.

"What about me? I'll take a turn." All heads turned to look at Cecile "Just because I'm a woman doesn't mean I'll let you down again."

They all knew she spoke the truth. She probably had more reason than all of them to do a good job.

"OK, Ceci, you and Denny can take a night, and then we'll all get two nights sleep. This could be a long drive."

They all scattered to find their bedrolls. Denny took the rabbits to the cart, tore them into sections, and hand-fed the dog. He had fashioned a collar from an old belt and he fastened it about the dog's neck. He attached a length of rope to the collar, and put the ramp in place on the back of the cart. Coaxing, he got the dog to his feet. The animal was unsteady, and he could not put his weight on the repaired hip joint, but he managed, painfully, to descend to the ground.

"Good boy, Devil," Denny crooned.

"What the hell you doing with my dawg?" Ace screamed from the wheel of the grain wagon.

"Come here, Deacon," Ace demanded.

The dog flinched and cowed to the ground. Denny was surprised to see a dog so huge turn into a scared rabbit. He kneeled beside the dog and crooned, "It's OK, Devil."

"Get your hands off my dog," Ace screamed.

Grady came running with the rest of the crew right behind him. "What the hell's going on?" He demanded.

"That's my dog." Ace's face livid with rage.

"Well, Mr. Ace, your dog nearly killed a very expensive cow of ours. Just one more little item to chalk up on the big list I got going against you. Now you hear me, fella. You don't own nothin' but that rope you got around your hands and feet. Denny's in charge of that animal until we get to a town where we can get rid of you. By that time we'll decide if we want to get rid of the dog also. Now shut up and go to sleep."

Ace glared at the trail boss, struggled against the ropes, and then sagged angrily against the wheel. He watched while Denny led the limping dog around the campfire, stopping to let the animal relieve himself. When they got back to the cart Denny tied the dog to the wheel, and when Devil, or Deacon, settled to the ground and softly licked a torn wound on his chest, Denny went to the grub wagon and brought back his bedroll.

He laid the roll out just out of reach of the jaws of the dog. He crawled in and was quickly sinking into oblivion, when he felt a warm body settle against his back. He reached out and felt the dog's coarse hair. A thump of the heavy tail answered back. Denny checked the collar and found the rope was secure. The big dog had just backed up until he could touch Denny. Denny inched the bedroll closer, allowing the rope to give, and let the animal rest his head on his big paws. The two were tired. They had been awake, staring at each other in distrust the night before. Tonight each had decided to trust the other. Dog and boy were soon asleep.

CHAPTER TWENTY-FOUR

Cook soaked his pot of beans, cussing under his breath as he added extra cupfulls for the uninvited guests, his experienced eye telling him all rations would have to be cut in half soon or they would not make it to the next outpost to restock. He would have to use more meat and save the beans and flour for treats instead of basic fare; that is, if Little Bear could provide the meat.

Now that they were nearing the timberline there should be plenty of deer, maybe even a quail or two. His mouth watered at the prospect. He spat into the fire, settled the shotgun into his hand, a finger resting lightly on the trigger, and made his rounds of the prisoners.

Both Ace and Luke were snoring, lying curled up in a fetal position, hands tied behind their backs. Yancy was leaning against a wheel. Even breathing indicated he was deep in sleep. Grady had come by before he went to bed and covered the men with blankets.

Cook lifted the blanket on each man and studied the knots on their hands and feet. The three men continued to sleep, their snores broken by the disturbance, only briefly. When Cook walked away, the steady rhythm returned.

Cragen, however, was instantly awake. He heard the cook's approach. The man's eyes never left Cook's face as the crusty old man pointed the shotgun inches from Cragen's face and lifted the blanket to check Cragen's ropes. Satisfied that this prisoner was going nowhere tonight, Cook returned to the fire.

He rinsed the beans a couple of hours later, put fresh water over them, seasoned them, and hung the pot over the fire. Before he went to waken Grady, he made the rounds of the prisoners again. The trip was much the same as before. He shook his head worriedly as he walked away from Cragen. The man's eyes had been on him every moment. He grumbled under his breath, "Damn night owl. Don't he never sleep?" Still grumbling under his breath he passed Grady's bedroll, gave the trail boss a gentle shove with one boot toe. "Watch, boss."

"OK, good night, Cook."

"I don't trust that man," Cook grumbled.

"Which man?" Grady asked as he sat up and drew on his boots. "The boss man, Cragen. He ain't missed a check-out tonight."

"Yeah, he's pretty cool. You're right, he's the one we got to watch."

"Night, boss."

CHAPTER TWENTY-FIVE

Grady picked up his hat and rifle and went to the campfire and poured himself a cup of coffee. The smell of the beans, as they began to boil, rose over the fire. The coffee was hot, and Grady was soon wide-awake.

He set out to tour the prisoners and check their ropes, just in case Cook had been fooled. He found Luke and Ace snoring soundly, hands and feet secure. Yancy had shifted to his side, and his soft snore was added to the others. Before he reached Cragen, a voice spoke from the darkness. "If you men plan on keeping me awake all night I could sure use a smoke." Cragen's voice was deep, and rich, and educated.

Grady bent down and the two men sized each other up as he rolled a cigarette, lit it, and stuck it in Cragen's mouth. Then he rolled another. The two men smoked in silence until Cragen's cigarette was spent. Grady took it from his mouth, dropped it to the ground, dropped his beside it, and stood up. One big boot ground both cigarettes into the dirt.

"Get some sleep. I won't be back around till Cook gets up."

"Doesn't matter. I'll sleep on the cart tomorrow," Cragen said.

"How's the leg feel?" Grady asked.

"Hurts like hell," he replied.

"I'll take a look at it in the morning."

Grady returned to the fire. He spent the rest of the night watching the men, but he didn't rise again to check each man. He didn't know if Cragen slept, but he gave him the chance, as he had promised. Grady woke Cook at four thirty and climbed back into his bedroll.

Cook's first job was to check the prisoners. They were just as he had last seen them, even Cragen, who was watching everything with those piercing eyes. "Shit!" Cook spat into the dirt and went to get breakfast started.

They had flapjacks, trail-driver size, that morning. The odor of the cooking batter got everyone up early. Even old Deadly came in from the herd when he smelled the familiar aroma.

After Grady had poured a dipper or two of cold water in the wash pan, sloshed his face, and finger brushed his hair, he grabbed a tin cup out of the pantry and headed for the coffeepot. It sat to one side of the fire, coals stoked against the iron grill it sat on, to make room for the four big camp skillets. The pot of beans had been set aside, done, after cooking most of the night. The fire coals had been scattered in such a way that each skillet nested on its own hill of coals, and an enormous skillet-sized pancake filled each one. In the middle of the four skillets, keeping simmering hot, was the syrup pot and dipper, filled with watered-down molasses, and beef tallow.

"Prisoners've been fed, except for coffee," Cook said as he flopped a pancake over in its pan.

"Good." Grady said." I'll take some hot water and soap, and the whiskey, and take a look at Cragen's leg."

"Pan of water's ready on the seat of the grub wagon." Cook replied.

Grady found the hot water, but he had to dig for the soap and whiskey. He found Cragen just as he had left him the night before, watching as he approached.

"Let's take a look," Grady said as he pulled up the torn pant leg to reveal the bandaged leg. Upon inspection, he found what he had suspected. The bandages had stuck in the dried blood on the leg. He poured warm, soapy water over the bandage. Letting it soak awhile, he went in search of clean bandages. More rummaging around in the grub wagon, and he returned, poured another shot of warm water over the bandages, and began to unwrap them. The warm, soapy water had made a difference in the condition, but there were still times when he had to take his knife and work the bandages loose. He looked to see how Cragen was holding up under the discomfort.

Cragen smiled when he saw Grady look up. "Hurts like hell."

"Looks like hell, too," Grady replied.

"Poison?" he asked

"I don't think so." Grady's attention was once again on removing the crusted bandages. Soon the last wrap was reached. He poured more warm, soapy water over it and rocked back on his heels and began the same ritual as the night before. First he rolled Cragen a cigarette, lit it, and stuck it in the man's mouth, then he rolled himself one, and they waited for the saturated rag to loosen.

When both men had finished their cigarettes, Grady said, "Ready?"

"Yeah, get it off."

Grady clamped his jaws tight, with a steady pull, removed the rest of the bandage, pulling dried blood with it, and fresh blood took its place.

Cragen had tensed up, but when Grady looked to see how he had held up, he was surprised by a boyish grin. "Hell, that's great, man. That's what was hurting. Those damned bandages glued on like that."

"We had to stop the bleeding," Grady said.

"Well, you sure did a good job of that. Man, does that feel better. You don't suppose I could get a cup of coffee and take a leak now?"

"I'll get you a cup as soon as I pour this whiskey over the open areas. It looks good, no red bad flesh around it. I'll just put a light cover over it to keep the trail dust off today."

Grady had the job done quickly. He put the pans and extra bandages away, and was soon back with hot coffee and cream for Cragen. He untied the man's hands, stepped back where he would be out of reach, and watched Cragen sip his coffee. When he had finished, Grady untied his feet and motioned with his pistol for Cragen to get up and walk about. Cragen did so, moving slowly on the injured leg.

He relieved himself, and Grady motioned for him to walk over to the wheel where Luke was tied. Luke was grinning from ear to ear.

"'Morning, boss. Sure good to see you on yore feet."

"Thanks, Luke. I understand you were the only one of the boys that wanted to come back for me."

"Ace come with me." Luke was overwhelmed with the attention Cragen was giving him.

"Well, I appreciate your loyalty, Luke. I won't forget it."

"Aw, that's all right, boss. You always been good to me. I didn't talk neither. I didn't tell those buggers a thing."

155

"That's good, Luke. Let's keep it that way." Cragen grinned and winked at Luke. Luke didn't understand Cragen, but he felt they had a secret between them. He winked back. Cragen returned to his ropes, and Grady tied his hands behind him.

"Well, that didn't tell me anything." Grady said.

"What did you want to know?" Cragen grinned.

"Where you're from. I gather a posse is after you, but which one?"

Cragen gave Grady the same confidential wink that he had given Luke.

Grady couldn't help but return the grin. "Sit down and take it easy. We'll be on our way soon and you can get some sleep."

Cragen chuckled as he sat down and leaned back against the wagon wheel. Grady tied him to the wheel and tied his feet together.

CHAPTER TWENTY-SIX

Everyone but Grady had eaten when he returned to the fire. The four riders were already breaking camp. Cecile was having her second cup of coffee. Cook plunked a giant flapjack on Grady's plate. Grady cut it into quarters and stacked three of the quarters on the side of the plate. He used his kerchief to grab the handle of the syrup dipper and poured steaming hot syrup and tallow over the quarter section. As soon as this quarter disappeared, he replaced it with another quarter, and a dipper of hot syrup. Soon the oversized flapjack was gone. He saw Cook had left one in a skillet nearby, in case he wanted a second, but one of Cook's "trail breakers" was enough for Grady.

Cook came over and tossed the cake to the big dog. It disappeared into the cavernous mouth. Grady and Cecile could hear Cook's words as he talked to himself while he packed up the grub wagon.

"A fellow ought to be told afore he hires on that he's expected to wet nurse a woman, feed an elephant, and ride night herd on a gang of outlaws. Don't seem unreasonable to me. A fellow ought to get some warning so's he can say no if he wants to."

Grady and Cecile looked at each other and laughed. "Lord, isn't this a mess," Cecile said when she gained control.

"I guess it could be worse, but I don't see how."

"What are we going to do?" she asked.

"We're doing OK so far," he replied.

"Come on, Grady. Don't treat me like a child. I know I'm not always bright, but a loony bin would know we are in a jam."

"I guess that's about as good a word as any you could use. J-A-M! King-size jam!" Grady didn't want to scare Cecile but she was right. Treating her like a child wasn't the answer either.

"Can't we send them back?" she asked.

"We're too shorthanded now. One man would have his hands full, and it would probably cost him his life. Bear's the only one I could even begin to count on getting them there, and I'm going to need him when I get to Indian country." Grady sounded desperate.

"Why can't we just leave them?"

"How do we do that? Tie them to a tree and commit four starvation murders?"

"Just take their boots away and turn them loose."

"Lady, we just got ourselves out of that one by capturing them."

"Of course, you're right, but there must be some way," she pleaded.

"I had hoped that posse would show up, but I'm afraid the rains covered their tracks, and I'm sure now that the farther south we go the better Cragen likes it. He's like a snake sitting and waiting to strike." Grady shook his head. "It's a real J-A-M."

"How far is it to the station?" She asked.

"The storm threw us way off track. It could cost us days to get back to the Butterfield Trail."

"How are we going to get through the mountains if we've missed the pass?" Worry lines furrowed her brow.

"The mountains aren't the problem. We'll get on the trail eventually and over the mountains. We're getting dangerously low on food. The extra mouths are taking a toll."

"What about a town ahead?"

"Nothing for several weeks. Janos is the closest, and we'll have to go farther away from the stage route to reach it."

"We'll be out of food by then." Cook's dour voice joined the discussion as he took the camp skillets, and one by one tossed a handful of dirt into each. He scoured the grease and batter from their rims, then hung them on the hooks on the side of the grub wagon.

As though his intervention was a signal, Grady and Cecile went to their waiting horses, mounted, and went to join Denny and Bear as they moved the cattle out.

CHAPTER TWENTY-SEVEN

The next few days followed much the same schedule. The herd traveled upward daily with Trumpeter struggling to follow. The cart was much too unwieldy now to carry the bull without injury. The big dog continued to ride in the cart, gaining strength and healing his wounds. At night Denny took him for long walks, keeping him out of Ace's range. The outlaw, out of boredom, antagonized Denny and the dog every opportunity he got.

Little Bear spent much of his time hunting meat. This became the main object for everyone, Devil included.

The crew grumbled, and the prisoners complained that the dog was tossed more than his share. He began to gain weight. No one thought it possible that the dog could get any bigger, but as fat and muscle replaced skin and bones, the dog became an awesome sight. His was the only happy face in the camp at night. The thump of his huge tail wagging was evidence of his contentment.

Deadly was tired of the tedious, monotonously slow drive, and things were not right in camp. His friend, Grady, had little time for him. He stamped his cloven hooves and swung his heavy horns, smashing accidentally into Reginald's stomach, expelling his wind, and scaring the half-blind bull. Reginald realized that the insult had not been intentional, but just in case, he moved away into the herd.

Deadly decided to make his trip to camp for his biscuit early tonight. Maybe Grady would have time for him tonight. As he rounded the trail and came into the light of the campfire Denny and the dog also entered the trail on the opposite end. The dog ducked behind the boy as Deadly waved a horn in his direction.

"It's all right, Devil. Cut that out, Deadly. You guys got to be friends."

The dog was an enemy to Deadly, and to Devil the bull was a demon. Deadly gave ground. The dog was with the boy, and Deadly knew the trail rules. He would wait until the dog was alone some time and then he would finish the fight. Turning, he went to the grub wagon and nudged a pan until it clanged against the wheel.

"OK, OK," Cook yelled and hurried to get the bull his biscuits. When the rough tongue had drawn them both into his mouth, he went in search of Grady. He found him walking Cragen and fell in step behind, waiting patiently for his friend to notice him.

Cragen and Grady had walked a little farther from camp tonight than usual. Cragen's leg was healing and the outlaw was nervous from the constant confinement of the ropes. The arrival of the bull was inopportune. Grady had to keep his eyes on Cragen. He had released both the man's hands and feet, lit him a cigarette, and was following at a distance. Deadly became impatient and disgruntled. He reached forward to give Grady a shove. His greeting was rougher than usual, hitting Grady squarely in the back with his forehead. The pistol went flying.

Cragen was on it. All lethargy gone, he moved like a panther. Grady dove on top of him, grabbed his arm, and grappled to keep the pistol pointed away. The two men were nearly a match. Cragen was bigger and more muscular, but he was stiff from the days of confinement and weak from the injury. But his freedom was at stake, and he fought like a wild man, rough and dirty.

The camp dinner gong was ringing. Cook had alerted the camp. In moments the crew had the two men circled and Little Bear's rifle was bruising Cragen's temple. The sudden burst of energy ceased. Cragen relaxed and let Grady take the pistol and toss it to Lou.

"Stand up," Grady yelled. Weeks of frustration and rage had built up and as Cragen got to his feet Grady yelled, "Let him fight," and he swung a savage blow from his knees.

Cragen took the sledgehammer blow solidly. He looked from face to face, shook his head, and grinned at Grady. "You sure you want it this way, Trail Boss?"

161

Grady pulled a fist up from his boots. Cragen moved his head sideways, and the blow slid across his shoulder, then he lunged and grabbed Grady about the middle.

Clenching his hands he buried his knuckles in Grady's backbone and began to squeeze. The air left Grady's body. He struggled to land a solid blow to Cragen's head. Luke, Ace, and Yancy were yelling encouragement to Cragen. The crew was rooting for Grady. Cook held his shotgun level and Little Bear had his rifle to his shoulder.

Cragen's strength, his dogged persistence, told Grady that this was a man of men, a leader, one men would die for. As he gasped for air he wondered if he would be one of the ones that died. He held his breath, gathered his strength, and brought a knee into Cragen's groin. A steel-toed boot caught the outlaw in the wound on his leg. The leg gave way, tearing Grady free of Cragen's hold. He fell to his knees, but was immediately up. Cragen was set to lunge. Grady stepped back and drew a deep breath into his tortured lungs.

As Cragen ran forward, an infuriated longhorn charged onto the battleground. Swinging the silver-mounted horns like lethal weapons he caught Cragen in the midsection with the right horn. All of the crew heard the wind leave Cragen's lungs as Deadly picked him up from the ground and tossed him over his back.

"Deadly, hold it!" Grady was having trouble getting enough air into his lungs to yell, but Deadly heard him. The bull had turned on his heels like a cat, intending to mash the man on the ground until the blood ran, but he slid to a halt at Grady's command. He had learned as a young calf that men had play battles, that sometimes his friend had to discipline the men he worked with. Impatient and disgruntled, tonight he had broken the rules. He had interfered. Now he stood over the man in indecision. From habit his hooves dug into the dirt, he snorted and bawled, and when the man moved, he threatened to pin him to the ground with a horn.

Aggravated as he was, he let Grady take a horn in his hand and back him away from the man. Grady wrapped an arm about the bull's neck and leaned on the strong animal while he drew air into his lungs. When he could talk he rubbed the bone between the dual horns and then slid his hand down to Deadly's rump to scratch the large area. "Thanks old fellow, but this was a friendly fight." Deadly basked in the attention. A good rump scratch was his favorite and he started swinging his rump from side to side in enjoyment, settling down to stand at Grady's side.

Cragen got slowly to his feet. Bent over with his hands on his knees, he fought to keep from throwing up. The air was filling his lungs so quickly the pain was nauseating. When he was drawing even breaths he looked up at Grady and grinned. "Hell of a second you sent in."

"Sorry about that, Cragen, but I sure was glad someone interfered."

Cragen's grin broadened, and a twinkle came into his eyes. "We'll get a go at it again."

"I don't think so, Cragen. I'm not sure I could take you, so from now on you're the prisoner, I'm the jailer. No carelessness, no losing my temper, and no more fights."

"Have it your way, Trail Boss." The grin turned into laughter. The nervous crew, now that the danger was over, laughed in relief, and turned to go about their earlier business.

Cecile walked back to the campfire. The episode had not been funny to her.

She had been terrified. When Cook began pounding on the dinner gong she had been afraid of fire, then she had seen Grady and Cragen rolling on the ground. She had pulled her pistol and run with the crew. She had the pistol cocked and pointed at Cragen's head when Deadly interfered. No way was she going to let that animal Cragen win any fight, or hurt Grady. Hate had filled her. The desire to pull the trigger had been so strong that now she was limp. What was happening to her? She had actually wanted to kill that man.

Cragen was returned to his bindings. The crew settled for dinner. Deadly, feeling better now that Grady had paid some attention to him, returned to the herd. Cecile, still shaken, did not eat, and went to her bedroll early.

CHAPTER TWENTY-EIGHT

The herd moved steadily up the mountain. They chose easy paths defined by deer and other wild game. Deadly took side trips to search under pinion trees for the bitter nuts that nestled under the pine needles. From time to time one or two of the crew dropped back to tie their ropes to the wagons and help the drivers over rises too steep for the teams of horses.

The four prisoners' feet were untied, and their hand ropes tied to the grain wagon irons. They were made to walk and help push when needed. Yancy and Cragen bent willingly to the chore. Luke and Ace grumbled and shirked until Cecile rode by and deftly flicked out her whip, snapping the air under Luke's nose, burning the tip of it.

"Next time anyone has to tell you gentlemen to push, I'll take it off."

She rode on up the hill as the men quickly put their shoulders to the load. She could feel Cragen's eyes following her as she rode away.

Each night the crew was exhausted. The higher they traveled the thinner the air became, and it was growing cold. Winter jackets were unpacked. Hot soups became the fare, both to save on the rapidly dwindling food stores and to warm the bellies.

The evening insults from Ace, over the dog, had given the animal the camp name of "Devil Deacon." Ace never failed to insult the dog, making the brute cower and whine. The dog had no way of knowing that Ace was bound and could not follow through with his threats. Devil Deacon gave Denny the credit for protecting him. Everyone in camp knew he must have suffered badly at the hands of his past master. Secretly this put them all on the side of the dog.

As the days passed, Devil had grown strong and well, preferring to travel alongside the cart instead of in it. At night, around the campfire, Denny had begun to turn loose of the rope to let the dog take food from the fingers of the others. When they were all convinced that the dog was not vicious, watching as he gently licked the nose of the little calf, which was a third his size, and did not try to harm it, Denny began to remove the rope and let him run free. The dog acted as though the rope still tied him to the boy. He followed the kid's every footstep.

As the days grew shorter and the grade steeper, the dog was allowed to run loose. Denny was delighted the first time a rabbit jumped in front of his horse and took off down the hill. Devil, who had been following Denny's horse, leaped with an agility belying the enormous size of the animal. Soon he returned with the rabbit in his jaws and laid it in the path of Denny's horse, his tail thumping, and his giant tongue lolling. If dogs can grin to show pleasure, Devil was grinning as Denny jumped off his horse and lovingly petted the big dog, careful to avoid the still tender ribs.

The boy used his knife and quickly gutted the rabbit, and hung it over his saddle horn. That was the beginning of the dog's workdays. He made it his chore to run down every rabbit he could find. Some days he earned his dinner; other days he fed the entire camp. Devil had begun to earn his way, and the crew accepted him as one of them.

CHAPTER TWENTY-NINE

The prisoners had been given blankets, large-eyed needles, and rawhide thongs to fashion themselves a cover, in the absence of coats. Luke took both his and Cragen's, and with the patience of the dull-witted and his obvious hero worship of Cragen, made them both very acceptable garments. Ace's cover was just that, a covering, no definite shape, a cape with sleeves. He resented Luke's effort on Cragen's behalf and not his, and he added Luke to his sharp tongue, taunting the halfwit until Luke would kill Ace if he ever got near him.

They began to tie Ace by himself, leaving Cragen and Luke to share their strange friendship. Yancy became more docile and obedient each day. Ace hated them all. He brooded his time away imagining just how he would get rid of each one of them.

That prissy missy, if he could get his hands on her he would squeeze her skinny neck in his hands while he screwed her to death. Grady, the trail boss, snobbish bastard—what the hell right did he have to ignore Ace? He never shared a cigarette with him as he did with Cragen. If he didn't bitch his head off none of the bastards would give him a smoke. He'd like to carve the trail boss up, one piece at a time. I bet he wouldn't be so snobbish after he'd lost both his ears.

He'd stuff that cranky cook so full of his own apron he'd choke to death. He chuckled to himself when he was thinking about the Indian. He would scalp him. Just a neat cut around the hair line and roll it up like a rug. Gimpy Lou, he'd cut off the other leg. Scratch, the slow, quiet one, a good pair with Luke. He'd tie the two of them back to back and cut off their balls.

The kid, Denny. Ace spent hours relishing his daydreams of the tortures he would use on that little bastard. Sometimes he used fire, branding irons. He even tied the kid and beat him to death with a stick. The end was always the same, death, but slowly, ever so slowly.

His hatred was most intense when he saw the dog. When he had used up his victims he added the dog to his dreams. The animal, abnormal in its growth, had always drawn attention to Ace. Men had respected him. He had trained the dog to attack man or beast, and that little bastard was turning his dog into a lapdog. The first thing he was going to do after he had disposed of the crew was to tie the dog and beat the hell out of him. Teach the son of a bitch who's boss.

As he passed his time in thought his fingers were nervously exploring his bindings. Some days they were looser than others. Twice he had nearly worked them free before someone came to check and tightened them. This encouragement kept him working at the bindings even in his sleep. He wore irritated places on his wrists that began to bleed. Then they healed, toughened. The more he worked to free himself, the closer the men watched him.

The grain load was dwindling, and when the injured dog had begun to heal and walk beside the cart, the load had been divided. When the dog was allowed to go free, Ace took his place, secured by the same rope that had secured the dog to the cart. They treated him worse than the damn dog. He hated them all, the sons of bitches.

Ace was deep in his pastime of feeling sorry for himself and killing everyone off, everyone about him, when he noticed as he pushed the cart occasionally, helping the team over and up an obstacle, that if he placed his hands just right along the side of the cart, the iron rim of the wheel touched the bindings on his wrist. The first time it happened, he jumped back as the turn of the wheel slid off the binding and burned his wrist. He had cussed and moved his hands farther back. Then he began to reason, if he could place his hands just right each time, maybe the wheel would wear through the rope. He tried over and over again to repeat the trick of laying his hands in just the right position for the bindings to hit the wheel.

For several days he practiced, burning his wrists, cussing in pain, but determined to free himself. He persisted, careful to touch the wagon only when it actually needed assistance. Like a fox, a sly fox, he practiced, and on the third day his chance came. The bindings were knotted in such a way that a strand around his right wrist was clear and the wheel hit just right to work away and fray the fibers. He could hardly wait until the noon break. He knew the routine. They would stop and rest, shove a piece of jerky in his mouth, test the ropes, give him a drag or two on a cigarette. They treated him like a dog, worse than a dog. He spent the morning imagining what he was going to do to that dog and the kid when he got free.

The noon break went very much as Ace had figured it would. He bitched and complained to slow-thinking Scratch until the man forgot to check his bindings. Ace could hardly contain his pleasure as Scratch climbed back on the cart and began the grueling upward climb. Ace tried not to be too helpful, but anticipation made him put his shoulder to the cart more often than usual. The terrain was so bad that Scratch had a rough job driving the team. He paid little attention to the prisoner.

Grady and Little Bear came back once and tied on to help pull the cart up a hill. They didn't take time to check Ace's bindings as the other grain wagon was waiting at the foot of the grade. Ace kept his hands pushing, his head down, and feet shoving as the cart rolled on. They wouldn't stop to check if he was working.

The rope continued to fray as the day wore on. They stopped a time or two and Ace dropped by the wheel, giving the impression of being tired and needing to rest. Denny brought them all a drink of water. Ace kept his eyes on the ground, and his hands under his blanket cover. He dutifully took several swallows and sent a few curse words at the dog. He had to act the same. Wouldn't do to let them see the hope in his eyes.

They came to a mountain spring, one fed by the recent rains. The spring fed a small stream in a valley where the cattle could graze and water. The crew on horseback, Grady, Little Bear, Cecile, and Denny, had gone to drive the cattle and horses farther into the canyon. Cook was gathering firewood. Lou checked the prisoners then went to get their night blankets out of the grub wagon. Scratch unhooked his team of horses, hobbled them and set them free. The dirty son of a bitch took care of the horses before he saw to Ace.

Scratch never knew what hit him. He was hanging the harness on a wagon when a rock crashed into his skull. Ace peeked over the cart and saw Lou returning to the grain wagon with the blankets. Ace knelt down and pulled Scratch's pistol from its holster and stuck it in his own belt. He slid a hand over the cart, under the seat, and felt for the rifle he knew Scratch kept there. His fingers found it, and inch-by-inch drew it over the side.

"Hey, Scratch, you need some help?" Lou called as he walked over to the cart. He saw Scratch's body on the ground just before the rifle slammed into his head. He fell backward into Ace's waiting arms. Neither man had uttered a word.

Snowflakes started to fall. Ace held the old man's body against himself and tried to decide what to do next. He hadn't figured an escape in his plans. He had concentrated so hard on freeing his hands that he hadn't figured out what he would do when they were free.

The crew would return soon. If he slipped off into the trees he might escape, but he doubted it. The Indian would get him, or he would freeze to death, or die of hunger. He needed some grub and a horse. Ace wasn't stupid. He knew if he took time to get what he needed he would be caught unless he had help. Shit! He'd have to free Cragen and Luke. Screw Yancy.

He watched the cook pick up a bucket and head for the stream. Searching Lou's pockets, he found a pocketknife. Then he dropped the body to the ground.

Cragen heard the body fall. He looked over his shoulder. His face expressionless, he watched as Ace crawled under the cart and on hands and knees scrambled for the grain wagon. He turned back to check on the whereabouts of the cook as Ace crawled quietly under the wagon and put the rifle barrel between Luke's shoulders. The halfwit flinched, but he knew the feeling of a gun held to his back, and he froze, turning only his eyes pleadingly toward Cragen.

Cragen watched as Ace battled with himself. He knew Ace didn't want to release them. He also knew that Ace couldn't get away without help, so he sat watching as Ace made up his mind. A noise down by the creek made Ace open the knife and cut the ropes from Luke's wrists. Luke was about to jump up and yell with joy.

"Shut up, dummy, sit still," Ace commanded, ramming the gun harder into Luke's back. When he was sure Luke was going to obey him, he freed

Cragen and gave him the rifle. Then he crawled back to the cart, went under it, and using it as cover ran into the woods and made his way around the camp toward the spring.

Snow was falling steadily now. The ground was getting slick underfoot. He heard Cook mutter under his breath as he cursed the cold weather and the slippery ground as he carried a sloshing bucket of water up the path. Cook was caught completely by surprise when Ace stepped in behind him and pushed the pistol into the fat around his belly. At the same time Ace grabbed the shotgun before Cook could react. He jerked the harness loose from the cook's shoulder and growled, "Keep it quiet, Cookie." The grumbling ceased, and the two entered the camp.

Cragen and Luke were where he had left them. "Why in the hell ain't you saddled them horses and packed some grub?"

"I think it best if we wait for the crew to return."

"You ain't boss here no more, Cragen. Get them horses and let's get out of here."

"They'll track us down. Remember the Indian, Ace? Why don't you take the cook over and let him get us a meal started. Take the shotgun and stay behind the wagon until they get in camp. Luke and I will stay here and make it look good."

Ace didn't argue. He knew Cragen was right, but it angered him the way the man took over his gig. "All right, but you ain't boss no more."

Cragen didn't answer as Ace took the cook to the grub wagon and directed him to get busy, but not to take one step beyond the campfire or yell out, or he would fire both barrels. The manner in which the cook set about doing as he was bidden bothered Ace.

"Cragen you still got that old gimpy man over there on the ground by you ?"

"You mean old Lou? Sure." Cragen answered.

"Well, if this cook makes a sound, put a bullet in that old man."

"You're the boss, Ace," Cragen replied.

Ace chuckled. That was more like it. He'd shown Cragen that he was as capable of giving orders as Cragen was.

Cook began cussing under his breath. The only sound in camp was that of the cook as he grumbled about his work. If the three tired people riding in noticed any difference, it was too late.

Cecile, Grady, and Little Bear had tied their horses and gone to the fire before Bear grabbed for his pistol.

"Hold it, Injun," Ace's voice came from behind the wagon. I got the sawed-off shotgun pointed right at your cook's head. Get their guns, Luke."

"Sure, Ace, sure." Luke ran to relieve the three of their pistols and frisk them for knives. Then he went to the saddle horses and took the rifles. He was taking the guns to Cragen when Ace's angry voice stopped him. "Put them guns over here, dummy."

Luke looked slowly at Cragen. Cragen nodded his head, and Luke took the hardware over and dropped it at Ace's feet. He kept one rifle, and returned to Cragen's side.

Grady had turned to look at Cragen, and found the man resting easily against the wheel. A rifle leaned against his knees, pointed at the group. On the ground beside him lay Gimpy Lou. Cragen had taken Lou's makings from his pocket, and was using one hand to roll himself a cigarette. The other hand rested on the trigger of the rifle. Cragen grinned. "So, Trail Boss, the worm turns."

Grady's jaw set but he didn't answer. This was one hell of a jam.

"Get off your ass, Cragen, and get them horses packed with grub," Ace's temper was growing. How dare Cragen sit there so calm? He was blowing Ace's escape.

"There's a man missing, Ace."

Cragen's voice was slow, his grin deceiving, his eyes searching as far into the darkness as they could reach, while at the same time keeping an eye on the crew around the campfire.

"I'll stay here a bit longer, if it's all right with you, boss," Cragen drawled.

The kid. Shit. How could he forget that fucking, mealy-mouthed little shit! Goddamn Cragen. He had put Ace down again. Steady, man. Wait until you're safe, and then you can blow him to hell. Where was that fuckin' kid?

Snow was falling harder now, and visibility was poor. Maybe that was the reason Denny rode into camp without realizing the danger. Devil growled just before Cragen called out, "Hold it, kid."

The boy stopped his horse, and stared in disbelief at the scene around the campfire.

"Get off your horse, boy. Get his rifle, Luke," Cragen ordered.

Goddamn Cragen, he had done it again, put Ace down.

"The kid's mine, Cragen!"

"Sure Ace."

Luke got Denny's rifle out of the scabbard, brought the horse over, and tied it to the other wheel of the grain wagon. He was about to join Cragen when he remembered and turned and walked to Ace and dropped the rifle on the pile of guns, then returned to stand by Cragen.

That halfwit bastard, when this was over he'd teach that son of a bitch a lesson. Ace's blood pressure was climbing. He stepped from behind the grub wagon and shoved the cook over to join the other four.

"Where's Scratch?" Cecile half whispered, half cried out.

"Right where yore all going to be, sister, in hell." Ace growled at her.

"My Dad," Denny cried out as he spotted Lou lying on the ground by Cragen.

"He's all right, kid," Cragen said, as he lifted the rifle, halting Denny from coming closer.

"He ain't all right neither, kid. I bashed his head in," screamed Ace.

Denny, in shock, began walking toward Lou on the ground. Cragen raised the rifle again to threaten the kid when the roar of a shotgun rent the air. For one short moment Cragen saw the kid on his feet with a hole blown through his body and a look of surprise on his face, then he fell.

A ferocious growl ended as Devil Deacon leaped and knocked Ace to the ground. The now useless shotgun, slid over the snow that was beginning to stick to the ground.

Ace tried to tear the dog's jaws from his throat. Luke's rifle rang out, and the dog jerked, but his jaws continued to grind on the man.

"Hold it, Luke." Cragen's voice stopped Luke from firing a second shot.

Ace screamed and tried a bear hug on the dog. It was his undoing. It helped the dog take a firmer hold on his throat, and a snap of the monstrous jaws broke Ace's neck.

"Now, boss?"

"Yeah, Luke."

The dog was standing over his victim, shaking the man like a rag doll as the second shot rang out. A bullet through the heart dropped the big animal on top of his enemy.

"Oh, my God." Cecile turned away from the grisly sight. She retched and threw up.

Lou was coming to. He groaned and turned over on his stomach, reached up to rub his head and flinched at the pain. He raised his eyes and saw, on the ground before him, his son. His beautiful son, ruined. Somebody had put a hole in his body. Blood was everywhere. He felt a rifle jab his ribs. Stunned, he turned his head and looked into Cragen's smiling face. "Easy old man. You want to live to bury that boy decently, don't you?"

Lou looked back at his son. "My God." He dropped his head to his hands and cried.

"OK, Luke. Tie them up. Start with the trail boss."

Luke hurried to obey. Soon all of the little crew left alive were tied and seated in a row about the fire. Cecile was sobbing, and Cragen rose for the first time since Ace had freed his hands, walked over and slapped her. The shock of the blow stopped the crying. She knew better than to resume. She fought to control herself, drawing deep breaths and letting out silent sobs.

"I'll watch our guests, Luke. Then you untie Yancy, The two of you eat, then load some grub on one of those horses, while I eat.

Luke scurried to obey. Blind loyalty. Cragen squatted across from Grady and smiled at him. He reached over and took Grady's tobacco from his pocket and rolled a smoke, lit it, and stuck it in Grady's mouth. Then he rolled and lit one for himself. "Degrading, isn't it?" Cragen asked as he took a deep draw on the cigarette.

Grady spat the cigarette onto the ground. He no longer wondered about the man. He was a man of men. It was a shame he was such a deadly killer.

Cragen grinned. "It looks like we have come to the parting of the ways."

"You're going to kill us?"

Cragen bent over, picked up the cigarette, lit it again, and stuck it back in Grady's mouth. "Smoke that Grady, and I'll think about it." He grinned as Grady shifted the cigarette to the side of his mouth, but didn't draw in. Cragen was content for him to hold it, letting the trail boss hang on to his pride by not taking a drag.

Luke worked faster than Grady had ever seen him move. The man might be half-witted, but he was trail wise. He chose the Indian's surefooted paint to load the supplies on. Grady wondered when he disappeared for a while, and had about decided he had gone to relieve himself, when Luke returned with the team's hobbles and tossed them in a wagon. The horses would be gone down the canyon.

Cragen dipped up a bowl of stew and ate slowly and deliberately, watching the faces of what was left of the crew. He studied the expressionless face of Little Bear. Good man, that one. The old man, Lou, was broken by the death of his son. Grady, good man there also. Still in command of himself even though he was about to become a dead man. Like me, Cragen thought. The woman, she was obviously scared. She expected to be raped. She kept her eyes down, pretending that if she didn't look at him, he would not notice her. She felt his eyes on her and she looked up and met his humorous gaze. He grinned, and she dropped her eyes to the ground.

Luke came over to the fire. "OK, boss."

Grady looked around the camp. Yancy held three horses saddled and packed for the trail. The others on the stake line had been released and scattered downhill. Each saddle on the horses had a rifle, and a rain slicker. Luke was wearing Scratch's winter coat.

"I guess you want my coat?" Grady addressed Cragen, who laughed out loud. He was enjoying this.

"No, Grady, you'll be needing your coat."

"What am I, a hostage?"

"No, you'll come willingly."

"Like hell I will."

"I figured it out," Cragen spoke softly and leaned forward grinning with eagerness, "See how this sounds."

Grady nodded, willing to listen.

"You and I didn't get to finish our fight, right?"

"Right. Go on." Grady answered.

"We'll finish it now. The fight will decide." Cragen grinned.

"Will you get the hell on with it," Grady exploded.

"If you win, Luke and Yancy go free with the supplies. You get to free your folks."

"Agreed." Grady answered through gritted teeth.

"If I win, you go willingly with us, and I won't kill your people, just leave them tied."

"What if I answer no? They could freeze in this weather before they got loose."

Cragen laughed. "'Then you go unwillingly, and I kill all four."

"What if I refuse to fight?"

"I kill you all right now." Cragen's grin spread.

"I guess I don't have a choice, then. It looks like I fight whether I like it or not."

"Yeah, Grady. Luke, do you understand the rules? Grady and I are going to have a fight. No matter who wins, the two of you get on those horses and take those supplies and get the hell out of here. If I win, and I may be in no condition to determine that, you load both Grady and me on horses and get us out of here. Leave the folks where they are, and stoke the fire for them. Repeat what I just told you."

Luke hung his head and glared at Grady. "If he wins we go. If you win I take you with me. I don't hurt the folks, and I build up the fire."

"Good boy. That's very good."

"Can he be trusted?" Grady asked.

"You should know the answer to that by now." Cragen grinned and patted Luke on the shoulder. "And Luke, if that longhorn shows up, put a bullet right here," he pointed his finger and touched Luke between the eyes. Luke grinned, licked his lips, and looked from Grady to Cragen.

Grady hoped Deadly stayed with the herd tonight.

Cragen turned and went to the trees, Grady presumed, to relieve himself. He wished he could do the same.

"You can't do this," Cecile sobbed.

"It seems to be my only choice. Otherwise, we all die."

"But we will die anyway. We'll freeze to death." Tears ran down her cheeks.

"Maybe not. I think I can beat him, but he's a lot stronger now than he was a couple of weeks ago. Walking and hefting that wagon has put muscles on him. I should have taken your advice, Little Bear, and put a bullet through all their heads when we first captured them."

"Stay away from him. Don't let him get hold of you," Little Bear spoke low.

"Watch that bear hug of his," whispered Cook.

"Oh God, this isn't happening. We can't just sit here," Cecile began to scoot along the ground. Cragen came out of the woods and she stopped as he walked toward them.

"Luke, take the girl and the old man and tie them to the grub wagon wheels."

Luke untied Cecile's feet and helped her up. He held her arms as she hung back. When they reached the wagon she broke free and ran for the trees. She could hear Cragen laughing as Luke chased her. She had no balance without her hands, and her foot slipped on the gathering snow. She fell and rolled, landing against a tree as Luke caught up with her. He was mad. She had made him look bad to Cragen. He picked her up and threw her over his shoulder, carried her back to the wagon, and lashed her tightly to the wheel, pulling her legs up and tying them to the wheel also. She could hardly move. Her eyes fled to Cragen. "Don't kill anyone else. I'll go with you."

"That's right kind of you, Miss McNamara. If Mr. Grady loses, I may take you along." Cragen chuckled.

He walked over to Little Bear and released his feet. "Up." The Indian rose. "That tree." Cragen pointed to a tree close to the camp. He tied the Indian securely, wrapping the rope several times about his body and legs.

Luke had dragged Lou to the other wheel and secured him.

He didn't want to be made a fool of again. The cook was tied to the yoke of the grub wagon. Cragen, satisfied that all the members of the crew had a ringside seat, motioned Luke to help him, and they dragged the bodies of Ace, the dog, and the boy down the hill toward the spring, leaving red trails of blood across the snow.

Lou watched Denny's body as it slid down the hill. Tears rolled down his cheeks. Cook cussed. Cecile stared in horror. Bear began to work his ropes up and down on the tree bark. Cragen and Luke came back up the hill into the camp. Luke took a stand with a rifle where he could watch both the fight and his prisoners. Yancy took a position across the campfire from Luke, securing the area so he could support Cragen.

CHAPTER THIRTY

Cragen removed his handmade blanket coat and slowly undid the buttons on his shirt. The garment was nearly a rag after the weeks of wear. He threw the shirt in the fire. Flexing strong, bulging muscles, he grinned and strolled around the fire, stretching, shadow boxing, and putting on an exhibition for the prisoners. He stopped in front of Cecile and made the muscles of his biceps leap into full power.

Cecile watched in silence, both hate and fear radiating to Cragen. He laughed and strolled over to Grady. A few quick flicks of a knife, and Grady stood free. He rubbed the circulation back into his hands.

"Take your time, Trail Boss. I'll have a smoke. When you're ready let me know." Cragen backed to the other side of the fire and crouched to his heels. Like an animal, his eyes shone red in the campfire light as he rolled himself a cigarette.

Grady went to the fire and crouched, warming his hands and body, removing the stiffness caused by the cold. He wanted to jump the man, beat him senseless into the soggy snow-wet mud, but he knew he needed to warm his muscles first. It would take more than desire to beat this man. It would take all the knowledge and strength that he possessed.

When Grady had warmed both his front and back, he removed his jacket, folded it and laid it over the grub wagon wheel. Then he removed his sheepskin-lined vest, folded it neatly, and put it on the coat. He began to unbutton his shirt; aware that Cragen's eyes were glued to his action.

Grady looked up, catching Cragen unaware, and saw the craven desire in Cragen's eyes as they traveled over his chest. Cragen saw Grady watching him, and the hungry look turned to laughter. Once again the grinning face was in command, but now Grady knew. He knew why Cragen chose to take him with him. He understood now the strange magnetism of the man, the control he had over his men. "You bastard," Grady snarled, "Take a good look, man, because that's all you'll ever get."

Cragen threw back his head and laughed uproariously. When he had collected himself he said, "I think not, Grady. Some things are inevitable. It's been a long trail drive, and I've waited patiently. Now it's my turn." The words were slow, but when the last word was spoken Cragen leaped across the fire, hitting Grady in the abdomen with his shoulder.

Grady was ready for the attack. He had held his breath, tightening his muscles and back, and had stepped back as Cragen crashed into him. The breath was not knocked out of him as Cragen had planned. Grady rolled free, bounding to his feet. Cragen, like a cat, recovered his feet a split second behind Grady. The two men stood slouched, eyeing each other, looking for an opening. Grady knew he had to stay away from Cragen's reaching arms, arms that could crush a man.

Cragen moved forward, and Grady danced back. Cragen laughed and lunged, reaching for Grady, who stepped aside, spun in a circle, and backed farther into the shadows.

Luke yelled, "Stay in the firelight, or I'll put a bullet in you."

Cragen lunged again. Grady sidestepped, this time jamming his fist into Cragen's nose as he passed, spun again, and backed back into the firelight. The light of the fire now to his back, Cragen had to come to him with the fire glow in his eyes, while Grady was a silhouette against the fire.

This time Cragen came forward slowly, dodging from one side to the other as Grady tried to avoid him. With the fire in back of him and Cragen advancing, Grady leaped in, slashed a fist into Cragen's jaw, and jumped back. Cragen laughed and advanced another step.

Grady turned, jumped the campfire, and wheeled to face Cragen. "What the hell kind of a face have you got? That blow should have dropped you."

"One of my better features. Come on, Grady, you can't run forever. I am going to give you a good thrashing."

Grady could see the gleam in Cragen's eyes. The man was actually looking forward to beating Grady senseless. Grady supposed the man had a
right to be bitter and seek revenge, but his eagerness put those reasons
aside. The man was really looking forward to beating Grady into submission. Submission to what? Grady knew. He could see the reason in Cragen's
eyes. Grady was fighting for a lot more than his life.

Cragen came around the fire, advancing slowly, dodging as before.
Grady backed away from him, watching for the catlike leap he knew Cragen was capable of. It came suddenly and before Grady could dodge. A
sledgehammer blow sent Grady reeling backward. He rolled as he fell, to
avoid Cragen, who intended to pin Grady to the ground. The accumulating
snow was cold to his skin. Grady grabbed a handful of snow as he rolled.
He gathered all his strength, got his feet under him, and moved quickly
away from Cragen's reaching hands. Grady rubbed the cold snow across his
face, shook his head to clear the ringing, and kept moving back as Cragen
rose and advanced.

Cragen leaped again. Grady's foot slipped on the snow as he tried to
dart sideways away from the grasping fingers. He fell to his back on the
ground, and Cragen was on him. Grady threw two quick, sharp punches to
Cragen's nose, feeling and hearing them hit soundly. Cragen didn't seem
to feel the punches. He was busy trying to grab the flying hands and pin
Grady's body to the ground. Grady twisted to his side, throwing Cragen off
balance, but the man grabbed Grady by the throat, and shaking him like a
rat, threw him back to the ground, Cragen once again on top.

Grady, using both hands, tried to pry Cragen's hands from his throat.
His breathing halted. He lifted a leg and threw it upward and over Cragen's
head. The spur on his boot dug deep into Cragen's cheek. Using all his
strength and back muscles, Grady began to pull Cragen backward, the spur
digging into the man's face, tearing a huge gash across the jaw and cheek.

As Cragen went over backward he clung like a leech to Grady's throat,
choking harder. Grady, eyes bulging, brought both arms straight up through
Cragen's arms, and with all his strength broke the hold. Cragen, switching from dogged tenaciousness to panther-like swiftness, rolled backward,
regained his feet, and leaped again, pinning Grady to the ground before he
could catch his breath or regain his feet.

Now, with his great strength, Cragen turned Grady face down, forced one arm behind his back, and pulled up one leg and locked it behind the knee of the other. With a leg, and his body weight he controlled Grady's legs. He used leverage on Grady's arm, threatening to tear the shoulder from the socket. Grady screamed in pain.

Cragen laughed. He reached under Grady's stomach and loosened his belt buckle. Grady struggled to free himself, and Cragen yanked on the arm. Grady screamed again, and waited in agony until Cragen let up on the arm. His other hand didn't cease. The fingers loosened the belt, the buttons, and Grady could feel them reaching, pulling hair as they reached under his clothing.

The son of a bitch. In anger Grady struggled to free himself. Cragen laughed, put pressure on the arm, bent over, and whispered in Grady's ear, "Don't fight it, man. You may like it."

"You fucking son of a bitch." Grady screamed.

"You're right, Grady, that's just what I am."

Grady cringed as the hand began to caress his stomach, moving slowly down to his groin. He cursed, tears in his throat, as his organ responded. In spite of his revulsion, his body reacted to the caresses.

Cragen was laughing, holding the extended organ in his hand, squeezing slowly, and letting go. Grady, humiliated, forgot the pain and struggled like a crazed animal. Cragen removed his hand to control the man, but now he was dealing with soiled pride. Grady was a man hardened to the trail, hours in the saddle, his muscles developed over years of hard work. And he was a man crazed with indignation.

The two rolled on the ground. Grady freed his legs and smashed with savage chops, over and over, into Cragen's neck and back. Cragen, not laughing now, struggled to regain control, but the man he fought was no longer fighting like a man. He clawed, and kicked, ripped with spurs. He knew it was useless to hammer at Cragen's head. Blows pounded into kidneys and groin, spurs raked, digging holes in Cragen's thighs. Cragen released his hold on Grady's arm and moved to escape, to roll away, but Grady, incensed with fury, wanted to kill. The desire was so strong that he grappled with Cragen, forgetting the powerful bear hug.

As Cragen's arms closed about him, Grady dug his thumbs into Cragen's eyes, and buried his teeth in Cragen's Adam's apple, grinding like a dog, feeling the blood as it ran from his mouth. The pressure, as Cragen's arms tightened, seemed far away. The fact that he couldn't breathe didn't seem to matter. All that mattered was his teeth grinding as he slid into unconsciousness.

When he came to Little Bear was squatting beside him. Instinctively he reached for the buttons to his pants. They were intact, and his belt was fastened. He blushed as he looked into the Indian's eyes. He surprised a rare glint of humor in them.

"You nearly lost yore virginity," the half-breed grinned.

Grady grinned back. "Damn, I think yore more white than Indian. Only a white man would think that's funny."

"Hell, man, even an Indian would laugh at that one."

The two laughed together. Grady sat up, found that Bear had used snow and washed the blood from his jaws. He looked over at Cragen's body. Blood still poured from the severed jugular vein. The laughter was gone, the face was frozen in surprise, and the eyes were staring lifelessly. Grady tasted blood. He didn't think he would ever rid the taste from his memory. He lifted his hand and waved Cragen's body away. Little Bear got up and dragged the body outside of the firelight. Then the Indian released all that were left of the crew, Cook, Cecile, and Lou. A few short hours ago Scratch and Denny had been alive. In such a short time four men had died.

Cecile helped Lou to the fire. He was a broken old man. Cook found the teakettle, filled it with water from the bucket that he had brought from the spring when Ace jumped him. He dug into the supplies and handed Grady a new sack of tobacco. Grady rolled Lou a cigarette then rolled himself one. He felt Cecile sit down beside him. He put his arm about her, and drew her close. The three people sat listlessly staring into the fire.

Little Bear grabbed a rifle and disappeared into the darkness. He followed the trail of the two saddle horses, and the packhorse. That packhorse was a friend of his. He traveled at a run. It was dark, but the trail in the snow was clear. The riders were traveling slowly, picking a trail through the wilderness. The packhorse hung back and fought the rope. Luke cussed, and beat him about the head, only making the animal more obstinate. The Indian's horse was trained to obey only the Indian. He didn't want to follow this man. He struggled to go back trail.

A shot rang out and Yancy dropped from the saddle. Luke released the paint and spurred his horse down the mountain. The paint wheeled and ran to meet the Indian. Both Little Bear and the horse were overjoyed when they met. Satisfied that Luke would hasten to put miles between him and the camp. Little Bear swung onto the horse bareback, without bridle, and the two returned to camp.

Cook stacked wood and made a fire on the other side of the grub wagon, away from the bloody battleground. Soon hot stew and biscuits were ready. Hot coffee odor filled the air. Grady and Cecile helped Lou to the new cook site, away from the blood-soaked snow. He sat in a stupor while Cecile spoon-fed him hot broth from the stew pot. He stared into the flames and like a child opened his mouth and swallowed each spoonful obediently.

Grady got Lou's bedroll and helped him inside it. Cook laced a cup of coffee with the laudanum they had given Cecile, and held the cup as Lou drank. Soon he was asleep.

When Bear returned the four weary people sat around the fire. Cook filled his bowl and sat quietly. Each harbored his own visions of the harrowing nightmare evening, finding comfort in the presence of the others. None of them were hungry, their stomachs were still rebellious. But they were hardy pioneers who knew their bodies needed the hot nourishment to keep going, so they forced down the stew.

Cecile held her bowl in both hands, hands that trembled, and sipped slowly from the edge of the bowl. The chunks of meat and potato she left at the bottom of the bowl. She couldn't swallow them. They would have come right back up.

Little Bear ate heartily. He needed the strength. The burden would be on Cook and him until Grady regained his strength, and lost his muscle stiffness from the fight. Old Lou was no more than the living dead. Bear's mother's people would leave the old man in the wilderness to die, to save food and energy for the living. But Bear was half-white, and Grady was white, and they would care for the old man.

Cook filled his bowl again. He was figuring what was left of the supplies. "Flour's gone, couple of bags of beans left. I got one tin o' coffee in my trunk. Snows will drive the game down the mountain. We can't stay here."

"No, we have to get down the mountains. The freezes up here will be setting in. We can only hope this is a brief storm. The first ones usually are. We've got one more climb before we can start down. We will need the rest of the grain to get the cattle off the mountain. Both wagons are nearly empty, but it would be too difficult to get one over the pass if we load it. But we're too short-handed to drive both wagons."

"I can drive one," Cecile offered.

"Cook's got the grub wagon. I need Bear to help drive the cattle. That still leaves one wagon."

"The grub wagon's near empty. If we crowd up the bedrolls and extras, we could throw a few bags of grain in there." Cook didn't like the idea, but he had the only solution.

"OK, let's get some rest. In the morning we'll bury our dead, and get the hell out of here."

Bedrolls circled the campfire. The falling snow was changing to driving ice as the temperature dropped.

CHAPTER THIRTY-ONE

When the cook rose and looked out the canvas cover of the cook wagon, he shook his head at the white scenery surrounding the camp. Movement caught his eye and he spotted Lou with a shovel, breaking his way through the snow and the frozen top layer of the ground. He watched as the old man doggedly dug, clearing rocks and brush to provide a burial area for the four men.

Cook climbed out of the wagon and started breakfast. He used some of the oats and made hot oatmeal, and coffee. Grady and Little Bear woke and helped Lou dig. The men dug silently. There wasn't anything they wanted to talk about. One big hole was dug for the two outlaws, and both men were dragged into it and covered. They dug Scratch and Denny separate graves.

Lou spoke for the first time, "Denny would want Devil buried with him. They was pretty good friends, and I'll feel better knowing he's got a friend with him."

Grady nodded, and the young boy and the dog were buried together.

When the graves were covered, a short service was held. Grady spoke over the graves, and Cecile put crosses she had made from tree limbs at the heads of Scratch and Denny's graves.

Breakfast was a sad, silent meal. Lou refused oatmeal, but drank several cups of hot coffee. When the rest were nearly finished eating, he spoke. "Denny was a good boy. I'll miss him. Only real thing I ever done in my life

I could be proud of." He seemed to shake a load from his shoulders. "Now we got a job to do. We got to get Miss Ceci home. This ain't no country for a lady. No lady should see the things that took place here. We got to take her home."

"Right, Lou, you're right. We are going over the pass and get these cows off this mountain. Do you think you can drive a wagon?"

"Hell, yes. I been driving one, ain't I?"

"You bet. Let's move on out. We'll trail the herd and the horses together."

CHAPTER THIRTY-TWO

The next few days were difficult. Intermittent showers of snow kept the weather damp and cold. Winds increased the chill factor. The little group was miserable. Food was meager and travel difficult. The trail was not defined. They would have lost their way as the snow grew deeper if it weren't for Deadly's instinctive sense of direction.

The only cheerful moment was the discovery of another young calf dropped during the night. This baby was purebred Hereford, a little heifer calf. This baby joined the first one in the back of one of the carts. At least they would have plenty of milk.

Deadly worked hard. The little cows didn't like climbing over snow-drifts, falling into blind holes covered with snow. The horses had to be loose hobbled to keep them from running off down hill and leaving everyone behind. Little Bear and Grady had to help the wagons, leaving Deadly to watch the herd. At night the herd crowded around the grain wagon to receive their meager allowance of oats. The supply was dwindling rapidly.

They made the pass and began the descent. Going down was not much easier than going up. The wagons strained at the brakes and required ropes tied to saddle horses to keep them from crashing down the mountainside. Grady and Little Bear had practically no time to watch the herd, so a method was worked out. Cecile joined them, and for several hours they would drive the herd, then slow it down and turn it over to Deadly. Then all three would ride back and take one wagon at a time to catch up with the herd. It was tedious, slow work.

Bear caught a few rabbits. No one seemed to mind the short rations. They were all too tired and cold. They climbed into their bedrolls early, too tired to carry on a conversation.

Grady knew they could not go on like this. He had to get them down the mountain where the storms would not be so severe, and Bear could find meat. Then he would have to go it alone.

Several days later the herd came into a mountain valley where the snow was shallow enough for the cattle to dig for grass. There was only enough grain to last another week.

Grady told the crew to make camp. "Throw up lean-tos. Dig in and get as comfortable as you can. You may have to shovel snow down to the grass to feed these cows before I get back. For the first time, I'm glad we are only driving seventy-two head. Cook, put me up some jerky, if we've got it. I don't need anything else. I'll leave first thing in the morning."

Little Bear began a log and branch shelter for the campfire. Miss Ceci could sleep in the grub wagon, but they would need a central area for warmth and food, out of the weather. He didn't get far that night. The corner posts were set and the cross posts tied to prevent them from falling. Grady had set about gathering what warm clothing he could find and was packing his saddlebags. He had raided the false bottom of the grub wagon and taken enough cash to purchase supplies and hire men. He wrapped a bandage around one of his thighs and hid the money in the cloth folds. He had seen men take everything a man owned, leaving him naked, and usually dead.

They were all up to see him off. All of them knew how critical things were. If anything happened to Grady, they might not all die, but the fate of the herd was certainly grim.

"Little Bear is going to keep meat in camp, but just in case none can be found you will butcher a cow."

"Of course we will. You mustn't worry about us. Just take care of yourself, and hurry back." A big tear ran down Cecile's face.

"Don't you worry none about us, boss. I'll see to Miss Ceci myself," Lou stammered. He had taken over the care and comfort of Grace Cecile McNamara, making her a substitute for his dead son.

Bear shook Grady's hand, and Cook waved a hand and motioned for him to get moving. He was about to turn to his horse when Cecile ran to him. He pulled her into his arms, and she wrapped her arms around him. She wept but her lips sought his. They clung to each other, and their kiss felt right.

"I don't want you to go," she whispered.

Grady was surprised by the kiss from Cecile, but he welcomed it. "Shoo, Don't cry, girl. I'll be back before you know it." This was not the proud and haughty woman he had met in San Diego.

This drive had nearly broken her spirit. What a shame he thought. He pressed his lips to hers in an effort to stop the quivering. She tightened her arms, drawing him closer to her, and hungrily returned his kiss. He could taste the saltiness of her tears, and the sweet promise of more kisses to come. Now was not the time. He gently removed her arms and held her from him.

"Ceci, you don't have to worry about me. That good-bye will keep me going, and looking forward to a kiss waiting for me will hasten my return." He bent over and kissed her lightly and felt her lips reaching for his again. Tearing himself away was hard, but he turned and swung to his saddle. "I'm taking Deadly with me. He needs the vacation."

As he rode from the clearing, he looked back and waved. Cecile had followed to the edge of the camp. She waved and blew a kiss. He could see her worried expression. He was worried also, but he smiled as he rode off.

CHAPTER THIRTY-THREE

Three days had passed. Grady rode over one more rise. Each day he dropped lower leaving the black storm clouds rolling heavily together, concealing the distant mountain ranges. Grady frowned as worry over the people he had left in the small valley continued to plague him. At night, after a meager fare of kettle tea, and jerky, he rolled in his blanket and stared at the flickering flames of the campfire, his thoughts drifting back to the valley.

In his imagination he felt Cecile in his arms and tasted her sweet mouth against his. As his body responded to his daydreams, the pleasant anticipation would turn into bitter humiliation as his thoughts would turn to the way he had felt when Cragen had cradled Grady's organ in his hand. He felt ashamed of his response. He would shake away the unpleasant thoughts and drift into exhausted sleep, awaking the next morning to repeat the grueling journey another day.

Deadly had been delighted when he realized he and Grady were traveling on alone. This was more like it. Just the two of them, like old times. The first day he had taken the lead eagerly, leaving the pending snowstorms behind him. When they stopped to make camp each evening, Grady shared his meager fare. He gave Deadly biscuits, but something was missing.

Frequently during the long nights Deadly would face the lofty mountain range and test the air. His instinct told him they had narrowly escaped a severe winter storm. He missed Trumpeter. He would lower his nose to Grady's bedroll and with tail to the wind doze until daybreak.

The fourth day out, the weary horse carelessly stepped in a crack in the rocky mountainside, and his right foreleg snapped with a loud crack, and sent the horse plunging headlong into a ravine. Grady was thrown into a hard bed of stones and rendered senseless. He came to in the familiar half-world of consciousness thinking he was once again in his bedroll suffering from an agonizing hangover. The familiar shape of Deadly moved as he attempted to rouse Grady from what he supposed was a sluggish sleep.

The thudding head pain took on the sharp pains of an injury. Deadly ceased to shove as his friend began to move. It was about time. He had about given up rousing the man. The horse had tired from trying to rise with the broken leg, and lay helplessly where he had fallen.

Grady rolled over and groaned as a sharp pain stabbed his shoulder. He must have fallen on the shoulder. His arm hung uselessly as he explored the dislocated shoulder with his other hand. An unconscious thought made him grateful it was his left shoulder that was hurt. He still had the use of his gun arm.

His stiff fingers struggled to loosen the knot of his kerchief. He worked slowly until the loop around his neck grew large enough for him to lift the limp arm and stuff it through the makeshift sling.

Satisfied that his friend was once again moving about, Deadly wandered off to find something to eat. He had found some dried grass to feed on when a pistol shot rang out. He jumped at the unexpected sound, then went on filling his belly. Men were always firing rifles or pistols. It was just one of the annoying things the bull had learned to put up with.

Grady put the pistol back in its holster and lay a comforting hand on the dead gelding. He patted and smoothed the hair along the animal's long, muscular neck. Out of acquired habit he catalogued in his mind that the horse had put on a growth of winter hair as the nights had grown colder. This had been a good animal. Nothing really outstanding about him, but he had responded to Grady's demands and given the man a good day's work without creating friction. He had earned the right to grow old on a good pasture. Grady didn't like the thought of leaving the animal for the coyotes, and wolves, but even without the injured arm he did not have time to bury the animal.

Rising, he unfastens the cinch and tugged to free the saddle from the horse. It remained firmly fixed where the horse lay heavily on the stirrup.

If Grady had had the use of both arms he could have lifted hard enough to free it.

Deadly would have to help. He reached for the lariat fastened to the saddle ties. The leather was stiff with cold. It had been wet from the snow and drizzle, and as it dried it had become stiff. Grady bent down and grabbed one of the ties with his teeth. He couldn't watch his progress. His fingers had to feel as they worked to separate the knotted ties. He was nauseated and his head was filled with pain. He was certain that he had a concussion.

Nausea threatened vomit, gagging him. He retched and let loose his bite on the tie to turn aside and gasp for control. Deep breaths helped and he returned to his effort on the tie. When they loosened, he freed the lariat.

When he had the lariat, he called Deadly, who left feeding, and obediently went to the man. His eyes and nostrils grew large as he picked up the scent of blood. He knew it came from the horse on the ground. He ran his tongue, over his nose, uncomfortable but he stood still and waited patiently for Grady's next move.

Grady looped the rope over Deadly's gleaming horns and tied the other end to the saddle. He put his hand on Deadly's horn and backed the bull away from the dead horse. Deadly paused as he felt the rope tighten. He had been taught not to pull away from a rope when he was tied, but Grady gave him a familiar command to back up and pushed firmly on his horn. Testing to find out if Grady wanted him to back up, the bull took one step and paused. The command came again, and Deadly braced against the tug of the rope and steadily backed, pulling the saddle from under the horse.

"Good, Deadly." Grady patted the bull's neck, fighting the dizziness and sick stomach.

Grady lifted the saddle blankets that had come loose with the saddle and tossed them over Deadly's back. The bull's tail switched in protest, but he did not move away. He had learned early in his life to carry anything attached to him. Before Grady had graduated to trail boss, he had spent many years as a poor cowboy. A good part of the time he was too poor to afford a seasoned horse to pack his grub, and Deadly had been elected to do so to pay his way.

Deadly had carried rattling pots and pans, and bleeding deer, and even firewood. He did not refuse to do these menial jobs, but he switched his tail. He would do it, but he didn't have to like it.

191

Grady removed the bridle from the horse and tied it to the saddle. Deadly would not need guiding. The bull knew the direction as well as Grady, and the bridle was one insult Grady had never tried on the bull.

Grady pulled himself into the saddle. Deadly shifted uncomfortably. This was not right, he bunched his legs to react. Grady patted his neck and crooned, "Easy boy, good Deadly." When the bull relaxed, Grady gave him another pat and said, "Move them out," a familiar order. Slowly, testing the added weight and balance on his back, he moved out. He gained confidence with each step and was soon moving rapidly down trail with his rangy trot, paying little attention to his passenger. He was free of having to pace himself to the horses' endurance.

Grady clenched his teeth, grabbed the saddle horn with his good hand, and tried to brace himself against the pounding jolt of the bull's ground-covering jarring trot.

As the hours wore on, the pain in Grady's head became intense. He wanted to stop the bull, slide off, and lie upon the cool ground. Fever was burning in him, but he held on. He feared he was going to pass out and fall to the ground.

The bull came to a halt to drink at a mountain stream. Grady struggled with one arm to pass his lariat over his head and arms and let it settle to his waist, then he passed the rope through the hole under the horn of the saddle, and back around his waist. He repeated this until the entire length of rope, secured him to the saddle. If he did pass out he could not fall.

As the bull moved on down the trail Grady relaxed in the security of knowing he was firmly attached to the saddle. The jolting trot made his head ring. The torn ligaments in his shoulder screamed with pain, and fever from the inflamed ligaments washed over his entire body. He was positive now that he had a concussion. He kept throwing up, leaning out, until he had nothing left to throw up.

He tried to think. Should he find a place and camp for the night? He pictured himself unsaddling, building a campfire, trying to saddle again. But the man he saw had two good arms. All the pain seemed to come together and blend into one unbearable hurt. Mercifully he passed into unconsciousness, his upper body falling forward over the saddle horn, his hips sliding as far as the ropes would allow down the side of the saddle.

CHAPTER THIRTY-FOUR

Deadly came to an abrupt halt as he felt the man lose his balance. He waited patiently for Grady to regain his seat. When the man didn't move, Deadly reached back and nudged his boot with his nose. There was no response. He tried a second time, harder, putting his nose under the boot and lifting the man's leg away from the bull's side, letting the leg slide off his nose to flop back against his side. Still the man didn't move.

Deadly switched his tail. Fine time for his rider to go to sleep, it would soon be dark and this was no place to stop. Deadly drew in a frustrated breath of air. He did need to catch his breath, but this was ridiculous. He braced himself against the pull of the weight in the saddle. If he didn't watch out the entire rig, man and all, would be under his belly. The giant tail whipped the air impatiently.

Deadly gazed down the trail. They would have been off the mountain soon, and in the foothills. A few more hours and they would be at the small village of Janos. The tail whipped back and forth. The silver horns tipped nervously up and down in agitation.

In the distance a howl sounded, and was answered by another howl off to the right. Deadly moved some grass out of his cheek and began to chew restlessly as he listened to this chorus. Other howls joined in and it became clear to Deadly that a pack was forming.

The sound was not new to him. He was familiar with the wolves that ranged these southwestern regions. There were several species, one of which was the powerful and vicious lobo that was both large and attractive. They had an independent air, self-confident and powerful. They were not sneaking and hangdog. They were large like a mastiff, with large white spots on their sides. They feared nothing. They mated eagerly with Indian dogs, forming large packs in the winter months of half wolf, half dog, wise in the ways of men, half-starved and vicious. They hunted through mountains and foothills like a plague, killing and devouring everything in their path.

Deadly shoved the cud back into the pocket in his cheek, and gingerly moved down the trail. He had to lean opposite the weight threatening to slide off of his back. With each step he felt surer that his load would stay put if he walked smoothly. His feet glided in an even rhythm, interrupted only when he had to hesitate and search for footing.

The howling of the wolves was growing closer. It seemed he was headed to meet them. He wanted to turn back up the trail and put miles between himself and the pack, but instinct told him he could not outrun the pack, and this was no place to stop and wait for them.

He wanted to increase his pace, but the unsteady burden protested by sliding dangerously more to the side, so he steadily worked his way along the trail as the sun went down and darkness took over. His eyes adjusted to the gradual light change as he continued to travel.

The howling had stopped and for a long while, maybe an hour, the only sounds he heard were his own hooves striking the rocks in the trail. But he did not forget the pack. They would be out there trailing him in the dark, at a safe distance, until hunger made them bold enough to close in.

He smelled water. His nostrils flared, reaching for the scent. Saliva slid from his mouth, his coarse tongue reached out to clean his nostrils in an attempt to sharpen their senses. He stopped and tested the air. The odor of water came from the right of the trail. He stood still, listening to the night, and from the corner of his eye he caught the flash of an animal as it passed between the trees. He swung his body in that direction and took another reading. The air now carried the odor of wolf. It was time, decision time. He had not come to a good place to fight. Openness was all around him, scattered with convenient brush to hide his enemies. What would he find if he left the trail? Did he dare do it?

He rapidly made a decision, turned and glided smoothly through the brush, winding his way among the brush. A furry body crossed in front of him, eyes gleaming red in the dark. He could hear growls now as they snapped at each other as they ran. The damp smell was stronger now. He would soon be on top of it.

Pain tore at his back leg. He kicked out and landed a solid blow on a furry body, which emitted a yelp of pain, struck the ground, rolled, leaped to its feet, and disappeared into the underbrush.

Then he felt the water splashing about his feet. It was a small stream, only a few feet across and maybe a foot deep at the most. Not much, but the time had come. They were attacking. He swung to face the wolves as they ran toward him.

The heavy horns swung low, catching a shaggy black mongrel under the stomach, lifted him off the ground, and hurled him into the stream. Pain shot through his shoulder. A big, dark-gray lobo clung tenaciously to the bull's hide, his teeth grinding slowly into the muscle. The bull used his teeth like the dog, biting solidly across the spine, snapping the backbones. The dog screamed, dropped to the water, its back legs useless as it tried to drag itself away from the desperate bull.

Three wolves were already working to gain a hold on the bull's back legs. Their teeth were grinding the flesh dangerously close to the hamstrings. Deadly whirled to protect himself. Grady swung limply off to the side. The saddle slid over the ridge of the bull's back and continued its path downward, and dumped Grady into the water.

The smell of man overpowered the sweat of the bull, and now became part of the mouth-to-mouth battle as the pack darted back and forth ripping at the bull. Now they were getting the taste of man. Frightened, one by one the Indian dogs of the pack pulled back to the dry bank; camp discipline strong in their subconscious. For the moment they retreated, but the true wolves eagerly increased their attack.

The pain of the sharp bites, and the water as it filled his mouth, brought Grady to his senses. He was strangling. The icy chill of the cold water was shocking. He had drifted back and forth into unconsciousness for hours. He had not fought it, as even in semi consciousness he was aware that Deadly was still on the trail and headed down hill. He had been aware that it was night and had not questioned Deadly's judgment to continue. But he must make himself come out of it. He was strangling, drowning. He was being dragged through water. His arms and legs struck out. The dislocated shoulder wrenched with pain and he cried out, his mouth filling with water. Something bit his leg hard enough to draw blood. He kicked out, struggling, and his feet hit the muddy floor of the creek.

Now he had direction. He tried to turn and get both feet under him, but he couldn't, and then he remembered he had tied himself to the saddle. Coughing and strangling, he felt for the rope. He hung down from the saddle that now swung on the underside of the bull. Reaching up with the good arm, he grabbed the saddle horn and pulled his head up out of the water.

Deadly swung, keeping the wolves on the bank in front of him and his back legs in the middle of the stream. Grady lost his hold on the wet leather and dropped back into the water. Coughing and cussing, he grabbed again for the handhold. His head was clearing, and he knew he had to keep his head up out of the water, or he was done for. He timed it when the bull stood still for a moment and shifted his handhold to the girth, around the bull's belly. He could hardly work his fingers under it, but he needed the security and the height from the water that the girth afforded.

His head safely out of the water, he worked his legs until he was on his knees, his body still tied to the saddle. Deadly swung his rear end the other way, and with sheer willpower Grady hung on to the girth as he sprawled again under the icy water.

Pulling himself upright, he let go a stream of cusswords directed at the bull. Then he saw them in the shadowy darkness. At first only a movement as the wolf darted forward, gaining confidence, the gnawing hunger taking precedence over the wolf's fear.

Wolves! Shit! Grady's eyes tried to pierce the blackness surrounding them. Another movement. There were at least two, maybe more—too many for Deadly to battle handicapped with the saddle, and the man, under his feet.

If he still had his gun they might have a chance. He struggled to get his feet under him again. He was still coughing from strangling in the cold mountain stream. Between fits of coughing he talked to Deadly. "Steady, fella. Easy, Deadly."

He tested his balance and found he was steady. He would try to let go of the girth and reach for the gun. If Deadly moved he could end up back in the freezing water. If there was no gun—Hell! He wasn't going to think that way. He had to take the chance.

When Deadly heard Grady's voice coughing and cussing he was relieved, it was about time the man woke up. He could use some help. He was confident Grady would have a solution to the problem. Grady's voice calmed and soothed him. He stood still listening to the voice, a wary eye on the wolves on the bank.

The pistol shot was loud in the darkness. Deadly heard the fatal yowl of a wolf, and smelled its blood as it spattered over the bank.

The man had a fire stick. The wolves fled and did not see the pistol fall into the water as the man dropped it to reach for the girth, before he was plunged, once again, into the icy water. Deadly had jumped at the sound of the pistol. Familiar with the results when a rifle or side arm was fired, he was not surprised when the wolves turned and fled. To his way of thinking, it was about time Grady did something.

Satisfied that the wolves were gone, the bull climbed to the dry bank and stopped. Although burdened by the dragging man, the switching tail was the only evidence of his annoyance.

Grady sagged to the ground. He was beyond uncomfortable. His waist was still secured tightly to the saddle and only his shoulders and knees rested on the ground. He could end up with a broken back if he didn't get free.

He felt for his pocketknife with frozen fingers, located it in his soaking wet pocket. He had trouble freeing it. It took several sawing motions with the small knife to sever the many wet strands of the lariat. When he dropped to the ground he scooted to get out from under the bull's hooves, exhausted. He passed out.

When he came to he did not know how long he had lain there freezing, shivering, his teeth chattering and his fingers stiff from cold. "Deadly," he called out for the bull.

Deadly had tried to get away from the saddle. He had walked sideways, tried backward, used a hoof, hit at it a few times, and then decided to put up with the discomfort. He had tried to waken Grady a time or two with a shove of his nose; then finally in resignation, he had gone in search of food. He had not wandered far, and he heard Grady's call. Returning to the man's side, he stood while Grady used the attached saddle girth to pull himself to his feet.

Grady was shaking from cold and weakness. His feet were numb from the wet boots. He was a goner. If he passed out again he could call it quits. There was something he had to do. He tried hard to remember, but the freezing cold made him pull his thoughts back to the predicament at hand. He tried to lift the saddle. He was so weak the effort brought him dangerously close to passing out. That would never do.

He sank against the bull until his head cleared, then felt his way around to the other side and located where the girth was fastened. His fingers were numb, and he had only one good arm. The girth had tightened from the weight of dragging the man, the wet leather of the girth resisted loosening.

Grady kept at it persistently, pulling and tugging, and resting against the bull when dizziness threatened to bring on a blackout. He was so cold he could hardly stand it, but he had to fix the saddle, and get back on his horse. He was well into delirium, no longer recognizing the bull. He couldn't remember why, only knew, it was life, or death.

The girth finally gave, and Grady worked loose the intricate knot that kept the saddle fastened on the horse. The saddle dropped to the ground, Deadly started to walk away from the aggravation that had caused him so much discomfort.

"Whoa, horse, Whoa, man," Grady crooned to the animal. He was out of his head. Habit caused him to pick up the saddle and lift it back in place over the bull's back. The saddle blanket had drifted with the rushing spring currents, the efforts to receive it beyond the ability of the injured man.

Deadly switched an impatient tail and dipped a horn in an annoyed gesture. Grady crooned soothingly and fumbled with his good hand to tighten the girth. Deadly swung his head around and gave Grady a rough shove.

"Whoa, boy," Grady crooned and continued to tug and shove, forming the intricate knot that would secure the saddle. When it was finally finished he grabbed the saddle horn, and with tremendous effort, dragged himself up onto the saddle, dizziness exploding in his brain. The fever became so strong that tremors began to rack his body, competing with the shivers of the freezing cold. He grabbed the horn with his good hand and slumped forward, his teeth chattering. He kicked the animal.

Deadly moved out, insulted by the kick. The man in the saddle swayed precariously, so Deadly slowed to a steady, easy walk that did not cover ground as fast as Deadly preferred to travel. But in a short time he could see the lights of the town. They were still several miles away, but the bull ambled steadfastly on, glad to know that soon there would be hay and grain.

CHAPTER THIRTY-FIVE

Grady pulled himself up to the rim of the tunnel where the light burst in a blinding splash across his brain. He shut his eyes and tried to filter the light in slowly. He had made this trip several times, but he always slid back into darkness. He knew there were people trying to reach him. He had cried out to them. It was important that they reach him. He had something to tell them.

At first there was only confusion. He kept seeing blood soaking into the snow, and there was the taste of blood in his mouth. He tried to spit it out. He was drowning in blood. Ceci wiped his face with cool rags. She was always crying out to him. He wanted to comfort her, but he kept sliding back into the blackness of the tunnel.

The effort to hold on to the rim of the tunnel made him break out in a sweat. He kept testing his eyes, letting a little light filter in each time. Ceci was reaching out to wipe off the perspiration.

He could see her through half closed lids. She looked like an angel, the light a halo around her head.

"Senor, you must wake up, Senor." A man's guttural voice came from the angel. It confused Grady, and he felt himself sliding back into the darkness.

"Leave the man alone. Can't you see he's trying to come out of it," a woman's voice spoke angrily. That was the angel speaking. Someone else was in the room. Grady fought to regain consciousness. He struggled to open his eyes. There were definitely two people by the bed. Disappointment covered him as he realized the woman was not an angel. She wasn't even Cecile McNamara. She had that worn, ageless look of the frontier women.

By the woman's side was a man wearing a huge, black, Mexican sombrero. It covered the head of a tall, slender, gray-haired Mexican. A colorful serape hung to his knees.

"Go find the doctor. You can talk to him later," the woman commanded. The sombrero obeyed and left the room.

"Now you just hang in there until Doc gets here. Don't you dare go back to sleep!" This was definitely a command. He didn't want to disobey, so he struggled to clear his head. Gradually the room took on form, and the woman leaning over him looked less like an angel as his eyes began to focus, and more like the saloon girls he had partied with in trail towns from Texas to San Diego.

Too much face paint, hair color, and stiff stays.

"That's it, honey. Open up those eyes and look at Candy. That's a good boy." She reached into the washbowl by the bed and pulled out a washcloth, steaming from the hot water it had been floating in. "Damn, that's hot," she exclaimed as she both tossed the rag from one hand to the other. When it reached a temperature she was comfortable with, she capably washed his face, not missing a crevice, or an earhole. The roughness of the cloth and her firm but gentle cleansing felt good, and he smiled, weakly, to show his thanks.

"Well, that's more like it. For a while we didn't think you were going to make it."

An elderly man entered the room, and came to lean over the bed. The girl moved aside so he could examine the cowboy, conscious now, but having to struggle to remain so. With skilled hands the doctor drew back Grady's eyelids and studied the insecure focusing of the pupils. The man stuck an instrument in his ear and placed the other end on Grady's chest.

"Hell, Doc. Tell us how he is," the girl demanded. "Shut up, Candy. Let me listen to his breathing."

The girl spun and left the room. The man in the sombrero moved closer and filled the space she had occupied.

"Sounds like a damned sawmill," the doctor growled out loud to himself. He straightened up and yelled toward the door. "Candy, bring him some chicken broth. Try to get it down him."

The girl returned with a cup, and Grady could smell the chicken broth, and realized that he was hungry. The first few spoonful's went down his chin and under his neck, but with practice he managed to coordinate opening his mouth in time with the woman's forceful attitude toward spooning the savory broth into Grady's uncooperative mouth.

"He'll mend now, Candy. You girls did a good job. Hadn't been for the care you took of him he wouldn't have made it through the first week."

"Just in a day's work, Doc. You know us gals specialize in caring for the gentlemen." A teasing laugh floated from her throat, and the doctor grinned an embarrassed understanding.

"He'll be up and around in a few weeks."

A few weeks! An explosion of white, blinding light flooded Grady's mind. He had been laying here a week? Two weeks? He had to get back to the herd. No telling how bad the weather was in those mountains, and they had very few supplies. He tried to push away the bowl, but his arms were weak and uncoordinated. He tried to lift himself up, fighting to breathe, pain in his head and stabbing pain in his chest. He screamed as he put weight on the now relocated and taped shoulder. He had forgotten about the shoulder, but the searing pain brought it back to memory.

Hands reached for him and forced him back on the bed. The light burst and scattered and turned into rainbows, then faded into darkness as he passed out. He sank back into the tunnel, but he could still hear the woman.

"Hell, Doc, you don't suppose he's going to be out for another two weeks?"

"No, I don't think so. He'll come around, but don't expect him to regain a lucid mind for several days. And keep those mustard plasters on his chest. He had enough to handle with a concussion, and that dislocated shoulder. No telling how long he was in those wet clothes. That pneumonia would've killed him if you ladies hadn't taken turns around the clock to keep him doctored. He purty damn near owes you girls his life."

"Senor Medico," the Mexican asked. "Will the cowboy be able to talk soon?"

"Don't know, Mr. Avilas. We'll just have to wait and see."

"I must talk to him. He keeps calling Miss Cecile's name, he calls for "Ceci". I know it is her and he knows where she is."

"I know, Mr. Avilas, I know. We've been over and over this ever since you came into town. I've let you stay in this room for days now so you could talk to him, and the man is trying to tell us. I believe that's what's kept him alive, and that may be what will kill him. He won't rest quiet. He keeps fighting to get up. She's out there somewhere, Mr. Avilas, and he's feeling responsible. But if he doesn't relax and get some strength in his body, he may never get out of that bed."

Relax, or he will never get out of that bed. Relax, or I'll never get out of bed. Relax, or I'll never get out of bed. The doctor's words kept ringing as Grady slid further into the tunnel. He responded by letting loose the sides of the tunnel. He ceased to claw and grab to pull himself up. Relax, or I'll never get out of bed. His mind picked up the ringing words, and his body responded. It sank down into a black pit, floating now, softly turning, slowly getting smaller and smaller. But he was no longer afraid of the tunnel. He welcomed its blanket of warmth and oblivion, and let the darkness cover him.

The doctor watched as Grady's body relaxed and sank limply on the bed. The man had lain motionless, in a coma, for a week, and had been burning up with fever. Now the doctor bent over and felt the man's forehead. "The fever's gone, and he's breathing evenly. Let him sleep. His body is exhausted. We will just have to wait until he wakes up to see if his mind is clear."

Candy saw the expression on the doctor's face and reached a hand to his arm to draw him up to face her. "What do you mean, Doc? I mean about his mind being clear."

"I've seen it happen before. Seen a woman once. Come out of a bad fever, strange, like all her past life was burned out of her head. Didn't know no one, her parents, her husband…didn't even know her kids. Weren't crazy, or nothing, just didn't remember a thing, or a body, after the fever."

"But Senor," The Mexican protested, "the whole time I sit here he talks, he remembers, he calls out. I know Miss Cecile's alive. He talks to her, and he talks to that bull that brought him out of the mountains. I know he remembers."

"That was the fever talking, the delirium, and it's that very fever that can burn the mind away. We just have to wait and see." The doctor left the woman and the Mexican standing by the bed, looking worried.

They both wanted the same thing, but for different reasons. The woman was fighting for a life; one she had helped nurse back to health. A job she had protested in the beginning when the doctor had moved the man into one of her best rooms over the small saloon below. She had made a good living and she had done well, for a woman, in this man's wilderness. The last weeks had given the last mother instinct inside her an opportunity to vent itself. She had fought with the instincts of a mother lion protecting her cub in order to bring this man back to life. She had threatened and driven the girls who worked the upstairs bedrooms, making them responsible for both her absence from the saloon and their chore of watching over this man.

Now there was a possibility that this boy's mind would be gone. This young man, he was probably no younger than she, but she felt so old, so much older. This life, this rugged land with its rugged men, this man, for surely he was a man, not a child, she was not his mother, only his nurse, but she couldn't bear the thought. She had worked so hard to keep him alive. She felt numb. Tiredness flowed through her body.

She lifted a hand and placed it comfortably on the elderly Mexican's arm standing beside her. He also wanted this man to regain consciousness with a sound mind. His reasons were different from hers, but she had learned how deep his concern was over his lost lady patron. This C.C. whoever she was, must be some hell of a gal to have two such men devoted to her.

"Mr. Avilas, I'm going to my room and get some sleep. Will you call me if he wakes?"

"Si, Senorita." The Mexican stood by the bed for a few moments after the woman left the room. He seemed to shrink from the straight, slender height his pride maintained around the others. The lines appeared on his face, and its ageless look was replaced with that of a tired and worried old man.

He sank slowly to one knee beside the bed. He removed the big, black sombrero with its intricate Spanish embroidery, and laid it on the floor beside him. He made the sign of the cross, bowed his head, and prayed. He wanted this man to live, and to live with a good mind, and he prayed for a speedy recovery. It could already be too late for Miss Cecile. Then he rose, replaced his hat, and returned to the chair to wait, as he had done now for days.

CHAPTER THIRTY-SIX

Cecile watched until Grady disappeared in the trees and falling snow. Emptiness filled her, and anxiety set in. She had come to trust and depend on this man's strength, and the crew obeyed his command. With him gone, who would watch over them? She shuddered, trying to shake off the gut instincts of looming disaster.

"Stop this right now, Grace Cecile McNamara." She talked to herself as she walked about gathering firewood. "You are your father's daughter. This is your herd. You are responsible for them, and besides, you have Lou, and Bear and Cook. It will only be a few days and Grady will be back with food and help, and the cattle need the rest." She felt better. Her spirit was bolstered both by the self-assurance and the activity. Her body warmed from the work and soon she had piled a much larger stack of dead branches, and burnable brush than was usually gathered for a night's fire.

She piled the fire up and its heat soon had a pot of water bubbling, its steam rising like smoke clouds in the cold atmosphere that was rapidly dropping in temperature. The storm clouds thickened and the snowflakes became larger and fluffier, falling steadily, building up on the ground until it was a struggle to walk. The hunt for wood became more difficult as the snow grew deeper.

Satisfied that Cook had enough wood to supply him for a while, she changed her wet gloves for a dry pair. She wished she had another pair of boots to change into but had to settle for dry socks. She hung the wet gloves and socks over a branch close to the fire.

Cecile studied the heavy snowfall and eyed the wet items steaming from the heat of the fire. She wondered if the fire's heat could defeat the snow as it fell on the drying items.

Cook had his daily pot of beans cooking. He had watched the girl at her wood gathering, and satisfied she was occupied, and doing a proper job, he went about preparing his area. He set about raising the grub wagon's foul weather canvas, preparing the wagon for the coming storm. Never know about these first snowstorms. Could pass right over. But he had seen them last for days, and when they passed, he had seen snow as deep as the wagon bed. The canvas created a snug area under it where the men could find a place of warmth, by the fire while they ate their meals.

The memory filled him with a sense of urgency. He was so pre-occupied with his work he gave the girl a brief hand wave when she said, "I'll go help the men."

Cecile realized Cook was racing the weather. She headed toward the small canyon's opening where Grady had had them drive the herd. It was an ideal holding pen for a few days. It had a running creek, small but steady, and plenty of forage for a week for the small herd.

She heard the sound of an axe long before she spotted Bear swinging it high over his head and then sharply down, slashing into the slender, but strong, branches of a fallen tree. She was surprised to see he had removed his coat and shirt. Big muscles rippled under his dark skin. She shivered from the cold, but he was working furiously, and the snow melted instantly as it landed on his perspiring skin. Lou was dragging the cut branches to a place where they could close up the entrance to the canyon. It was crude, but effective, brush was piled high, between trees and post that had been added where needed. The Herefords would stay in the little canyon. They would not climb the rocky sides as long as they had food and water.

She tugged at a loose branch, and dragged it over to Lou, who smiled his approval, took it, and worked to lodge the branch into place. She returned for another. The three people worked in this fashion the rest of the day, both the old man and the girl stopping frequently to catch their breath. They marveled at the endurance of Little Bear who worked methodically, pacing himself; he never hurried, never slowed down, and never stopped until they had put the last barrier in place.

That night around the warmth of the campfire Cook ladled out a heaping pile of beans into each pan, then helped himself.

Hot bread sent its heavenly aroma into each hungry soul. All three, tired, ate in silence, sopping up the bean juice with the heavy pan baked bread.

Cecile remembered her gloves and looked for the branch she had hung them on. Cook seeing her, reached over and lifted the lid on a pot sitting on the ground close to the fire. Inside were her gloves and socks dry as toast and just as warm. She smiled, too tired to talk. She pulled off her boots and wet socks, removed the dry socks and gloves from the pan, and put the wet ones in their place. Tucking the dry gloves in her pocket, she crawled under the wagon and into her bedroll. Cook was such a dear. He had laid it out for her. She was so tired. Tomorrow she would thank him.

The men sat quietly around the fire. Lou rolled a cigarette, stuck it in his mouth, and sat staring into the fire, too tired to reach for a stick to light it. His thoughts kept running to his boy lying in the blood soaked snow.

Bear pulled a small clay pipe out of his coat pocket, reached over and pulled Lou's tobacco out of his pocket, filled the pipe, then returned the tobacco to its owner. The old man was lost in thought. Not good to remember. White men had a hard time burying their dead. He liked the Indian custom better.

He found a twig and stuck it into the fire, then touched it to the tobacco, drawing deeply until it caught and he could draw the acrid smoke from the pipe bowl into the stem, letting it out slowly into the night air. Lousy white man's tobacco. He wished he had some peyote nuts to add to it, but he relaxed his body and took what pleasure the pipe gave.

Cook poured another cup of coffee and studied the snowfall. It had been steady all day. It was already a foot deep. As far as he could tell it would snow most of the night. In the pitch black of heavy clouds it was impossible to see if there would be any let up. If it did keep up all night they were in trouble. The cattle would have a difficult time digging down to graze. If old Deadly was here he would teach them prissy cows how to do it. If there was anything Cook hated worse than riding herd on cows, it was working on the end of a shovel. If this storm kept up they would all be shoveling to feed Miss Cecile's cows.

The men took turns feeding the fire during the night. The pile of brush gathered by Cecile earlier in the day disappeared, and each man in his turn made trips into the dark in search of something to burn. Little Bear located a dead tree. He felled it in the black night with the driving snow whipping about him. He chopped by instinct, separating the dead, dry limbs and dragging them closer to the grub wagon. By putting an end into the fire and sliding it forward as it burned, he was able to doze and keep the fire going until morning.

The men woke to a white world. They let Cecile sleep. It would be warm in the bedroll. Cook commenced to dig out his pots and pans. To accomplish the job he had to take the shovel and clear a path around the wagon. The work and the cussing soon warmed him. It wasn't long before coffee water was hot, and the last of the oatmeal was simmering over the fire.

Lou had gone to check on the cattle, and Little Bear had taken the axe and gone in search of more firewood.

When the oatmeal was done and the tallow and sorghum heated, Cook rang out the grub wagon dinner gong, and soon they were all gathered for breakfast.

"The cattle are fine," Lou reported. "The snow's pretty deep, but the canyon's protected enough that there is still some grass showing. If we get much more we're going to have to clear ground for them. Today we better get some kind of lean-to in the canyon, and stock up on firewood here and down there." Lou talked between spoonfuls of oatmeal.

Cook began where Lou ended, "I don't want to scare no one, but that's the last of the oatmeal. There's enough flour for a few more meals but beans are low, a few days maybe. Everyone better keep their eyes open. Anything that moves in this weather we better nail it, even if it's skunk." He smiled to take the sting out of the warning, but they all realized the seriousness of the situation.

"How long do you think it will take Grady to get to a town and back?" Cecile asked. No one answered as she looked from one face to another. They avoided her eyes, concentrating on their oatmeal.

Little Bear reached for the coffeepot and poured a cup of weakened coffee into his cup. Cook was using yesterday's grounds again to save coffee. He spoke quietly, "The Indians have a name for this kind of storm. It's called 'Winter Ghost.' The White Buffalo is fighting with the White Wolf. If the buffalo wins, the storm will pass. If the wolf wins, he will feed on the buffalo, and he can last out the storm even if the snow buries his den."

"If you are trying to scare me, Little Bear, you're doing it. This can't continue. It has to pass."

The men didn't answer. Bear reached forward and stirred the fire. "Grady can't travel in these snow drifts. If this keeps up it could be weeks before he returns." Silence met her amazed disbelief. "Are you telling me we could get snowed in with no food? But we've got the cattle, we can kill one for beef."

All eyes met hers in stubborn defiance. "Oh, no, you don't, not any of you. I'm still the owner of that herd. I am not going to have anyone starving when we have prime beef cattle here." Her chin set and her eyes met theirs glaring with equal stubbornness. "The last thing I want is to have to lose any more of these cows, but your lives are more important than my financial future."

"We won't need to eat yore cows, Miss Ceci. Just forget it. Bear can shoot a deer or something. You just relax. We ain't going to have a Ghost Winter." Lou attempted to sooth her fears.

"Don't pamper me. Don't lie to me. Oh, I'm sorry, I appreciate your concern, but you must all promise me, if it gets bad we will kill a beef. Besides, it's better that we eat them and live than have them starve to death." Tears were in her eyes and her voice trembled, but the men knew she was right.

"Well, I'll take stock of the food and see how many days we can manage. In the meantime, keep your eyes open and your guns ready. And you wear your gun all the time, Miss Ceci," Cook growled. His words had more meaning than just hunting for food.

"What are you afraid of?" she demanded.

Little Bear spoke up, "We won't be the only hungry ones if this storm continues. Bears will hole up for the winter, but the wolves will gather in packs, and with that much meat on the hoof we could be sitting pigeons for the White Wolf." Little Bear sent a look of warning to each face around him.

"Oh my God, you're right. I never gave it a thought. What can we do?" she begged.

Little Bear spoke, "First we do what Lou says. We get shelters made, one here and one in the canyon. That means more firewood. We find anything that will burn, dry brush, dead trees. I'll find some close to camp and clear the area so we can't be snuck up on, and we put the logs up close to both lean-tos, both for convenience and windbreak. Miss Ceci you climb into the grub wagon and rearrange things and make yourself a bedding spot off the ground. Cook can take your place under the wagon, and Lou and I'll share the lean-to we put up in the canyon. We'll all take turns with the fires. Keep it low when we aren't cooking, or warming ourselves, save our fuel as much as possible. We better get moving." Little Bear rose, picked up the axe, picked out a tree close to camp and swung the axe.

"That was the most I've ever heard that Injun talk," Lou said as he rose and left the camp to search for fallen tree limbs.

CHAPTER THIRTY-SEVEN

Cecile went quickly about sorting out the inside of the grub wagon, setting aside anything that might be needed if the weather continued to remain ugly. Sorting the contents of the wagon into piles, occasionally she cried out happily as she uncovered a can of sorghum that had become buried under a pile of rope, or a jar of tomatoes someone had carefully wrapped in a pair of long underwear and stuffed into a bucket. She became amused at herself for becoming excited over these ordinary items, so much more valuable now than the ornate silver and turquoise saddle so carefully wrapped in a blanket to hide its glistening treasure. It was a treasure that had cost Denny his life, and almost cost all of them their lives. Shuddering, she turned her back on the hidden saddle, putting the thoughts out of her mind, but remembering the blanket in case they needed it.

Several times she climbed from the wagon to warm her hands at the fire. It seemed to be getting colder as the day wore on.

All the men came and went. A lean-to of sorts began to take shape on the other side of the fire from the grub wagon.

On one of her trips to warm her hands she found all of the men gone at one time, so she turned, backing up to the flames until she felt the warmth through her heavy skirt. Soon the cloth was so hot she had to rub her backside to keep it from burning. The flesh was tight from the cold, and the heat felt good.

She had not realized when she left her ranch, months ago, that it would be such a long time before she saw it again. She was homesick. How she wished she were standing in the living room of the hacienda, in front of the massive stone fireplace. She could picture a pig turning on the spit in the huge mouth of the fireplace and hear the music of her people strumming their guitars. She could almost smell the pig as its juices dripped into the fire.

"Yore going to catch that skirt on fire if you don't move." Cook's gruff, embarrassed voice announced his arrival. She jumped and realized she was smelling the scorching material as it hit her flesh and burned uncomfortably for a few minutes. She rubbed violently up and down her legs to ease the heat.

Embarrassed also, she grinned at him. "I was daydreaming. I was at home, and there was music, and a pig roasting in the fire-place."

He could sense her homesickness. "Won't be long, Miss Ceci. It's been a rough trip, but I've seen a lot worse. Why, we haven't seen an Indian or had a real stampede. Course them outlaws slowed us down quite a bit. Should have put a bullet through all of them when we first caught 'em. Saved a lot of time and trouble." The cook talked to cover up her embarrassment until he realized he had sent her memory sliding backward to bad memories instead of the happier ones of home and comfort.

"This is a heavy snow for this early, but it should clear soon and give us time to get on home with yore cows. How's the housework coming?" he asked to get her mind off the problems.

"I found some sorghum and a jar of tomatoes, and a sack of salt, and a jar of peaches." She brightened, pleased to report her finds.

"Well, now, we got more goodies than I figured. Let's keep it a secret for a while. We might need a lift if we have to eat beans morning, noon, and night. I got enough to last about a week.

She smiled and returned to the wagon. She arranged everything around the outer edges of the wagon to give her more protection from the cold, and plugged up a tear in the canvas that let in cold air. She noticed her breath clouding up thickly from the increasing cold.

When she had settled her bedroll and thrown some extra saddle blankets on top, she headed once again for the warmth of the fire. The lean-to was taking shape. Most of the frame was made, and Lou was dragging up full branches of fir trees to weave into the frame and make a solid shed against the falling snow. She pulled her gloves on and went to help stack the wood Little Bear had cut into manageable sizes.

As she worked, the log barrier rose to aid in sheltering the campfire from wind and drifting snow. The evening beans had sent their fragrance into the air in spite of the continuous snowfall.

Little Bear soon ceased swinging the axe, and the silence made her realize darkness was coming.

The men headed for the canyon to check on the cattle and horses. Cecile helped Cook. She went to the spring after a bucket of water, and set it to heat by the fire, for later use. It was dark when the men returned. Cecile had started to worry, and her eyes constantly searched the darkness for them. They were nearly in camp when she saw them and breathed a sigh of relief. She was surprised that she had been unable to see farther through the falling snow.

CHAPTER THIRTY-EIGHT

There was an ominous aura that filled the area around camp that night. The winds were bringing the chill factor down to dangerous levels. No one lingered over the fire. They all searched out their bedrolls that had been carried and stacked by Cecile close to the fire to warm.

Cook stood the first watch, ending it several hours later by picking up a long branch, with one end on fire. It glowed some in the dark and gave enough light to make the trip to the canyon. He located the cattle, all huddled together. The horses, hobbled to keep them from easily climbing the canyon walls and escaping, stood restlessly with their tails to the wind. The animals shivered from the drop in temperature, and icicles were beginning to form around their nostrils. The hair under their bellies, where the snow melted from body heat, ran down their sides and froze instantly into jagged icicles.

The glow from the branch faded. The cattle seemed to be settled for the night. Cook woke Lou and hurried back up the trail to climb into his own warmed bedroll.

Morning found the winds blowing with gusty violence. The temperature had dropped so low the falling snow had stopped, but a heavy freeze had set in. The deep piles of snow ceased to drift with the wind, and glazed over, solid.

Little Bear had stood the last watch, and had worked to keep two fires going. Many of the cattle had sunk to the ground. They were crowded together searching for warmth. After the summer heat, they were unaccustomed to this severe cold with snow freezing solidly to their backs, and icicles hanging for inches from the breath of their nostrils.

The Indian had gathered wood and lit a fire as close to the animals as he could without having them move away. He prodded them to their feet, and made them move about to increase their blood circulation. He had to travel farther into the canyon to cut branches to burn. The building of the fence line had denuded the closer areas of brush and trees.

The snow was over his knees, it was difficult to make his way over it and with the freezing of the crust it became slippery, adding to the effort to gather more wood. He crushed and disturbed the freezing crust enough as he worked to make digging down for feed easier for the cattle. The heat from the fire helped some and he kept piling it higher and higher with quickly flammable brush, and then throwing on heavier logs that would keep burning while he chopped down and dragged in another shrub. Each trip back, he prodded any animal that had sunk to the ground and made the herd mill about, and on trips back to the camp he threw enough logs on the campfire to burn until he could return. He grabbed a shovel and used it each trip to keep the path clear between the canyon and the camp.

CHAPTER THIRTY-NINE

When Lou woke, shivering in his bedroll, it was near daybreak. The cold, snapping and crackling about the camp told him he had better get up and about the task of survival. He climbed the path to the upper camp and found Cook already up trying to dig out the grub wagon, cussing as he shoveled, the atmosphere fogged from his breath as he worked.

Lou warmed himself by the fire, got a cup of coffee, and spat the first mouthful out as scalding water with barely a taste of coffee burned the roof of his mouth. He cuddled the tin mug in both hands, warming them, letting the steam from the hot liquid bathe his face as he tested it and sipped slowly. His eyes studied the laden skies.

The snow had ceased to fall as the temperature dropped, and the wind was building, pushing heavy clouds sluggishly across the sky. The thickness and color of the clouds, along with their solidity, gave no immediate hope for relief. The crackling that had wakened him was the solid freeze that seemed to grow before his eyes.

Branches, heavy with snow and dampness, had turned to brittle ice that broke and plunged to the frozen snow below. He observed that their weight did not sink into a soft cover, but shattered on the frozen crust, sending icy particles scattering.

The liquid in his cup was barely warm as he swallowed the last of it. Cook's barrage of cusswords joined with the clanging of pots and pans as he dug them out of the snow that had piled high about the wagon. Lou figured it would be some time before food would be prepared.

He returned to the canyon. He found Little Bear breaking the frozen snow crust. The canyon floor looked like a battlefield. Everywhere, several feet apart, the Indian had dug down to the frozen grass, just enough to uncover it so the cows could find it. Some had already learned to dig out the next clump. The horses had climbed as high as the hobbles would allow, searching for grass on the protected side of the mountain.

Reginald dogged the Indian, pulling at the easiest clumps of grass. Trumpeter followed, pulling at the remaining stubs. Lou could see that Little Bear was exhausted. The old man grabbed the axe that had been left by the embers of the fire. He climbed up the side of the canyon and chopped free, and sent rolling downward, all the brush he could loosen. If this freeze continued another fire would be needed by nightfall.

An hour later the Indian beckoned, and the two men headed for camp, both winded and in need of rest. They found a pan of camp bread and a skillet of gravy made with milk, meager fare, but hot and plenty of it. The steaming coffeepot, weak with pre-used grounds, had been sweetened with a tablespoon of sorghum. Not as satisfying as a strong cup of coffee, but better than just hot water.

Cecile was keeping the fire burning, the gravy from sticking, and had a pot she was filling with snow to provide hot water to clean up with later. She had been afraid to leave the gravy to go to the spring for water. She answered the question before it was asked. "Cook is finding some branches to close in underneath the wagon. I guess he nearly froze last night. He needs a windbreak. I told him I'd manage breakfast. I'm sorry, but bread and gravy is all I could find."

"Sounds good to me." Lou grabbed a pan, sliced off a hunk of bread and ladled gravy on top of it. Bear followed. Cecile filled their tin cups and watched the men eat. They were exhausted. She studied Bear's strong face, finding it drawn with weariness The old man would have a heart attack if he kept up this pace. She was deep in thought and the two men were so weary that riders had entered camp before anyone was aware that visitors were coming.

Startled at the sound of horses snorting as they cleared the icicles from their nostrils, Cecile looked up into the painted faces of Indian braves. Her gasp caught Bear's attention. Following her frightened stare, he reached forward and caught her arm, warning her by pressure to sit still.

Trembling, she obeyed his silent message. Her eyes were locked on the group of riders sitting quietly on the horses, studying the campground. They were dressed in buckskin leggings, and moccasins laced to the knees. Heavy fur robes covered most of their bodies. The one that she thought was the leader wore a buffalo robe, slit for his head and falling loose over the rump of his horse.

His buckskin-clad arms held the reins through slits in the thick hair hide. His eyes found hers and softened as he studied her, recognizing her beauty under the heavy coats. Her hat had fallen to her back, held by the stampede strap around her neck, letting her black hair loose to curl in the winter dampness. Her cheeks, flushed from the fire, gave radiant color to her face.

A commotion distracted everyone as half-a-dozen mongrel camp dogs joined the riders, dropping to the ground and panting from the run to keep up with the riders in the deep snow.

Bear filled his cup with the sweetened liquid, rose and walked slowly to Buffalo Hide, and offered him the cup. The Indian stared into Bear's eyes, surprised to see an Indian in white man's clothing at a white man's camp.

One of the dogs, a big, white-frosted animal, rose and growled menacingly at Bear as he approached the horses. Bear spoke gruffly, in guttural words, and the dog sank to the ground, but kept his eye on Bear as he spoke to the rider on the horse.

Cecile tried to understand what was being said, but the two men spoke in their own language. She looked at Lou. He smiled a warning and continued to eat slowly, as if Indian visitors were an every day occurrence. With trembling hands Cecile reached forward and stirred the gravy. The fire needed a stick of wood, but her knees were too weak from fright to lift her, so she sat and stirred the gravy.

Buffalo Hide looked over Bear's shoulder, and Cecile was paralyzed by the steadiness of his eyes as he studied her. Bear turned to her and spoke angrily in Indian, gesturing toward the woodpile. Lou whispered, "Get up and get some wood and put it on the fire, quick."

She obeyed, trembling, afraid she would stumble with fear, but she piled her arms high and returned to the fire. She turned her back on the

Indians and worked to move pots and build up the fire, then put the pots back in place.

"Go on about dumping snow in the pot," Lou whispered between bites. She obeyed, keeping her back to the riders.

She heard the horses turn and the riders leave the camp, but she couldn't believe they were leaving. She had expected them all to be slaughtered. She jumped as Bear reached her side and roughly put an arm about her waist, and pulled her to him. He turned her, with him, and raised his right hand, palm out, in answer to the man in the buffalo robe, who turned and followed the braves as they rode out of camp. The dogs followed, snarling and snapping at each other as they ran.

Bear released her and returned to his place at the fire. He picked up his plate and scooped a hot ladle of gravy onto the cold food on the plate, and resumed eating.

Cecile jumped, startled, as Cook came from behind the wagon and leaned the shotgun he carried against the wagon wheel.

"Were you there all the time?" she asked.

"Yes, ma'am," he replied.

"I wish I had known. I might not have been so scared."

"Sorry, ma'am, but I thought it best. Might give us an edge if they return."

"Will they? Will they return?" Frightened she turned to Little Bear. She had her answer from the weary slouch and his eyes trying to avoid hers.

"What will we do?" Stunned she sank to the log by the fire. "What was that all about? What did they want?"

No one answered her. "What did they want?" she demanded.

Little Bear looked her squarely in the eye, "What all savages want Miss Ceci. Food, horses, women. The hunting is going to be bad soon. The braves are stocking the camp for the White Winter."

"What tribe was that?" Lou asked.

Little Bear shifted his eyes to his plate and sat quietly debating whether he should answer.

"Looked like Apache to me," Cook replied.

Bear raised his dark eyes and looked into Cecile's worried gray ones. "Cochise," he said through clenched teeth.

Cecile caught her breath. Cook whistled and Lou briskly rubbed his hands as he warmed them over the fire.

"He's on the run. Johnny Ward rescued a Mexican girl with an Apache child. A bunch of hot-blooded young warriors raided the Ward ranch and drove off some cattle and carried off the child. Ward rode to Fort Buchanan and reported the incident. A new lieutenant was put in charge of sixty troopers to find the cattle and the child. The Cochise camp has befriended the Butterfield Station, sells them wood. Bascom is a cocky, arrogant, son of a bitch. He went to Butterfield's Station and accused Cochise of the kidnapping and demanded the return of the child and the cattle, or Cochise would be arrested. Cochise escaped and some of his warriors were captured. In retaliation he attacked the Overland mail coach and killed the passengers. The stage station is shut down. Cochise's tribe is wearing war paint, and these mountains are dangerous as hell right now."

"Why did they leave?"

"Out of respect, ma'am, for my woman. My woman who owns the sacred cows. I explained to them that the little red cows were rare as the white buffalo, and whoever harmed them had the Winter Ghost to answer to. I explained that we also are hungry and look for the deer. It is forbidden to kill a sacred cow for food."

"Did he believe you?"

"For now. It will depend on the camp hunger."

"Thank you, Little Bear."

"My pleasure, ma'am. Sometimes it doesn't hurt to have mixed blood." He set his plate aside, rose, and went to the lean-to. The weary droop of his shoulders was very different from his usual strong stride of pride.

"My God," she sobbed, letting her face rest in her hands. "What will we do if they return?"

"They are not the immediate danger, ma'am," Lou spoke up. "The freeze is our enemy. We must spend the day stockpiling wood and shrubs for fire, here and in the canyon. Little Bear can't keep up the pace by himself."

Cecile looked toward the lean-to, wiped the tears from her eyes, and stood up. Reaching into her coat pocket she pulled out her gloves. "Let's get busy."

"Yes, ma'am," he answered, swallowed the last of his sweetened liquid, and rose to follow her.

They worked all day. When Cecile became so exhausted she wanted to quit, she remembered the swarthy Indian faces and the steady stares. She imagined them undressing her, torturing her. She would shake off the daytime nightmares and work harder to keep the nightmares from returning.

In the afternoon, Little Bear joined them. Cook took a shovel and went to the canyon to dig more holes in the deep snow. Clouds, heavy, black, laden with snow, rolled in so low it became hard to see through the thick haze. The temperature began its downward journey as darkness arrived.

Supper was mostly a bean soup, but they were all so tired no one complained. They were too tired to be hungry.

"We won't have a first watch tonight. It's too cold for company. Lou and I will take the midnight watch. Lou will stay and keep the campfire going. I'll keep the canyon fire going. If I need help I'll come and get you. Miss Ceci will keep the campfire and Cook the canyon fire on the early morning shift. Get as much rest as you can. We'll know tonight whether the White Buffalo or the White Wolf is the Winter Ghost."

Hours later Lou awakened Cecile. She could hardly move. Her muscles ached so badly she wanted to cry, but the sight of Lou's exhausted face kept her from doing so.

The wind was howling across the mountain range caught in an early winter blizzard that white men and Indians were to remember for many years.

Little Bear did not sleep at all that night. He and Cook worked to keep the cows on their feet. The fire aided by throwing off some light to work by, but its heat was overpowered by the blasts of snow and wind.

Cecile struggled to keep the campfire burning. She worked with freezing hands, dragging wood from the stockpile, fighting the whipping winds, blinded by the driving snow. She was so involved in keeping the fire burning that at first she wasn't sure she had heard the howl of a wolf. It had probably been the wind.

Filling her arms with wood, she turned wearily to struggle back to the fire. Head down, she fought against the wind. Then she heard it again, closer now. It was the wolf, the Winter Wolf. She had heard it. It was not the wind. Faster she struggled to reach the fire. Throwing the wood on the flames, she went to the wagon, picked up a rifle, and returned to the fire. Thank God it was nearly morning. She didn't think she could hold up much longer. Exhaustion and fear were taking their toll.

CHAPTER FORTY

When Grady awoke his head hurt, but it was clear. He could focus his eyes and study the room about him. It must be early morning. The house seemed quiet, and the Mexican sleeping in the corner was snoring soundly.

Grady tested his strength and tried to sit up, but dizziness threatened to swallow him, and because he feared passing out again he lay back, letting the dizziness pass.

He lay there remembering, putting it all back together, the herd, Cecile, the outlaws, days on the trail. How long had he been in bed? One week? Two? He was consumed with urgency.

"You," he called softly to the Mexican but was answered with a snore. "Hey," he called louder. The man jumped and was instantly awake. When he saw Grady's eyes were open he rose quickly and came to the bed.

"You are awake, Senor?"

"Yes. I think so. I'm not too sure any more if I'm awake or not," Grady answered.

"Miss Cecile?" The name was a question.

"What about Cecile?" Grady asked, afraid of bad news. "Where is she?" Relief filled him, "Why do you ask?"

"I am responsible for her. Her father told me to take care of her. I should never have let her leave the hacienda alone."

"You are a friend?" Grady hoped it was true. He needed a friend now.

"She is a daughter to me. My godchild. You must tell me if she is safe."
The old man was begging.

"Yes. Yes. At least, when I left her she was all right. How long have I been here?"

"This is twelve nights, Senor."

"It must have taken me several days to come down the mountain. I can't remember. I dislocated my shoulder, and I was unconscious much of the time."

"Si, Senor. You were unconscious when the bull brought you in."

"Deadly. Where is he?"

"He is in the barn behind the house, that is, except when he escapes. Then he stands by the back porch."

"Good old Deadly. He could have led you to Cecile," Grady exclaimed.

"I tried, Senor. He would not leave the yard. He threatened to fight any of us who tried to make him go."

"He can be a pain at times. I wish he had chosen another time. I've got to get out of this bed. Help me," Grady said as he tried to raise himself to his elbow.

The Mexican gently put a hand on his shoulder saying, "Wait, Senor, do not strain yourself. We cannot risk another blackout. You must tell me where she is. I will go for her."

Grady lay back. The man was right, of course. He could not risk another blackout. "What is your name?"

"I am Juan Avilas, Senor."

"OK, Juan. I moved the herd off the trail into a canyon. I don't think you can find it, but Deadly can. He will take you if I go with you."

"But Senor, you cannot ride. You are too ill," Juan Avilas protested.

"You got that right," Grady agreed. "But I have to make it somehow. We need food and men and a wagon. I'll stay here quiet in bed. You find those items and when you are ready to travel, fix me a place in the wagon."

"I don't think you can make it, Senor."

"It doesn't matter if I pass out in the wagon, Juan, if Deadly knows I'm in it he will lead the way back. All you have to do is show him that you are putting me in the wagon."

"Senor, I will find a wagon, and I will get food, and prepare for the journey, but I am not sure I can get men."

"There's always someone hanging around needing work, Juan. You know that."

"Si, Senor, but there has been talk of a war between the states, and many men have gone to fight. Those who have not left talk of leaving. It may be a problem."

"Try, Juan. We are shorthanded, and if we don't hurry, there could already be more danger than we know. I have been gone too long. You must hurry."

"Si, Senor, I shall try." Juan hurriedly left the room, stepping aside for the red-haired woman as she came through the door.

"Well, where is he going in such a hurry?" she asked when she saw Grady was awake.

"I have sent him to buy supplies and find some men to work. I have a herd back on the trail, and it's important that I return as quickly as possible."

"Do you realize how ill you've been?" she demanded.

"Lord, lady, I can't remember when I felt worse than I do right now, but if I don't get back we may lose the herd. I left a short crew."

"Seems you left more than that," she laughed.

"I don't understand," he replied.

"Tell me what a C.C. is," she grinned.

Grady flushed, and then he grinned also. "How do you know about Ceci? Of course, old Juan told you."

"No, honey, you did. Why, you've been out of your head hunting for that girl for a week now. Most of the time you thought I was her. I was tempted to crawl in beside you a time or two, hoping that would give you some comfort and you'd quiet down. But somehow I didn't get the feeling that Miss C.C. was that kind of woman, and it might not have calmed you."

Grady flushed again. "I thank you, ma'am, for your care of me. I know I was a handful."

"Handful, that ain't the half of it. Regular disruption of business you were. Kept all my girls busy taking care of you."

"I really thank you, miss."

"Candy. Just call me Candy, honey, everyone does."

"Well, thank you, Miss Candy. I really appreciate your help."

"You're welcome, honey. You got some money locked up in my safe downstairs. You're going to need it to buy those supplies."

Grady was surprised, and Candy laughed.

"Not all us dance hall girls are thieves, Mr. Grady. Some of us are real ladies."

"You don't know how thankful I am that I fell into the hands of one who is a real lady," he replied sincerely.

"You need lots of rest now if you want to try and make that trip. I'll get you some breakfast, and then you better sleep as much as you can and let that concussion rest."

"Thank you, Candy, that sounds like good advice." His voice drifted off, and his lids closed. He was once again in a deep slumber by the time she had left the room.

CHAPTER FORTY-ONE

Juan Avilas walked about the town. It was not a large town. Juan went first to the only eatery in town and ordered the breakfast special. He had not eaten regularly since he had arrived, and he was hungry. When the steak and eggs, country gravy, and biscuits were set before him, the steak was tough, the gravy greasy, and the biscuits hard, but the eggs were done right for him so he ate it all in silence, while he studied the room and the street outside the window.

It was early. It was possible that many of the border town's occupants were still sleeping off last night's debauchery at Candy's saloon, but he doubted it. There had been a steady evacuation of the town for days. Even some of the girls at Candy's had taken the stages headed east. There would be money for them in the towns close to the battlegrounds.

Two men came down the street and entered the eatery. Juan dismissed the two with a glance. One he recognized as the elderly man who ran the stables, the other man he did not know, but his age eliminated him for trail driving.

Finishing his breakfast, he stepped out onto the boardwalk and stopped to lean against a tie rail. He took brown Mexican cigarette paper from an inside pocket, in his serape. His fingers fondled a knife in its scabbard as he felt for his tobacco pouch. With the expertise of many years of practice his fingers filled and rolled the tobacco in the brown paper. At the same time he studied the sleepy street and the buildings facing it. His eyes came to rest on the Border Patrol office that had been established to aid in controlling the raids of Cochise's Apache renegades into Mexico. For a second his hands were still, and then he completed the roll, lifted it, and moistened the paper. He stuck the dark cigarette in his mouth and headed for the office.

In the office he found a uniformed army officer sipping a cup of coffee, his feet propped up on a chair, warming them in the heat from the iron stove.

"Senor, may I look at your prisoners?"

"What for, Mex?" The officer looked over the rim of his coffee cup at the old Mexican standing in the middle of the room. These border bums irritated him. They were lazy, and more than often ended up in the jail for theft.

Juan Avilas didn't like this gringo. He had met his kind before. But he had a chore to do, and he could not let personal feelings interfere, so he played the part the officer expected.

"My son, Senor, he has not come home for many days. I think maybe he is in your jail."

"Well if he was, Mex, he would stay there, but I ain't got no Mexicans in the lockup right now."

The old man slouched a little under the serape, but didn't move.

"Hell, I ain't lying to you, old man. Ain't nobody locked up now but the town drunk. Ain't even got many vagrants these days." He was getting impatient with this conversation. It was interfering with his morning coffee.

"This drunk is old?" Juan asked timidly.

"Hell, I ain't lying to you. Go on and get out of here. Try Carmella's bordello. Your kid is probably just having a good time."

"Carmella's?" Juan shrugged his shoulders.

"Don't know the town, eh?" The officer had that look as if any vagrant in his cells was better than none.

Juan slowly pulled the knife from its scabbard, his hands hidden under the heavy folds of the woven wool serape. Nonchalantly he brought the weapon into sight, and began to use its gleaming blade point to cut the nails on his left hand. Particles of nail flew as he passed the sharpened blade through the nails' growth.

Juan's eyes locked into those of the officer, and the man saw in them a warning. He stared back, daring the Mexican, but the steady, brown eyes did not falter. The light from a lantern glistened on the blade of the Spanish dagger. The officer lowered his eyes, distracted by the flash, and saw that the blade had been honed to razor sharpness. The way the Mexican handled it, he knew the knife had been used for purposes other than nail cutting. His attitude changed to that of placation.

"I'm sorry your son's missing, old man, but I ain't raggin' you about Carmella's. I was down there last night, checking it out on my rounds."

Juan knew. This kind of white man scum would use his rank to profit him. Juan nodded his understanding and waited for the man to complete the directions to Carmella's.

"I seen several strangers. If they ain't there in the daylight, the girls would know who was there and answer some questions for you. If they don't, just tell 'em you'll speak to Lt. Carn about the man that ran the stables, hem, and they'll talk to you." The braggart left no doubt in Juan's mind that the girls at Carmella's survived only because they catered to Carn's demands.

"You haven't told me where to find this Carmella's, Senor." Juan spoke with careful respect. He knew how to feed this white man's ego.

"Go out the east road towards Cottonwood Grove. There's a pile of rocks, big ones, stones. Took twenty men to lift them on top of each other. Just follow the trail to the right and you won't miss it. You'll come to the main house first, but don't let it fool you. Them cottonwoods are filled with one-room cabins. There's about eight in all. That woman's a smart one. She can hide out a rustler in that maze by just moving him from one cabin to another." He chuckled, remembering some of the wild goose chases he had made at Cottonwood Grove.

"Thank you, Senor. I will look for my son at Carmella's and I will appreciate the use of the name of so important a man as Lt. Carn." Juan played the part, sweeping the large sombrero off his head and clasping it to his chest as he bowed.

This was more like it, a little respect from the Mexican bum. Lt. Carn lowered his feet to the floor, rose, and refilled his cup from the coffeepot, sitting on the stove keeping warm. "Just doing my job, Mex." He sat back in the chair feeling his importance.

"One more question, Senor."

"Well, hurry it up. I don't want this cup of coffee getting cold yapping with you."

"I'm sorry, Senor, I spoil your coffee. But the drunk, he is an old man?"

"Hell, you don't believe me, do you? Go on back and take a look at him. Satisfy yourself he ain't no Mexican, but don't get smart. I got my eye on you all the way. Take your look, and get the hell out of here."

"Thank you, Senor." Juan bowed, and backed, bowing out of the office into the hall between the cells. He turned and located the man lying in one of the back cells. The door of the cell had not even been closed. Juan stared down at the dissipated face, so typical of the alcoholic beggars that swept up the floors of the saloons in payment for drinks. The man probably hadn't been on a horse for years. He was in no condition for the job ahead.

Juan left the Border Patrol office quickly, leaving off the sleepy attitude of the Mexican peon the white men were used to seeing. He went quickly back to the saloon where he had kept his horse tied, ready to ride, ever since he had entered the town. He had fed, groomed, and walked the animal while he waited for Grady to regain consciousness, but he had kept the horse saddled and waiting. Now he loosened the tie rope, slipped on the bridle that had hung from the saddle horn, swung up into the saddle, and moved the gray mare out of town on the east road.

The mare moved with grace and natural speed. Her age, and the shaggy winter coat, hid the excellent quality of her breeding. Juan had chosen her for the inherent endurance of the Arabian. He could have selected a younger horse, but knowing the direction he would be traveling, a Mexican riding a spirited Arabian would be suspect. Besides, the mare was an old friend and a comfort to the old man.

Juan recognized the stone landmark at once. It was unmistakably a man-made landmark. He followed the road to the right, but when the first house came into view Juan turned the mare into the woods, working his way in a circle around the house. When he came to a secluded clump of brush, Juan dismounted and tied the mare. On foot he looked for paths that would lead to the cabins. One by one he located each cabin, and checked it out. In two he found girls sleeping soundly. Four were empty. One contained a man and a woman. Looking through the window, Juan saw the man's shoes by the chair at the foot of the bed. Homesteader's shoes. Probably one of the farmers traveling across the country looking for free land on which to settle, build a mud house, and dig up the ground. The eighth cabin was filled with storage, furniture, cases of bottled whiskey, and barrels of beer.

Juan returned to his horse, mounted and retraced his trail to the road where he continued on to the main house. As he tied the mare to the rail in front of the porch, the door swung open and a Mexican woman stepped out onto the porch. She was dressed in a plain dress, proper in every way, made of expensive black fabric covered tastefully with black lace. Her face was ageless. Her black hair glistened with cleanliness. The woman wrapped her Spanish shawl tightly about her shoulders warding off the winter's cold air and waited serenely for the Mexican gentleman to tie his horse and climb the stairs. She stepped aside and motioned him into a large living room made from crude milled lumber, but refined with drapes made of satin from Spain, and silks from the Orient. Rugs covered the rough plank floor, some oriental, some fur, but all blended to give an atmosphere of luxury.

The room had the smell of exotic imported perfumes not unfamiliar to Juan Avila. His friend and patron, Senor McNamara, had imported such perfumes for his wife, Juan Avila's only love. Juan had never married. He had never questioned his position in life. He was a servant. Estralita was a princess; at least to him she was a princess.

They had grown up together. He had taught her to ride, and he loved her more than any person in the world. So he was happy when she fell in love and was allowed to marry Senor McNamara. He knew she loved this man more than her life, and he, Juan, could not bear the thought of her marrying the son of Andréa Fernandez whose ranch was four days drive from the hacienda. His son's name was Carlos.

He had hated Carlos Fernandez because Carlos always teased him and sent him away like a peon when they came to visit. Estralita would always sneak away and find Juan. She also disliked Carlos. The two of them would hide and giggle watching his fat legs trudge from one barn to the other, searching for her.

They had loved each other as brother and sister, and Juan had served her and her family all his life, transferring that love to Cecile and Ramon. Little Cecile looked so much like his Estralita and had so much of her spirit, and the strength of her father.

"I see you approve of my house." Carmella's voice was husky with only a slight hint of accent in the cultured voice. Her words brought Juan from his memories back into the room with the drapes, rugs, and rough-hewn plank. The large fireplace had a welcoming fire burning in it.

"It was the perfume, Senorita. It brought back memories." He smiled an apology.

She smiled and reached to take his hat.

"No, Senorita, I did not come to you for comfort. I need help."

The woman wrapped the shawl tighter about her shoulders. She stood waiting, wary of anyone that entered this house for any purpose other than for the comfort of the women in the cabins. The Mexican man standing in her living room was of high class. Her trained eye saw the fortune in silver engravings attached among the elaborate embroidery of the sombrero. His boots were of the finest cowhide, hand styled by Mexican artisans. If he removed the heavy serape she would bet he wore the hand-tailored suit of the highborn Latin gentry.

Juan removed his hat, holding it in both hands in a position of respect. He smiled warmly at the woman in an effort to set her at ease. She remained motionless, waiting for an explanation.

"In the mountains is lost someone I love very much. I need help. Riders, vaqueros, cowboys, anyone that can ride with me to bring her out of the mountains."

"A lady? Is she your lady?"

"She is my patron, and my godchild."

"What can I do to help?"

"I had hoped you would know men who would hire out to ride with me."

"Why is it that because I run a house, everyone comes to me when they are looking for men? I should open an employment agency." She was aggravated. Juan realized he was handling this situation wrong.

"No Senorita, I did not come to you because you run a bordello. I came to you because you are a countrywoman. I had hoped I could trust your judgment."

She looked in his eyes and found truth. Relaxing, she reached out and took his hat.

"All right. Remove your serape and let's go into the kitchen. We will discuss this problem over coffee."

The kitchen was more comfortable than the living room. Several girls sat around the table. Unlike the girls at Candy's, these girls were fully clothed, and wore sensible, warm robes. They rose as if on cue and left the kitchen when Juan and Carmella entered.

"Sit, Senor. Introduce yourself and we will talk," she said as she hung his hat and serape on a peg by the door. She had been right. He wore a suit made of soft, black leather, and expensive black woven fabric outlined in embroidery, styled slim in the legs. The coat, broad at the shoulders, came only to the waist, a waist trim from active years. She saw a distinguished Latino gentleman, not the bum Lt. Carn had seen.

"Excuse me, Senorita, my name is Juan Avilas, from the Hacienda del Ciela near San Antonio de Bexar."

"I am pleased to make your acquaintance, Senor Avilas. I am Senora Carmella Smith."

"Smith!"

"Smith."

They saw the humor in each other's eyes, laughed together, and became friends. The coffee was good, the kitchen was warm, and the two were comfortable together.

CHAPTER FORTY-TWO

Two days had passed. Grady had grown stronger. He still could not stand without dizziness overtaking him, but if he raised himself by degrees, he could reach a sitting position, and if his head was propped he could feed himself.

He had not heard from Juan Avilas. He was beginning to believe he had misjudged the man. Time was so valuable. He kept flexing his muscles, stretching his legs, using muscle tension to strengthen his good arm. He ate everything Candy brought him, even when he felt like throwing it all back up, he forced himself to keep it down.

The evening of the second day Juan Avilas strode rapidly into the bedroom. Grady's heart filled with relief. He had been afraid the man had deserted him, and he alone would have to make the trip back to bring in the herd.

"Senor, forgive me for the delay. It is most impossible to find trustworthy help in this town, and I had to wait for outside help to ride in. I have two men. They are young, but they are skilled with cattle."

"That's good. Can we leave tomorrow?"

"We must leave tomorrow, Senor, as early as light will permit. I have learned some news that alarms me."

"Tell me quickly. What did you hear?"

"I have a friend, Senor. She runs a bordello out on the edge of town. Last week a man came several nights to visit one of her girls. The man kept talking about a saddle mounted with silver, and when he became drunk with wine he would strike the girl, and scream abuse at her. He would yell, 'It's all your fault.'

"My friend forbade him to visit the girl when she found out. She told me the last time the man had visited her bordello, he had brought another man with him, one she did not like. This man did not take his pleasure with the ladies. He sat in the living room by the fire, and cleaned and oiled his gun while he waited for his friend. I trust her judgment, Senor. She said he breathed of evil. Until I came asking for help to bring Miss Cecile out of the mountains, she had just thought the pair were run of the mill perverts that show up at houses of prostitution, but she felt such overwhelming evil their memory had not erased from her mind."

"Luke," Grady exploded. He threw back the cover and tried to get out of bed. Dizziness whirled and he fell into Juan's arms, clinging to his shoulders for support. His legs sank from under him.

Juan struggled to lift the younger man back into the bed. Even with the weight Grady had lost from illness, he was a solid six-foot, muscled, outdoor man, and the elderly man had to struggle to get him back into the bed.

"Hey, what's going on?" Candy came into the room as Juan was attempting to lay Grady's body back onto the bed.

"Help me, Senorita. He tried to stand up."

Candy hurried to help lift Grady back into bed. She removed the covers so Juan could swing Grady's feet back onto the bed, then she pulled the covers over him and reached for the smelling salts the doctor had left. She wafted it under Grady's nose until he began to move, then she grabbed the washrag floating in the hand pan and bathed his face with cold water.

Grady opened his eyes. For a moment he could not remember where he was. Then he recognized the two concerned people working over him, and he remembered his fear.

"Luke," Grady stammered, once again struggling to rise. Both Avilas and Candy held him down.

"Wait, Senor. We cannot afford to have you keep passing out on us."

"That's right, Grady. You've got to behave yourself. The doc says you aren't ready to travel, but that if you insist, you got to do it by wagon, lying down until this dizziness passes. It will pass in time, but you got to give it time."

Candy's concerned voice quieted Grady. He realized she was right. He had to stay awake. "All right, I'll stay down. I've got to keep awake. But you must realize there is real danger. I mean real danger!" He went on to tell them about Cragen and the outlaw prisoners. He saw the agony in Juan Avilas face when he told of the encounter. "There's no telling what he will do to her if he finds her. He's not bright, he's slow. Cragen was special to him. If he blames Ceci for Cragen's death, it won't be the saddle he's after. It will be Ceci. But if there are other men with him they will have treasure on their minds, and they will find the canyon."

Candy looked at Juan Avilas and was shocked to see how white his face had grown. He had become a very old and helpless man in a matter of minutes. For a moment she felt instant hatred for Cecile McNamara. Any woman who could strike such concern in men as strong as these two must be very precious, or else she was a witch.

"Well, that does it," Candy said. "I'm going with you and don't try to stop me. I've lost half my girls to the boys in uniform. My bartender gave notice this morning. He's joining the North. In another week I won't have a business here anyway. I have a wagon and team and most of the supplies. We can leave as soon as first light."

She continued, "Boy, am I anxious to meet this paragon of virtue who men will lay their lives on the line to defend. I wouldn't miss this trip for a brand new saloon right smack dab in the middle of the war zone." Finished with the angry tirade, Candy turned and flounced out of the room.

CHAPTER FORTY-THREE

Cook struggled into camp as the night's darkness was lifting and another day began. "Trumpeter's down. I can't get him to his feet," he panted, slumping to his knees by the fire and holding out his hands to warm them.

Cecile, who was sitting by the fire, rose wearily and walked to the grub wagon. She rummaged around and returned with dry socks for both Cook and herself. Cook groaned at the thought of removing his boots, but he knew she was right. A man could lose his toes in weather like this. Freeze them suckers right off. Break like the iced branches. Cussing, he got to his feet and found a log in the fire pile, with a forked branch sticking out. He put the heel of one boot in the fork, and with the other foot stood on the branch. Struggling and cussing he worked the boot off with this makeshift bootjack.

Cecile watched, and then she removed her boots the same way. The makeshift bootjack saved energy. Cecile flopped her wet socks into the pan by the fire that already held Cook's wet ones.

"What should we do?" she asked.

"Got to get him up," Cook replied.

"I'll wake Lou and Bear," she said, and rose to do so.

Cook had put some beans to soak before he had gone to the canyon. A crust of ice had frozen over them even though he had left the pot protected in the wagon. He grabbed a handful of salt and sprinkled a sufficient amount on top of the ice, then set the pan on the fire. Cecile returned to

235

the fire. She threw some logs on, wrapped up in a blanket, and immediately went to sleep, still sitting up, her arms folded over her knees.

By the time Lou and Little Bear climbed from their bedrolls, pulled on their boots, and gathered by the fire, Cook was turning the first flapjack. Sorghum was heating in a pan with a hunk of frozen tallow, unyielding until the syrup became warm enough to begin it's slow melting. Water was hot in the coffeepot, with milk and sorghum added to it.

"Last of the flour. Figured it was time for one of them special occasions." Cook winked at Cecile. She had wakened when Lou and Bear stomped about the fire.

"What special occasion, the celebration of us all freezing to death?" Lou complained, stomping his feet to keep them warm.

"Oh, Lou, don't say that. I'm so cold." Cecile pleaded.

"I'm sorry, Miss Ceci, but I nearly froze my buns off last night. This freeze better break soon."

"You better get your tins and eat these flaps before they freeze solid," Cook growled.

"We're all snapping everybody's head off." Cecile was near tears. "And Trumpeter's down."

Lou and Bear looked at her then turned their eyes to Cook. He nodded, verifying the girl's words. The cook filled a tin plate and poured hot sorghum and tallow on the flapjack. He fed the men first. They had work to do. Then he fed Cecile and sent her to climb into her bedroll in the grub wagon.

As she snuggled down into the bedroll, her feet struck some-thing hard, and warm. She smiled and settled into the bedroll, pulling it over her head. Bless his heart, cranky old Cook, he had heated a rock and wrapped it in something and put it in her bedroll to warm her feet, sweet, cranky old man. She drifted off to sleep feeling delightfully warm and comfortable after so many miserable, freezing days of fighting the storm. She thought she heard the Winter Wolf howl, but decided it was a dream.

Cook scooped some snow into the dirty pots and set them by the fire. Bear threw on some logs to keep it burning. Cook rose wearily, "Let's get moving."

The three men picked up shovels, and an axe. They cleared the accumulation of snow from the rough places of the path they had worn walking back and forth to the canyon.

The winds were relentless and made the chill factor so much more extreme. The cattle huddled together, the ones on the outside fighting to crowd back into the inside to escape the wind. Several were down.

Cook had put the calves in the lean-to, and dragged some branches across its opening to hold them, and protect them. Their mothers stood together on the windward side of the lean-to. The horses were not in sight.

The men lifted, pulled, whacked, cussed, and threatened the cows that lay in a stupor, until the cattle feared the men more than the freezing wind, and climbed to their feet, and slowly began to mix with the herd.

They found Trumpeter. They had to dig him out. The snow accumulation had covered him since Cook had left the canyon in the early hours.

Trumpeter's eyes were closed, frozen shut. There were fogs of breath fighting their way past the icicles that had formed about his nostrils. He was alive. Shock had not set in. The men worked furiously to get the old bull to his feet, pounding on him to get the blood circulating, and breaking away the icicles so that he could draw more oxygen into his lungs.

Years of obedience to man won over the freezing hands of death. The old bull had obeyed man's commands for too long. He made every effort to rise to his feet. The effort encouraged the men. They increased their shouts and put their shoulders under him and lifted to help him gain his feet. Once he was up, they continued to push, pull, and shove until they had moved him to the lean-to. Protected now on three sides from the wind, and the fire blocking out the cold on the other side, they let him sink to the ground. The men built up the fire, and trudged back up the path to the camp. Cook put on some water to heat, and joined the two on the log by the fire.

"Did anyone hear them wolves last night?" Lou asked, letting smoke sift out with his words.

"Yeah. Didn't want to say anything before to scare Miss Ceci."

"Indian dogs," Little Bear said. The contradiction was final.

"They traveling with company?" Lou asked.

"No. Indians will be holed up in weather like this. They let the dogs in for warmth, but food is rationed and the dogs don't get enough scraps to live, so they hunt. We worry when the storm stops, and the Indians hunt."

"Them cows is an easy mark," Cook said.

"Just keep your eyes open. You better get some sleep, Cookie. From the looks of this weather we got another night of it." Lou was resigned. He didn't wait to see if Cook did as he suggested. He picked up the shovel and went down the trail to dig out some feedholes so the cattle could eat. Might take their minds off freezing to death.

Cook did not sleep. He worked about the camp. Cecile slept and they did not wake her. Someone would need to be alert tonight.

The jar of tomatoes had frozen. Too bad, Cook thought as he dug the frozen mass out of the jar and dropped it in the beans to add seasoning. The tomatoes would have been tasty alone, and might have helped disguise the small portion of beans each person would get for this meal.

Cook had divided the last of the beans to provide one more meal, hoping the boss would make the round trip back as expected. Grady should have been back in camp with supplies long before now, Cook worried. Then he pushed the bad thoughts away.

CHAPTER FORTY-FOUR

Two weeks passed. The freezing temperature held. In the years to come, in history books, this winter's record freeze would be known as the worst in history for the area.

Little Bear, stronger than the others, carried the load. They tried to help him but the cold began to wear down their endurance. He worked around the clock, grabbing catnaps when exhaustion overtook him. There was no time to hunt. The rations were gone. It was time to butcher a cow. The meat would give them strength to fight the bitter cold. The half-breed made up his mind. In the morning he would select one of the weaker cows, one that might not make it anyway.

He threw wood on the campfire, and with weary legs trudged along the path to the canyon. He had made this trip so many times the past two weeks he felt he could shut his eyes and his feet would travel by themselves. He didn't need the torch, but from habit he had carried it to use in case the other fire had gone out.

He almost didn't see the shadowy form that crossed the path ahead of him. Weary eyes, half closed, did not instantly register the movement. Then another form darted across and Little Bear halted and lifted the torch overhead, straining to see into the darkness in front of him. The light from the torch illuminated red eyes flashing from the blackness. The Indian camp dogs, they had finally come. Little Bear knew they would. He had heard their howls the past week as they banded together to hunt. No longer would there be enough scraps around the Indian camps to feed them. Wild game was becoming harder to find. The half-breed could testify to that himself. The deer had moved off the mountain and the smaller game was staying in their burrows.

The leader of the pack would be Buffalo Hide's white, shaggy half wolf. The dog knew where the herd was and Little Bear had been expecting him. Tiredness faded away as the adrenaline of danger entered his mind. His tired body shook off its lethargy and he ran along the well-worn path as fast as its slippery surface would allow him to travel.

He heard the restless herd bawling, and milling in fear, long before he reached the bed ground. The pack had already singled out a victim. He could hear their snarls and growls as they fought over the meat. Mouths full they ripped and gulped hunks of meat, desperate to swallow as much as possible before another snatched it away. Later they would regurgitate it and present it to their empty bellies in a more digestible form.

This manner of feeding had been the reason Little Bear had not heard the danger before. Camp dogs differed from wolves.

The dogs used their voices only to call the pack together. Their training from infancy, by their Indian masters, was to hunt in silence. They had crept silently in the dark, among the cattle chosen a cow already weak and down. She may have tried to bawl when she felt the jaws close over her windpipe, but she was quickly and quietly silenced as several of the big dogs ripped away her jugular vein and continued to eat through the flesh of her throat and neck.

Bear fired a shot and the dogs disappeared, shadows slinking away in the dark. They would not be back tonight. Afraid of man's fire stick, and their hunger assuaged for the time, they would seek the warmth of the Indian camp, creeping silently into their masters' teepees to curl up on the deer skins provided for them.

Little Bear built up the fire just in case a hungry straggler hung about. He dragged one of the shrubs from the stockpile he had accumulated over to the blood-soaked ground. Touching the torch to a branch, he waited for the heat to dry the branch enough to catch fire. When it finally caught, it began to burn rapidly, its flames lighting up the area.

He built the fire with branches until it would last long enough for him to salvage as much of the meat as he could. He worked quickly, separating the torn shreds from the bone, throwing the pieces into a pile of undisturbed snow. He saved every edible thing he could find, including the brain, and tongue. The skull had protected these from the tearing teeth. He was able to salvage most of the hindquarter and shoulder, which lay on the ground. Little of the exposed topside of the cow was left.

Before he could finish the grisly chore, Cook, Lou, and Cecile had joined him. The gunshot had brought them all running, rifles and pistols in hand, ready to do battle, only to find the enemy had already struck, and disappeared, leaving the remains of the cow.

Cook returned to camp for flour sacks. They all worked silently sacking the meat, and carrying it back to the upper camp.

Cook sliced thick chunks of meat and strung them on iron stakes to roast over the fire while he sorted through the sacks of meat, cutting the badly damaged into stew meat, slicing steaks, and meal-sized roasts. Once the meat was sorted and repacked into the flour sacks. It would freeze into solid hunks. Tired as he was, the cook finished the job before he hung the meat out of the reach of hungry animals.

It was a sorry crew that waited around the fire for the meat to heat enough to eat. Cecile hated herself for being so eager to devour one of her cows, but the smell of the meat roasting made the saliva glands work in her mouth. She could hardly wait to sink her teeth into the nourishing steak. Tonight she would move her bedroll to the lean-to in the canyon.

Bear felt relief. He disliked the white-man feelings that had filled him earlier. He had not wanted to butcher one of Miss Ceci's cows. For days he had used up much of his waning strength to search for wild game. He was glad the dogs had done the job for him, the sneaky bastards. He wondered how many cattle they would destroy in the dark of night. From now on he would sleep with the cattle.

The sight of the dead cow saddened Lou, but he had the sensible feelings of wisdom. Without nourishment to keep them going there would be no one to protect the herd. Tonight he would sleep with the cows.

All of them in their own thoughts decided to stand guard over the cows. With this resolution they sank their teeth into chunks of hot meat, still partially uncooked. The blood ran through their fingers as they tore the meat apart with their teeth. Bear's sense of humor returned as he watched them devour the chunks of meat. They ate Indian fashion, with their hands, not waiting for tins, or tools to cut and shove meat pieces into their mouths, white-man fashion.

Bear's humor turned to discontent as he watched Miss Ceci squatted by the fire, disheveled, bundled in layered garments far too large, ones she had salvaged to ward off the freezing winds. Her face was chapped, her lips covered with fever blisters, and cracks. Her hands were callused and scratched from the constant battle to provide the hungry campfire, with fuel. He recalled the proud woman who rode out of San Diego. It was hard to imagine this bedraggled camp squaw was the same Grace Cecile McNamara.

The cook had lost the fat around his middle. His usual irritable disposition had disappeared days ago. He had done a remarkable job of coming up with something to fill their bellies while also working beside them to care for the herd. The crotchety cook was using muscles he had not used since he was a boy. He ached, and there was no time to complain. The situation had become too futile to cuss at it. Without his usual frown he looked his age, and pallor was in his skin that disturbed Little Bear.

The old man, old Gimpy Lou, seemed to continue in the same shape he had always appeared to Little Bear. Except for the evening of Denny's death old Lou had worked steadily. The gimpy leg slowed his work, but he pulled his load, and he took care of Miss Ceci. It was this transference of devotion that kept the old man going, and his aid to Cecile kept her going. He kept warm stones in her bed at night, kept her gloves and stockings dry, and carried her meals to her when she was too tired to bother. He was always close if she needed help with a heavy log, or a job too hard for her to handle. The two working together made a good pair, almost putting out the work of one good man.

They had meat now. They could hold out for several days if they had to. Grady should have been back. He had run into trouble or he would be here. These people would not hold up much longer. Little Bear made a decision. As soon as the storm broke they would move out.

That night it seemed a higher being had heard the Indian's decision. The angry fury of the freezing winds increased. It became impossible to keep both fires burning. They moved their bedrolls to the canyon. All four worked through the night to keep the fire in the canyon burning. Little Bear kept the cattle moving and on their feet. Cecile kept Trumpeter tied to the outside of the lean-to close to the fire. This cleared the lean-to for their bedrolls She spent most of her time, when she wasn't hauling burnable material, rubbing his hide to keep the circulation flowing.

She kept an eye on the calves. Cold and miserable, they bawled constantly. The mothers trampling about the lean-to answered, but the space was so crowded Cecile kept them out. The pacing kept them warm. When the calves tried to lie down and give up she swatted their sides, and bodily lifted them to their feet.

The night dragged on. The crew could hardly move. Fingers were numb with cold. Constant drying out and changing of gloves did not help. The freezing winds were adding the possibility of frostbite to ears, noses, toes, and fingers.

Cecile couldn't stand it any longer. The men were half dead. She had come to love all of them. It was killing her as she watched them exhaustedly fighting to keep her tiny herd alive. Suddenly she hated the little cows. She hated herself, how could she ever have thought these animals were worth the losses they had suffered, Denny, Scratch, and surely Grady. She knew he wasn't coming back. He would have been here by now. She couldn't bear the fear that built up in her when she wondered what his fate had been, for she knew in her heart that he would have returned if he could.

"Stop it! Stop it! Stop it!" she screamed.

She tried to tell the men to stop worrying over the cattle, to take care of themselves. She felt arms lifting her. She repeated, stubbornly, for them to stop, as she slid into unconsciousness.

Cook made a trip back to the grub wagon for meat and a pot. Lou stayed with Cecile and kept the fire stoked as Little Bear searched for more firewood.

Snow was melted, meat put on to boil for broth, and stones heated and put around the bedroll where Cecile lay in the deep sleep of total exhaustion. In this weather she would have frozen to death had she been alone. She tried to wake as Lou spooned warm broth into her mouth. In delirium, she thought it was her turn for night watch. She tried to open her eyes, but they were too heavy. Deathly tired, she quit fighting and drifted back into deep slumber.

CHAPTER FORTY-FIVE

It had been a scramble to get horses hitched, supplies loaded, Grady's bed made, and him loaded. They had to wait for Candy. Juan tied his horse to her wagon and held her team. If it hadn't been for her red hair in a braid hanging down her back and the rouge on her cheeks and lips, she might have passed for a young man in men's riding pants. They hugged her bottom, and the men could see she had long slim legs. Astonished their mouths hung open. Lance let out a long slow whistle.

"Knock it off! I don't intend to fight those petticoats. Get used to it. Let's get this show on the road." Juan moved aside. She picked up the reins and cracked her whip and the caravan pulled out with Deadly in the lead.

Candy's wagon was lightweight, and traveled faster than the wagon driven by Carmella's youngest son. Glancy Smith was sixteen. He had his mother's fiery dark eyes, but the crop of red hair he had inherited from his father. Lance, his older brother, had escaped the red hair. His dark good looks were those of Carmella's Spanish blood. At eighteen he had already won all the ladies' hearts around Janos.

Lance rode a big muscled Morgan gelding. His tack was not only in good condition, but expensive and showy. He was dressed in clothing that had seen plenty of wear, but it fit his muscular body like a glove. The feather stuck in his black hat gave him a cocky look.

A few days earlier, when Juan Avilas introduced Grady to Carmella's boys, he knew the trail boss felt regret that they were not older, more experienced trail hands. Juan was grateful that Grady had not shown his feelings to the boys. Grady shook hands and expressed his gratitude that the young men were traveling with him.

After they left the room, Juan said, "They are young, Senor, but they are skilled cattlemen. I was so long because it took time to ride with their mother to find them. The bordello is only the front of a very large cattle ranch. The boys have run the ranch for their mother since their father died. They know cow ranching, Senor."

Grady relaxed on the bed. "I trust your judgment, Juan. Thank you. But it's not their cattle experience I'm worried about. Ten-year-olds could drive that herd. It's Looney Luke and whatever trouble he has created for us that worries me. We need gun hands, or at least men who will risk their lives for pay. I'd hate to bring Carmella's boys back to her in a box."

Juan Avilas's chin set, and a worried frown creased his forehead. "I know, Senor, I refused Carmella's offer many times, but she was very persuasive. She insisted that if we needed men we could trust, her boys were the only ones she would recommend. She said to tell you, Senor, not to let their ages deceive you. They are men in every way. The running of a bordello is not an easy life, and those boys know what life is all about. I checked their skill with rifle and pistol. They are both accurate with both weapons. It is my opinion, Senor, the older boy would only flash that charming smile while he put a bullet between a man's eyes."

"If that's the case, can we trust them?" Grady asked.

"They obey one person, Senor. Carmella. She told them to protect you and do your bidding. I think you will have two men you can trust, and just to be safe, I took a precaution. Carmella has three sons, Senor. The other is older. He's equally talented, but he helps his mother at the bordello. I sent him to Rancho del Cielo to bring back help I can trust. My men will be in Janos when we return with Miss Cecile and the herd."

Grady reached out his hand and Juan grabbed it in a firm handshake. "Thank you, Juan, you have done well."

"Thank you, Senor, I just hope my help will be in time to reach Miss Cecile. We have not told you before, Senor, for fear it would interfere with your healing. We are locked in a freeze. The worst winter I have ever experienced, and I am not a young man. I know the mountaintops are suffering from one of the worst blizzards this part of the country has ever known. Every day we delay may be the death of those you left behind."

Pain filled Grady's face. He was tormented as he remembered the falling snow, and the dropping temperature. The panic that filled his mind and body caused his hands to tremble.

Juan quickly leaned over Grady and put his hands on Grady's arms to still the trembling. He pushed his own weight down to hold the man still. Angry determination spewed from Juan's mouth. "Senor, you must stop this minute. We cannot afford to lose the time you will cost us if you are ill. You must be ready to travel in the morning."

Grady took a deep breath, fighting to control the shaking of his body. As it began to still, he opened his eyes to look into the determined glare of the older man. He could not blame this man for hating him. He had taken on a job to bring Cecile McNamara and her herd across country safely. He had failed. Juan Avilas should hate him. Grady had a job to finish, and he would need all the strength he could muster to do it.

"Tell Candy to bring me a thick steak, some potatoes and gravy, and some hot coffee. I'll need something besides that gruel she keeps pouring down me if I'm going to be any help."

CHAPTER FORTY-SIX

As they followed Deadly, Lance's horse pranced behind the bull, eager to pass, and lead the procession. The boy riding the impatient gelding held him in check. Patience showed in his eyes whenever he turned his face with its flashing smile, to see if the caravan was following him.

Candy drove a pair of matched black geldings. They moved the light wagon over the wet and dripping trail with ease. Grady half lay and half sat in the wagon bed. Juan had broken the legs off one of the more comfortable chairs, and set it in the wagon bed. Its back was braced against the tailgate so Grady could sit up when he felt like it, and watch Deadly and the trail ahead.

Glancy handled the team of four mules well. His ability was incredible for his age. Juan was proud of the boy as he rode in the rear to keep an eye on the trail behind. The gray mare responded to his touch on her sides with his knees and legs. Under his serape his hands firmly clasped a rifle. He was prepared for trouble, but he did not expect it until they reached Grady's camp. If Luke and his friends were following them, Juan wanted to know it as soon as possible. He prayed they were following, but he feared that they were ahead, already at the camp. The fear came into his throat like bile.

Grady studied the mountains ahead as they began to climb.

He had been shocked at the bite of the wind as the young boys carried him from the warm bedroom and tucked him into the bed of the wagon.

He noticed the soft mattress he lay on, and the chair, thoughtfully arranged so he could watch the trail ahead.

They had not been able to move out of town until Deadly had been brought to the wagon, and Grady had greeted him with familiar words, patted the massive head, and rubbed the raised bone between the horns. Grady held out a biscuit he had saved from his morning meal. The rough tongue swept it into his mouth and Deadly was ready to travel at Grady's command, "Lead out, Deadly." Deadly was glad to see the direction was back trail. He had missed old Trumpeter.

Glancy's wagon was laden with food supplies and sacks of grain. The four-mule team had plenty of pulling strength, and could keep up with the lighter wagon. At times Deadly had tried to cut corners and leave the beaten trail. Grady had to redirect him to allow the wagons to follow.

Nervously Grady played with the weapons stacked beside him. Extra rifles and pistols had been loaded and wrapped in a blanket. He checked and rechecked, to be sure they were all loaded. As the day wore on, the weather dropped in temperature as the wagon climbed higher into the mountains. Grady became tired and slid down to cover his head and drift into fitful sleep. Afraid Deadly would take off across country and leave the slower wagons, he did not stay down long at a time, just enough to settle his pounding head and warm himself. He couldn't believe the freezing temperature. If it was this bad at the base of the mountains, what could it be like higher up?

By dark he was exhausted, and relieved when Candy called a halt. He could feel the tension in the camp. The two young men had a fire made, the horses rubbed down and grained, and all of the saddles and equipment where it was needed, or protected under a wagon. Juan was right; they were teenagers going on forty.

Candy handed him a bowl of soup to sip and said quickly, "Don't worry, Grady. I got some red meat coming in a jiffy." He grinned his thanks, drank the hot soup, and slid into the bedding, and into sleep. Somewhere he thought he heard a guitar playing. Beautiful, he thought as he drifted into sound sleep.

The second day of their climb brought them into the full fury of the freezing blizzard. The extra clothing and blankets they had brought would not be enough to hold warmth in the blowing, icy wind.

248

Grady felt helpless and guilty as he sat under the covers. The freezing wind made his chest ache. He was no help and would be even less if the pneumonia returned. The journey would have to depend on Deadly. He hoped Deadly understood that.

He tried to remember how many days he had traveled before his horse fell. He kept going over each night he had camped. He remembered his dreams of Ceci, and always Cragen would enter those dreams. The laden wagons could not travel as fast. He had to allow for a difference in time, and he could not figure the time that he was unconscious. He kept going over the events, but he could not get a clear, definite idea of how long it was going to take them to reach the camp on the mountain where he had left Ceci.

The sharpness of the air began to clear Grady's head. Each day he sat up longer and worked the muscles in his arms and legs as the wagon bounced over the rough ground. He was glad he had the chair to brace against. He practiced handling his pistol and a rifle until his fingers hurt from handling the frost covered steel of the weapons. When he tired of this, he talked to Candy, who was already regretting her offer to make this trip.

"Hell! Damn! Shit! Grady, my damned fingers are frozen," she fumed.

"Did you know the weather was this bad?" he asked her.

"Shit, Grady, I didn't even know weather could be this bad. Sure I heard the people complaining, but hell, people always complain. I had no idea it was this bad. I would never have offered, much less insisted, on making this trip." Her teeth were chattering.

"Have I thanked you for the help, Candy?"

"Hell, no. All you've done is worry over Grace Cecile McNamara, whatever that is," she grumbled.

Grady smiled. He had grown used to Candy's gruff exchanges. "Grace Cecile McNamara is the prettiest woman I ever saw besides you, Candy."

"I figured she had to be pretty. She's probably a lot younger than me, too."

"No, I don't think she's younger in age, Candy, just in living life. You know what I mean."

"Yeah, you mean she's a virgin. Weren't we all at one time," she pouted.

The left black gelding slipped to his knees, and her attention was absorbed in getting his feet back under him on the icy trail. When she looked back Grady had slid under the covers and was probably sleeping again.

"Gawd," she said to herself, as she tried to see through the driving sleet. It struck her cheeks with stinging sharpness. Branches covered with ice were constantly breaking, and dropping into the trail. Lance's big gelding no longer pranced and fought the bit, but worked steadily with his rider to clear the trail so the wagons could pass.

Each evening as it drew time to stop, Lance had ridden ahead and found a camp area where frozen branches could be turned into the warmth of a campfire. Some man, that kid! Candy wished she were a few years younger. She had known Carmella's kid since he wore diapers, but she would bet he carried more in his drawers now than he did then.

She laughed out loud at her ribald daydreams, and tucked the reins under her bottom so she could pound her hands together and try to get some circulation moving in her fingers. She yelped and squealed at the pain, but kept rubbing, and clapping them until the fingertips began to burn.

Glancy spent all his time fighting the mules. The ice on the trail was so hard and thick that the cleats he had added to the iron shoes on the mules could not penetrate it. They had a hard time getting a foothold so they could set and pull the loaded wagon. He was thankful he had added the cleats. The mules spent most of the time on their knees as it was. Without cleats they could all forget this trip. As it was, Glancy wasn't too sure how many more mountains they could scramble up. Both of the lead mules had bleeding knees. He wished he were home by the fire. This had not turned out to be as exciting as it had sounded.

Juan Avilas had holstered his rifle the second day out. It became obvious that the mare would need a steady rein to lean into if she slipped on the icy trail. He continued to try to keep an eye on the back trail, but it soon became obvious that the loaded wagon ahead needed his help. He spent most of his time helping the mules get to their feet. As they climbed pelting rain had turned to driving sleet, and he could no longer see beyond the end of the wagon ahead.

Desperation was driving Juan. He wondered how long the others would battle this bitter cold. There was no real reason for them to endure these elements. If it was much farther to this canyon he expected all the others to turn back. He would go on alone. His child was out there. Not the child of his loins, but the child of his heart. Estralita's child. He had promised Estralita to care for her baby. He should never have listened to this crazy scheme. He should never have allowed Cecile to leave the rancho.

CHAPTER FORTY-SEVEN

The pallor of Cook's face deepened and a rattling cough began to shake his once massive body. Fever burned inside him. He was never cold anymore. The driving wind felt good at times, cooled him off. Perspiration would pop out on his forehead, only to freeze into little solid ice balls that he wiped away before they froze to his skin.

He knew he was ill. He had doctored enough trail hands to know the symptoms. He gargled regularly with salt water. Good thing they had plenty of salt. He always carried plenty of salt. One thing a man always needs is salt on his meat. Don't matter what the meat is, salt always makes it better.

Damn shovel, made so many blisters in his hands they would hardly close. Damn cows. Stupid little sons of bitches, you would think they would learn how to find their own feed by now. Indian dogs should have killed all the stupid little sons of bitches.

It was time to fix dinner again. Hell no, it was time to fix breakfast. Oh shit, don't matter anyway. Whatever meal it was would be the same. He gargled and spread some of the horse liniment over his throat. The fiery fumes irritated his eyes and drifted up his nose to his sinuses.

He pulled the pot off the fire and filled it with icicles that hung from the lean-to. More solid water in them, than in the snow. He dumped in a chunk of cut-up stew meat frozen together in one solid lump. Hell, he wished he had a potato. They were all going to end up with scurvy. He already had the damn runs.

The stones were steaming. He used a stick and raked them out of the coals. He plucked the cold ones from around the girl and replaced them with the already cooling ones from the fire. Cecile groaned, moved her head back and forth, words coming through the cracked lips. He thought he heard Grady's name. Damn trail boss. Hell of a fix he left them in. Oughta had better sense than to take this drive. Wish he had some honey. He'd make some snow ice cream. Cool off this fever.

He started to rise and something hard stuck into his back. "Hold it right there, buddy," said a gruff, unfamiliar voice.

Denny's bloody body flashed in front of Cook's eyes. He saw Cragen and Grady rolling in mortal combat on the snow. No way. Not again. He lunged up, turning to meet his opponent. The gun went off so close the flash blinded him. He felt the bullet plow through his chest. Oh, hell. Now he'd done it. It was called Bite the Bullet. He had watched many a man die of gunshot.

Not many cooks died of gunshot, though. Maybe he should've told the man he was the cook. Too late now, he thought, as he died before he hit the ground.

Little Bear and Lou heard the shot. Bear motioned the old man to hide behind the closest cover, then he whipped his knife out of its scabbard, placed it between his teeth, grabbed his rifle, and crawled away from the herd into the swirling mist of the blizzard.

He climbed the canyon wall and ran crouching down, along the top of the ridge, dodging snow covered brush and trees until he was close enough to the abandoned camp. The wind shifted the snow and sleet as it fell. Noises in the brush ahead halted him. Slowly, inch-by-inch, he crept forward. He made out the forms of horses held by one man. He counted seven horses, one loaded with grub. At least six men. The man was not an Indian. Could be the posse that wanted Cragen.

Still he hesitated to show himself. He retraced his way to the canyon He inched in the direction of the campfire. He could smell the odor of burning flesh. Dropping into the ravine he crawled until he was behind the lean-to. He crept up the bank of the ravine and slowly raised his head until he saw the campfire and the cook with his blood seeping into the trampled ice, and one hand lying in the fire.

Three men ignored the cook, and warmed their hands at the fire. Two men were trying to waken Cecile. One of them drew back his hand and slapped both sides of her cheeks. She groaned, and mumbled, limp in their hands, safe in her exhaustion. The man who had slapped her dropped her back to the ground where she lay, an inert bundle.

Little Bear crawled back to Lou. "Six men, five in camp, one with the horses. Cook's dead. It's a cinch you will be, too, if they see you. Miss Ceci's unconscious. She don't know what's happening.

Now you listen to me, old man. Don't go near that camp. The only chance that girl's got is if they don't know we're here. Unless it's her life, don't play hero. I'm going for help."

"Where? How?" Lou asked.

"Indian camp."

"It's too far."

"You got any better ideas?"

"No, except I seen your paint down the canyon a ways, with Miss Ceci's mares, when I was wood hunting today. I don't know what good it will do. You got to pass that bunch to get out of here."

"Thanks, Lou, and do as I say. Stay hidden. Here's my jacket. I'll be moving so I won't need it. Try not to freeze to death before I get back. And stay away from those men."

"Don't worry, Little Bear, I'll take care of Miss Ceci. But hurry," he pleaded as he watched Little Bear disappear in the storm.

Getting out of the canyon without the men seeing him had not been hard. They had been so eager to get warm by the fire that the horse traveling high on the canyon in the swirling gusts of sleet was never seen.

Little Bear knew the direction of the Indian camp. He had learned that from Cochise. The howling of the dog pack had reinforced those directions. The distance was uncertain. He had no idea how far. The terrain was hazardous. The Indian walked much of the way, trying to save the horse, but the horse was less exhausted than the man whose energy had been sapped by weeks of punishing labor. Soon Little Bear had to rely on the paint.

They traveled the rest of the day lost in driving sleet, the, half-breed clinging to the horse, his arms wrapped about the horses neck, his legs around the barrel in an attempt to absorb as much of the horse's body heat as he could.

He heard the camp noises before he saw the campfires in the driving sleet.

CHAPTER FORTY-EIGHT

Deadly switched his tail with the impatient whipping back and forth that he had continued since they had left Janos headed back up the trail. The pace of the riders and wagons was much slower than he wanted to travel. His only consolation was the stop each evening when Grady fondled him and gave him his nightly biscuit. The bull had stayed by the wagon most of the nights, grazing during the days as he waited for them to catch up with him. Feed was scarce, buried deep in frozen snow. Deadly was tired, hungry, and irritated when he came over the rise and saw the snow-covered outline of the grub wagon. The campfire was cold, and snowdrifts covered the camp area. He had left the wagons behind at lunch break when he knew he had reached journey's end. He was not far from Trumpeter, and he was anxious to see his friend.

Deadly was disappointed when he found the camp cold. He sniffed and puffed about the grub wagon. Satisfied no one was around he took the path to the canyon. The cold wind carried cattle sounds to him. Not strong, weakened by the wind, but he knew they were there. He passed some horses tied together.

He surprised the men huddled about the fire in the canyon. They scattered, several reaching for pistols, as the huge bull thundered down the path. A gunshot whizzed past his ears, but Deadly wasn't worried. Men were always firing their pistols. Besides, he smelled Trumpeter's odor about the lean-to. The men had run the old bull down to the herd, and like a hound, Deadly followed the old bull's odor that led into the canyon.

Lance heard gunshots. He pulled up the gelding to listen. He had been following the trail left by the bull. He tied the gelding, pulled his pistol, and followed the tracks left by Deadly. When he spotted the wagons by a dead campfire, he circled around the camp checking it out. When he was satisfied that the camp was deserted, he picked up the bull's trail and followed it into the canyon. He went slowly, testing the air for sounds. He strained to see through the storm, his pistol ready in his hand.

The sound of horses off to one side made him detour to look them over. He counted seven tied together. He could hear men's voices down canyon. No one was on guard with the horses.

Wary, he slipped down into a ravine. The slide down was soundless except for the small avalanche of sleet that lay on the snows surface. The young man sat still waiting to see if the slight sounds had reached other ears. Satisfied he had not revealed himself; he put down his free hand to lift himself to his feet. The hand was laid on a soft body.

Lance jerked his hand back and looked at the body lying in the bottom of the ravine. The dead body did not frighten him. He had seen death many times. He had even caused men's deaths a few times. He had just not expected to share the small ravine with a dead man. The apron on the man indicated he could be a cook. There was a bloody hole in the man's chest, and one hand was burned.

Lance remained low and worked his way down the canyon until he was close to voices. He crawled quietly to the top of the ravine. The winds seemed to be dying down, and when snow shifted, he saw the campfire and the lean-to. Moving slowly from brush cover to rock cover, he slowed as voices reached him.

"Luke, you stupid bastard, when is that stew going to be done? I ain't had a good meal since we left town," a surly voice growled.

"We brung grub with us. You ain't starving."

Lance figured the voice that answered was that of Luke. Another with more authority cut in, "Both of you shut up. I'm tired of hearing complaints."

The camp was noisy, the banging of pots and pans, the bawling of cattle, and the voices of men arguing. Lance figured he could get closer without being heard. He crawled until he could see inside the lean-to. He tried to count the men. One stood over the fire. That was probably Luke. Two squatted by the fire. One man came in with an armful of firewood. There was a man sitting in the lean-to with his back against the braces. Someone lay in a bedroll inside the lean-to.

The man who had entered the camp with the firewood dropped it by the fire and walked to the lean-to. He kicked the bedroll. It's occupant groaned and lay still.

"What's wrong with her," the man said giving the roll another kick.

"How the hell should I know," answered the man that sat in the lean-to.

"What are you gonna do with her?"

"Leave her lay."

"She'll freeze to death."

"Who the hell cares? I didn't come out here for no Goddamned woman. I sent you to find that saddle and whatever else is worth taking. Where the hell have you been?"

"Stuff's up the canyon. That abandoned campground, couple of wagons. Stuff's in one of them." He lowered his voice. "Better not let them bums see it. It's worth slitting our throats over."

"Luke's the one told me about it. I wouldn't be surprised if all the boys been told. Might as well bring it down and divvy it up. Luke don't want nothing but the woman. Says he's got a score to settle for a friend of his, and I don't think he intends to settle it with a toss in the bedroll. He'll probably slit her throat."

"What about them cows? Funny looking critters, suppose they are worth anything?"

"Yeah, dummy, a hangman's noose. Leave the livestock here with the girl."

"Even the horses? Mine's pretty tuckered. I could use a fresh horse."

"Hell, man, that's horse stealing. You can go to jail for that," the man said jokingly, and laughed at his fun. The other man laughed and joined the two by the fire.

Lance began his slow retreat. He crawled as swiftly as the icy ground would permit. He had counted five men; there had been seven horses. He was careful. Could be a couple on watch. When he felt safe, he ran for his horse, untied the reins and leaped aboard, kicking the horse into as fast a pace the frozen ground would allow.

He found Candy's wagon had halted, waiting for Glancy to catch up. Juan Avilas hurried his horse up the hill to hear Lance's report to Grady.

"There's trouble up there. I think the lady is alive. I saw her, but she's unconscious in a bedroll. The man I saw, the one that sits beside her is the Evil One that visited Carmella's with Luke. Luke is there. Besides those two there are three others that I saw. But I counted seven horses. There is a man, probably a cook, dead in a ravine back of the camp. He has been shot in the chest, and his hand is burned

"Could you tell how long they've been in camp?" Grady asked.

"Not long enough, Senor." Lance knew what Grady had asked. His concern was for Cecile. "But they have located whatever they are looking for, and the Evil One plans to let Luke torture the lady. It will probably be tonight. They will leave by early morning."

"They must be stopped. Get this team unhitched, and put my saddle on a horse," Grady commanded the young man.

"Grady, you can't ride. You're not strong enough," Candy cried.

"I have to. You don't understand men like these, Candy. They don't like women. Luke will put her through hell before he kills her."

"The hell I don't understand men like that. They walk into my place every day, sadistic bastards, beating the girls and cutting tattoos into them with their knives. You are not strong enough to ride into a mess. By the time you get there you will collapse before you can save her. You stay put. Lie down and hang on. Candy's heading out." She picked up her whip and cracked it over the horse's heads. They jumped and lunged, feet slipping and sliding on the frozen ground. Then they dug in, and the wagon moved. Gaining momentum they lunged and plunged on the trail, the wagon bouncing along behind them. Grady braced himself and hung on.

"You crazy broad, are you trying to kill me?" he said.

"You better shut up, or you'll let the enemy know you are attacking," whispering, she laughed as she cracked the whip again over the horses' heads.

Lance rode back to Glancy's wagon. The kid leaped to the back of Lance's horse, and put one arm tight about his brother. The other hand held his pistol ready to fire.

Juan had followed Candy's wagon up the trail. He caught up with her and passed, waving her on. Lance's horse flew by her wagon and Grady cussed. They were being left behind.

When the wagon reached the grub wagon and the old camp Grady crawled forward and pulled Candy backward into the bed of the wagon. Stopping the horses, he unhooked the harness and with effort climbed bare back on one of the blacks.

"You get under cover and stay there," his order was quiet but firm. He rode into the canyon.

"You get hurt again after all the hours I put in on you, Grady, and I'll kill you myself," she wanted to yell at him but refrained. She was the only one to hear her threat.

Grady was weak. His legs refused to cling to the back of the horse. Grady fought to stay on the animal. Shots rang out in the canyon. Several horses fled past him. They were riderless and none looked familiar.

Grady saw his three companions spread out, firing into the canyon. A barrage of answering shots whizzed past his head convincing him to slide off the horse and join Juan behind some rocks.

"What did you find?" he whispered.

"The kid is right. Six men. My guess is Miss Cecile is in the bed-roll," Juan whispered.

"Where the hell is my crew?" Grady asked, this conversation was all being said in whispers.

"I saw your cook. They could all be in the ravine, Senor."

"I hope not," Grady said.

Juan nodded agreement. "They cannot get past us, Senor, but they have leverage we do not have. They have Miss Cecile."

"This bunch will kill her before they strike any bargains, just for the pure hell of it." Grady was gritting his teeth in an effort to control his nerves.

Candy crawled up beside him, dragging a rifle.

"I told you to stay put," he hissed at her.

"Not on your life, man. I'm here to protect my investment. I don't intend to let all those hours I put into getting you on your feet be destroyed now. Besides I can shoot the head off a match at fifty feet. Want to see me?"

"You shut up and stay put. That's an order," Grady hissed and turned to crawl closer to the campfire.

"Careful, Senorita, you will send him into battle with his mind scattered. He will get killed. Do as he says. Be ready to shoot anyone that passes you, except me, of course." He smiled and touched her cheek, then turned and crawled after Grady.

"Conceited jackasses," Candy fumed. Dragging the rifle she followed at a safe distance, not letting the two men know she was behind them.

Lance had cut the tethers on the outlaws' horses, and sent them moving up trail, out of the canyon mouth. Then he circled the camp and found a boulder where he settled down to observe the ground about the campfire.

Glancy climbed higher on the canyon rim and found a rock that over-looked the campfire. He hoped the freezing wind would continue to quiet down so he could see more clearly into the canyon.

Lou could hardly stand the cold as he lay under the brush cover, hidden from the unwelcome intruders. He had endured the cold for such a long time that he had almost gotten used to not having any feeling in his feet and hands. The gimpy leg hurt like hell though. Good thing. As long as he could feel the pain he figured he wasn't frozen.

Bear had been gone for a long time. Lou lost track of time, but he must have lain there several hours. In the beginning of the wait, Lou had been anxious for Miss Ceci and tried to crawl close enough to the camp to see what the man were doing. He was able to get close enough to hear voices, but the severity of the blizzard made it impossible to see.

The brush and trees had been cut for fence and fire until there was no cover he could use to crawl closer. He knew he would be no good to Miss Ceci if he got himself killed; however, he feared he would go to sleep and freeze to death. He was so tired. The pain in his leg had helped keep him awake, at first, but it was getting exceedingly difficult to keep his eyes open.

He would try to remember things. That helped keep his mind off sleep, but he would bring himself back just as his mind would see Denny lying in the snow, red blood and pieces of flesh scattered over the white ground. He was determined this was not going to happen to Miss Ceci. He was ready to give his life for her, but the wisdom of his age held him back. He knew there would be a critical time for her. He must not die before that time came.

Men had passed him collecting firewood. He feared they would try to use the brush he was hiding under. It's tough, angular roots had saved it from being pulled up before this, but burnable material near the camp was scarce, and it would only be a matter of time until someone would tackle his brush with an axe.

His teeth ceased to chatter. He fought sleep, finding the struggle so hard he was beginning to forget the reason he must stay awake.

At first he didn't recognize the gunshots. The sounds were muffled by the storm. They were an intrusion on the constant howling of the wind. Lou struggled to wake himself. He fought to make his brain register what he heard. His eyelids had begun to freeze together. He had to rub away the icy particles sealing them.

He was confused. He did not know if the men in the camp were shooting at someone else, or each other, or maybe they had shot Miss Ceci. His determination to protect the girl gave old Lou the strength to move. His fingers had remained still for so long they were stiff, making it difficult to pick up his rifle.

The wind seemed to be dying down. The driving sleet was mixed with the soft kiss of snowflakes. His vision was still hampered, but Lou was surprised to see how close he actually was to the camp. He located himself behind the lean-to. Now he could see the woven branches of the structure. That's where he had left Miss Ceci.

His mind was beginning to sharpen. The gunfire was continuing. There was a battle, but who were the opponents? He began to crawl toward the lean-to, one elbow at a time, pulling himself over the frozen ground. He would stop to peer into the falling snow, searching for movement before he made the next move forward.

He reached the lean-to. His fingers were so cold and stiff that they were too painful to pull apart the branches. He loosened the knife he carried in his belt scabbard, a large, well-sharpened hunting knife. It would separate the branches if his hand could hold it. Slowly, and silently, he dug through what appeared to be an area where leafy branches had crisscrossed and frozen together. Sleet had piled on top. He chopped and dug away with the knife until he had created a hole in the lean-to that he could look through with one eye.

The first thing that attracted his attention was the blazing campfire. Next, a man looked dead near the fire. Lou spotted fresh blood on the floor of the lean-to. It gave him a fright. Whose blood was it?

A pistol shot went off nearly in his ear. There was someone in the lean-to firing at whoever was out there. He prayed, and slowly and carefully began to enlarge the opening so he could get a wider view. Not knowing who was in the lean-to, he worked as quietly as possible.

When he looked through the opening again, he could see the floor of the lean-to. The bedroll that held Miss Ceci was where he had left it. The girl moaned, unconscious, but disturbed by the guns firing about her. A voice in the lean-to yelled out, "The next bullet that's fired, I'll put a hole in the gal's head."

Silence answered from the cover of the storm.

Shifting his body, Lou was able to see the big man crouched by the side of the lean-to. The man held his pistol a few inches from Cecile's head.

"Hold your fire. I'm coming in, "yelled a familiar voice. Lou recognized Grady's drawl. Thank God. Lou sank his head onto his arms and gathered strength from the knowledge that Grady was alive and had finally returned. The old man drew a deep breath in an effort to still his trembling body. He had to be ready at the right moment. His position could be critical help for Grady. He lifted his head to look through the opening. A heavily dressed man was coming toward the lean-to, his hands lifted high. When he reached the glow of the campfire, Lou could see that the man was Grady, but the face was thin and white. This was not the face of the man who had left them weeks ago. He wondered what had happened to make such a change in the trail boss.

Grady spoke. "I've got this camp surrounded. You get your men on their horses and ride out of here, and I'll guarantee your safety,"

"You got it wrong, mister. My men are out there, and I have your lady under my gun. Now who's riding out, mister?"

Grady was quiet. He seemed to weave a little, unsteady on his feet. Then he spoke quietly, controlled.

"We have you outnumbered."

"Hey, Luke. You got this bastard covered?"

Luke's crazy laugh sounded eerie in the swirling winds of the blizzard.

"If there's one more shot, Luke, blow his head off."

"Hell, let me do it now," Luke yelled back. The eagerness in Luke's voice scared Lou.

"Naw, we don't want no murder on our hands, Luke. Just self-defense," the man laughed, amused at his own sick humor.

Grady called softly into the wind, "Juan, you got Luke covered?"

"Si, Senor, I got a little spot right in the middle of his forehead picked out. I put a neat hole in it."

"Shit," Luke's voice could barely be heard as he crashed to the ground, searching for cover.

The man in the lean-to laughed and said to Grady, "I'll bet your man ain't got him covered no more."

Grady smiled and called out, "Glancy, you got a man covered?"

"Yes, sir!" Glancy called.

The smile slipped on the man's face, but he remained cool. "So you got a couple of men. Don't matter. I shoot the girl first if any of them move. You guys hear me? If any of these bastards come near me or fire a shot, I'll put the girl to sleep permanently."

Silence, except for the howling wind, Grady stood still. Lou watched the grin on the man's face. It reminded him of Cragen. The man carried evilness like a cloak. The old man knew this man was enjoying the situation. He was in control. Grady's face was deathly white. Lou could see his arms trembling in the air. He could sense the effort Grady was making to keep them lifted.

A hand touched Lou's shoulder. He would have jumped and rolled to fire at the man, but one hand grabbed his rifle, and the other softly closed over his mouth. Lou held his breath and turned his head slowly, to look into the eyes of Little Bear. Lou's body sagged with relief. Little Bear squeezed his shoulder. Using signals he pointed to the rifle, and then to the hole Lou had made. Then he touched his chest and pointed into the blizzard beyond the edge of the camp. He made a circling movement. Lou nodded his understanding, and Little Bear disappeared into the storm.

Soon after Little Bear had faded into the storm, Lou heard the howl of a timber wolf somewhere in the direction he had gone.

The old man, with a silent, but heartfelt sigh of relief, put his eye to the hole, his rifle held ready to fire.

From the opposite side of the canyon another wolf answered. Down canyon another howl joined the first two. Up the canyon a drawn-out howl made a shiver run up Lou's spine, even though he knew Little Bear had brought help. He hoped the help would know the good guys from the bad guys. Grady's trembling stopped. A smile touched his lips.

"What the hell is going on," exclaimed the Evil One. "Indians. Looks like we all lose."

Grady grinned wider. "Injuns, shit. That was wolves."

"That's right. The Winter Wolf. Looks like the Winter Buffalo lost this fight," Grady said as he sank to the ground.

"What the hell are you talking about," screamed the man in the lean-to.

Grady lowered his arms and rested his hands on his knees. His eyes held those of the man. He could see the insanity in the man's eyes. Fear would trigger a tantrum that could cause the pistol in his hand to fire into the bedroll at his feet.

"Easy, man. We may need all the bullets we both have to stay alive," Grady crooned, his voice soothing.

"Luke! Luke!" the man screamed.

Luke began an answer. His voice stilled in the middle of a word. Luke had been silenced. A wolf howled.

Lou was watching the Evil One's finger on the pistol. He saw it's slight move to tighten. Lou aimed. He pulled slow and steady. The rifle fired. The bullet hit. A small, neat hole appeared in the man's left temple. The pistol fell.

Lou watched as the man's body sagged; he fell onto the frozen puddle of blood.

Grady slumped into a faint. Lou saw Grady fall forward. He thought a bullet had hit him. He expected gunfire to fill the air, but only the howl of the wind came to his ears.

"OK, Lou. It's over," Bear called from a distance.

Lou rose slowly to his feet. Numb with cold he stumbled around the lean-to. Stepping over the dead man, he knelt by Cecile's side. She was alive. His hands were cold, too cold to feel the fever in her cheeks, but the flush told him she had a heavy one. He rose and went to Grady, rolled him over, and examined him for a gunshot wound. He found none. Grady was alive. He was breathing irregularly. Lou could see the struggle for breath.

Lou looked in the direction he had last heard Little Bear and yelled, "Bear."

"I hear you, Lou."

"I need help," Lou replied.

"Have to wait a bit."

"Can I move about?" Lou asked.

"Sure," Little Bear answered, then yelled out in guttural Indian. He was answered in the same tongue.

"Get some wood on the fire, Lou," Bear yelled.

Lou lifted Grady under the arms and pulled him to the fire. Then he turned to go in search of wood, but stopped short. The carcasses of the two calves hanging from the corner poles of the lean-to explained the blood puddles. They had been gutted.

The butchery had been interrupted. They were not skinned and guts were in a pile where they dropped.

"Shit," Lou said as he passed the lean-to and selected a branch from the piled wood. He dragged it to the fire and stuffed an end into the heart of the coals.

A pot of water by the fire had boiled dry. Finding enough icicles, and chunks of frozen snow to fill it again was difficult for the old man with the crippled leg and frozen fingers, but he worked with determination. He cut a hindquarter off of one of the calves, skinned the hide and cut a few strips into the water. He braced the rest of the calf's leg over the fire to roast.

The wind ceased to howl. A gentle snowfall replaced the driving sleet. The storm had broken.

Lou bathed Cecile's face with his kerchief. Her swollen lips, parched and cracked, moved constantly in delirium. She needed medicine, but Lou was afraid to head up the canyon to the grub wagon. Most of the supplies were gone anyway. He found a dipper and held it, full of hot broth, to her lips. She swallowed as it flooded her mouth. She threw her head back and forth, coughing deep in her chest. Lou didn't like the sound of it. He kept making her swallow until she relaxed from the warm broth and fell into a fitful slumber.

Then Lou turned to Grady. The old man didn't know what was wrong with the boss, but the only thing he could do was force some warm broth down his throat. Grady coughed, choked, and struggled to open his eyes. At first he didn't know where he was. Then he remembered. He looked around the camp and saw Cecile.

"Is she all right?"

"She's alive, boss, but she's very sick." Lou answered.

Grady looked at Lou. He hardly recognized the old man. His face was thin, his beard was long and shaggy with icicles hanging from it, and the old man had turned gray, almost white, since Grady saw him last.

"Cook?"

"Dead. Them squirrels shot him."

"Bear?"

"Out there somewhere. Got the Injun nation with him."

"Hell, Lou, I got men out there." Grady tried to sit up.

"Hold it, boss. You better use your mouth. Don't get out of this camp until you talk to Bear, or you might lose yore scalp."

"Bear," Grady yelled.

"Yeah, boss?" came back an answer from a distance.

"I got people out there."

"Bringing them in, boss," Bear answered, the voice closer.

They appeared, growing clearer as they drew nearer to the camp. Candy, Juan, Glancy, and Lance were tied. They were all frightened. Grady didn't blame them. The half-dozen fur-covered Indians who half carried, half shoved them into the clearing looked like serious wild savages. The leader wore a ragged buffalo robe over his shoulders. Tied to his lance were fresh, bloody scalps—five of them. Little Bear strode into camp from the opposite direction followed by a dozen Indian braves. War paint on his face and a ragged fur cape thrown over his shoulders made it difficult to tell him from the Indians who surrounded him.

He strode to Buffalo Hide and spoke in his language. Buffalo Hide pointed to the dead man Lou had drug away from the lean-to. Little Bear nodded and one of the braves removed the man's scalp and hung it with the rest on the lance carried by Buffalo Hide.

Little Bear gestured down the canyon and spoke many words. Grady knew Bear had offered the Indians beef for their help.

Buffalo Hide shook his head, spoke for a long time, and pointed again to the calves. Bear walked over and removed them from the posts. He threw them to the braves. They whooped and ran for their horses that were hidden in the canyon.

Buffalo Hide waited for a brave to bring his horse to him. Bear walked to him and in white-man fashion, held out his hand. Buffalo Hide looked impassively at the hand, then into Bear's eyes. Then he took Bear's hand in his and pressed firmly. With head high, he walked to his horse and swung onto the bare back. He raised his lance in the air, and a war whoop filled the canyon and echoed between the mountains. The braves answered, and the war party turned and rode away into the diminishing storm.

"What the hell was that all about?" Lou asked.

"Cochise didn't want any bad luck. He refused the gift of the sacred cows of my woman."

"Your woman?" Grady stammered.

"Easy, boss. Just a little joke. Indians like to joke, too, or didn't you know that," Bear grinned tiredly.

"Indian, hell. That paint doesn't fool me. You're a white man, through and through."

"Is that a compliment?" Bear asked.

"Hell, yes. Will you untie those folks?" Grady lay tiredly back on the ground. He watched as Lou and Bear freed the four captives.

Candy hurried to his side. "I thought I was a goner," she said with much relief in her voice. "Are you all right?"

"Take care of Cecile. I'll be fine. I'm just dizzy. Too much hero stuff I guess," Grady said to her. Candy rose and went to inspect the girl.

Grady introduced Juan and the two boys to Little Bear, who nodded to the men and returned to squat by Grady. The boys dragged the body of the Evil One away from the camp, and then went with Juan to get the wagons.

"You hurt?" Bear asked Grady.

"Dislocated collar bone, concussion, and a bitch of a cold. Pneumonia they tell me," Grady answered. He studied the Indian's tired face. He saw the silent suffering from a body worked past endurance. "Better get some rest, or we will need a hospital to hold us."

Bear nodded, walked to a corner inside the lean-to, and squatted, his back to the wall. He crossed his arms on his knees and laid his head on them, and was instantly asleep.

When Juan and the boys returned with supplies from the wagons Juan found a bedroll and handed it to Lou. The old man looked at Cecile, hesitating to let up his guard over her.

"Senor, you have done a good job keeping my godchild alive. I owe a deep debt of gratitude to you. You must get some rest yourself. She may need all of us to get her home." Juan spoke kindly. Lou knew he was right. He was no good to Miss Ceci when he was so tired. He was asleep as soon as he pulled the bedroll about himself.

CHAPTER FORTY-NINE

The big longhorn ignored the calls of the young cowboy as he neared the camp and eagerly trotted ahead to find his friend, Trumpeter. The longhorn startled the strangers as he trotted through their camp. Some of the men pulled their pistols and fired after him, but Deadly did not alter his course. Men were always firing guns. Soon he was in the midst of the small herd of cattle. He sniffed noses and pushed his way in and about the herd until he located Trumpeter lying in a pile of ice and snow. Only the steam from the old bull's breath indicated that Trumpeter was alive. He had been more fortunate than the mothers of the calves. The boss man had chased the bull from the lean-to to clear it for himself. Not long after the bull had ambled away to join the herd, the man had ordered the calves butchered, and the cows shot to stop their bawling. The cows had been run into the ravine behind the lean-to, and shot. The hindquarters had been removed and hung to freeze. The small group of men would be well supplied when they rode away from the camp in the canyon.

Deadly snorted around Trumpeter, pawed the ground then tipped his horn and swung it into Trumpeter's side. The old bull groaned and let out a cloud of steam from breath forced from his lungs. Deadly repeated the punishment until Trumpeter bellowed in protest, but circulation was beginning to pump through his cold body. Deadly circled and pawed the bed of ice that had settled about the older bull. He nudged Trumpeter with his nose and swung his horns again, driving the ball tip hard into the bull's flesh.

Trumpeter struggled to get to his feet. It took several attempts with Deadly continuing the punishing blows, until the old bull lunged to his feet, and tried to face his antagonist. His stiff old legs clumsily slipped on the frozen footing. Deadly continued to threaten the old bull to keep him moving. The circulation built up in the older bull's legs, and he moved to escape the pain of the silver-tipped horns.

Angry now at the continuing punishment, Trumpeter lunged, head down, at Deadly. Deadly lowered his head and met the old bull head on. As they crashed into each other Deadly began a steady push. Heads locked together, the old bull lost ground, backing up slowly. Deadly forcing the bull to strain, encouraged the flow of blood to limbs that had begun to freeze when the bull had lain inert in the ice on the ground.

Deadly would relax and let the old bull gain a foothold, and shove Deadly back. The ground became churned under the sharp hooves as this mock battle continued.

As abruptly as he had begun, Deadly quit antagonizing the old bull. He left the bull snorting in fury, and began to paw at the churned ground where their hooves had loosened the ice. Soon he had a hole dug in the layer of frozen snow. He walked to Trumpeter and touched his nose. Trumpeter snorted in anger, but settled down when Deadly flicked out his tongue and ran it across Trumpeter's nose. The old bull followed Deadly to the hole and nosed at the meager blades of frozen grass.

Deadly began a new hole nearby. Reginald joined him and soon several of the cows began to dig through the crusted snow and layers of sleet.

The smell of blood, and the haranguing voices of the strange men, had caused the small herd of Herefords to move deeper into the canyon. Deadly was able to find undisturbed areas where the men had not dug for feed for the herd. Many of the cows had learned to dig for feed, but some were too weak from hunger and cold. These waited until grass was uncovered, then attempted to feed with the stronger cows, which fought to protect the meager blades of grass.

Deadly ignored these herd squabbles. His size and strength were to his advantage. He opened up the ice with sharp cloven hooves, and moved on, letting several of the weakened cows feed on the uncovered grass. Steadily he worked down canyon, knowing that soon he would reach the closed end of the canyon, but he preferred to put distance between his herd and the rowdy men, and the smell of blood at the camp.

Deadly ceased his labor from time to time, hot air billowing from his extended nostrils, his sides heaving from exertion.

His rough tongue swiped clean the moisture dripping from heated nostrils. He tested the air often, searching for some scent of his friend, Grady. He knew the grain wagon would come with his friend. He looked forward to a good pile of grain, and maybe a biscuit.

Gunfire again, back at the lean-to, caught his attention. He stood staring into the blackness toward the faint flicker of the campfire. He would wait longer in the canyon before back trailing to search for his friend. The gunfire didn't scare him, but Deadly didn't like the noise. He would stay with Trumpeter until the night was quiet.

CHAPTER FIFTY

Candy studied the childlike face, which was all that could be seen because of all the extra cover the sick girl was buried under. Candy warmed her hands by the fire then touched the girl's forehead. It was burning with fever. The touch disturbed the delirious girl, and she jerked her head back and forth, mumbling through swollen, parched lips.

Carefully, the saloon girl unwrapped her, uncovering more layers of filthy, work-worn clothing. The odor emanating from the filthy bundle told Candy the girl had lain for several days in the bedroll under the extra layers of tarps and miscellaneous horse blankets and coverings that some-one had packed about her to keep her from freezing. Body odor combined with urine made Candy gag, but she used water from the pot by the fire and careful not to expose the flesh long in the freezing air, bathed the girl piecemeal, one limb and part at a time. She replaced the filthy clothing with clean ones from her own bag from the wagon that Glancy had fetched for her.

Soon Cecile was placed in a fresh bedroll, and warm broth laced with whiskey, strong brown whiskey from Candy's personal stock, filled her belly. She drifted into a peaceful sleep. The first in many weeks.

Grady had dragged himself closer to the fire, and Juan had thrown a bedroll over him. He also slept. His was the sleep of exhaustion. He had gathered strength from his deepest reserve to ride to Ceci's rescue. Now he knew she was alive, and in safe hands, Candy's hands. The excellent care she had lavished on Grady gave him the peaceful knowledge that Ceci would be cared for, so he slept and let the strong young men, and Juan, worry over the herd.

Candy was tired. Her muscles had ached for days. She hadn't spent that much time driving a team and wagon since she was a kid on her pa's farm. Even though she had worn gloves to hold the reins she felt blisters sting when she dipped her hands in the warm water in the pot by the fire. The blistered areas burned like fire when she rubbed a strong liniment on the girl's chest.

When Candy was satisfied that she had done all she could for the sick girl, she inspected Grady to be sure he was just resting and had not slipped back into fever. Then she sat on a saddle by the fire and sipped a mug of broth that would have been tasteless without the strong shot of whiskey she poured into it. The whiskey was warming her when the man squatting behind Cecile against the back of the lean-to raised his head and stared at her.

The movement startled her. She had forgotten about him. When she was ministering to the girl's needs she had been aware of the man as she moved carefully about so as not to bump or step on him, but he had remained immobile for such a long time that she had ceased to be aware of him until he raised his head.

Now she stared into piercing brown eyes. She shuddered at the vision she saw. His face was covered with war paint that he had applied as Cochise's men prepared themselves for the skirmish with the white men. His unkempt black hair hung long about his shoulders. His black western hat was all that suggested the man had any white blood in him. To Candy he looked all savage. He didn't have the beard, or stubble, of the white man, and his skin was smooth and brown. She observed the strong set of his jaw, and for a fleeting moment thought to herself that, cleaned up, the man might be a handsome fellow.

She lifted her mug toward him, "If you can hold your liquor I'll fix you a cup of hot broth and whiskey."

Bear glared at her, instantly furious at the bigoted white man's notion that Indians could not drink liquor without reverting to heathenism.

"Don't glare at me, man. Wash your face if you want me to treat you like a white man," Candy said as she glared back. Tired, aching, and sleepy, she was in no mood to pacify a man.

A stoic Indian expression passed over Bear's face as he put this woman out of his mind, lowered his head and drifted back to sleep. For a short moment Candy resented being dismissed in such an insulting manner, but she was too weary to worry about it. She pulled herself into a bedroll. Her last memory was of Glancy piling wood on the fire.

Candy woke to a hustle around the fire. The storm had ceased. The view of the white canyon walls was stark. The snow had been so heavy nothing was left without a coat of white, except the scars left by the axe, and the churned and dirty bed ground the herd had spent so many nights forming.

She raised herself on one elbow, moaning from stiffness. She had not moved all night, thanks to the whiskey, but now she felt the bruises from the uneven ground she had lain on, and the sore muscles that had hardened into unyielding pain.

The men were breaking camp. The Indian she did not recognize at first. All vestiges of war paint were gone, as well as the ragged fur cape. His black hair had been controlled, and stuffed under his black hat. She had been right last night. Under the war paint was a good-looking man.

Bear felt the girl's eyes on him. He refused to recognize her and continued to strap Grady to the makeshift travois he had fastened to his horse. The men had agreed that the higher camp, where the grub wagon sat, would be more convenient to care for their needs as they rounded up the herd and prepared to move them out.

Lou was tenderly spooning hot cereal into Cecile's mouth. The girl was awake, but she was so weak she could hardly open her mouth to accept the delicious, hot oatmeal. She did not know that Grady, and help, had come. She recognized old Lou and wondered where he had found the cereal. She drifted back to sleep. So tired, she was so tired. Would she ever want to rise again?

Candy groaned and cussed, but made sore muscles move until she was sitting up. The bedroll still encased her hips and legs.

Old Lou filled a pan with oatmeal and poured a generous amount of maple syrup on it. She could see his delight at the luxury. These people had gone through hell. She hoped she would never have to feel the hunger, and freezing weather they must have endured. She smiled her thanks and hungrily ate the hot gruel. Before she spooned in the last bite, Lou handed her a cup of hot coffee.

"I could learn to love you," she said to the old man.

"I'd be proud to have you fond of me, ma'am," he returned with a grateful smile.

As she sipped the hot coffee, she watched Bear through half-opened eyes and caught him sneaking sidelong glances at her. Self-consciously she tucked loose strands of hair under her hat. Bear grinned to himself, but Candy saw. She knew he was laughing at her. "Shit," she said under her breath, and continued to sip her coffee, but now she lifted her eyes and winked impishly the next time he glanced her way. His face colored as he turned to mount the horse and ride up the worn trail, moving slowly and carefully so as not to hurt Grady, who lifted a hand and waved to her. She waved back and watched until they were out of sight.

The noise of horses approaching from down canyon made her turn to watch Glancy riding a gray stallion and leading a gray mare. Even under the dirty, shaggy, winter hair she recognized good horseflesh.

"Come on, Miss Candy. I'll give you a lift up to the grub wagon."

Candy cringed at the thought of mounting the mare bareback, but decided she preferred to ride up the trail rather than walk up. Lou gave her a leg up and she swung onto the mare's back. She was glad she had worn the men's riding pants. .

The mare's back was damp from falling snow for she had gone under loaded tree branches. Candy had little time to feel the discomfort as the mare lunged to keep her footing as she climbed up trail. Candy grabbed a sodden clump of mane and held on. They reached the camp right behind the travois. Before Glancy could dismount and help Candy down, Little Bear, was beside the mare with arms lifted to help her.

She leaned over so he could get a secure hold under her arms, placed her hands on his shoulders, and slid into his arms. She felt strong muscles move under her hands. She looked into black eyes in a face devoid of expression. She grinned, thinking about the fun she would have teasing this man. She said, "I think I'm falling in love."

The black eyes remained expressionless as the half-breed set her firmly on the ground, then turned back to remove Grady from the travois.

Candy backed up to the fire to dry her damp bottom while she observed the camp. The boys, or Juan, had shoveled the snow out of the lean-to, and out from under the grub wagon.

The camp was pitiful, but it was better protected than the small lean-to in the canyon. The Indian helped Grady walk to the fire and steadied him until he was seated with his back against a log. Candy was amused when the Indian glanced up to see her rubbing vigorously on her bottom to keep the heat from the fire from growing too warm. She winked and watched with amazement as the color built up in his face. He turned and swung into the saddle, and pulling the travois behind, he rode back into the canyon.

"You're one hell of a sport, Candy," Grady said to the girl.

"Gee, thanks," she answered sarcastically.

"You mad at me?" he accused.

"Hell, no, Grady, I'm not mad at you. I just get tired of being a 'hell of a sport.' Why don't you tell me I'm a hell of a lady, or some peach of a woman? What the hell is wrong with me, Grady? Don't I have all the right parts in the right places?"

"Sure you do, girl! You're a fine figure of a woman, and you're also a lady. A nice lady."

"But you're in love with Little Miss Muffet down in the canyon," she pouted.

"I hadn't thought about it, but I think you're right. I might be in love with her. I've been so worried I never really thought about it. I guess we all love her though, Juan, old Lou, Bear."

"Yeah, I noticed," she said again sarcastically.

"Is she all right, Candy?"

"I don't know, Grady. She's pretty worn out, and I suspect they have all been on short rations. She's pretty thin. I guess we'll just have to see how some good food and rest affects her before we'll know for sure. I better find the beans and get something on for dinner," she said, and left the fire to search through the stocked wagon they had brought with them.

Engrossed in her task working about the wagon, she knew when Bear returned with Cecile on the travois, but she saw the old man was with them, hovering over Cinderella like an old mother hen, so she ignored their arrival and continued to prepare a meal. Dutch oven bread, slices of floured steak, thick gravy, and a pot of nourishing beans were ready when all of the men gathered for a hot noon meal.

Trumpeter once again occupied the lean-to, and Deadly stood patiently behind Grady, waiting for a piece of the pan bread.

Everyone settled back with full stomachs. Some of the men rolled cigarettes and relaxed. Young Glancy closed his eyes and was instantly asleep. Lance relaxed and stared into the fire with droopy eyes. Cecile was once again in a sound sleep, and old Lou was enjoying his cigarette. "How soon can we travel?" Grady asked, not addressing anyone in particular.

Juan Avilas answered him, "Cows are in poor shape, half starved. They should be grained for a few days before we travel with them, but I want to get Miss Cecile out of these mountains before we get caught in another storm."

"Can we get it together to pull out in the morning?" Grady asked.

"I think so, Senor. I'm going to need the boys to help herd. We'll have to leave some wagons behind. Travel as light as we can, but carry all the supplies we might need if the weather turns bad again."

"All right, Juan, it's up to you and Little Bear to get us out of here. Use your judgment. Mine's not too good yet. Head still hurts like hell," he said.

"Lance, you boys help load all the supplies and all the bedrolls, and anything you think we might need, in the larger grain wagon. We'll load Grady and Miss Ceci in the light wagon. Miss Candy can drive it, and Lou can drive the grub wagon if he feels up to it," Juan said, looking questioningly at the old man.

Lou sat a little straighter and said, "Hell, yes, anything beats tramping back and forth on that canyon path. It will be a real pleasure to ride for a change."

"Little Bear and I will throw some sacks of grain on the travois and go give the cattle a good feeding tonight, and another early in the morning before we pull out," Juan said, as he snuffed out his brown paper cigarette and rose to tackle the job of loading grain on the travois. Bear rose and joined him. Soon they disappeared down the trail into the canyon.

Lou helped Candy empty the food supplies left in the old grub wagon. Cecile woke and Candy went to see to her needs. She tried to spoon some gravy into Cecile's mouth, washing it down with strong coffee. She frowned when she saw Grady rise weakly, and move closer to the girl. Candy resented the worried look on his face as he sat watching Cecile.

Grady was worried. Cecile seemed to be in a coma. Her eyes lacked luster, and did not focus on anything. Her body hardly moved, as if the effort to move was beyond her endurance.

Grady was grateful the herd had not suffered a much larger loss. He had some idea of the hell his men, and Cecile, had gone through to protect the herd. He studied the scarred forest around the camp and tried to imagine what it must have been like for them to struggle ever farther from camp each time to replenish the fuel to keep the fires going.

Grady studied the girl's face. Her mouth was unrecognizable, swollen, cracked, in a face with chunks of skin breaking loose, from frostbite. She was a Cecile that he did not remember, a stranger who spoke deliriously from fever.

Cecile's arms and hands had been restrained in the bedroll. Even in delirium her fighting spirit caused her to strike out at those who were trying to help her. Candy lost all patience with her. She had managed to bathe the girl, put clean clothes on her, and wrap her in clean blankets, but it had been a struggle, and in spite of the bitter cold, Candy's forehead gleamed with perspiration. Cecile refused to swallow the gravy, and spewed it back as she garbled unintelligibly.

Candy tried to catch most of the gravy as it ran from Cecile's mouth and force it back between clenched teeth. In exasperation she threw the spoon into the bowl and handed it to Grady. "Here, you feed her. There's no sense in both of us wasting time with her." She shoved the bowl into Grady's hands, angrily rose, and returned to loading the grain wagon.

Grady freed himself from the blankets Candy had thrown about his shoulders and set the bowl closer to the fire to stay warm. He had moved from the bed in the wagon to the campfire where he could be near Cecile. Now moving closer, he pulled the girl into his arms. She struggled to free herself. He tightened his hold about her, hugging her frail body to his chest. He felt like crying as he held her to himself. He felt such gratitude that she was alive and in his arms.

He also felt worry and guilt at her condition. She was so ill. Could she survive until they reached the town and a doctor? He talked to her, soothing her. "Hush, honey, you're safe. Old Grady's holding on to you. I won't let you die. You hang in there, you here me?" He crooned endearments in her ear, comforting her, reassuring her.

Her body began to relax in his arms. Her eyes searching his face still held a vacant look, but the muscles in her jaw unclenched and her arms quit struggling to free themselves.

Continuing the crooning cadence, Grady held her close with one arm, and reached for the bowl of gravy, putting it near enough to reach with the spoon. He filled the spoon half-full and raised it to the girl's cracked lips. Gently, crooning while he held her close, he laid the spoon on her lower lip. For a fraction of a moment her jaw tightened, then her eyes closed. He felt her body completely relax and mold into his arms. Her mouth opened, he tipped the spoon and watched the loose, creamy gravy slide into her mouth. She swallowed with difficulty. Grady figured she probably had a sore throat and hoped the ailment did not go into the chest and lungs.

Patiently he fed her until she ceased to swallow, and he could tell from her relaxed face that she had slipped into a peaceful sleep. He continued to hold her close; afraid to lay her down for fear she would waken and return to anxiety. He wanted her to rest in peace with a feeling of safety. Most of all, he wanted her in his arms. He wanted the comfort of knowing she was safe in his arms.

Candy threw pots and pans together. She was angry, but she wasn't sure why. She watched Grady as he tenderly held the girl in his arms. The anger flared as she saw him hug her to him and nuzzle his face into Cecile's neck. The soft crooning voice, as Grady talked to Cecile held a tenderness she had never heard in any man's voice.

Candy realized where her jealousy was coming from. She realized she had grown fond of Grady in these many weeks, but she was intelligent enough to know from the devotion he had shown in his efforts to recover and return for the girl that she, Candy, would never be more than Grady's friend.

She was envious of that devotion. She had spent a lifetime pleasing men, but she would give it up in a moment if she could share that feeling with just one man. She felt empty inside. She tried to busy herself, but frustration filled her eyes with tears. Her fingers were cold and stiff, and she dropped pans and blankets didn't fold right and had to be redone. She stamped her foot, angry at herself. She had more pride than this. Standing still she closed her eyes and drew cold air deep into her lungs.

She let pride flow through her body. She felt it fill her lungs. She wiped her eyes with the back of her hands, took several more deep breaths, and refolded the blankets and stored them in the grain wagon.

When she had the grain wagon packed, she carried the cover she had dried and warmed by the campfire to her light wagon and made a bed for

Grady. She smiled softly as she smoothed the bedrolls over the floorboards of the wagon. She smoothed several blankets on top and then covered them with a heavy canvas that would hold in the warmth.

That night after the evening meal, Candy put water on to heat for a bath. She felt crummy. Some clean drawers would lift her spirits. She hung a blanket on the opening of the lean-to and put her bucket of hot water inside. The bull that was occupying the lean-to shifted his rear to the back of the area as she put a shoulder firmly into his side, and pushed. "Move over, you hunk of beef, and don't step on my feet," she snapped.

It was too cold to undress. She washed piecemeal as she had bathed Cecile the night before. She shook from the cold, but took pleasure in soaking a rag in the hot water, wringing it out, and holding it to her face, letting the steam soak into her flesh. She dug the dirt from her ears, and scrubbed the skin of her body until she once again felt clean. She left the bucket of water, already beginning to chill, for the bull, and gave him a parting pat. She removed the blanket and threw it around her shoulders. Tired, she sank to the log placed by the fire.

She had grown soft. A lot of years pampering herself in saloons had spoiled her. She could hardly wait until she could sink her sore body into a tub of suds, and soak. A noise caused her to look up and see the man called Little Bear come into the firelight, his arms full of wood for the fire.

"I thought Indians were silent and crept up on you," she said teasingly.

"I'm only half Indian so one foot is heavy like the white man's," he replied in a dry voice.

It took her a moment to realize that he had a sense of humor and had not been serious. She laughed lightly, pleased to see a smile form on his face. "Hey, you've got a dimple when you smile," she teased.

"Took that after my father," he answered, as he squatted on his heels and put his hands out to the fire to warm the palms.

"Was he the Indian or the white man?" she asked, curiosity replacing her previous sense of humor.

"My mother was Indian. I was raised by her people."

"Are you a bastard?"

Silence greeted Candy's blunt question.

"I'm sorry," she apologized. "Don't answer that if you don't want to. I am. A bastard that is. My pa raised me. My ma and pa never married. She left with a drummer fellow one day, so Pa raised me until I was old enough to find work."

"What kind of work do you do?" he asked.

Silence again filled the air. Candy was surprised at herself. She was ashamed to tell this man her occupation.

"You don't have to answer that, either, if you don't want to," he said, mimicking her previous teasing tone.

"Oh hell, I don't hide it anymore. I don't guess I ever did. I was proud to earn my way, keep myself in nice clothes, and eat decent meals. Didn't matter how I did it. It was easier on me when I finally came into enough money to set up my own saloon, and let other girls work for me."

"No, I'm not," he said, cutting short her self-conscious effort to be honest.

"Not what?" she asked.

"A bastard," he replied. "My mother and father had two ceremonies, a white man's, and an Indian ritual. I'm more legally born than any white man I know, or any Indian I know," he said with a chuckle.

"I didn't know Indians laughed."

"You'd be surprised how funny we find life," he said, smiling. She saw the dimple in the fire's glow.

"And besides, I'm half-white. Could be the white half has the sense of humor."

"How come you speak such good English if you were raised by Indians?"

"Until my father was killed in a gunfight I attended white man's school. After he died we went to live on the reservation where my mother walked with me to attend the mission school. She knew he wanted me to fit into his world."

"Do you?" she asked.

"Hell no. I don't fit in either one." He spat contemptuously into the fire. "I can't drink in a white man's saloon, and I can't live in an Indian hovel. I can't look at a white woman without getting hung, and I see Indian squaws when I look at an Indian girl."

"So you just live on the trail then?"

"Sure, why not? Grady's a good man. He don't see white or Indian when he looks at me. He sees a man."

"But what about your sex life? How do you handle that if you can't have one, and don't want the other?"

Silence again.

"Oh hell, I'm sorry." Candy said, "I'm so used to talking about things that decent folks consider not nice that I forget sometimes to mind my own business. I'd better get to sleep. Tomorrow will probably be another holy terror."

"Would you go to bed with me?" he asked softly, his voice gentle, prepared for a negative answer.

"Now?" she asked.

"Now," he repeated.

"Here?" she asked.

"Over there," he nodded into the darkness beyond the campfire. "But it's freezing cold," she said doubtfully.

"Are you in love with Grady?" he asked.

"Hell!" she exploded. "Can't you stick to one subject at a time?"

"I think maybe you are," he said.

"Like hell I am," she hissed. She was surprised at the strength of her denial. Was she really in love with Grady, or was she just possessive because she had nursed him back to life?

Little Bear rose and turned to walk away.

"Is that it?" she asked, not believing the conversation ended.

"Now you have your answer," he said over his shoulder.

"What answer?" she asked, bewildered.

"The one about my sex life," he said, and walked away into the darkness.

"Wait. I'm coming with you," she spoke in a loud whisper.

"Good. I'll keep you warm."

Candy followed his light laughter until she felt his hand touch her arm. She took hold of his arm and ran her arms up until they circled his neck. She felt his arms gather her gently to him. His mouth covering hers, exploring, searching for sensations he knew were still there even after years of controlled sex.

Candy was both surprised and delighted. This half-breed—dirty Indian, most people would call him—smelled of ice water and soap. His breath held the faint scent of cloves.

"Why you conceited jackass. You took a bath. You planned all the time to get me in bed with you."

He laughed and swung her lightly into his arms. "Well, now you have the answer as to how I manage my sex life."

She pulled his head to hers and lightly bit his ear. He hugged her to himself, and bent his head threatening to bite through her clothing to her nipple. She squealed softly in his ear, and said, "Wait until you remove my clothes."

He stopped walking and sank to his knees. Gently he lowered her to the ground, but instead of the icy hardness of the frozen snow, she felt the soft warmth of fur. He pulled a fur robe over her then rose and walked away. She listened for his return while her hands swiftly loosened her clothes and removed them, pushing them with her feet to the bottom of the pallet.

She did not hear him return, but she felt his cold, naked body slide in beside her. She was cold, but a feverish need shielded her from the cold. "You rat, you even made the bed," she said, reaching for him.

"Shut up, woman. It's time for lovemaking, not talk." His mouth closed over hers. She ran her hands over his body. Exciting herself as she explored with her fingertips, gasping as he gently massaged her back, sliding his hands smoothly to areas that made her faint with desire. She was nearly frantic when he quit teasing her, roughly drew her under him, and began the search for the warmth between her legs. She opened up, welcoming him, and nearly screamed aloud with delight as he entered her with such slow control that she strained upward, urging him to meet her.

He continued to tease her, plunging deep, thrusting fast, then holding at the opening until she fought like a wild woman to draw him back deep into her.

Never had she felt so wanton. This was not just sex. This was heaven, and she wanted him so badly that she hurt. She clung to his back, crying and begging for him to thrust deeper. And when he did, her entire body responded as she entered the dream world of orgasm. Her mate continued to thrust until he felt her body rock with shudders, then he released himself and joined her. In that ethereal world, they floated together in ecstasy.

CHAPTER FIFTY-ONE

Camp came alive, excited activity was everywhere. The air was cold and crisp from the low night temperature. Fog rose from the breath of working men and animals. Mules stood in the traces, waiting for the driver to crack his whip and give the word to lean into the harness and pull. The herd had been moved out of the lower canyon and headed along the downhill trail. The young drovers were moving slowly, not pressing the cows, giving them time to set their feet firmly on the frozen ground.

Cecile woke to the sound of the morning bustle of breaking camp. At first she thought it was a normal morning and she had overslept. Her intention to get out of the bedroll was halted by dizziness, and an aching body. Confused, she lay back and closed her eyes.

"Miss Cecile." A familiar voice spoke over her. She opened her eyes. The face and beard looked familiar, only the face was so thin and the once dark-gray hair was now white as the surrounding snow.

"Lou?" she questioned timidly.

"Yes, ma'am. It's old Lou."

"Where are we, Lou?"

"Still in the canyon, miss," he replied.

The canyon. Memory slowly returned. She remembered the men working so hard. She knew she had been ill. "How long have I been sick, Lou?"

"About a week, miss."

"Oh Lou, I'm so sorry. I've been such a burden." Her voice was weak.

"No, ma'am. You ain't been a bother, and I got a surprise for you." He walked away to return shortly with Little Bear.

"Good to see you awake, Miss Cecile." Bear grinned at her. We are about ready to move out. You eat some breakfast and I'll get you loaded in the wagon."

She noticed for the first time a dimple in one cheek. These men had grown so dear to her. Lou returned shortly with a bowl of oatmeal.

Candy wrapped stones that had been piled close to the fire. She placed the stones under the blankets that she had arranged for Grady so the bed would be warm for him. She then went to find Little Bear.

An excitement filled her when she remembered the night in his bed. He had more than satisfied her. He had brought her to climaxes she had never before experienced with a man. He had played with her, found her most vulnerably sensitive areas, behind her knees, in her groin, and the tips of her nipples.

She could feel her nipples shrinking under her heavy clothing, a reaction to remembering the Indian's fingers as they softly circled her breasts, traced the fullness to the darker areas at the base of the nipples, and lightly fingered the tips. He slid smoothly under the covers to run his tongue across her chest, and with its damp touch, follow the pattern of the path his fingers had traveled before ending with gentle teasing of the nipple with his tongue, sucking and nipping with his teeth, never enough to hurt, only to drive her into a desire so strong she had strained for his touch.

Candy stopped, breathless from her thoughts, as she spotted Little Bear working with a shovel. He had removed his shirt and the bronzed shine of his body, wet with perspiration, was beautiful to watch as muscles rippled across his back. She leaned her back against a tree to catch her breath as she watched him work. He was nearly finished burying the cook.

The pick stopped as the Indian turned, aware of her approach. He had felt her eyes on his back. He grinned when he saw the hungry look on her face. The look aroused him and the hard swelling began between his legs. Laying the pick aside, he walked to her and pulled her to him, crushing her to his chest. He took her hand and guided it to the swelling. She trembled as she felt its rising and smelled the masculine odor of perspiration, and the spicy fragrance he had covered himself with before joining her in bed the night before.

"You're a hungry woman," he groaned, pressing her closer against him, enjoying the sensual feeling as her body rubbed against his.

"I'm a starved woman. Do you think I'll ever get enough of you?"

"We'll have a few days' travel to find out," he replied, and lowered his head to press his mouth over hers. He ran his tongue around her lips, coaxing passion from her, nursing the kiss until her body quivered, and she panted with desire.

Slowly he drew his mouth from hers. "That will have to hold you until camp tonight."

"I don't think I can wait, and you sure don't feel like you can either." She laughed and gently squeezed the organ.

He gave in to the pleasure of her caress and pressed harder, pulling her hips to meet his. "We must. The cattle are already moving. Today is going to be a bitch. We are going to have to clear a path for the wagons. We may be able to follow the ruts you made coming up, but getting the wagons out will be difficult. I've instructed the boys to move the cattle on down trail, and return to help us pull the wagons through."

"Camp's packed up," Candy replied, "except Grady and Miss McNamara. That's why I came after you. I need help getting the girl in the wagon. Lou is not strong enough to lift her. We are the only one left in camp."

"So you've just been toying with my affections," he grinned, teasing her. "You need a strong back, and I thought you needed me."

She laughed, stood on her toes, grabbed his head and with her arms pulled it down to hers, and returned the sensual kiss he had given her earlier. Still kissing him, she ran her hands over his chest and around his back. Clutching him to her, she pressed her body firmly against his, and easily, softly, suggestively, rotated her hips, pressing against him with the promise of better things to come.

Given time, she would delve into her years of experience and repay him for the pleasures he had taken the time, and restraint, to give her. Hand-in-hand they returned to the fire, releasing their hold before Grady looked up and saw them.

Glancy had hitched the horses to Candy's wagon, and it was ready to move out as soon as Grady and Cecile were loaded.

"Time to move you to the wagon, Grady," Candy said.

285

"I can ride today. The men will need help to drive the cattle," Grady replied.

Candy was exasperated and fire glinted in her eyes. Little Bear spoke up with authority. "Today you need to watch Miss Ceci, Grady. The cattle will be OK for a few days. They will follow the grain wagon until we get to a lower elevation and find some grazing. Candy will drive her wagon, Lou will take the grain wagon, and Glancy, Lance, Juan, and I can handle the herd while you keep Miss Ceci covered up. She may already have pneumonia. Someone has to take care of her."

Grady was still weak and ill himself, but male stubbornness would make him pull his load. Little Bear's argument sounded reasonable so Grady agreed by nodding his head. He watched as Bear lifted Cecile and carried her to the wagon.

Candy helped Grady to his feet. He leaned on her and followed the Indian. He watched while Little Bear and Candy laid the girl in the wagon, covered her, and tucked her in. Then Candy turned back the blankets beside Cecile to allow Grady to lie down. Grady sat on the end of the wagon, and Little Bear helped move him slowly and painfully into position.

Cecile stirred beside him. She had drifted back to sleep after breakfast.

He ran one arm under her neck, the other across her waist, and pulled her closer to him. "It's all right, Ceci. You're safe," he crooned softly. Cecile moved closer to the warmth of his body, became still, and slept until the men returned to move Candy's wagon.

Candy climbed onto the wagon seat, took up the reins, and snapped them across the team's withers, yelling, "Get up. Move it. Hup!" The horses strained to release the wheels from the frozen snow. The men's ropes snaked out to grab hold of the wagon and leaned into their saddles, urging the horses under them to strain with the team.

A cracking noise rent the air as the wheels broke loose and the wagon jumped forward. They worked in this manner until they had covered the distance to where the herd and the other wagon awaited their arrival to begin the treacherous trek off the mountain.

The blizzard that had dominated the mountain for weeks had diminished, but the mountain was not to escape more of winter's onslaught. This storm of record was just the beginning of a long, cold winter. Early in the winter's birth the savagery of the Winter Wolf had struck, leaving snow and ice piled high, only to be smothered again and again as the winter settled into its normal cycle of storms.

But for today, all of the people from the camp at the mouth of the small canyon felt relief. The winds had stilled, lifting the chill factor, and white clouds rose above the mountain, giving distance to vision once again. But the sun did not shine through the slow-moving clouds and there was no warmth, as winter was truly upon the high mountain range.

Grady had risen onto his elbow so he could observe the moving of the wagon, and had several times given orders and suggestions. He felt great relief when they arrived at the herd and he spotted Deadly Deadly waiting patiently by Trumpeter's side.

A movement by Cecile, still resting in his arms, made him look down. He looked into clear eyes, eyes that studied his face in disbelief.

"Grady?" The question was barely audible. Her voice was raspy and faint. "Grady, is it really you, or am I dreaming again?" she pleaded.

"You're not dreaming, darling. I'm real flesh and blood."

"I knew you would come, but it was so long. I began to think you were dead. That maybe you could not come back. I was so worried."

"I know, love. So was I. You're tired and ill now, but when you are better, I'll explain. You must rest and get well."

"I will. Please don't leave me. Hold me," she begged.

He pulled her closer to him, tucked the blankets in tight around her, and kissed her eyes closed. "Shush," he whispered. "Just rest. I won't let go of you again."

She smiled and settled into his embrace, snuggling close to feel his face against her forehead.

The wagon bed was hard, but Candy had done a good job of making it comfortable and warm. Grady could feel the tension leave his body. He relaxed as the girl snuggled into his arms.

He called, "OK, Deadly. Lead them out."

20531850R00181

Made in the USA
Charleston, SC
16 July 2013